A Christmas Family Miracle

BARBARA HANNAY **DONNA ALWARD** **ALLISON LEIGH**

MILLS & BOON

A CHRISTMAS FAMILY MIRACLE © 2023 by Harlequin Books S.A.

A VERY SPECIAL HOLIDAY GIFT
© 2014 by Barbara Hannay
Australian Copyright 2014
New Zealand Copyright 2014

First Published 2014
Second Australian Paperback Edition 2023
ISBN 978 1 867 29585 3

CHRISTMAS BABY FOR THE BILLIONAIRE
© 2019 by Donna Alwood
Australian Copyright 2019
New Zealand Copyright 2019

First Published 2019
Second Australian Paperback Edition 2023
ISBN 978 1 867 29585 3

THE RANCHER'S CHRISTMAS PROMISE
© 2018 by Allison Lee Johnson
Australian Copyright 2018
New Zealand Copyright 2018

First Published 2018
Second Australian Paperback Edition 2023
ISBN 978 1 867 29585 3

Except for use in any review, the reproduction or utilisation of this work in whole or in part in any form by any electronic, mechanical or other means, now known or hereafter invented, including xerography, photocopying and recording, or in any information storage or retrieval system, is forbidden without the permission of the publisher.

This book is sold subject to the condition that it shall not, by way of trade or otherwise, be lent, resold, hired out or otherwise circulated without the prior consent of the publisher in any form of binding or cover other than that in which it is published and without a similar condition including this condition being imposed on the subsequent purchaser.

All rights reserved including the right of reproduction in whole or in part in any form. This edition is published in arrangement with Harlequin Books S.A. Cover art used by arrangement with Harlequin Books S.A. All rights reserved.

This is a work of fiction. Names, characters, places, and incidents are either the product of the author's imagination or are used fictitiously, and any resemblance to actual persons, living or dead, business establishments, events, or locales is entirely coincidental.

Published by
Mills & Boon
An imprint of Harlequin Enterprises (Australia) Pty Limited
(ABN 47 001 180 918), a subsidiary of HarperCollins
Publishers Australia Pty Limited (ABN 36 009 913 517)
Level 19, 201 Elizabeth Street
SYDNEY NSW 2000
AUSTRALIA

® and ™ (apart from those relating to FSC®) are trademarks of Harlequin Enterprises (Australia) Pty Limited or its corporate affiliates. Trademarks indicated with ® are registered in Australia, New Zealand and in other countries. Contact admin_legal@Harlequin.ca for details.

Printed and bound in Australia by McPherson's Printing Group

CONTENTS

A VERY SPECIAL HOLIDAY GIFT 5
Barbara Hannay

CHRISTMAS BABY FOR THE BILLIONAIRE 169
Donna Alward

THE RANCHER'S CHRISTMAS PROMISE 343
Allison Leigh

A Very Special Holiday Gift
Barbara Hannay

Reading and writing have always been a big part of **Barbara Hannay**'s life. She wrote her first short story at the age of eight for the Brownies' writer's badge. It was about a girl who was devastated when her family had to move from the city to the Australian Outback.

Since then, a love of both city and country lifestyles has been a continuing theme in Barbara's books and in her life. Although she has mostly lived in cities, now that her family has grown up and she's a full-time writer she's enjoying a country lifestyle.

Barbara and her husband live on a misty hillside in Far North Queensland's Atherton Tableland. When she's not lost in the world of her stories she's enjoying farmers' markets, gardening clubs and writing groups, or preparing for visits from family and friends.

Barbara records her country life in her blog, *Barbwired*, and her website is: www.barbarahannay.com.

Recent books by Barbara Hannay:

SECOND CHANCE WITH HER SOLDIER
MIRACLE IN BELLAROO CREEK*
THE CATTLEMAN'S SPECIAL DELIVERY
FALLING FOR MR. MYSTERIOUS
RUNAWAY BRIDE**
BRIDESMAID SAYS, "I DO!"**

*Bellaroo Creek!
**Changing Grooms

This and other titles by Barbara Hannay are also available in ebook format from www.millsandboon.com.au.

Dear Reader,

When I first started this story I planned to set it in my country—Australia. But when my editor asked for a Christmas theme I found myself wanting to write a "fantasy" Christmas. As an Australian, I'm used to Christmases that are hot and often spent at the beach—and, while these Christmases are always wonderful, I found this time that my imagination had developed a hankering for a traditional cold climate festive season. I wanted my characters to wear coats and scarves, and to eat hot dinners and see beautiful snow.

So my fantasy took my characters to London, a city I love (as some of you might have guessed from other books I've written). When I added a drop-dead handsome and rich boss to the story mix, a superconscientious PA, plus a newborn baby, I had all the ingredients for my favorite kind of Christmas.

I had so much fun writing Chloe and Zac's story. Thank you for picking up the book, and I hope you enjoy it. I would love to hear from you if you do.

Warmest wishes,

Barbara

For Elliot, with huge, *huge* thanks for your unfailing faith in my writing....

It would never have happened without you.

CHAPTER ONE

THE PHONE CALL that changed Chloe Meadows's life came when she was poised on tiptoe, on a chair that she had placed on top of a desk in a valiant attempt to tape a loop of Christmas lights to the office ceiling.

It was late on a Wednesday evening, edging towards nine p.m., and the sudden shrill bell in the silent, empty office was so unexpected Chloe almost fell from her precarious perch. Even so, she slipped as she scrambled down awkwardly in her straight grey business skirt and stocking feet.

She was slightly out of breath as she finally grabbed the phone just as it was due to ring out.

'Hello? ZedCee Management Consultants.' She wondered who would call the office at this late hour. On a Wednesday night.

There was a longish beat before she heard a man's distinctly English voice. 'Hello? I'm calling from London. Could I please speak to Mr Zachary Corrigan?' The voice was officious, like the command of a bossy teacher.

'I'm sorry. Mr Corrigan isn't in the office.' Chloe politely bit back the urge to remind the caller that it was well after office hours in Australia and that her employer was almost certainly at a social function.

On any given week night, Zac Corrigan was likely to be socialising, but that possibility had become a certainty *this* week, the week before Christmas, when almost everyone was at some kind of party. Everyone, that was, except Chloe, whose social calendar was *quiet* even at this busy time of the year.

Sadly, the red letter date in Chloe's festive season was the office Christmas party. This was the third year in a row that she'd put up her hand to be the party's organiser. She'd ordered the champagne, the wines and beer, as well as a selection of delicious canapés and finger food from François's. And she'd been happy to stay back late this evening to decorate the office with festive strings of lights, shiny balloons and bright garlands of tinsel and holly.

Secretly, she loved this task. When she'd first landed her job at ZedCee she'd also moved back home to care for her elderly parents, who weren't overly fond of 'gaudy' decorations, so this was her chance to have a little Christmas fun.

'To whom am I speaking?' the fellow from London barked into the phone.

'I'm Mr Corrigan's PA.' Chloe was used to dealing with bossy types, matching their overbearing manner with her own quiet calm. 'My name's Chloe Meadows.'

'Ms Meadows, this is Sergeant Davies from The Metropolitan Police and I'm ringing from The Royal London Hospital. I'm afraid the matter is urgent. I need to speak to Mr Corrigan.'

'Of course.' Instantly alarmed, Chloe forgave the policeman his bossiness and reached for a pen and paper. She was appalled to think that this urgent matter was in any way connected to her boss. 'I'll call Mr Corrigan immediately and tell him to ring you.'

Sergeant Davies dictated his number, Chloe thanked him and her stomach clenched nervously as she connected straight to Zac Corrigan's mobile.

The zip in the young woman's black silk dress slid smoothly downwards and the fabric parted to reveal her delightfully pale back. Zac Corrigan smiled. She was lovely. Tipsy after too many champagne cocktails and without very much to eat, but at least they'd escaped the party early, and she was quite irresistibly lovely.

With a practised touch, he caressed the creamy curve of her shoulder and she giggled. Damn. Why did champagne make girls giggle?

Still. Her skin was soft and warm and her figure was exquisite and, for a repeat of the night they'd shared last weekend, Zac could forgive her giggling.

With a firm hand cradling her bared shoulders, he leaned closer to press a kiss to the back of her neck. His lips brushed her skin. She giggled again, but she smelled delicious and Zac's anticipation was acute as he trailed a seductive line of kisses over her shoulder.

The sweet moment was spoiled by the sudden buzz of his mobile phone and Zac swore beneath his breath as he sent a frustrated glare in the direction of the armchair where he'd dumped the phone along with his jacket and tie.

'I'll get it!' the girl squealed.

'No, don't bother. Leave it.'

Too late. She'd already wriggled free and was diving for the chair, laughing excitedly, as if answering his phone was the greatest game.

Chloe suppressed a groan when she heard the slightly slurred female's voice on the line.

'Hi, there!' a girl chirped. 'Kung Fu's Chinese Takeaway. How can I help you?'

'Hi, Jasmine.' Chloe was unfortunately familiar with most of her boss's female 'friends'. They were usually blessed with beauty rather than brains, which meant they were always ringing him at work, and Chloe spent far too much time holding them at bay, taking their messages, placating them with promises that Mr Corrigan would return their calls as soon as he was free, and generally acting as a go-between. 'Hold the jokes,' she said now. 'And just put Zac on.'

'Jasmine?' The voice on the end of the line was slightly sloshed and distinctly peeved. 'Who's Jasmine?' Her voice rose several decibels. 'Zac, who's Jasmine?'

Oops. Under other circumstances, Chloe might have apologised or tried to reassure the silly girl, but tonight she simply spoke loudly and very clearly. 'This is Mr Corrigan's PA and the matter is urgent. I need to speak to him straight away.'

'All right, all right.' The girl was sulky now. 'Keep your hair on.' There was a shuffling, possibly stumbling sound. 'Mr Corr-i-gan,' she said next, sounding out the syllables in a mocking sing-song. 'Your PA wants you and she says you'd better hurry up.' This was followed by a burst of ridiculous giggling.

'Give that here!' Zac sounded impatient and a moment later he was on the line. 'Chloe, what's up? What the hell's the matter?'

'An urgent phone call has come through for you from London,' she said. 'From the police. At a hospital.'

'In *London*?' There was no missing the shock in his voice.

'Yes. I'm afraid it's urgent, Zac. The policeman wants you to call him immediately.'

There was a shuddering gasp, then another sound that might have been—

No. It couldn't have been a sob. Chloe knew her ears were deceiving her. During three years in this job she'd never detected a single crack in Zac Corrigan's habitual toughness.

'Right.' His voice was still *different*, almost broken and very un-Zac-like. 'Can you give me the number?'

Chloe told him and listened as he repeated it. He still sounded shaken and she felt a bit sick. Normally, she refused to allow herself any sympathy for her boss's personal life, which was as messy as a dog's breakfast, as far as she was concerned. But this situation was different. Frightening. She couldn't recall any connection between her boss and London and she thought she knew almost everything about him.

'I'll let you know if I need you,' he said.

Zac was as tense as a man facing a firing squad as he dialled the London number. This emergency *had* to involve Liv. He was sure of it. He'd been trying to convince himself that his little sister was an adult now and quite capable of running her own life, especially after she'd ignored his protests and left for England with her no-hoper boyfriend... But...

Liv.

His baby sister...

All that was left of his family...

His responsibility...

'Hello,' said a businesslike English voice. 'Sergeant Davies speaking.'

'This is Zac Corrigan.' His voice cracked and he swallowed. 'I believe you're trying to contact me.'

'Ah, yes, Mr Corrigan.' The policeman's tone was instantly gentler, a fact that did nothing to allay Zac's fears. 'Can I please confirm that you are Zachary James Corrigan?'

'Yes.' What had Liv done? Not another drug overdose, surely? When he'd rung her two weeks ago, she'd promised him she was still off the drugs, *all* drugs. She'd been clean for over a year.

'And you're the brother of Olivia Rose Corrigan?'

'Yes, I am. I was told you're calling from a hospital. What's this about?'

'I'm sorry, Mr Corrigan,' the policeman said. 'Your sister died a short while ago as the result of a road accident.'

Oh, God.

It wasn't possible.

Shock exploded through Zac, flashing agonising heat, threatening to topple him. Liv couldn't be dead. It simply was *not* possible.

'I'm sorry,' Sergeant Davies said again.

'I—I see,' Zac managed. A stupid thing to say, but his mind was numb. With terror. With pain.

'Do you have any relatives living in the UK?' the policeman asked.

'No.' Sweat was pouring off Zac now. Vaguely, he was aware of the girl, Daisy, with the black dress dangling off her shoulders. She was hovering close, frowning at him, her heavily made-up eyes brimming with vacuous curiosity. He turned his back on her.

'Then I take it you'll be prepared to be our contact for any arrangements?'

'Yes,' Zac said stiffly. 'But tell me what happened.'

'I'll pass you onto someone from the hospital, sir. The doctor will be able to answer all your questions.'

Dizzy and sick, Zac waited desperately as the phone went through several clicks and then a female voice spoke.

'Mr Corrigan?'

'Yes,' he said dully.

'This is Dr Jameson from the maternity ward.'

Maternity? She was joking, surely?

'I'm very sorry, Mr Corrigan. Your sister was brought to our hospital after a vehicle accident. There were extensive head and chest injuries.'

Zac winced. Head and chest. The worst.

'Olivia was rushed to theatre and we did our very best, but the injuries were too extensive.' A slight pause. 'I'm afraid we couldn't save her.'

Zac went cold all over. So there it was. Two people had confirmed the impossible. His greatest fear was a reality. After all these years when he'd tried and failed with Liv, he'd now failed her abysmally...

And it was too late to try again.

He couldn't breathe, couldn't think. Horror lashed at him as he fought off images of Liv's accident. Instead he clung to a memory of his beautiful, rebellious young sister from years ago when she was no more than sixteen… He saw her on the beach, during a holiday on Stradbroke Island, her slim tanned arms outstretched, her dark gypsy hair flying in the sea wind, her teeth flashing white as she laughed and twirled with childlike joy.

He remembered it all so clearly. With her brightly coloured sarong over a skimpy yellow bikini, she'd looked so tanned and beautiful. Innocent, too—or so Zac had thought—and, always, *always*, so full of fun.

That was how he'd thought of Liv back then—full of fun and life.

Now…he couldn't believe that her life had been extinguished.

'But we were able to save the baby,' the English doctor said.

Baby? Now Zac sank in weak-kneed horror onto the edge of the bed. What baby? How could there be a baby?

'Are you there, Mr Corrigan?'

He swallowed. 'Yes.'

'You're listed as your sister's next of kin, so I'm assuming you knew that Olivia was pregnant?'

'Yes,' he lied when in truth he'd had no idea. When he'd phoned Liv only two weeks ago, she hadn't said a thing about being pregnant. Right now, he felt as if the world had gone quite mad.

'Your sister was already in labour,' the woman said. 'We believe she was on her way to hospital when the accident occurred.'

'Right.' Zac sagged forward, elbows on knees. 'So—' he began and then he had to stop and take a shuddering breath, which wasn't much help. He forced himself to try again. 'So—this baby. Is it OK?'

'Yes, a beautiful baby girl, perfectly unharmed and born by Caesarean section only a couple of weeks before her due date.'

Zac pressed a shaking hand to his throbbing forehead. His stomach churned. He was sweating again. This woman was trying to tell him that some crazy twist of fate had snatched his beautiful sister's life and left a baby in her place. How bizarre was that?

He wanted to drop the phone, to be finished with this absurd conversation. No way did he want to deal with the gut-wrenching news that had just been so calmly delivered.

But, of course, he knew he had no choice.

With a supreme effort, he shut off the hurt and pain and, like the cool-headed businessman he usually was, he forced his mind to confront practicalities.

'I presume you've contacted the baby's father?' he said tightly, recalling the man who'd convinced Liv to run away with him. A guy from a band—a band no one had heard of— an older man with dreadlocks streaked with grey and restless eyes that could never quite meet Zac's gaze.

'Your sister wasn't able to tell us the name of the baby's father. There was a man in the car with her, but he assured us he was only a neighbour and not the father, and our blood tests have confirmed this.'

'But he could tell you—'

'I'm afraid he doesn't know anything about the father's identity.'

'Right.' Zac drew a deep, shuddering breath and squared his jaw. 'So this baby is, for all intents and purposes, my responsibility?' Even as he said this, he knew it hadn't come out right. He'd sounded uncaring and hard. But it was too late to try to retract his words. He could only press on. 'I'll...er...make arrangements to come over to London straight away.'

Chloe had just finished pinning the last decoration in place when her boss rang back.

'Chloe, I know it's late, but I need you to book me a flight to London.' His voice was crisp and businesslike, but tight, too, the way people spoke when they were fighting to keep their emotions in check. 'You'd better make it the soonest flight possible. First thing tomorrow morning, if you can.'

'Of course, and would you like a hotel reservation as well?' Chloe hoped she didn't sound too surprised, or worried... If there was a crisis, the last thing Zac needed was an anxious, fussing PA.

'Yes, book a hotel room, please. Somewhere central.'

'No problem.' Already she was firing up her computer.

'And I'll need you to sort out those accounts with Garlands.'

Chloe smiled to herself. 'All done.'

'Already?' He sounded surprised. 'That's great. Well done.'

'Anything else?'

'Could you ring Foster's and tell them that Jim Keogh will represent me at tomorrow's meeting.'

'No problem.' Chloe paused, in case there were any more instructions. 'That's all then?'

'Actually, Chloe...'

'Yes?'

'You'd better book two flights to London. Just two one-way seats at this stage. I'm not sure how long I'll need to be over there.'

Ridiculously, Chloe's heart sank. An annoying reaction. Why should she care if her boss wanted to take the giggling girl who'd answered the phone with him on an all-expenses-paid trip to London? Of course, she couldn't help wondering how much use the girl be would if Zac had been called away to something urgent.

'What name for the second ticket?' she asked smoothly as the company's preferred airline's website came up on her computer screen.

'Ah...good question. Actually...'

Another pause. Chloe began to fill the boxes on the flights search. Point of departure... *Brisbane, Australia.* Destination... *London, UK.* Date of flight...

'How busy are you, Chloe?'

'Excuse me?'

'Could you spare a few days?'

'To fly to London?'

'Yes. This is an emergency. I need someone...capable.'

Chloe was so surprised she almost dropped the phone. Was Zac really asking her to go to—to London? *At Christmas?*

'I know it's short notice and it's almost Christmas and everything.'

Her head spun, first with shock and a fizz of excitement, and then with dismay as she thought about her elderly parents at home, waiting for her, depending on her to look after the shopping and to cook Christmas dinner and to drive them to church. They would never cope without her.

'I'm sorry, Zac. I don't really think I could get away at such short notice.'

As she said this, there was the sound of a door opening behind her and she jumped. Turning, she saw her boss striding into the office. Of course, he'd had his phone in the hands-free cradle while he was driving.

As always, Chloe's heart gave a pitiful little skip when she saw him, but at least she was used to that nuisance reaction now. She knew it wasn't significant—pretty much the automatic reaction shared by most women who encountered Zac Corrigan's special brand of tall, dark and handsome.

This evening he looked paler than usual and his grey eyes betrayed a shock he hadn't been able to shake off.

'If you can come with me, I'll pay you a hefty Christmas bonus,' he said as he strode across the office to Chloe's desk.

But he'd already paid her a generous Christmas bonus. 'Can you explain what this is about?' she asked. 'What's happened?'

What's happened?

Zac lifted his hand and rubbed at his brow, where a headache had been hovering ever since he took the call from the hospital and now throbbed with renewed and vicious vengeance.

'Are you all right, Zac? You look...'

Abruptly, Chloe pulled a swivel chair from the nearest desk and pushed it towards him. 'Here, sit down.'

He held up a hand. 'It's OK, thanks. I'm fine.'

'I'm sorry, but I don't think you are.'

To Zac's surprise, his PA took a firm grasp of his elbow, gripping him through his coat sleeve. 'I think you should sit down now before you fall down.'

Zac sat.

'Can I get you a cup of tea?'

If he wasn't feeling so strung out, he might have smiled at this old-fashioned response from his conservative and over-conscientious PA. She was dressed in one of her customary businesslike suits. Her white blouse was neatly buttoned and tucked in, and there wasn't a strand of her light brown hair out of place. Good old, reliable Chloe.

He was so relieved to see her tonight. He'd been desperate to get away from the giggling Daisy and, by contrast, cool, collected Chloe was a reassuring and comforting sight.

'I don't need tea,' he said. 'I'd just like to get these flights sorted, and I could really do with your assistance in London.'

'I assume this is all because of the phone call...from the hospital.'

'Yes.' Zac swallowed, trying to clear the sharp, persistent pain that seemed to have lodged in his throat. 'I'm afraid it wasn't good news,' he said with quiet resignation. 'It was bad. Really bad. The worst.'

'Oh, no... I'm so sorry.'

Sorry... Zac was sorrier than he'd ever thought possible. He looked away from the sympathy in Chloe's soft brown eyes. Then, staring bleakly at a spot on the grey office carpet, he told her the rest of his news...

When he finished, Chloe took ages to respond. 'I... I don't know what to say,' she said at last. 'That's so terrible. I... I never realised you had a sister.'

'Yeah...well...' He couldn't bring himself to admit his estrangement from Liv, or that he hadn't known about the baby, that Liv had never even told him she was pregnant, that she almost hadn't told him about going to England.

How could he admit to this prim and conscientious cliché of a secretary that his reckless sister's pregnancy was just another of the many secrets she'd hidden from him?

'I guess you'll need help...with the baby girl...if they can't find her father,' Chloe suggested awkwardly.

'Yes. I'll be it's... I mean...*her* guardian.' He knew this, because the one thing he'd insisted on after Liv's overdose was that she made a will. He'd hoped that a measure of reality would shake some sense into her. 'I couldn't possibly manage on my own.'

Babies had never registered on Zac's radar. He'd always supposed they were a dim possibility in his far distant future...when he eventually settled down and chose a wife and all that went with a wife... But, even though he was a godfather twice over, he'd never actually held a baby. There had always been plenty of women with willing arms and he'd been more than happy to buy expensive gifts and the best champagne to wet the baby's head and then stay well in the background...

'I'm sure we can find someone.' Chloe was busy at her computer screen, scrolling through some kind of spreadsheet.

'Find someone?' Zac asked, frowning. 'How do you mean? What kind of someone?' He didn't need to *find* someone. He had Chloe.

She turned back to him with a smile that was almost sympathetic. 'This is a list of your personal female contacts.'

'You have them on a spreadsheet?'

'Well, yes. How else do you think I manage to—?'

'All right, all right.' He gave an impatient wave of his hand. He knew Chloe was a marvel at managing his female friends—sending them the appropriate invitations or flowers, birthday or Christmas presents, get well cards, even, at times, offering excuses on his behalf...but he'd never given any thought to how she kept track of them.

'What about Marissa Johnson?' Chloe said now. 'She always struck me as sensible.'

'No,' Zac said curtly, remembering the awkward way he and Marissa Johnson had broken up. He jumped to his feet, seized by a fit of restless impatience. 'Look, there's no point in looking at that list. I don't want any of *them*. I want you, Chloe. We've worked together for three years now and I know you'd be perfect.'

To his surprise her cheeks went a deep shade of pink—a becoming shade of pink that unsettled him.

'I don't know very much about babies,' she said.

'Really?' Zac frowned at her. She was female, after all. 'But you know enough, don't you? You know how to put on a nappy. And when it comes to bottles and that sort of thing, you can follow instructions. It's just for a few days, Chloe. There's a remote possibility that I might have to bring this child home. I'll need help, just till I have everything sorted.'

Not that he had any idea how this problem could be sorted. At the moment he was still too shocked. Too sad. He didn't want to think about a little new life when Liv was—

'I'm sorry,' Chloe said quickly. 'I'd like to help, but I'm not really free to rush overseas at the drop of a hat. Not at this time of year. I have my parents to consider...'

'Your parents?' Zac frowned again. Why would a woman approaching thirty be so concerned about her parents? Then again, he knew he was out of touch with the whole family thing. His own parents had died when he was eighteen and he'd been managing without them for almost seventeen years.

But now there was a baby...a niece...another little girl who was his responsibility. A slug of pain caught him mid-chest. History was repeating itself in the most macabre way.

'It's Christmas,' Chloe said next, as if that explained everything. She looked up at the surprisingly attractive decorations she'd arranged about the office. 'Would you like me to look into hiring a nanny?'

Zac let out a weary sigh. 'The last thing I need now is to start interviewing nannies.'

'I don't mind doing the interviews.'

'No,' he snapped. 'We don't have time.'

Besides, for this delicate operation, he needed someone he already knew, a woman who was loyal and trustworthy, and sensible and efficient—and a woman who wouldn't distract him with sex.

Chloe Meadows ticked every box.

CHAPTER TWO

CHLOE COULDN'T QUITE believe it was actually happening. Here she was in the executive lounge of Brisbane International Airport, enjoying coffee and croissants with her boss, with a boarding pass for a flight to London in her handbag, a grey winter jacket and rosy pink scarf folded on the seat beside her, and a neatly packed carry-on bag at her feet.

She still wasn't quite sure how Zac had convinced her to do this, but from the moment he'd learned she had an up-to-date passport the pressure had begun. He'd argued that the company was winding down for the Christmas break anyway and, thanks to her superb organisational skills, the office Christmas party could run brilliantly without her.

He'd brushed aside her concerns that she knew very little about babies. After all, the child's father might yet be found.

To Chloe's amazement, even her very valid concerns about her parents had been duly considered by her boss and then swiftly and satisfactorily smoothed away.

She'd been stunned when he'd asked last night if he could visit her parents. She'd tried to protest. 'Sorry, no. Mum and Dad will be in bed already.'

'Why don't you ring them to check?' he'd said confidently.

To Chloe's surprise, her mother and father were still up,

watching *Carols in the Cathedral* on TV, and, even more surprisingly, they said they'd be happy for her boss to call in, if he didn't mind finding them in their dressing gowns and slippers.

Zac said he didn't mind in the least.

'Chloe, there's sherry in the pantry and we can break open that box of shortbread you bought last week,' her mother suggested, sounding almost excited.

Zac had poured on the charm, of course, and, when it came to being charming, her boss was a genius. Even so, when he offered to put her parents up in the Riverslea Hotel, all expenses paid, with all their meals, most especially Christmas lunch, included, Chloe was sure they would refuse. It would be all too flash! They didn't like flashiness.

But, before her parents could object, Zac had thrown in a car with a driver to take them to church on Christmas Day, or to the doctor, or anywhere else they needed to go, and he'd offered to hire a nurse to check daily that they were keeping well and taking their correct medication.

Chloe's mother had looked a bit doubtful about this, until she'd received an elbow in the ribs from her dad.

'It would be like a holiday, love,' he'd said.

Still, Chloe had expected her parents to have second thoughts and say no. But then Zac also told them with commendable sincerity how extremely important, no, *invaluable,* their daughter was to him and how much he needed her for this very important mission in the UK.

Somehow he'd struck just the right note, which was clever. If he'd praised Chloe to the skies, her parents would have been suspicious and he would have blown it.

Instead, by the time he'd finished, they were practically squirming with delight, like puppies getting their tummies rubbed just the way they liked it.

And now...this morning, her parents, with their out of date, simple clothes and humble, shabby luggage, including her dad's walking frame, had looked a trifle out of place in the luxurious hotel suite with thick white carpet, floor-length cream linen curtains, golden taps in the bathroom, not to mention panoramic views up and down the Brisbane River...but the grins on their faces had said it all.

'Chloe, you go and look after your nice Mr Corrigan,' they'd said, practically pushing her out of the door. 'Don't you worry about us.'

Chloe had closed her gaping mouth.

Remembering her parents' delight, she could almost imagine them exploring their hotel room like excited children, checking the little bottles of shampoo and bubble bath, flushing the loo and bouncing on the king-sized mattress. Zac Corrigan had achieved a minor miracle.

And Chloe was going to London!

Right. Deep breath. She only hoped she wasn't making a very serious mistake. After all, she knew why her boss had been so keen to avoid asking any of his female 'friends' to accompany him on this very personal journey. He liked to keep his relationships casual and this sojourn to London would be anything but casual.

Chloe also knew why her boss regarded her as a suitable choice. She was capable, conscientious and uncomplicated, and he trusted her to remain that way. Which suited her just fine. It did. Really.

Yes, there was a danger that those annoying longings she sometimes felt for Zac would surface, but she'd had plenty of practice at keeping them in check and she was sure she could survive his close proximity for a few short days.

So perhaps it was OK now to admit to herself that she was a tiny bit excited, or at least she would be if she wasn't concerned for Zac and the sad ordeal that still awaited him when they landed.

Eventually, they boarded and took off, making the long flight across Australia, and now they were, according to the map on the screen, flying high above the Indian Ocean...

The cabin lights were dimmed, Zac and Chloe had eaten an exquisite meal and had drunk some truly delicious wine, and their business class seats had been turned into beds.

Beside Chloe, her boss appeared to be asleep already, stretched out in jeans and a black T-shirt, with his shoes off and his belt removed and his feet encased in black and purple diamond-patterned socks. He had also plugged in earphones and was listening to music and he had slipped on the navy silk eyeshade the airline provided.

He was used to flying and she supposed he would sleep now, possibly for hours. He'd probably had very little rest during the previous night and she was sure he needed to sleep. Actually, Chloe's night had been sleepless as well, so she knew it would be sensible to try to follow his example. Otherwise, she'd end up in London, useless with jet lag, with a boss who was ready and raring to go.

Unfortunately, however, Chloe was too *wired* to sleep. The past twenty-four hours had been such a whirlwind and the thought of London was simply too exciting. She'd acquired her passport in happier times, when she'd thought she knew exactly where her life was heading...

But she'd never used it. So she'd never been on an international flight before, had never flown business class, and had certainly never been to England. It was hard to believe she would soon be seeing the famous Tower Bridge and Big Ben and Buckingham Palace.

Needing to calm down, she fished in her bag for the magazines she'd bought from the airport newsagent while Zac was busy with a phone call. The mags were all about mothers and babies and parenting and Chloe hoped to find an article or two about caring for newborns. Just in case...

Luckily, there were plenty of stories and columns covering all kinds of newborn issues. Chloe soon discovered what to do if a baby had colic, jaundice, an umbilical hernia...and masses of information about bath time, skin care, crying, feeding, burping...

She read the information conscientiously, trying to take it all in, wondering if she would actually be called on to apply any of this in practice and hoping she'd remember the important details. Her real-life experience of babies was limited to admiring her friends' offspring, and she'd found them cute to cuddle or play with and then she'd been happy enough to hand them back to their mothers.

After her life turned upside down several years ago, she'd given up her own dreams of motherhood, so she'd never given much thought to the finer details of green nappies or colic or projectile vomiting.

Even now, she blocked those images. Not every baby had those problems, surely?

Instead, Chloe allowed herself to picture a tiny, warm, sweet-smelling bundle in her arms, a dear little baby girl, with soft pink skin and perhaps dark hair like Zac's. A darling rosebud mouth.

'Aren't you sleepy?' murmured a deep voice beside her.

Startled, she turned to see that Zac had lifted his eyeshade and removed an earplug, and was watching her with marked curiosity.

Chloe's insides began to buzz—an annoying reaction to having him so close. 'I...er...thought it might help if I read for a bit first,' she said.

Zac leaned closer, frowning. 'What on earth are you reading?'

The magazine in her lap was unfortunately open at a full-page picture of a tiny baby attached to an enormous breast.

Chloe felt her cheeks heat. 'I...um...just thought...in case... you know, the baby...it would be handy to have a few clues.'

'It would indeed.' Zac spoke smoothly enough, but his eyes once again held the bleak shadows that had arrived with the terrible news about his sister. 'Good thinking, Ms Meadows.'

Chloe swallowed. It was more than a little unnerving to find herself lying so close to her boss's disconcerting, sad grey eyes. She could see his individual thick, dark eyelashes and the grainy texture of the skin on his jaw. She hadn't been this close to a man since—

'I'm sure I'll be sleepy soon,' she said quickly, before her thoughts could be hijacked by haunting memories.

'Tell me something you've learned,' Zac said, keeping his voice low so he didn't disturb the other passengers, many of whom were sleeping. 'I'm intrigued.'

'Something about babies?' Chloe whispered back.

He cast another glance at the photo in her lap. 'Or breasts, if you prefer.' He gave her a teasing smile.

Despite the rising heat in her cheeks, Chloe sent him a drop-dead look and closed the magazine.

'Babies then,' Zac amended, his lips still twitching in a smile. 'Tell me what you've learned about babies.'

In truth, she'd learned an awful lot that she hadn't really wanted to know—about a newly delivered mother's hormonal fluctuations, the stitches she might have in awkward places, her leaking or sore and swollen breasts.

'OK,' she said as she remembered a snippet of practical information that was safe to share with him. 'Did you know that you should wash the baby's bodysuits and nightgowns in hypoallergenic dye- and scent-free detergent?'

'Fascinating.' Zac yawned, clearly already bored.

Good, he might leave her in peace.

Chloe waited for him to replace his eye mask. Instead, he pointed to one of the magazines in her lap. 'Do you mind?'

This time, she didn't try to hide her surprise. 'You want to read one of these? A mother and baby magazine?'

Her corporate executive playboy boss could not be serious. The Zac Corrigan she knew wouldn't be caught dead with such an incriminating piece of reading material in his hands, not even in the relative anonymity of an international flight.

'Yes, please,' he said, holding out his hand and smiling blandly. 'I'd like to be educated.'

Lips compressed to stop herself from making a smart retort, Chloe handed him a magazine that focused on a baby's first six months. She supposed he was probably teasing her, but he might be trying to distract himself from thinking too much about his sister.

It was even possible that he genuinely wanted to learn. After all, if a father for Liv's baby couldn't be traced, Zac might soon find himself in complete charge of a newborn.

For a while they both read in peaceful silence, the small glow of their reading lights making golden cones in the otherwise darkened cabin. But Chloe couldn't relax. For one thing, she was too curious about how Zac might be reacting to the contents of his magazine.

But it wasn't long before he leaned close, speaking softly. 'Did you know that babies can stare at you while they sleep?'

'Excuse me?'

He smiled. 'It says here that they can sleep with their eyes half open. It looks pretty spooky, apparently.'

Although his smile, up close, was dangerous for Chloe's heart health, she couldn't help smiling back at him. 'Well, the article I'm reading warns that babies sometimes don't sleep at all.'

'No.' Zac feigned complete shock. 'That can't be right.'

'Well, I guess they sleep eventually, but some stay awake for much longer than they're supposed to.'

'A bit like us,' he said, looking around the business class cabin at all the other passengers, who appeared to be contentedly sleeping.

Chloe sighed. 'I guess we really should turn our lights out and try to sleep.'

'Yes, we should.' He closed the magazine and handed it back to her. 'Thanks for that. Most enlightening.'

By the time she'd stowed the magazines away, Zac had turned

off his reading light, pulled down his eyeshade and folded his arms over his wide chest. 'Goodnight, Ms Meadows.'

He usually only addressed her this way when he was in a playful mood, which wasn't very often, mostly when he'd pulled off some extraordinarily tricky business coup. Chloe wondered if the playboy was coming out in him now, simply because he was lying beside a young woman who was close enough to touch and kiss.

That thought had no sooner arrived than her body reacted, growing warm and tingly and tight.

Oh, for heaven's sake.

Where had such a ridiculous reaction sprung from? Chloe gave herself a mental slap and glared at Zac.

'Goodnight, sir,' she said icily.

'And try to sleep.' He spoke without lifting his shade and he sounded now like a weary parent. 'We've a long way to go.'

Chloe didn't answer and she was relieved that she would not have to speak to her boss again until morning. She pulled on her own eye mask and tried to settle comfortably, hoping that the steady vibration of the plane and the hum of its engines would soothe her.

Her hopes were not realised.

She couldn't relax. She was too upset by her mental slip about kissing and touching her boss. Too busy delivering a good, stern lecture to herself. After all, she knew very well that Zac had asked her to accompany him on this trip precisely because he needed a female companion to whom he was *not* sexually attracted.

Her momentary lapse had no doubt been brought on by her over-tiredness. She knew nothing like *that* would happen. Zac had spent a good section of almost every working day in the past three years in her company without once trying to flirt.

Besides, she didn't want it to happen. She was far too sensible to ever fall for her boss's superficial good looks and charming wiles. Apart from the fact that she'd had her heart broken once and never wanted to experience that pain again, there was no way on this earth that she would allow her name to end up on the spreadsheet of his *Foolish Females*.

Unfortunately, her attempt to sleep only lasted about ten or fifteen minutes before she had to wriggle and fidget and try for a more comfortable position. Beside her, she heard a weary sigh. 'Sorry,' she whispered.

Zac lifted the eye mask again and pinched the bridge of his nose.

'Sorry,' Chloe said again. 'I disturbed you, didn't I?'

He shook his head. 'Not really.' He yawned. 'I'm dog-tired, but I have a feeling I'm not going to sleep tonight.'

'Do you normally sleep on long haul flights?'

'Eventually.'

She wondered if he couldn't stop thinking about his sister. Was he simply too upset to sleep? She wished she could help.

'I don't have any brothers or sisters,' she said tentatively.

Zac frowned.

'Sorry,' she said quickly, wincing at her third apology in as many minutes. 'I just thought you might want to talk, but I shouldn't have—'

'No, no, it's OK.' He sighed again, and lay staring into space, apparently thinking...

Chloe waited, not sure what else to say.

'Liv was eight years younger than me,' he said quietly. 'When our parents died, she was only ten, so I felt more like her father at times.' His mouth was a grim downward curve. 'She was my responsibility.'

Chloe stared at him now as she tried to take this in. Was the poor man blaming himself for his sister's accident? Did he feel completely responsible? 'But you must have been very young, too,' she said.

'I was eighteen. An adult.'

Only just, by the skin of your teeth. 'How awful for you to lose both your parents so young.'

'Yeah,' he agreed with another sigh.

Chloe didn't like to ask, but her imagination was running wild. 'How did it happen, Zac? Was there an accident?'

He shrugged. 'We'll never know for sure. My parents were sailing somewhere in Indonesia when their boat just disappeared. My father was a geologist, you see, and my mother was a marine biologist and they were mad keen on science and exploration, always on the lookout for a new discovery. I suppose you'd call them nutty professors. Eccentrics.'

So they'd just disappeared…? Poor Zac. How terrible to have his parents simply vanish, to never know if they'd been taken by pirates, or capsized in a tropical storm, or drowned when their boat struck a coral reef…

'They—they couldn't be still alive, living on some jungle-clad island, could they?'

Zac's mouth tilted in a wryly crooked smile. 'I've played with that fantasy, too. But it's been seventeen years…'

Chloe couldn't imagine how awful it must have been for him—a mere eighteen years old and forced to carry on living without answers, just with terrible possibilities.

'Right from the start I was worried about Liv,' he said next. 'I couldn't bear to see her disappear into a foster home, so I applied to be her guardian. I dropped out of uni and got myself a job, so we could live together and I could look after her.'

'Goodness,' Chloe said softly, hoping she didn't sound as surprised as she felt.

Zac's lips curled unhappily. 'It was possibly the stupidest decision I ever made.'

'Don't say that. I think it was incredibly brave of you.'

She was stunned to realise that Zac had sacrificed his own goals to try to keep what was left of his family intact. All she'd ever known about his private life was the revolving door of lookalike leggy blonde girlfriends. He'd never seemed to really care about any of them beyond their sex appeal and she'd assumed the 'care factor' gene was missing from his DNA.

But it was clear to her now that he'd cared very deeply about Liv.

'I couldn't keep her on track,' Zac said, so softly Chloe almost missed it. 'Liv never really looked on me as a parent. She wouldn't accept me in a fathering role, so I had very little influence, I'm afraid. I think she was mad at our parents for disappearing the way they did and she saw me as an inadequate substitute. Before she was out of her teens she was into drinking and trying drugs. And then she was like a nomad, never wanting to settle. She didn't want to study and she would never stay in one job for long enough to get any real skills. She was like a butterfly, always searching for a brighter flower.'

'Might she have inherited that urge from your parents?'

'Quite possibly, I guess.'

He stared unhappily up at the cabin's ceiling and Chloe wished she could offer him wise words of consolation.

She did her best. 'Honestly, I don't think you should blame yourself for this accident, Zac.'

But he simply shook his head and closed his eyes.

It was ages before Chloe drifted off to sleep and when she woke a soft grey light filled the cabin and flight attendants were bringing around hot towels to freshen their hands and faces, as well as glasses of orange juice.

'Morning, sleepyhead.'

Zac's seat was already back in the upright position and he looked as if he'd been to the bathroom and washed and shaved.

Chloe yawned and hoped her hair wasn't too messy. In a minute she would follow his example and freshen up. 'What time is it?'

'Seven forty-five. That's Greenwich Mean Time, of course. If we were still at home it would be five forty-five in the evening.'

So...her parents had almost completed their first day in the hotel. Chloe hoped they were still enjoying themselves.

If she'd been in Brisbane, she would be putting the final touches to the office's decorations and making last minute checks about the drinks and ice.

'I hope you're not worrying about your parents.'

'No, I'm not.' She knew they were in good hands and she'd left the hotel desk, the hired nurse and the chauffeur with all the phone numbers and information they could possibly need. 'I was thinking about the office Christmas party tonight, actually.'

'Really, Chloe?' Zac was frowning at her now, although his eyes glinted with puzzled amusement.

'I was looking forward to the party,' she admitted, no longer caring if this revealed her inadequate social life.

'You were looking forward to watching half the office staff get plastered and then staying behind to clean up their mess?'

She opened her mouth to protest.

Zac's smile was gently teasing. 'You're going to see London at Christmas. I promise you that's a thousand times better than the office do.'

'I suppose it would be. When should we get our first glimpse of England?'

'Oh, in about an hour.'

CHAPTER THREE

IT WAS RAINING when they touched down at Heathrow, but somehow that couldn't dim Chloe's excitement. As business class passengers with only carry-on baggage, she and Zac didn't have to hang around in long queues and soon they were outside, suddenly very grateful for their warm overcoats and scarves.

While they waited for a taxi she made a quick phone call to her parents.

'We're about to go down to the dining room,' her mum told her excitedly. 'We've already checked out the menu and we're having lamb cutlets and then rhubarb crumble. Give our love to Zac.'

They were having the time of their lives and, within moments, Chloe was climbing into a proper shiny black London taxi and her excitement mounted as they whizzed along busy rain-slick streets filled with other taxis and cars and bright red double-decker London buses. Ahead, on a pedestrian crossing, people huddled beneath umbrellas glistening with rain.

Zac asked the taxi driver to stop at their hotel to leave their luggage and Chloe caught a brief impression of huge glass doors, massive urns filled with greenery and enormous gold-framed mirrors in a white marbled foyer.

'Now, we'd better head straight to the Metropolitan Police,' Zac said when he returned.

'Yes.' Chloe dug out her phone and checked the arrangements she'd made for Zac to meet with Sergeant Davies. She gave their driver the address and then they were off again.

Three blocks later, they had stopped at traffic lights when she saw the trio of soldiers. The tall, broad-shouldered men were simply standing and chatting as they waited to cross a road, but all it took was the sight of their camouflage uniforms and berets to bring back memories of Sam.

It could still happen like that, even though she'd had three and a half years to recover. The smallest trigger could bring the threat of desperate black grief.

Not now... I can't think about him now...

But now, on the far side of the world with her handsome boss, this painful memory was a timely reminder of the heartache that came with falling in love. Chloe knew she had to be super-careful...and she was grateful she'd trained herself to think of Zac as nothing but her boss...glad that she'd become an expert at keeping a tight lid on any deeper feelings...

At the police station, Sergeant Davies was very solicitous as he ushered them into his office. He told them that Liv's death had been clearly accidental and there was no reason to refer it to the coroner.

'The young man who was driving your sister to the hospital is definitely in the clear,' he added. 'He's a Good Samaritan neighbour. He was injured, but he's going to be OK. A badly broken leg, I believe.'

Zac sat stiffly, his face as grim as granite, as he received this news.

'We'll be laying serious charges against the driver of the other car,' the sergeant then told them.

'Driving under the influence?' Zac asked.

This was answered by a circumspect nod of assent.

Zac sighed and closed his eyes.

***

Outside, Chloe wanted to suggest that they found somewhere for a coffee. She was sure Zac could do with caffeine fortification, but perhaps she shouldn't have been surprised that he was determined to push on with his unhappy mission. At work he always preferred to confront the unpleasant tasks first. It was one of the things she'd always admired about him.

Within moments of hitting the pavement, he hailed another taxi and they were heading for the cold reality of the Royal London Hospital.

Once there, Zac insisted on seeing his sister, but as Chloe watched him disappear down a corridor, accompanied by a dour-looking doctor in a lab coat, she was worried that it might be a mistake. Her fears were more or less confirmed when Zac returned, white-faced and gaunt, looking about ten years older.

She had no idea what to say. There was no coffee machine in sight, so she got him a drink of water in a paper cup, which he took without thanking her and drank in sips, staring at the floor, his eyes betraying his shock.

Eventually, Chloe couldn't bear it. She put an arm around his shoulders and gave him a hug.

He sent her a sideways glance so full of emotion she felt her sympathetic heart swell to bursting. He offered her a nod, as if to say thanks, but he didn't speak. She was quite sure he *couldn't* speak.

For some time they sat together, with their overcoats bundled on the bench beside them, before one of the hospital staff approached them, a youngish woman with bright red hair. 'Mr Corrigan?'

Zac lifted his gaze slowly. 'Yes?'

The woman's eyes lit up with the predictable enthusiasm of just about any female who met Zac. 'I'm Ruby Jones,' she said, holding onto her bright smile despite his grimness. 'I'm the social worker looking after your case.'

'Right. I see.' Zac was on his feet now. 'I guess you want to speak to me about the...the child?'

'Yes, certainly.' Ruby Jones offered him another sparkling smile, which Chloe thought was totally inappropriate. 'Am I right in imagining that you'd like to meet your niece?'

'Meet her?' Zac looked startled.

'Yes, she's just on the next floor in the maternity ward.'

'Oh, yes, of course.' He turned to Chloe. 'You'll come, too, won't you?'

'Yes, if you like.'

Ruby, the social worker, looked apologetic. 'I'm afraid—in these situations, we usually only allow close family members into—'

'Chloe is family,' Zac intervened, sounding more like his usual authoritarian self.

Chloe stared at the floor, praying that she didn't blush, but it was a shock to hear Zac describe her as family. She knew it was an expedient lie, but for a crazy moment her imagination went a little wild.

'I'm sorry.' Ruby sounded as flustered as Chloe felt. 'I thought you mentioned a PA.'

Zac gave an impatient flick of his head. 'Anyway, you couldn't count this child's close family on two fingers.' He placed a commanding hand at Chloe's elbow. 'Come on.'

Chloe avoided making eye contact with Zac as the social worker led them to the lift, which they rode in silence to the next floor.

'This way,' Ruby said as they stepped out and she led them down a hallway smelling of antiseptic, past doorways that revealed glimpses of young women and bassinets. From all around were sounds of new babies crying and, somewhere in the distance, a floor polisher whined.

Zac looked gloomy, as if he was hating every minute.

'Have you ever been in a maternity ward before?' Chloe asked him out of the side of her mouth.

'No, of course not. Have you?'

'Once. Just to visit a friend,' she added when she saw his startled glance.

Ahead of them, the social worker had stopped at a glass door and was talking to a nurse. She turned to them. 'If you wait here at this door, we'll wheel the baby over.'

Zac nodded unhappily.

Chloe said, 'Thank you.'

As the two women disappeared, Zac let out a heavy sigh. His jaw jutted with dismal determination as he sank his hands deep into his trouser pockets. Chloe was tempted to reach out, to touch him again, to give his elbow an encouraging squeeze, but almost immediately the door opened and a little trolley was wheeled through.

She could see the bump of a tiny baby beneath a pink blanket, and a hint of dark hair. Beside her, she heard her boss gasp.

'Oh, my God,' he whispered.

The trolley was wheeled closer.

'So here she is.' The nurse was middle-aged and hearty and she gave Zac an encouraging smile. 'She's a proper little cutie, this one.'

Chloe couldn't help taking a step closer. The nurse was right. The baby was incredibly cute. She was sound asleep and lying on her back, giving them a good view of her perfectly round little face and soft skin and her tiny nose—and, yes, her perfectly darling rosebud mouth—just as Chloe had imagined.

The baby gave a little stretch and one tiny hand came out from beneath the blanket, almost waving at them. There was a hospital bracelet around her wrinkled wrist. Chloe saw the name Corrigan written on it and a painful lump filled her throat.

Zac was staring at the baby with a kind of awestruck terror.

'So what do you think of your niece, Mr Corrigan?' asked Ruby, the social worker.

He gave a dazed shake of his head. 'She's tiny.'

'Her birth weight was fine,' the nurse said, sounding defensive, as if Zac had directly criticised her hospital. 'At least seven pounds.'

The social worker chimed in again. 'Would you like to hold her?'

Now Zac looked truly horrified. 'But she's asleep,' he protested, keeping his hands rammed in his pockets and rocking back on his heels as if he wished he could escape. For Chloe, by contrast, the urge to pick the baby up and cuddle her was almost overwhelming, as the maternal yearnings that she'd learned to suppress came suddenly rushing back.

She saw a frowning look exchanged between the nurse and the social worker and she worried that this was some kind of test that Zac had to pass before they could consider handing the baby into his care.

'Go on,' Chloe urged him softly. 'You should hold her for a moment. You won't upset her. She probably won't even wake up.'

Zac felt as if the air had been sucked from his lungs. He couldn't remember when he'd ever felt so out of his depth. The nurse was peeling back the pink blanket to reveal a tiny baby wrapped tightly in another thinner blanket. This was going to happen. They were going to hand her to him and he couldn't back out of it.

'Our little newborns feel safer when they're swaddled firmly like this. It also makes them easier to hold,' the nurse said as she lifted the sleeping bundle.

Reluctantly, Zac drew his hands from his pockets and hoped they weren't shaking.

'Just relax,' the nurse said as she placed the baby in his arms.

Relax? She had to be joking. It was all right for her. She did this every day. He was still getting over the agony of seeing Liv. And now he was so scared he might drop her baby...

She was in his arms.

He could feel the warmth of Liv's baby reaching him through

the thin wrap. Could feel her limbs wriggling. Oh, dear God, she was so real. Alive and breathing. He forced himself to look down into her little pink face, so different from the deathly white one he'd so recently witnessed...

And yet...the similarity was there...

He found it so easily in the baby's soft dark hair, in the delicate curve of her fine dark eyebrows, and in the tiniest suggestion of a cleft in her dainty chin.

'Oh, Liv.'

His sister's name broke from him on a desolate sob. His vision blurred as his throat was choked by tears.

Chloe's heart almost broke when she saw the silver glitter in Zac's eyes.

Even now, under these most difficult circumstances, it was a shock to see her boss cry. Zac was always so in control. In the day-to-day running of his business, it didn't matter how worried or upset or even angry he was, he never lost his cool. Never.

He usually viewed any kind of trouble as a challenge. In fact, there were days when he seemed to thrive on trouble and conflict. Twice, to her knowledge, he'd taken his company to the very brink of economic peril, but he'd never lost his nerve and had emerged triumphant.

Of course, there was a huge gulf between the challenges of the business world and a personal heartbreaking tragedy.

Now Zac Corrigan, her fearless boss, was caught in the worst kind of heartbreak and he was shaking helplessly as tears streamed down his face.

'Here,' he said, thrusting the baby towards Chloe. 'Please, take her.'

Her own emotions were unravelling as she hastily dumped their coats to accept the warm bundle he pressed into her arms. The poor man had been through so much—*too* much—in such a short time and, on top of everything else, he was dealing with jet lag. But, even though he had every reason to weep, Chloe knew he would be mortified to break down like this in public.

She wasn't at all surprised when Zac turned from them and strode back down the corridor, his head high and his shoulders squared as he drew deep breaths and fought for composure.

Watching him, she held the baby close, inhaling the clean and milky smell of her. She thought how perfectly she fitted in her arms.

Beside her, Ruby, the social worker, said, 'It's such a very sad situation.'

Indeed, Chloe agreed silently.

The baby squirmed now and beneath the blanket she gave a little kick against Chloe's ribs. Chloe wondered if this was how it had felt for Liv when she'd been pregnant. *Such a short time ago.*

Oh, help. If she allowed herself to think about that, she'd start weeping, too.

Perhaps it was just as well that she was distracted by Zac's return. He seemed sufficiently composed—although still unnaturally pale.

'I'm so sorry for your loss,' the nurse said.

Zac held up a hand and gave a brief nod of acknowledgement. 'Thank you.' His manner was curt but not impolite. Then he said, in his most businesslike tone, 'I guess you need to bring me up to speed.' He shifted his now steady gaze to the social worker. 'What's the current situation? Has anyone been able to locate the father?'

Ruby shook her head. 'I'm afraid we've had no luck at all.'

'You've definitely ruled out the fellow who was in the car with Liv?'

'Yes.'

At this news, Zac looked bleaker than ever.

'We've also interviewed the people who lived in the share house with your sister,' Ruby said next. 'But they haven't been able to help us. They said Olivia wouldn't tell anyone the father's name. She simply told them that he wouldn't be interested in a child and she didn't want anything more to do with him.'

Zac stared at her for a long moment, his grey eyes reflecting a stormy mix of emotions. Eventually he nodded. 'That sounds like my sister, I'm afraid. But there was a boyfriend. I'm pretty sure Liv was still with him last Christmas. An Australian. A singer in a band.'

'Bo Stanley?'

Zac nodded grimly. 'Yes, I'm pretty sure that's his name.'

Again, she shook her head. 'A housemate did mention him and he's still in the UK, so we made contact and had him tested. It was easy to disqualify him. He's completely the wrong blood type.'

This time, Zac stared at her as if he was sure she had to be mistaken, but eventually he gave an unhappy shake of his head and shrugged. 'I guess he's off the hook, then.'

In Chloe's arms, the baby gave a little snuffling snort. When Chloe looked down she saw that her eyes had opened. The baby blinked and stared up at Chloe, straight into her eyes.

How much could those newborn dark grey eyes see? The baby's expression was definitely curious. Trusting, too. Her intense, seemingly focused gaze pierced Chloe's heart and she was enveloped by a rush of warmth, a fierce longing to protect this tiny, sweet girl. *It would be so easy to love her.*

She realised that Zac was watching her.

His gaze lingered on her as she stood there with the baby in her arms. Surprise flared in his eyes and then a softer emotion. Chloe held her breath and for a winded moment her mind played again with hopelessly ridiculous possibilities...

Fortunately, Zac quickly recovered. 'OK,' he said, looking quickly away and becoming businesslike again. 'I guess my next question is about the baby.'

'What would you like to know?' the nurse asked guardedly.

'Is she healthy?'

'Perfectly.' She sniffed as if his question had offended her. 'You would have been informed before now if there was a problem.' Then, more gently, she asked, 'Do you have a particular concern?'

Zac grimaced uncomfortably. 'My sister had a drug habit, or at least she used to.' He shot a quick glance to Chloe and then looked away, as if he was embarrassed to have his employee hear this admission. 'It was some time back,' he added quickly. 'And Liv assured me she's been clean ever since, but I assume you've run the necessary tests?'

'Yes, Mr Corrigan. I can reassure you there were no signs that the baby has been adversely affected by alcohol or drugs.'

'Well, that's good news at least.' He swallowed. 'So…' Looking from the nurse to the social worker, he summoned a small smile, a glimmer of his customary effortless charm. 'What's next?'

Ruby, the social worker, was clearly surprised. 'Well…as you're next of kin and you've been named as guardian—'

'Yes, I've brought a copy of my sister's will if you need to see it.'

'And you've come all the way from Australia,' Ruby continued. 'I—I mean *we* were assuming that you planned to care for the baby.'

Zac nodded and his throat worked as he swallowed again.

Chloe knew he felt overwhelmed. He'd fielded successive shocks in the past twenty-four hours and she felt compelled to speak up. 'We've only just arrived from Heathrow and Mr Corrigan hasn't had any time to adjust, or to buy any of the things the baby will need.'

The nurse nodded. 'Of course. I understand.'

Shooting Chloe a grateful look, Zac added, 'If the baby could remain in your care for a little longer, I'd be happy to pay for any additional costs.'

This could be arranged, they were told, and Zac was also given a list of funeral parlours, as well as the name and address of Liv's share house, so that he could collect Liv's belongings. On that sobering note, they departed.

Outside the hospital a brisk December wind whipped at them, lifting their hair and catching at the ends of their scarves. Standing on the footpath on Whitechapel Road, Zac almost welcomed the wind's buffeting force and the sting to his cheeks. He dragged in an extra deep lungful of chilled air, as if it might somehow clear the raw pain and misery that roiled inside him. But there was no way he could avoid the two images that kept swimming before his vision. The pale, bruised, lifeless face of his beautiful sister and the small, red, but very much alive face of her tiny newborn daughter.

His niece.

His new responsibility.

The frigid air seemed to seep into Zac's very blood along with this chilling reality. This baby, this brand new human being had no other family. He was *it*. She would be completely dependent on him.

He shot a glance to Chloe, whose cheeks had already turned quite pink from the cold. The high colour made her look unexpectedly pretty and he thought how fabulous she'd been this morning. In fact, his decision to bring his PA with him to London had been a stroke of pure genius. On the long flight, at the police station and again at the hospital, Chloe's no-fuss efficiency and quiet sympathy had been exactly the kind of support he'd needed.

'I vote we go back to the hotel now,' he said. 'We can check in and get a few things sorted.'

Chloe nodded. 'I'll check out those funeral parlours, if you like. It might be hard to find a—a place—with Christmas and everything.'

Zac was about to agree, but then he remembered the heartbreaking decisions he might be required to make. 'I'd better talk to them, Chloe. Anyway, you're probably exhausted.'

'I feel fine, actually.' She smiled. 'Being outside and grabbing a breath of fresh air makes all the difference.'

You're a breath of fresh air, he almost told her, and then thought better of it. Even minor breaches of their boss-PA boundaries seemed to make Chloe uncomfortable and now that she'd given up her Christmas and had come all this way, he didn't want to upset her. Instead he said, 'And I'll also make contact with the share house people.'

'Yes, it might be worth finding out what Liv's already bought before you start shopping.'

Zac frowned. Suddenly, his mega-sensible PA wasn't making any sense at all. 'Shopping?'

'For the baby.'

'Oh.' He gulped nervously. 'Yes, of course.'

A vision of a mountain of nappies and prams and tins of formula mushroomed in Zac's imagination. He felt overwhelmed again as he raised a hand to hail their taxi.

In a matter of moments, they were heading back into the city centre. Chloe leaned back in the seat and closed her eyes. She was probably worn out, even though she'd denied it. Zac had never seen her like this—with her eyes closed, her dark lashes lying softly against her flushed cheeks, her lips relaxed and slightly open.

She looked vulnerable and he found his attention riveted...

This wasn't the first time he'd entertained the idea of kissing Chloe, of making love to her, but, just as he had on the other occasions, he quickly cut off the thought.

From the start, when he'd first employed Chloe, he'd quickly recognised her value as his PA and he'd set himself clear rules. No office affairs. Ever.

Of course, there'd been times when he'd wished to hell that he wasn't so principled where Chloe was concerned. More than once they'd been deep in a business discussion when he'd been completely distracted by her quiet beauty, but it was almost certainly for the best that his common sense had always prevailed.

And now, once again, Zac dismissed ideas of tasting her softly parted lips and he wrenched his thoughts back to his new responsibilities.

A tiny baby...such an alarming prospect for a commitment-shy bachelor. If he took Liv's little daughter into his care, she would rely on him for everything—for food, for shelter, clothes...love. As she grew older she would look up to him for wise guidance, for entertainment, for security. She would require vast amounts of his time and patience.

No doubt she would view him as her father.

Her daddy...

The thought brought shivers fingering down Zac's spine. He couldn't deny he'd been hoping that the baby's biological father would emerge and make a claim, but he'd also been worried by the prospect. Knowing Liv, the guy was bound to be a no-hoper. Now, the possibility of a father galloping up on a white charger to save the day was fast disappearing and this left Zac with a different, but equally worrying set of problems...centring on his own, very real inadequacies...

He was very aware that his personal life was at best...haphazard...but there was a good reason for that—in more recent years he'd been making up for lost time.

Liv had been so young when their parents died, and for many years Zac had made her his first priority. He'd juggled several part-time jobs so that he could be at home for as much of Liv's out-of-school time as possible.

It was only *after* Liv had turned eighteen and struck out on her own, that he'd decided he might as well have some fun, so when it came to dating women he'd been a late starter. By then he'd also discovered he had a head for business as well as a talent for attracting gorgeous girls. He'd enjoyed the combination of work and play so much that he hadn't felt a need to settle down.

Now...as he stared out at the busy London traffic, at the towering modern buildings and the occasional ancient stone church hunkering within the skyscraper forest, he wondered if adoption might be the best option for Liv's baby.

It wasn't the first time Zac had toyed with the idea. Ever since the first shocking phone call from London , the possibility of adoption had been there, nagging at the back of his thoughts.

A huge part of him was actually quite willing to hand the baby over, and not because he was keen to shirk his responsibility, but because he was so totally scared of failure. With Liv, he'd tried his damnedest and he'd failed spectacularly, so how could he hope to be any more successful with her baby?

And yet...

Zac dragged an agonised hand over his face as guilt squirmed unpleasantly inside him. Could he really bring himself to hand that tiny bundle, that little 'mini-Liv', over to strangers?

After all, his sister had named him as guardian of her children in her will, and surely she wouldn't have made that weighty decision if she'd wanted her baby to be adopted.

Problem was...if the child was *not* adopted, there were very few alternatives. He certainly couldn't care for a baby on his own and he shuddered at the idea of a procession of housekeepers and babysitters and nannies.

He had to find a better solution. Fate had handed him a second chance to care for a member of his family and he simply *had* to get it right this time.

Liv's child needed security and continuity and she needed someone else besides him, someone who would balance his strengths and weaknesses. But a baby also needed someone who would really care about her and love her and, most importantly, stay with her...

What the poor kid needed was a mother...

With a heavy sigh, Zac closed his eyes, recalling a long ago image of Liv as a baby. He could picture their house in Ashgrove in a street lined with Bunya pines. Their mother was bathing Liv in a special little baby bath on the kitchen table, holding her carefully in the crook of her arm as she squeezed water from a facecloth over her fat little tummy.

Their mum had made a game of it and every time the water touched Liv's tummy, the baby would laugh and splash. Zac remembered the happiness of that squealing baby laughter, remembered the shining joy and impossible-to-miss love in his mother's face.

At the time he'd been a bit jealous and oh, so aware of the vital importance of a mother's love.

Oh, Liv, Liv...you should have been a mother, too.

Watching from the seat in the taxi beside Zac, Chloe saw his face twist with pain. He was looking away, out of the window, and he had no idea he was being observed. His mouth was trembling and then he grimaced and bit down hard on his lip as if to hold back a sob, and she could see tears again, could see the raw, agonising pain in his face. She longed to reach out, but she knew he would hate to be caught on the brink of breaking down yet again.

Still staring bleakly through the window, Zac's weary mind threw up a picture of Chloe at the hospital this morning. He remembered how perfectly the baby had fitted into the cradle of her arms, remembered the warm glow in Chloe's chocolate eyes as she looked down at her. He remembered the equally warm, melting sensation that he'd felt as he'd watched the two of them.

So natural and right...

Yes, there could be no question. What the baby needed most definitely, *absolutely*, was a mother.

And suddenly, arriving with the lightning jolt swiftness of every great idea, Zac discovered the perfect solution.

'You know what this means, don't you?' he announced in sudden triumph.

Beside him Chloe jumped and blinked as if she'd been woken from sleep. 'What?' She was frowning. 'Excuse me?'

'This baby,' Zac said impatiently. 'Liv's baby. There's only one way to take proper care of her.'

Despite Chloe's puzzled frown, her eyes widened with curiosity. 'What is it?'

'I'll have to take the plunge.'

'What plunge?'

'Into wedded bliss.' He tried to sound more excited. 'I'll have to get married.'

CHAPTER FOUR

MARRIED?
Zac Corrigan married?

Chloe stared at her boss, too stunned to speak. There was every chance she wasn't breathing and she had huge doubts about her hearing.

Surely she must have dreamt that Zac, the serial dater, truly wanted to get married?

He was watching her with a smile that didn't quite reach his worried eyes. 'Don't look so shocked,' he said.

She gave a dazed shake of her head, as if to clear it, and sat up straighter. 'Sorry. I think I must have nodded off and didn't hear you properly. What did you just say?'

'I've found the perfect solution to the baby problem.'

'Which is...?' she prompted cautiously.

Zac lifted his hands in a gesture of triumph, as if he was announcing the latest boost in company profits to a group of delighted shareholders. 'It's obvious that I need to get married.'

Good grief. She had heard him correctly.

For no more than a millisecond the word 'marriage' uttered by Zac Corrigan sent a strange thrill zinging through Chloe, skittering across her skin and lifting fine hairs. But, almost immediately, she came to her senses. He was pulling her leg, of course. If she hadn't been so tired she would have seen the joke immediately.

'Marriage?' She laughed. 'Yeah, right.'

'I'm serious, Chloe.'

'Yes, of course you are.'

'I mean it.' He said this forcefully, as if he was growing impatient with her. 'It's the perfect solution.'

For some men, possibly, but not for you, Zac.

Clearly, jet lag had caught up with her devilishly handsome playboy boss. Jet lag plus too many personal shocks in a short space of time.

Unless...

Chloe supposed it was possible that Zac had fallen deeply in love very recently, without her knowing. 'I should have asked,' she said quickly. 'Do you already have a lucky lady in mind?'

Please, don't let it be that giggling girl who answered his phone the other evening.

Perhaps it was just as well that their taxi pulled up outside their hotel at that precise moment. Zac didn't answer Chloe's questions and the crazy conversation was dropped. Instead, he turned his attention to signing for the fare, making sure it included a generous tip.

Then a young man, resplendent in a uniform with tassels, opened the taxi door for Chloe. She had an almost film star moment as she went up the short flight of stone stairs with Zac to enormous glass doors, opened for them by another man in livery.

Once inside the glamorous high-ceilinged foyer with an exquisitely decorated soaring Christmas tree, they were greeted by more smiling staff who attended to the business of collecting their luggage and checking in.

It all went super-smoothly, with a level of service that exceeded Chloe's experiences on previous business trips. She'd certainly never stayed anywhere this glamorous before.

Zac had interrupted her last Wednesday evening, when she'd been about to make the hotel booking.

'Hang on,' he'd said, as he hunted in his desk and produced a business card. 'Try this place. I stayed there once. It's central and rather good.'

It was much pricier than his usual budget, but Chloe hadn't liked to argue and now, here they were, in a lift with an intricately tiled floor and mirrored walls, taking them silently swishing upwards...

Seconds later, they were standing in the carpeted hallway outside their adjoining rooms. 'Take your time settling in,' Zac said. 'Perhaps you'd like to rest up for a bit?'

Chloe was tempted, but she knew it wouldn't be wise. 'If I fall asleep now, I'll probably find myself wide awake and prowling around at midnight.'

To her surprise, he responded with a sparkling-eyed, slightly crooked smile.

She frowned. 'Did I say something funny?'

'No, as always you were eminently sensible, Chloe, but I have a very curious imagination. I couldn't help playing with the idea of my Ms Meadows on a midnight prowl.'

To her dismay, her mind flashed an image of the two of them meeting out here in the corridor when she was wearing nothing but a nightie and heat flared as if Zac had struck a match inside her. 'Don't be ridiculous,' she snapped.

He wiped the smile, but irritating amusement still lurked in his grey eyes. 'Seriously, it's probably best if you can manage to stay awake until this evening. How about we meet in half an hour for lunch?'

'Sounds fine. Would you like me to make you a cup of tea, sir?' She added this in her most deferential manner, to remind them both of the very clear lines drawn between his status and hers.

Zac's response was another unsettling smile and, for a moment, he looked as if he was going to make yet another inappropriately playful remark, but then he gave a slight shake of his head and the amused light in his eyes died. 'No, thanks. I'll manage.'

Chloe was annoyed that she still felt unsettled as she slid the key in her lock and went into her room.

But she was soon distracted by the room's jaw-dropping gorgeousness. It had an enormous bed, a thick, pale carpet and comfortably padded armchairs, as well as vases of roses. Everything was in tasteful shades of pink and cream, and the view was beautiful, too, through elaborately draped windows to green English parkland with enormous ancient trees spreading winter-bare branches above smooth velvet lawns.

She set her bag down and took off her coat and scarf and laid them carefully on the end of the bed. She slipped off her shoes, and when her stockinged feet sank into the deep pile carpet she gave a blissful little twirl and then a skip.

She thought of her parents back in Brisbane, enjoying their lovely hotel stay, which was also courtesy of Zac. It seemed wrong somehow that both she and her parents were enjoying a luxurious and other-worldly experience for such a very sad reason.

Sobered by this thought, she located the tea-making facilities hidden discreetly behind white-painted doors. Soon she had the jug boiled and a bag of Lady Grey tea brewing in a delicate china cup and, with milk and a half-teaspoon of sugar added, she took the cup to an armchair. For the first time in days, she had a little time to herself, to relax and unwind. But she couldn't stop thinking about her boss and the difficult phone calls he was making right next door.

As an only child, she didn't know what it was like to lose a sibling, but she knew all too well what it was like to lose someone she loved...and, without warning, she was swamped by memories.

Once again she was feeling the crushing weight of the raw grief caused by Sam's death. It had sent her retreating home to her elderly parents and, once there, their increasing age and health issues had become her excuse to withdraw from the pain of her old life...

Now, curled in the armchair, clutching the lovely cup to her chest, Chloe wept for Sam, her fiancé...and for her lost dreams...and also, in a more complicated way, she found herself weeping, as well, for her boss.

'Are you sure you're OK, Chloe? You're looking a little peaky,' Zac commented when they met again thirty minutes later.

She looked surprised. 'I'm perfectly fine, thanks.'

He might have quizzed her further, but he knew he probably looked rather pale and drawn, too. He'd certainly felt flattened after his discussions with the funeral director.

'Liv's share house is in Islington,' he said, referring to one of the other phone calls he'd made. 'It's probably just as easy to take the Tube and we can go out there first thing in the morning.'

Chloe nodded.

'I was hoping you'd come, too.'

'Yes, of course.'

The enormity of his relief was out of all proportion but, with that small issue settled, they headed for Oxford Street, hunting for a place to eat. Or at least that was Zac's plan until Chloe was completely captivated by the extravagant Christmas displays in the shops' windows.

He was patient enough while she admired them—blinding white snow scenes complete with pine trees and clever mechanical toys, glittering tables laden with sumptuous feasts, fantastic fashions displayed against a stunning snowy backdrop.

He knew the shop windows were incredibly inventive and artistic, but he found it difficult to enjoy them. He was finding it impossible to shake off the burden of his new and weighty responsibilities.

He'd been slightly miffed that Chloe had laughingly dismissed his brilliant solution of marriage without giving it so much as a moment's thought. He was also surprised she'd been so forthright. Usually, if his PA disagreed with him, she kept her opinions to herself, unless he specifically asked for her input.

Of course, he'd never discussed his private life with Chloe until now, but everything had changed last Wednesday evening. And it had changed again this morning when he saw his sister's tiny baby. He was overwhelmed anew by the huge pressure of his *duty*, and now, as Chloe turned from a clever display of robots made from children's building blocks, he was gripped by a new kind of urgency.

'You know, I'm at a loss about this child,' he said. 'I can't possibly care for her on my own.'

Perhaps he spoke a little too loudly. A woman rushing past them, laden with shopping parcels, sent Chloe a distinctly disapproving glance.

Fortunately, Chloe ignored her and simply stepped closer to Zac, lowering her voice. 'You can have all kinds of help with a child, you know. There are nannies and—'

Zac cut her off in a burst of impatience. 'Nannies come and go. I want—' He sent another glare to the steady stream of Christmas shoppers flowing around them and gave an impatient shake of his head. They couldn't talk about this here, and the cafés in Selfridges were bound to be packed at this time of the year.

'Come on.' He tugged at her coat sleeve. 'I've remembered a pretty good pub just around the corner.'

As Zac charged off, Chloe almost had to run to keep up with him.

She soon forgave him, though, when he located the pub. It had a very appealing wonderfully 'old English' atmosphere created by small paned windows with white trims, a green door and a window box spilling red, white and purple petunias.

Inside, the dark, timber-panelled space was as warm and cosy as the outside had promised. Appetising aromas drifted from the kitchen, and there was a friendly buzz in the room as diners, who were taking a break from their Christmas shopping, chatted quietly at tables covered in white linen.

Chloe and Zac took off their coats and scarves and hung them near the door, which was quite a novel experience for Chloe after subtropical Brisbane, and a friendly young waiter showed them to a table in a corner.

Several of the female diners turned and unashamedly followed Zac with their eyes. Chloe was used to this, of course, but Zac hardly seemed to notice them.

As they made themselves comfortable, Chloe was tempted to relax completely and soak up the centuries-old atmosphere, but she was too conscious of the tension coming off Zac in waves. She wondered if he was still stewing over his crazy marriage idea. Surely he would soon wake up to himself?

At least he didn't try to raise the delicate subject until after they'd ordered. Chloe chose a Stilton and potato soup with a glass of white wine, while Zac ordered a beef and Guinness pie and half a pint of beer.

With that settled, Chloe decided that she should at least humour her boss. 'So are we still discussing this marriage plan, Zac?'

His grey eyes narrowed. 'On the assumption that you're prepared to be reasonable.'

'Of course I'll be reasonable, but you never did tell me if you had a future wife in mind.'

'Well...no.' He smiled a little ruefully. 'I'll admit that's a problem.'

Chloe stomped on the ridiculous flush of relief that swept through her.

'But I'm still quite sure marriage is the perfect solution.'

'Because...?'

'The baby will need a mother,' Zac said simply.

Ah, yes...

In a heartbeat, Chloe was remembering the sweet little bundle in her arms, the warm weight of Liv's baby, and she was reliving that amazing moment when she'd looked deep into the baby's bright little eyes and had felt her heart turn over.

The memory made her throat ache and she had to swallow before she could answer. 'Finding a mother would be the ideal solution,' she said, hoping the emotion didn't show in her face. 'But plenty of babies have been brought up by nannies.'

Ridiculous tears threatened and she looked away quickly to the end of the dining room. What on earth was the matter with her? She had to be very careful that she didn't become too emotionally caught up in Zac's problems. There was no point in becoming maudlin just because she'd given up her own dreams of a family when she'd gone home to her parents.

She turned her attention to the far wall, where a huge mantelpiece lent the restaurant a gracious Victorian air. With her gaze centred on it, she said lightly, 'Wasn't the British Empire practically raised by nannies in its heyday?'

Zac's jaw stiffened, a clear sign that he was annoyed. 'Let's stick to the twenty-first century.'

She tried again, in placating tones. 'I believe the modern nannies are very well trained.'

'But no nanny these days is going to stick with a child until she's an adult.'

'That might be a stretch.' Across the table, Chloe eyed her boss boldly. 'Then again, modern marriages don't always last very long either.'

A stubborn light gleamed in Zac's eyes as he stared unblinkingly back at her. 'I still think marriage is the most sensible option. I want this child to have stability, parents who'll stick around, perhaps a little brother or sister—a life as close to normal as possible.'

Such an alluring picture...

Chloe took a deep breath. Zac wanted to give the baby everything Liv had lost. He wanted this quite badly, and desperate times required desperate measures. 'You have to do what you think is right, Zac. It's none of my business, anyway.'

'Actually...that's not quite true...'

Her heart began a frantic hammering. What did he mean?

'I thought you might be able to help me,' Zac said.

'Really? How?'

'You have that spreadsheet. We could go through it together—take another look at the possibilities.'

The spreadsheet... It was so ridiculous to feel disappointed in him. Why on earth might she have thought...?

'Please tell me you're joking,' she said quickly.

'I'm not. I'm deadly serious.'

'But trawling for a wife through a database is so—' *So wrong on so many levels.* 'So unromantic.' Chloe had to look away again.

She was remembering the day Sam proposed. They'd been walking in the rain along a cliff top, with the sea crashing and foaming on the rocks below. Sam had produced a ring and he'd actually gone down on one knee. It was *so-o-o-o* romantic. He'd told her how madly he loved her and their kiss in the rain had been the most exciting moment imaginable...

'I mean,' Zac was saying. 'For all we know, these modern marriages might fail for the very reason that they're based on romantic notions instead of common sense and logic.'

'So what are you saying now, Zac? That you don't believe in romance?'

Before he could respond, the waiter approached with their drinks.

'Meals won't be long,' the young man said cheerfully.

Zac thanked him and, as the waiter left, he raised his glass and smiled. 'Anyway...here's to you, Chloe Meadows, best PA ever.'

It was such a sudden turnabout, she knew she looked flustered and was possibly blushing. Again.

'I'm extremely grateful to you for agreeing to come here at

such short notice,' Zac went on. 'And at such a difficult time of the year.'

As they clinked glasses, his smile was so sincere that Chloe gave a little laugh to cover her reaction.

'How could I turn down an all-expenses-paid trip to London?' she said, but she was actually wondering how Zac could be so exasperating one moment and then so charming the next.

After a sip of wine, which was exceptionally fine, she veered back to their previous discussion. Now that Zac had raised the thorny subject of marrying someone with the aid of a computer spreadsheet, it was like a prickle buried in her skin that she had to dig out. 'So I take it you don't believe in romance?' she challenged him again.

He shrugged. 'I think romance is problematical. I don't see how people can make a decision that lasts a lifetime based purely on their feelings. It's highly possible that there would be more successful marriages if everyone took a more practical approach.'

'Like arranged marriages?'

'Why not? They seem to work quite well in many cultures.'

Chloe took a deeper sip of her wine as she considered this. She had to admit it was true that arranged marriages often worked. Her parents' neighbours from Afghanistan were prime examples. The Hashimis' marriage had been arranged by their parents when they were still in their teens and they'd been happily together for forty years. In fact, Mr Hashimi seemed more devoted to his wife than ever.

'You know, you're *almost* making sense,' she said. 'Except—'

'Yes?' Zac prompted eagerly, but then the waiter appeared again with their meals.

Chloe was grateful for the interruption. She'd been about to say that she couldn't imagine many Australian women falling for Zac's scheme, but then she'd remembered the names in the list of his *Foolish Females* and she knew that quite a few of those girls would probably leap at the chance to marry her boss. After all, Zac Corrigan was exceptionally eligible.

'So it sounds as if you'd like to approach this marriage like a business strategy?' she said instead as she sprinkled croutons over her soup.

Zac nodded as he cut into his crusty pie to reveal rich dark meat and gravy. 'As a starting point, at least.'

'And how would you make your choice? Draw up a list of the attributes you want in this wife? Then try to find the perfect match from the *Fool*—from the list of girls you've already dated?'

'Exactly,' he said with a grin. 'I knew you'd come on board.'

An hour later, they were still in the pub.

Having finished their meals and drinks, they were onto their second cups of coffee, hoping to keep jet lag at bay for a little longer, and Chloe, to her own amazement, was helping to draw up Zac's list of wifely qualities.

'OK, let's see what you have so far.' She read from the notes she'd typed into her phone. 'We—I mean *you*—want someone who's sensible—' She'd been majorly surprised that this had headed his list. 'Smart, sympathetic, reliable, has a sense of humour, likes kids, is not too loud...'

Zac nodded. 'That sounds about right.'

What about size eight and blonde? This described most of the girls he liked to date, but somehow Chloe restrained herself from asking this and took a kinder approach. 'I don't think you really need a database, Zac. You must already know which of your girlfriends has these qualities.'

A deep frown furrowed his brow as he stared at his coffee cup. 'It's hard to find them all in one person, though, isn't it?'

When he looked up, he seemed genuinely perplexed. 'Angie Davis has a great sense of humour and she's probably good with kids, but I'm not sure she's all that reliable. And Sasha Franks would run a terrific household, but she's a bit...cold.'

'What about Marissa Johnson?' Of all Zac's girlfriends, Chloe had liked Marissa the best. She was a very friendly young woman who worked in a sports store on the Gold Coast, and she had short dark hair and a natural, make-up-free glow of the outdoors about her, which made her a little different from his usual choices.

Zac, however, was shaking his head. 'Why does Marissa's name keep cropping up? You told me to invite her here to London and I said no then.'

Chloe shrugged. 'I just think she's really nice, the sort of girl I could be good friends with.' She smiled sheepishly.' But I don't suppose that's helpful to you.'

'Actually, you're probably right about Marissa.' He sighed heavily. 'But of all the girls I know, she's probably the least likely to be interested in marrying me.'

'Are you sure?'

He nodded. 'I'm afraid I stuffed things up with her. I…er… kind of forgot to mention that I was still seeing someone else.'

Chloe groaned. 'For heaven's sake, Zac.'

He shrugged. 'The other girl was in Melbourne and it was only ever occasional, but Marissa still gave me the boot.'

Good for her, Chloe thought, but she kept the thought to herself. Instead, she found herself saying, 'You never know, she might forgive you if you asked very nicely. Putting a ring on her finger could make a world of difference.'

She wished she felt happier about offering that last piece of unasked-for advice. It didn't help that Zac's response was a gorgeously brooding smile that made her wonder what he was thinking.

Was he actually in love with Marissa?

Why should I care? It's not as if I want him for myself. Chloe knew she was far too sensible to make such a foolish mistake.

'I've never actually asked about *your* credentials,' Zac said suddenly.

'Mine?' A zap, like an electric spark, shot through Chloe. 'Wh-what d-do you mean?'

'Well, here I am seeking your advice and I don't even know if you're qualified. I know nothing about your social life. You're such a private girl, Chloe. I've never heard you mention going on a date.' He was looking at her now as if she was a very amusing riddle. 'For example…is there a boyfriend I should have apologised to when I dragged you away at Christmas?'

Chloe gulped. 'No—there's…er…no one at the moment.'

'You're a lovely girl…so there must be an explanation.'

Stifling her delight at his use of the word 'lovely', she decided that she wouldn't tell him about Sam. How could a man who didn't believe in romance possibly understand her pain, or why she'd retreated so completely from the dating scene?

Zac was still smiling, but the expression in his grey eyes was piercing now. It seemed to skewer her. 'You're not going to share that explanation, are you?' he said.

'No, I'd rather not.'

He frowned and, for the longest time, he regarded her with a look that was unexpectedly sympathetic, but, to Chloe's intense relief, he dropped the subject.

They walked back to their hotel through the gathering gloom of a wintry London afternoon. Street lights had already come on and the window displays made eye-catching splashes of colour.

Zac was beginning to feel a little better after a warming meal and a reasonably profitable chat with Chloe, as if he'd been trapped in a nightmare but was gradually finding his way out. He would certainly give the Marissa option more careful thought.

'I suppose you might have to think of a name for the baby,' Chloe said suddenly when they were about a block from their hotel.

'A name?' With a soft groan, Zac threw back his head and

stared helplessly up at the dark lowering clouds. 'I wouldn't have a clue where to begin.'

'Oh, I'm sure you'll have fun once you get started, Zac. There are so many pretty girls' names.'

'I guess.' But when he tried to think, he could only think of past girlfriends' names and he didn't want any of them. Beyond these, however, his mind drew a blank. 'Do you have any suggestions?'

Chloe laughed. 'Where do I start? Mind you, I'm no expert, but I think all the old classic names are still very popular—names like Emma and Sophie or Rose. Or, let me see, there's Isabella or simply Bella.'

'Bella's cute,' Zac admitted, thinking of the tiny pink-cheeked baby he'd been handed at the hospital.

'I guess you'd also want to choose something that went well with Corrigan.'

'Would I? Yes, I guess...'

'For example, Chloe Corrigan would sound a bit off.'

Inexplicably, Zac's chest tightened. 'Would it?'

'Definitely,' Chloe said gruffly. 'Too many Cs and Os. Although Kate or Katy might work. Katy Corrigan sounds catchy. Or maybe something pretty starting with M like Megan or Molly or Mia—or, if you wanted to be modern, you could go for something like Mackenzie.' His PA was obviously warming to this task.

'Molly,' Zac said quickly. 'I don't mind that. I don't know why, but the baby sort of looks like a Molly, doesn't she?'

Chloe turned to him. She was smiling, but her brown eyes were so soft and warm with emotion that the band around his chest pulled tighter.

'Molly's very cute,' she said. 'Or if you wanted to tie in a Christmas link, you could always go for Holly.'

'No, I'm warming to Molly,' Zac said. He liked to arrive at firm decisions. 'Molly Corrigan sounds all right, doesn't it? Or are there too many Os?'

'Molly's great.'

'Or Lucy. What about Lucy Corrigan? That sounds better, doesn't it?'

'Yes, Lucy's lovely,' Chloe said softly.

'Lucy Francesca Corrigan,' Zac refined, proud of his sudden inspiration.

'Oh, Francesca's gorgeous. What made you think of it?'

'It was my mother's name, although most people just called her Fran or Frannie.'

'It would be very fitting to name the baby after her grandmother. Lucy Francesca's so pretty. I love it!'

'Excellent. We can sleep on it and see if we still like it in the morning.'

For a moment, Zac thought he saw a glistening dampness in his PA's eyes, but she turned quickly to study another shop window, so he couldn't be sure.

He wondered if he'd said something wrong.

CHAPTER FIVE

ZAC WASTED NO time in getting to the share house the next morning. Having finally succumbed to jet lag on the previous evening, he and Chloe had opted to skip dinner in favour of much needed sleep and, consequently, they'd both woken early. A hearty hotel breakfast and a Tube ride later, they stood outside the house Liv had shared for the past twelve months.

Zac had no idea what to expect, but he wasn't totally surprised when his knock was answered by a girl with purple hair and a silver ring through her nose.

'Good morning,' he said rather formally. 'I spoke to someone called Skye on the phone.'

'Yeah,' the girl said. 'That's me.'

Zac lifted the empty suitcase he'd brought to collect Liv's belongings. 'I'm Zac Corrigan.'

Skye's face broke into an unexpectedly warm smile. 'Lovely to meet you, Zac.' She offered her hand, complete with black nail polish. 'Liv told us so much about you.'

'Really?' He couldn't hold back his surprise.

'Yeah, of course she did. She was dead proud of you, you know.'

But as she said this, her eyes filled with tears and—dammit—Zac felt his own eyes begin to sting.

'Come on in,' Skye said in a choked voice, blinking hard as she opened the door wider and stepped back to make room for them. 'Pete and Shaz have both left already for work.'

'We're not holding you up, are we?'

She shook her head. 'I don't work Saturdays.'

In the narrow hallway a faint smell of incense lingered. Zac introduced Chloe.

'Pleased to meet you.' Skye smiled now and regarded Chloe with interest. 'Are you Zac's girlfriend?'

'PA,' Zac and Chloe said together.

The girl gave a slightly puzzled frown, then shrugged and headed down the hall, nodding for them to follow.

'We miss Liv so much,' she said over her shoulder. 'But you must know that, Zac. You know what she was like. Such a live wire and always so lovely and kind.'

'Yes,' Zac said faintly as they entered the lounge room, which wasn't nearly as dilapidated as he'd expected.

The furniture was almost certainly second-hand and the sofa was draped in a hand-knitted shawl of red and purple wool, while the walls were hung with huge amateurish paintings in equally bright and gaudy oils. But everything was clean and tidy and the overall effect was surprisingly appealing. Artistic and cosy.

'Before I show you Liv's room,' Skye said, 'I thought I should mention that Father Tom dropped by last night.' Her eyes widened with the importance of this news. 'He said he could squeeze in a funeral on Monday morning, even though it's Christmas Eve…' The girl looked from Zac to Chloe. 'That is, if you'd like a church funeral.'

Zac hoped he didn't look as surprised as he felt. Avoiding Chloe's gaze, he asked, 'Did—did Liv attend church?'

'Oh, yeah.' The look Skye gave him was almost pitying. 'Every Sunday morning and on Wednesday evenings as well. We all go together. It's lovely.'

'Um…what kind of church?' he dared to ask.

'Oh, you can check it out for yourself, Zac. It's the little chapel around the corner. Father Tom's marvellous. You should see the work he does in the streets around here.'

'I see.' Zac swallowed. 'I'm afraid I had no idea about this. I've...er...made arrangements with a funeral director for a cremation.'

'But wouldn't you want a church service with Liv's friends as well?'

He realised he'd given no thought to the friends Liv might have made. She'd only been in England a year and he'd somehow pictured her wandering around with the guy from the band, pretty much alone and drifting...

Somewhat dazed, he looked Chloe's way and she immediately smiled and sent him an encouraging nod.

'A church service would be...perfect,' he said.

'Wonderful. I'll give Father Tom a ring, shall I?'

'Thank you.'

'Right. It's this way to Liv's room.' Skye was pointing. 'Feel free to take any or all of her things. Anything left, we can sort out.' Her voice wobbled and suddenly there were tears in her eyes again and her nose was distinctly pink. 'And stay as long as you like.'

'Thank you. You're very kind.' Still feeling dazed, Zac went to the doorway and then came to an abrupt halt when he saw his sister's room.

As a teenager, Liv's bedroom had always been a dive, with the bed unmade and clothes left lying on the floor where she'd climbed out of them, the waste basket overflowing with scrunched balls of paper and drink cans. For Zac, the messy room had been a constant battleground, but in the end he'd hated carrying on like an Army sergeant major and he'd given up trying to get her to tidy it.

In this room, the bed was covered by a smooth, spotless white spread and there was an arrangement of bright flowers in a vase on the bedside table. On top of a chest of drawers sat a small yellow teddy bear and neatly folded piles of baby clothing. Beside that a collection of toiletries...talcum powder and baby lotion and a glass jar filled with snowy cotton wool balls.

Taking pride of place in the corner stood a white bassinet of woven cane made up with clean sheets and with a soft pink blanket folded over one side, ready and waiting for a tiny occupant.

Stunned, Zac sagged against the doorpost.

The room said it all. His little sister had grown up and changed beyond recognition. Liv had found a true home here in London and she'd obviously been looking forward to motherhood. All evidence pointed to the fact that she'd planned to be a perfect mother, until fate cruelly robbed her of that chance, that *right*.

Without warning, he was swamped by a fresh deluge of sorrow and his chest swelled to bursting point as he felt his heart break all over again. He had no hope of holding back his tears.

It was a while later when he heard Chloe whisper softly behind him, 'Zac.'

He felt her hand on his arm, rubbing him through his coat sleeve, and he found her touch unexpectedly comforting.

Straightening, he scrubbed a hand over his face. 'Sorry. I'm afraid I lost it again.'

'Oh, don't worry,' she said, swiping at her eyes. 'I've been blubbing, too.'

'It was such a shock.' He waved a hand at the room. 'I wasn't expecting this. Everything's so damn...*neat*.' He managed a broken laugh.

'It's charming,' Chloe said. 'Picture perfect.'

'The little monkey. Liv would never tidy a thing for me.'

They both laughed shakily, and stood looking about them. Then, drawing a deep breath, Zac set down the empty suitcase on a mat at the end of the bed. 'If only I had a clue where to start.'

Chloe crossed the room to the chest of drawers. 'I guess

you'll definitely need these baby things.' She picked up the top item of clothing and held it out to him.

It was the tiniest singlet he'd ever seen. 'Wow, it's so little.'

'It's minuscule,' Chloe whispered, sharing his awe.

'I can't imagine trying to dress a wriggling baby in that,' Zac added with mild alarm.

Chloe smiled, but made no comment and he thought how lovely she looked. Actually...what man wouldn't be entranced by those shapely legs, that shiny, touchable hair? And how could he ignore the lovely warmth of her dark brown eyes? Bizarrely, in the midst of these saddest of circumstances, Zac found himself wondering why he'd always been so black and white about the boundaries he maintained with his PA.

'I'll get started, shall I?' she said, turning to open the top drawer. 'I'm assuming you'll only take the baby clothes?'

'I think so.'

'There are plenty here. It looks like Liv was well prepared.'

Zac nodded and pledged to concentrate on the task at hand. 'If we set Liv's clothes to one side, Skye will know what to do with them.'

'But you'll want to keep things like this, Zac.'

'Like what?'

Chloe was holding out a small blue album. 'Take a look,' she said, sending him a significant glance.

It was a photo album, he quickly realised as he turned to the first page. It showed a professional photograph of his family taken in a studio when he was around ten.

His mother had used this photo to make a personalised Christmas card, he remembered. And there his mother was... looking youthful and beautiful with short dark hair and lively grey-green eyes, and wearing her favourite dress of tailored green linen.

Beside her, his father was wearing a white business shirt and dark trousers with a maroon tie. His father's hair had already started to grey at the temples, but his face was tanned from all the time he spent outdoors in the bush, tracking down the plants and animals that were endangered by extensive mining.

His mum had dressed them all in Christmas colours, so Zac was wearing a dark red polo shirt with pale chinos, while Liv, aged two, was in a white dress with a green and red tartan sash. Zac smiled, remembering how hard it had been to get Liv to sit still for the photo.

Now...they were all gone.

He was the only one left...and, suddenly, looking at the photo was unbearable. He shut the album with a snap. He'd had more than enough heartbreak for one day.

Without speaking, he walked over to the suitcase and dropped the album into it. Chloe glanced at it and then up at him, but she didn't say a word. Her eloquent dark eyes told him that she understood. For that, he almost hugged her.

It was as they were leaving and thanking Skye yet again that Zac remembered to ask, 'Do you know if Liv had any names chosen for the baby?'

Skye laughed. 'She had hundreds. You should have seen the lists. Liv knew she was having a girl, of course.'

'Did she have a favourite name?'

'Not as far as I could tell. The name seemed to change almost every day. The only thing Liv was certain about was that she wanted her mother's name, Francesca, for the middle name.'

'Ah...' Zac caught Chloe's eye and they shared a smile and he felt an unexpected glow inside. It was incredibly reassuring to know that his first important decision about the baby had been on the right track.

'Are you going to check out the church?' Chloe asked when they were once again outside.

'Yes, good idea. I wouldn't mind meeting this Father Ted, too, if he's around.'

'Tom,' Chloe corrected. 'Father Tom.'

Zac grinned. 'Thanks, Ms Meadows. I suppose the chances of finding him on a Saturday morning are slim.'

They saw the tiny stone church as soon as they rounded the corner. Surrounded by a narrow fringe of green lawn, it was like a relic from the past, smack bang next to a row of brightly painted modern shops.

The front door of the church was open, offering an enticing glimpse of a nativity scene, complete with a stable and straw and a plaster donkey. When Zac and Chloe detoured around it, they found two women in the church's darkened interior, arranging white gladioli and bunches of holly in tall copper urns.

'I was hoping to find Father Tom,' Zac told the nearest woman.

She nodded towards a small wooden arch-shaped door in the far wall. 'Over there in the vestry.'

'Thank you.'

'He's very busy with Christmas and everything, and there'll be a wedding here in an hour or so.'

'I won't take up much of his time.'

As he turned to head off, Chloe held out her hand for the suitcase. 'I'll look after that.'

'OK, thanks.' Leaving Chloe sitting in a pew, Zac realised how quickly he'd become used to having her right beside him. *Almost as if...*

He cut off that thought before it distracted him from the task at hand.

At the vestry he gave two short knocks and the door was opened by a young sandy-haired fellow in jeans and a black knitted sweater.

'Hi there,' he said. 'How can I help you?'

'I was hoping to speak to Father Tom.'

The young man grinned. 'And so you are.'

This was Father Tom? Zac swallowed his shock. He'd expected a grey-haired old fellow, possibly stooped and wearing spectacles. This Father Tom, with his designer stubble and flashing blue eyes and no hint of a dog collar, looked more like a rock star than a priest.

'How can I help you?' Father Tom asked.

'I'm Zac Corrigan. I—'

'Zac, of course, of course... Wonderful to meet you. Come on in.' The young priest opened the door wider and stepped back. 'Take a seat,' he added as he scooped a pile of hymn books from a chair.

Once the books were deposited on a crammed shelf, he held out his hand. 'Please accept my condolences.' His hand gripped Zac's firmly. 'Liv was an amazing girl, just wonderful. We're all devastated.'

'I'm very grateful that you've offered to fit in a funeral for her at such short notice.'

'Only too happy to help.' Father Tom sat behind his desk, pushed some paperwork aside and leaned forward, hands clasped. 'Is there anything else I can do for you while you're here?'

Zac deliberately tried to relax, with an ankle propped on a knee. 'I know you can't break confidence,' he said carefully. 'But I wondered if Liv ever spoke to you about the baby's father.'

'About his identity?'

'Yes.'

Father Tom shook his head. 'I had no luck there, I'm afraid. Of course, I did raise the question with Liv. I asked her if the father was going to be able to help her or at least support her. She was straight upfront and said that this was *her* baby and she would be the one to care for it. The father was completely out of the scene.'

Zac realised he'd been holding his breath and now he let it out slowly, surprised by an unexpected sense of relief. He wasn't sure how or when it had happened but, some time in the past twenty-four hours, he'd arrived at a point of acceptance and his feelings about the baby had changed. He would be disappointed now if a strange man stepped up to claim her.

'Of course I did talk to Liv about the challenges of being a single mother so far from home,' the priest said. 'I was concerned about her secrecy and I probed to make quite sure that she didn't want the father's help. She assured me that the baby's father hadn't abused her in any way. In fact, she impressed on me that he wasn't a bad guy, but she said she'd put a lot of thought into her future and she knew exactly what she was doing.'

He fixed Zac with a steady gaze. 'She liked to talk about her family and she told me all about you.'

'Her annoying big brother.'

Father Tom gave a smiling shrug.

'She never told me about her pregnancy.'

'Ah, yes, Liv admitted that. She seemed to think she'd given you enough worry over the years. She knew you would have felt compelled to rush over here and to—'

'Interfere,' supplied Zac, tight-lipped.

This brought another sympathetic smile. 'Micro-manage, perhaps.'

Zac nodded. He knew Liv was right. He would have been over here like a shot, bossing her around, trying to order her to come home.

'Liv certainly planned to tell you once the baby was born. She said—I want to show Zac that I can be a brilliant mum and I want him to be finally proud of me.'

Finally? Zac cringed and the back of his neck burned. 'I was already proud of her,' he said gruffly. 'I might have been bossy, but I—I loved her.'

Damn it, he was *not* going to break down again, and certainly not in front of this man.

'I know you loved her,' Father Tom said gently. 'And I'm sure Liv knew it, too. She was looking forward to showing you her baby. She told me that she couldn't wait to meet you at Heathrow and she fantasised about the moment she handed you your little niece.'

Oh, God. Zac groaned with the effort of holding himself together. Somehow he managed to lurch to his feet and thank Father Tom for his time. They spoke briefly about the service on Monday.

'Thanks for calling in, Zac. I'll see you then.'

They said farewell and Zac was still shaking inside as he strode back through the church to Chloe.

'No leads on the baby's father,' he said tersely and he was infinitely grateful that Chloe didn't press him with further questions as they went outside, where the clouds had parted at last to reveal a glimmer of pale English sunshine.

Chloe knew Zac was tense after his discussion with the clergyman. As the Tube train rushed back into the city, she tried to talk about practical things.

'I don't think we need to buy many more clothes for the baby, unless we see something *really* cute. I've done a little research on the Net and, for now, I think we probably only need formula and bottles and a steriliser, although we should check with the airline to see what they provide for babies on long haul flights.'

'Yeah, and I suppose we'd better ring the hospital and arrange a time to collect Lucy.' Zac looked a little self-conscious as he said the baby's name and Chloe gave him an encouraging smile.

Unfortunately, the look in his eyes when he returned her smile made her stomach drop as if she'd plunged from a great height.

Which was a definite problem. She'd had a few too many of these moments recently. Spending so much time with Zac was taking its toll.

She told herself that it was only natural, that sharing his personal tragedy was bound to have an impact on her own emotions. But now she was beginning to worry about the future. After this time in London, it was going to be so hard to return to their former strictly boss-PA relationship.

It would be hard for her, at least. She would remember all

the emotional moments when her feelings for Zac had felt so much deeper and sweeter. Quite possibly, Zac would have no difficulty, though. He was pretty much an expert at keeping his business and personal life in separate compartments.

For Chloe, however, it had become increasingly clear that the sooner she got back to Brisbane and normality, the better. She was thinking about this when she asked, 'Would you like to collect Lucy this afternoon?'

'I don't think so,' Zac answered slowly, as if he was giving the matter careful thought. 'I hope this doesn't sound selfish, but I feel as if I need a little more time to adjust.'

'How much time?' Chloe asked cautiously.

'A decade?'

She must have looked shocked and Zac laughed. 'A joke, Ms Meadows. Don't worry. I'll speak to the hospital about collecting her tomorrow. In the meantime...' His eyes suddenly gleamed with unexpected merriment. 'I think we've earned ourselves a night out, don't you?'

An unhelpful fizzing raced along her veins, as if they were filled with champagne. 'I... I'm not sure,' she said. A night out sounded risky.

Zac frowned at her. 'Surely you don't want to squander this perfect chance to enjoy a Saturday night in London town?'

Even to sensible Chloe it did seem like a wasted opportunity, and she found it especially difficult to voice her very reasonable concerns when her less sensible self was jumping up and down like an excited child.

'Of course you don't,' Zac answered for her. 'We'll have a fabulous night. It's my last night of freedom and it's your duty as my employee to help me enjoy it.'

Before she could summon an effective protest, the train pulled into Oxford Circus and Zac launched to his feet, so the subject was dropped until they'd battled their way out of the crowded Underground and found themselves once more on the footpath.

By then Zac had it all planned and he was quite exuberant. Even though it was at the last minute, he was sure he could wangle a table for two at a good restaurant.

'And what about theatre tickets?' he asked Chloe now, his eyes shining with expectation. 'What sort of show do you feel like seeing? I must admit I could do with a little comedy.'

'Definitely comedy.' Clearly, there was no point in trying to argue about going out with him for the evening. 'We've had enough of real life drama.'

'Great.' Zac was almost boyish in his excitement. 'We'll go shopping this afternoon to buy clothes—for ourselves, not for the baby. We don't have to worry about sticking to carry-on luggage for the journey home. We'll have the suitcase with Lucy's things, anyway, so why not lash out? I'll pay for your new outfit, of course.'

'No,' Chloe said swiftly and firmly.

Zac stopped abruptly and a pedestrian hurrying behind them almost bumped into him. 'Don't be silly, Chloe.' He reached for her hand, but she slipped it into her coat pocket.

'Now you're being stubborn. This night out is my idea.' Zac ignored the pedestrians streaming around them. His attention was solely on Chloe. 'Let me buy you a dress and hang the expense. Think of it as a thank you gift for everything you've—'

'No,' Chloe said again, even more firmly to make sure he got the message. 'Thank you very much, Zac. It's an extremely kind offer, but I can't let you buy me clothes.'

This was one line she knew she mustn't cross. It was the difference between being his PA and a member of his chorus line of girlfriends.

'It's just a dress, Chloe.' Zac's smile was charming now. Bone-meltingly charming.

Chloe could feel her skin warming and her limbs growing languorous. It would be so easy to give in, but she had to remember that this was the special smile Zac used to conquer his countless female victims.

'Chloe, come on, loosen up. You're in London, for heaven's sake. You can't be in London without buying at least one new dress.'

He was right about that, she conceded. She would regret it later if she arrived home without some kind of memento, and what better than a chic new dress from London's famous Oxford Street?

'I was planning to buy a dress anyway,' she said.

Without dropping the smile, Zac narrowed his eyes at her. 'No, you weren't.'

'Of course I was.' She lifted her chin for emphasis and kept her expression deadpan. 'It'll be my Christmas present to myself.'

CHAPTER SIX

BY THE TIME Chloe carried her shopping bags back to her hotel room she felt quite sick. She couldn't believe she'd spent so much money. On one dress.

The expense was almost obscene. She should never have tried the dress on, but as soon as she'd entered the store she'd been seduced, and she hadn't looked at the price tag until it was far too late.

The knee-length dress with cap sleeves had looked so simple and demure on its hanger. Admittedly, it was a bold red and Chloe had never worn such a bright colour before. She usually stuck to soft pinks or browns, but it was Christmas after all, and she was in a mood to be daring. And as soon as she'd stepped into the changing room and slipped the dress on, her senses had instantly fallen under its spell.

The silk lining whispered against her skin like a lover's kiss and when she closed the underarm zip, the dress settled around her like a second skin. Then she'd turned to the mirror and experienced a true *oh-my-God* surprise.

Was that really her?

How could one dress make such a transformation? The bright red seemed to give her complexion a fresh glow and the scooped neckline enhanced the line of her collarbone and décolletage so that she looked...amazing.

As for the fit of the dress, Chloe had no idea how the designer had done it, but he'd managed to give her an hourglass figure. In a blink she'd become positively vain. She couldn't help it. She twisted this way and that, looking at herself from every angle. She'd never dreamed she could look so good and she knew there was no question. She simply *had* to have this dress. She couldn't possibly walk out of the store without it.

It was only after she'd arrived at this decision that she reached for the label and tried to read the price with the help of the mirror. At first she thought she'd made a mistake—she'd read the price upside-down, or back to front or something—so she was still feeling reasonably calm as she took the dress off, once again delighting in the cool slide of the silken lining over her skin.

With the dress back on its hanger, she looked at the price tag again. And almost had a heart attack.

Just as well there was a seat in the changing room or she might have keeled over.

Huddling on the seat in her undies, Chloe wanted to cry. She'd fallen in love with the red dress. While she was wearing it, she'd been quite certain that the designer had dreamed it up just for *her*.

But, dear Lord, the price was horrendous. Normally, she could buy six dresses for that amount and, with the current exchange rate, it would be even worse in Aussie dollars.

A small voice whispered: *That's why this dress looks ten times better on you than any of your old ones.*

And then, in the next breath, Chloe pictured the expression in Zac's eyes when he saw her in this dress, and that was probably about the time her synapses fused and she stopped thinking clearly. She simply got back into her clothes, marched to the counter and handed over her credit card.

Now, as she hung her purchase in the hotel wardrobe, she tried to ignore the sick feeling in the pit of her stomach. She consoled herself that she'd got a bargain with the black platform heels she'd bought to complete the outfit. And she told herself she'd atoned for her sins by buying a beautiful expensive silk scarf for her mother and an equally costly cashmere pullover for her dad.

And now the only sensible thing was to make sure she enjoyed this evening. Surely that couldn't be too hard?

In fact, it was impossible not to enjoy herself. Zac had bought himself a new dark grey suit which he teamed with a fine grey turtleneck instead of a traditional white shirt, which meant that his already devastating good looks now took on an extra sexy European appeal. Chloe found herself staring. And staring some more.

Of course, Zac did quite a bit of staring, too, especially when they arrived at the romantic candlelit restaurant in Piccadilly and Chloe removed her coat.

After he recovered from his initial dropped-jaw shock, he stared at her with an almost bewildered smile, as if he couldn't quite get over the surprise of seeing her all dressed up.

Illogically, Chloe wanted to cry. The look in Zac's eyes was so out of character. So unguarded and intimate…and *unsettling*.

'Ms Meadows, you've outdone yourself,' he murmured and he didn't drag his shimmering gaze from her till the waiter cleared his throat.

'Sir? If you'll come this way, I'll show you to your table…'

'Yes, yes. Thank you.' Zac sent Chloe a wink, as if to cover any embarrassment, and he touched his hand to her elbow ever so lightly to indicate that she should go ahead of him.

To her dismay, his touch set off flashes and sparks and she almost tripped as they wound their way through the tables.

It was a relief to be finally seated but, throughout the meal, Zac's eyes revealed a range of emotions as his initial shock gave way to amused delight, and finally to a more serious smouldering heat that stole Chloe's breath and set her pulses drumming.

Later, she could barely remember the meal although, of course, everything was delicious. She was too absorbed in the experience of being with Zac in such a romantic setting. Everything was so different—their vast distance from Australia, her red dress, the romantic Christmas decorations—and for one night she stopped thinking of herself as his PA. She was a woman very much enjoying the company of an exceptionally handsome and charming man.

Zac was, not surprisingly, an excellent conversationalist, and once they'd been through the typical chat about favourite books and movies, Chloe encouraged him to talk about himself. He told her how, when Liv was three, his family had lived on an island on the Great Barrier Reef for two years while his mother studied, among other things, the nesting habit of sea turtles.

His father couldn't be with them all the time, apparently, because of his work in the central Queensland coalfields, so he used to fly in and out from the island in a seaplane, which also delivered the family's provisions.

To Chloe, who'd only ever lived in the same small house in a Brisbane suburb, this life sounded wonderfully adventurous and romantic. Zac had lived in a timber cottage perched on a hill overlooking the Coral Sea, and from his bedroom he could reach out of the window to pick coconuts. His mother had taught him how to skin dive, and at night she'd built campfires on the beach and, while Liv was curled asleep in her lap, she'd taught Zac all about the stars and planets.

'It's a wonder you didn't become a scientist, too,' Chloe said.

Zac shrugged. 'I started out studying marine science but, after my parents' boat disappeared, I—' A corner of his mouth tilted in a briefly awkward smile. 'I needed to try something completely different.'

'At which you're equally brilliant,' she told him warmly.

His eyes shimmered again as he smiled at her. 'Thank you, Ms Meadows,' he said with exaggerated modesty.

But Chloe was sure that talking about his family couldn't

be easy and, as they dug their spoons into a shared dessert of sinfully divine chocolate mousse, she directed the conversation to Lucy. 'Would you like her to have an adventurous childhood like yours?'

'You know, I almost want her life to be boring,' Zac said.

Chloe couldn't help herself. 'That would be such a shame.'

'But boring's safe.'

'It might be safe,' she responded, perhaps a little too vehemently. 'But it's certainly not fun.'

Now Zac regarded her thoughtfully before he helped himself to another spoonful of mousse. 'Sounds to me like you're speaking from experience.'

'I'm afraid I am.'

Of course, he wanted her to explain about this, which was how she ended up telling him about her parents—how her dad had worked in a hardware store and her mum was a teacher's aide, how they'd married late and never expected to have a family, so when baby Chloe arrived at the last moment, she had been a complete and bewildering surprise for them.

'My parents were already very set in their ways, so it was a very quiet life,' she said. 'Mum gave up work to stay at home with me and we didn't have much money, so we didn't go out very much, or entertain, and we only went on holidays every second year. Then it was always to the same place, Maroochydore. I love the beach, of course, but I was too shy to make new friends, so I used to sit under a beach umbrella with my parents and watch the other kids having fun.'

She rolled her eyes. 'I know, I know...that makes me sound like such a loser.'

'A loner, perhaps,' Zac said kindly. 'But hardly a loser.'

'It's not what you'd want for Lucy, though.'

He smiled. 'I guess I'll have to aim for some kind of middle ground.'

A picture flashed into Chloe's thoughts of Zac and Lucy with Marissa Johnson, sharing a new 'middle ground' life together.

She found the thought incredibly depressing, so it was probably just as well that they'd reached the bottom of the chocolate mousse and Zac checked his phone for the time.

'We'd better get cracking,' he said. 'Our show's starting soon.'

He took Chloe's hand as they left the restaurant. She knew it was only practical to hold hands as they hurried through the crowds in Piccadilly Circus but, as they passed beneath a dazzling wonderland of Christmas lights, she was excruciatingly conscious of his strong fingers interlinked with hers. She'd almost forgotten the heart-zapping intimacy of even the smallest amount of skin contact.

Then they were in the warmth of the theatre, taking off their coats and settling into comfy velvet-upholstered seats, with all the attendant excitement of the lights being dimmed and the curtain rising…

'My sides are aching from laughing so much,' Chloe said as they stood outside afterwards, waiting for a taxi.

'Mine, too,' said Zac. 'I can't remember the last time I laughed so hard.'

'I'm so glad you picked a comedy.'

'Yeah, laughter's certainly good medicine.'

They were freezing on the footpath, but the air was crystal-clear. Above them stretched a network of lights in the shapes of stars, snowflakes and angels that made the night even more enchanting.

Chloe was still feeling relaxed and happy when they reached their hotel, which was probably why she didn't object when Zac suggested a nightcap in the bar.

'Here, allow me,' he said, stilling her hands with his as she was unbuttoning her coat.

At his touch, she froze, and her heart began thumping as she looked up at him.

The world seemed to stand still and she was trapped by his smiling silver-grey eyes.

'I've been dying to do this all night,' he said softly.

She couldn't breathe as she dropped her gaze to his hands, as she watched his long fingers slowly undo each button, as he gently slipped the coat from her shoulders and let his gaze travel deliberately over her.

'You know this dress is...magnificent.'

Chloe could feel a blush rising from her neck to her cheeks.

'I'm so glad you wouldn't let me pay for it,' Zac said.

'Why is that?'

'You would have chosen something sensible and inexpensive and not nearly as attractive as this.'

Now she couldn't help smiling. Seemed her boss knew her only too well.

'Actually, I have a better idea,' Zac said next as he looked around him at the rather crowded bar. 'Let's not have a drink here. We should go upstairs and get room service.'

And, just like that, alarm bells began clamouring in Chloe's ears—loud and clear—a reality check as effective as the clock at midnight for Cinderella.

There was no way she could share late night drinks in her playboy boss's hotel room. But, before she could insist on staying at the bar, Zac took off for the lift, still carrying her coat. She hurried after him, planning to drag him back, but the lift doors were already opening and there were other guests inside. She didn't want to make a scene so she held her tongue until they reached their floor and were out in the corridor.

'Zac, I don't need a nightcap,' she told him quietly but decisively as they arrived at the door to her room.

He tipped his head to one side with the look a parent might give to a troublesome child. 'You're not going to be a spoilsport.'

Chloe sighed. She should have guessed that this would happen and she should have had a strategy already planned. 'Look, tonight's been wonderful. I've had a fabulous time, but we both need to remember this isn't a date.'

'But it so easily could be.'

This was true and in the confined space of the hallway Chloe could smell Zac's cologne, musky and expensive and very masculine. When she looked up, she saw that his jaw was now lined by an attractive five o'clock shadow.

Help! She was still tingling and zapping from having him take off her coat. Anything more intimate would probably cause her to self-combust.

This was such a dangerous moment. She only had to give the slightest hint of acceptance and Zac Corrigan would be kissing her. And she couldn't pretend that she didn't want to be kissed. It was such a long, long time since she'd been in a man's arms... and this wasn't just any man. It was *Zac!* His lips were so close, so scrumptious, so wonderfully tempting.

The air between them was crackling and sizzling. At any moment, he was going to lean in...

Now she was struggling to remember why this was wrong.

I'll only be another of his Foolish Females.

'Zac, we can't—'

'Shh.' He touched her arm, sending dizzying warmth washing over her skin. 'Forget about the office for one night.'

'How can I? How can *you*?'

'Easy,' he said as his thumb rode a sensuous track over her bare arm. 'Tonight you're not my PA and I'm not your boss.'

'But we—'

'Chloe, you're an incredibly sexy woman in a gloriously sexy red dress and I'm the poor, helpless guy who's absolutely smitten by you.'

His words sent shivery heat rushing over her skin. She longed to give in. She was only human after all and Zac was a ridiculously attractive man and she'd been half in love with him for the past three years.

And in the past few days she'd learned so much more to like

about him. She'd seen past the handsome façade to the vulnerable boy who'd lost his family and still longed for the safety and security of belonging.

But the yearning that filled her now had little to do with respect or friendship. It was pure and simple lust and all Chloe wanted to do was say yes... She was sinking beneath an overwhelming temptation to close her eyes and lift her face to his.

Why shouldn't she? Just about any girl in her situation would. *What the heck?* they'd say. *Why not have some fun for one night? What happens in London stays in London...*

Problem was...while Chloe had been half in love with Zac for all this time, she'd also felt smugly superior to the girls who'd fallen head over heels for him. She'd watched those girls from the sidelines and she knew all too well that one blissful night could so easily lead to weeks and months of regret.

There were so many ways that love could hurt and she'd taken ages to get over Sam's death. She was terrified of risking another version of that heartbreak and pain.

It was so hard to be sensible though. So hard when Zac was a heartbeat away from kissing her... When he was looking at her with a breath-robbing intensity.

'Chloe, has anyone ever told you, you have the most amazing—'

In panic, she pressed a hand to his lips, shutting off the rest of his sentence—which was a pity because she was actually desperate to hear why he thought she was amazing. But it was time to toughen up, time to summon every ounce of her willpower. She lifted her face. 'I have one word for you, Mr Corrigan.'

Zac smiled. 'Please, let it be yes.'

She eyed him sternly. 'Marissa.'

His smile vanished as if the name had landed in his chest like a smart bomb.

'Or, if not Marissa,' Chloe went on, needing to make her message clear, 'substitute the name of whichever girl you decide to marry. *That girl* is where your focus should be.'

She felt terrible though, especially when she heard the shudder of Zac's indrawn breath.

'Good shot, Ms Meadows,' he said softly, and then, with a heavy sigh, he took a step back. From a safer distance, he regarded her with a shakily rueful smile. 'I should have remembered that I can always rely on you to be sensible.'

'That's what you pay me for,' Chloe said crisply and then she turned quickly to open her door. 'As I said, I've had a fabulous evening, so thanks again, Zac, and…and goodnight.'

Without looking back, she stepped inside and closed the door swiftly before she weakened and did something very foolish.

Safely inside, she sagged against the closed door and saw her lovely lamplit room in front of her. *Don't think!*

On the other side of the door Zac was still holding her coat, but it was too bad. She would collect it in the morning. She couldn't see him again now. Not when stupid, stupid tears were streaming down her cheeks.

That was a very close shave.

Zac was scowling as he stared at Chloe's closed door. He'd almost lost his head and broken his own golden rule.

Tonight you're not my PA and I'm not your boss.

How could he have said that?

How could he have been so crass? With Chloe, of all people? His invaluable, irreplaceable Chloe.

He knew she already had zero tolerance when it came to his love life, and now he'd just proven to her that her low opinion was justified.

Damn it. How the hell had his plans to marry someone like Marissa slipped so easily out of his head?

Of course, everything might have followed its proper course tonight if Chloe had stuck to being Chloe. But she'd morphed into a goddess in the sexiest red dress on the planet.

Sure, Zac had always known that Chloe was an attractive young woman, but she'd always been safe as his conservative, efficient PA. Beautiful, yes, but a bit distant and shy. He'd never guessed she had the confidence to dress so glamorously, to reveal herself as a truly sensual, feminine woman.

Tonight's dress had been perfect on her. The rich red had given extra glowing warmth to her complexion, enhancing the lustre of her hair and the dark beauty of her eyes.

And as for the figure-hugging lines and the beguiling scooped neckline...

Zac had been stunned. Transfixed. It was the only explanation he could summon for why he'd stepped over the boss-PA line. For a moment there, he'd allowed himself to acknowledge his secret desire for Chloe. Truth be told, his feelings had felt way deeper than the mere desire he felt for his usual girlfriends.

But Chloe had promptly broken the strange hypnotic spell that gripped him and all it had taken was one word.

In a blink he was thudding back to earth, to his real life, to his new responsibilities, to the way the world would be for him from now on and for ever after.

He supposed he should be grateful to Chloe for reminding him, and for remaining so consistent and sensible. He *was* grateful, or at least he probably would be grateful...eventually...

Now, with a sigh of frustration, Zac unlocked the door to his room and went inside, tossing his and Chloe's coats into an armchair. He let out another sigh as he stood, hands on hips, staring down at the coats as they lay in a pool of lamplight—entangled—with a sleeve of Chloe's coat looped over the shoulder of his coat. Like an embrace.

Mocking him for his foolishness.

It was back to business at breakfast in the hotel dining room next morning. Last night's flirtatious smiles and warm camaraderie were safely relegated to the past.

Chloe was pleased that Zac was cool and serious again—at least she told herself she was pleased, just as she told herself she was relieved that he made no teasing or personal remarks as she started on her melon and yoghurt, while he tucked into his full English breakfast.

Apparently, Zac had even been up early and had already made phone calls to both the airlines and the hospital.

'I've decided that we don't need to buy a car seat while we're here,' he said, getting straight down to business. 'The requirements for fitting them into vehicles are slightly different from country to country. And apparently it's easy enough to get a taxi that's set up for a baby. As for the airlines, they provide bassinets and facilities for heating bottles or whatever.'

Chloe nodded. 'Let's hope Lucy doesn't cry too much during the flight.'

'Indeed,' he agreed gravely.

It was a daunting prospect, flying to the other side of the world with a brand new baby.

Zac frowned. 'Do you think three days will be enough time for us to get used to managing her here before we fly home?'

'Three days? Does that mean you're planning to fly home on Boxing Day?'

'As long as the passport comes through in time. Thank heavens you had the forethought to contact that brilliant agency before we left Brisbane. They've broken all records in fast-tracking Lucy's passport, because of our special circumstances. So do you think Boxing Day will work?'

'It should be fine, I guess.' Chloe was quite sure they shouldn't delay their London stay for a second longer than necessary. And she knew Zac must be eager to get home. He had a great deal to organise when he arrived in Australia—including the procurement of a suitable wife. 'As Lucy's so tiny, she might do a lot of sleeping,' she suggested hopefully.

'Yes, fingers crossed.' Zac handed her a sheet of notepaper. 'I asked the hospital about bottles and formula et cetera. Apparently, we should have collected a checklist, but I've jotted down the things we'll need.'

Chloe scanned the list as she sipped her coffee. Fortunately, she was used to reading Zac's scratchy handwriting. She nodded. 'I noticed there's a pharmacy nearby, so I'll get all these things straight after breakfast.'

'Great.' Zac lifted the coffee pot. 'Like a top-up?'

'Just half a cup, thanks.'

As he concentrated on pouring, he said, 'There is one other difficulty that we haven't discussed.'

'What's that?'

He kept his gaze focused on the coffee pot as he filled his own cup. 'We need to decide where Lucy should sleep.'

'Oh, yes.' This problem had occurred to Chloe, but she'd promptly dismissed it as far too awkward. Now it had to be faced.

Obviously, while they stayed in the hotel, Lucy would be installed in either her room or Zac's. But the big question was— which room was appropriate? Zac was Lucy's official guardian and uncle, but could a bachelor be expected to cope with a newborn baby on his own? Zac had been terrified of simply holding Lucy at the hospital.

'I understand small babies wake at all hours of the night,' he said. 'I read in one of those magazines of yours that newborns sometimes need feeding every two to three hours, even at night time.'

Chloe nodded carefully, certain she could see where this was heading. 'I wouldn't mind taking care of Lucy through the night.'

'No, no,' he said, surprising her. 'I wasn't angling for that. It's asking too much of you.'

'So you think you'll be OK looking after her?'

His mouth squared as he grimaced. 'Frankly, no. I imagine I'll be pretty hopeless.'

'Then, unless you hire a nanny, we don't really have an alternative.'

Zac watched her for a long moment and the smallest hint of

a smile played in his eyes. 'Actually, we do have an alternative, Chloe, but I'm afraid you're not going to like it.'

In an instant she was sitting straighter. 'You're not going to suggest we share a room.'

'But it makes sense, doesn't it?' His smile had disappeared now and Chloe could almost believe that he wasn't teasing. 'Neither of us knows much about babies. We both need moral support.'

She groaned. Of course she was remembering last night's close call when Zac had almost kissed her, when she'd almost let him…when she'd so very nearly welcomed him into her arms…and of course the memory stirred all the yearnings that she'd spent an entire night trying to forget. 'Honestly, Zac, don't you ever give up?'

'Calm down. There's no need to get all stirred up and old-maidish.'

'*I am not an old maid,*' Chloe hissed in a rush of righteous fury. Actually, she might have yelled this fact if they weren't in a refined hotel dining room filled with dignified guests.

'I stand corrected.' Straight-faced, Zac pushed his empty plate aside and rested his arms on the table as he leaned towards her. 'I certainly wasn't going to suggest that we share the same bed,' he said, lowering his voice so that she also had to lean in to hear him. 'I've actually looked into hiring a suite with two bedrooms, but the hotel's fully booked with special Christmas deals, so there's nothing like that available. And we really don't want to have to start hunting for another place at this late stage.'

Chloe had to give him credit—there wasn't a trace of a smile or a smirk.

'So what do you have in mind?' She wished her voice didn't sound so shaky.

'Well, it's easy enough to break up a king-size bed into twin singles and then our problem's solved.'

'Solved?' *So we'd be sleeping side by side?* 'What kind of a solution is that?'

'I'm only trying to think of what's best for the baby.' He actually sounded genuine. 'I swear there'll be no funny business, Ms Meadows. I'll be on my best behaviour.'

'I'm sure you have good intentions, Mr Corrigan, but I'd much rather—'

Chloe stopped. She'd been about to say that she would much rather look after Lucy on her own, but then she realised how selfish that sounded, and she would be denying Zac an important chance to get to know his baby niece and possibly to bond with her.

Maybe she *was* being a trifle prudish. After all, if Zac had really wanted to seduce her, he wouldn't have given up so easily last night. And if he could resist her in last night's red dress, he wasn't likely to pounce on her as she walked the floor at midnight with a fretful baby in her arms.

'Look, all right,' she admitted reluctantly. 'I suppose your plan makes a crazy kind of sense. I'll… I'll give it a go.'

Her boss rewarded her with one of his spectacular smiles. 'I knew I could rely on you to be unfailingly sensible. I'll organise for the beds to be changed, and for a cot to be sent up to my room. And I certainly won't let your room go. You'll need it as a bolt-hole, at least to escape to for long hot baths.'

His grey eyes shimmered and she couldn't be sure if he was teasing her again.

CHAPTER SEVEN

'SHE'S AN ABSOLUTE ANGEL, isn't she?'

Zac stood by the cot set in a corner of his hotel room, aware that he wore a sappy smile on his face as he stared down at the sleeping baby. As far as he could tell, Lucy Corrigan was perfect.

She'd been sound asleep when he and Chloe collected her from the hospital and she'd slept all the way during the taxi ride. She hadn't even stirred when they arrived back at the hotel, where he'd rather clumsily extracted her from the car seat before the excited hotel staff rushed to make a huge fuss of them.

Now the three of them were alone. Chloe was in an armchair by the window, reading yet another magazine about mothers and babies, and Zac was pacing the floor on tenterhooks, waiting for Lucy to stir and wake for her next feed.

Standing ready in the bar fridge were a row of bottles of formula that Chloe had made up and which she was going to heat with a special travelling contraption she'd found at the pharmacy.

Zac wasn't entirely happy about this. He'd planned to ask the kitchen staff to prepare the baby's formula and he'd been quite pleased with the idea of Lucy's bottles arriving via room service. He was rather amused by the prospect of signing for a baby's bottle delivered on a covered silver tray.

But Chloe, sensible as always, had wanted to be certain about the hygiene of the bottles and about getting the temperature of the milk exactly right, so now Zac's bathroom housed a sterilising unit as well as the heating gear and a collection of baby bath gels and lotions and wipes.

Still, he liked to think of himself as tolerant—and at least Lucy was very well behaved. Not a peep out of her so far. Then again, a quiet, sleeping baby was rather boring for a guy who wasn't used to sitting around…

'Isn't she due to wake up for a feed?' he asked Chloe as he checked the time yet again. By his reckoning, Lucy had slept twenty minutes past her mealtime.

Chloe looked up from her magazine. 'I suppose she'll wake when she's ready.'

'Isn't that a bit vague? I thought there was a schedule.' Schedules were usually his PA's forte. 'Isn't it important to get a baby into a routine?'

'Zac, give her time. She's only a few days old. She'll probably wake soon.'

Disgruntled, he picked up the TV remote and pressed the 'on' button. A loud blast of music erupted and Lucy gave a start, throwing one tiny arm in the air.

'Sorry,' he muttered as Chloe glared at him while he hastily searched for the 'mute' button.

Ridiculously, his heart was pounding now. No doubt he'd terrified the baby. He held his breath, waiting for her wails of terror. But, to his amazement, she was already asleep again, lying as still as a doll. Perhaps she'd never really woken.

Zac dropped into another armchair and began to flip restlessly through the channels with the sound turned down, but there was nothing he really wanted to watch and he found his mind meandering back over the previous night…

Rather than chastising himself yet again, he allowed himself to dwell on the pleasures of the evening. And there had been many. Chloe had been such good company—so relaxing and easy to talk to at the restaurant—and at the theatre she'd laughed uproariously, even at risqué jokes that he'd feared might upset her.

As for the red dress... Zac feared he was scarred for life by that dress.

He knew that from now on, every time Chloe walked into his office, he was going to remember the tormenting way the dress had hugged her delicious curves.

Why on earth had he paid such scant attention *to* those curves before now? He was beginning to regret that he'd been so disciplined from the day Chloe first joined his staff, never allowing himself to think of her as anything but his PA.

Of course, office romances were messy and bad for business—Zac had seen several of his mates fall by that particular wayside—but, last night, it was as if he'd had laser surgery and his vision had suddenly cleared. And today, even though Chloe had changed back into a sweater and jeans that he'd seen many times before, he was aware of her body in a whole new and entirely distracting way.

He couldn't help noticing the lush swell of her breasts and the dip to her waist, or the sweet tempting curve of her butt.

Which was hardly conducive to a good working relationship, especially now that they were spending so much time together, including sleeping side by side in the same room. Clearly his brain had been out to lunch when he'd come up with *that* bright idea. He'd presumed the baby would keep them fully occupied...

With a heavy sigh, Zac switched off the TV, pushed out of the armchair and began to prowl again. If Lucy slept for too much longer he would have to take off—go for a hike—hope that the freezing winter weather outside might chill his inappropriately lustful thoughts.

'Are you quite sure we shouldn't wake her?' he demanded after yet another circuit of the room.

Chloe rose and came over to the cot. Her sweater had a V-neck that exposed the soft pale skin of her neck and a hint of the perfection of her collarbone.

'I'm not totally sure,' she said. 'Most of the information I've read is for breastfed babies.'

Zac wished she hadn't mentioned breasts. He was all too aware of the way hers swayed gently beneath the soft knit of the sweater when she walked.

He tried to concentrate on the tiny girl as they stood together, looking down at her. Lucy was lying on her side, giving them a view of her profile now—the newborn slope of her brow, her snub little nose and slightly pouting red lips.

She was so still. So quiet. So *tiny*.

A tremor of fear rippled through Zac's innards. 'I suppose she's still breathing?'

He saw his fear reflected in Chloe's dark eyes. 'Of course. Well... I—I think so.'

Zac's fear spiked to panic. 'Should we check?'

'OK.'

One of Lucy's hands was peeking out of the blanket and his heart hammered as he reached down and touched it with his finger. 'She feels a little cold.'

'Does she?' Chloe also sounded panicked now and she gave the baby a prod with two fingers.

Lucy squirmed and made a snuffling noise.

'Oh, thank God,' Zac breathed and he nearly hugged Chloe with relief.

Then they both laughed, shaking their heads at their foolishness, but, as their smiling gazes connected, Zac's heart thudded for a very different reason.

He felt a deep rush of gratitude for this woman. In the past few days he'd experienced some of the darkest moments of his life and Chloe's presence had been like a gently glowing candle, a shining light just when he needed it. Actually, he suspected that this feeling comprised something way deeper than gratitude.

Perhaps Chloe sensed this, too. Confusion flashed in her eyes and she hastily looked down. 'Hey,' she said suddenly. 'Zac, look.'

From the cot, two small bright eyes were staring up at them.

Zac grinned. 'Well, well...hello there, Lucy Francesca Corrigan. Aren't you the cutest little thing?'

'I guess we can pick her up now,' Chloe said. 'She probably needs changing. Do you want to do the honours?'

Zac swallowed. The nurse had handed the baby to Chloe when they left the hospital, which was fine by him. He'd planned to be an observer. Then again, he'd never been one to chicken out of a challenge.

'OK,' he said bravely, peeling back the top blanket. To reassure himself, he added, 'No worries.' But he held his breath as he carefully lifted the tiny bundle.

'You can change her on the bed,' Chloe said.

'Me?'

'Why not?' Her smiling dark eyes were daring him now. 'I've spread towels for you.'

'Right, sure.'

Anyone would think he was defusing a bomb, the way he gingerly set the baby down and began to unwrap her bunny rug. Beneath this, he found that she was wearing an all-in-one affair, like a spacesuit, so his task now was to undo countless clips.

Beside him, Chloe was on standby with baby wipes and a clean disposable nappy.

'Maybe you should take over,' he suggested. 'You're probably an expert. You've done this before.'

She shook her head. 'I haven't actually, but I've watched friends change babies, and I'd say you're doing a fine job.'

Soldiering on, Zac eventually managed to free Lucy from her nappy and it was a bit of a shock to encounter her naked lower half. Her hips were minuscule, her legs thin and red as she kicked at the air.

'She's like a little frog,' he said in awe.

'She's beautiful,' reproached Chloe.

'Well, yeah. A beautiful little frog.'

Chloe handed him a wipe. 'You can put on a new nappy and dress her again while I heat her bottle.'

'Right.' Zac felt a stab of alarm as Chloe disappeared, but then he took a deep breath and manfully got on with the job and, although it was tricky getting tiny limbs back into the right sections of the garment, he was absurdly pleased with himself when he had Lucy properly dressed again by the time Chloe came back with the bottle.

'She hasn't cried at all,' Chloe commented.

'No, she's frowned and looked cross-eyed at me once or twice,' Zac said. 'But not one wail.'

'Isn't she good?'

'Amazing.' In a burst of magnanimity, he said, 'You can feed her if you like. I'm happy to watch and learn.'

But Zac soon realised this wasn't such a great idea. The picture Chloe made as she settled in the armchair with Lucy made him choke up again. This was partly because he was suddenly thinking of Liv and the fact that she should be here with her baby. But also…even though he was missing Liv, he knew that Chloe looked so damn right in this setting.

Perhaps it was something about the tilt of her head, or the way the light from outside filtered through the hotel's gauzy curtain, making the scene look soft, like a watercolour painting.

Or perhaps it was the fondness in Chloe's face as she looked down at Lucy, and the way Lucy looked straight back at her, concentrating hard, so that she almost went cross-eyed again as she sucked on the teat.

He was damn sure those two were forming a bond.

'I should put the kettle on and make you a cuppa,' he said, wishing his voice didn't sound so gruff.

Chloe flashed him a brilliant smile. 'Thanks.'

As Zac went to fill the kettle he couldn't remember the last time he'd made a cup of tea for anyone else. He knew he should be dismayed by the sudden domestic turn that his life had taken, but the craziest thing was that he actually quite liked it.

Chloe was secretly amazed that the first day with Lucy went so smoothly. After the baby was fed and burped she went straight back to sleep again and she continued to sleep while Chloe and Zac watched an entire DVD.

Now, the short winter daylight had disappeared already and the dark streets outside once again flashed with traffic lights and neon signs and Christmas decorations.

'This baby-raising is a piece of cake,' Zac declared as he poured two glasses of the Italian wine he'd ordered from room service and handed a glass to Chloe. 'How much do they pay babysitters and nannies for sitting around like this?'

'I don't really know,' Chloe said. 'But I'm quite sure they earn it.'

'I can't see how.' Zac was grinning as he lifted the cover on the cheese platter he'd ordered to accompany the wine, and Chloe guessed he wasn't really serious. Then again, it was hard to argue that their new responsibility was onerous as they clinked glasses in a toast to the sleeping baby in the corner.

Their afternoon had been surprisingly pleasant. She and Zac had established clear ground rules and he'd been on his best behaviour...and this evening promised ongoing pleasantness.

They planned to have dinner here in Zac's room and perhaps watch another movie, having discovered an unexpected mutual liking for sci-fi. It was all very agreeable. Zac was so much more at ease about caring for Lucy now and Chloe was genuinely pleased for him. He'd been through so much turmoil over the past few days and he still had to face his sister's funeral in the morning, and heaven knew what challenges awaited him when he got back to Australia.

A quiet, relaxing evening was exactly what he needed and so they'd planned for dinner at seven-thirty, allowing plenty of time for Lucy to wake and be changed and fed and settled back to sleep again.

Chloe always felt better when she had a clear plan...

'Is that someone knocking?' Zac shot a frowning glance to the door. He couldn't really hear anything with a baby screaming in his ear. 'What's the time?'

'Seven-thirty,' said Chloe, who'd been pacing anxiously beside him.

'That'll be our dinner.' Zac, who was fast becoming an expert, deftly shifted Lucy, plus a hand towel to catch spit-up milk, to his other shoulder. 'We should have rung through and told them to hold the meal till we got her down.'

Chloe winced, knowing that normally she would have thought of this. 'I guess I'd better answer the door.'

'Wait till I take Lucy through to the bathroom. We don't want to blast the poor guy's ears off.'

Chloe's stomach was churning as she watched Zac disappear with the red-faced, yelling babe. This had been going on for over an hour now and they weren't quite sure how or why Lucy was so upset.

She'd woken from her sleep and together they'd bathed her and changed her into clean clothes from head to toe. This had taken a little longer than it probably should have and by the time they'd finished Lucy was desperately hungry and letting them know. When Zac offered her the bottle—they'd decided it was his turn—she had sucked quite greedily and the milk had disappeared in no time.

'Piece of cake, this looking after babies,' he'd said again, smiling smugly as he laid Lucy back in the cot.

Thirty seconds later, the wailing had begun. Lucy kept pulling her little knee into her stomach as if she was in pain.

'She needs burping,' Chloe decided. 'There's a diagram of

what you have to do in one of the magazines.' And, following the instructions carefully, she'd sat Lucy on her lap, holding her tummy firmly with one hand while she gently rubbed her back.

It hadn't worked—and neither had walking up and down with Lucy. The hoped-for burp never occurred and after more than an hour of valiant efforts to calm her, her cries still hadn't stopped.

Despite the closed bathroom door, the yells could be heard all too clearly now as their room service dinner was wheeled in...

Chloe gave the fellow a generous tip.

'Thanks.' His eyes were wide with curiosity and he sent more than one worried glance to the closed door.

'Colicky baby,' Chloe told him with the knowledgeable tone she imagined a nursing sister might use. 'She'll settle soon.'

The fellow nodded and hurried away and Chloe hoped they weren't going to be reported for creating a disturbance.

She opened the bathroom door for Zac and he emerged looking somewhat haggard, although Lucy's howls had finally begun to quieten to whimpers.

'Do you think she's settling?'

Zac's shoulders lifted in a shrug. 'I have no idea. From now on I'll admit to total ignorance and I take back everything that I said about nannies and babysitters. Whatever they're paid, it's not enough.'

Chloe couldn't help smiling and, although this wasn't the right moment, she also couldn't help noticing how utterly enticing a strong hunky man could look with a tiny baby in his arms. Moments like this, she could almost imagine...

But no. She reined her thoughts back. Imaginations were dangerous.

'That dinner smells amazing,' Zac said, casting a longing glance to the trolley.

'I know. My tummy's rumbling.' Zac had ordered a Greek lamb dish for both of them and Chloe doubted any meal could smell more tempting. 'I wonder when we'll get to eat it.'

At that moment, Lucy's knee jerked upwards again and she let out another heart-rending yell.

'She's definitely in pain,' Zac said. 'Maybe we should ring someone. Do you think there's a helpline?'

'I'm pretty sure she just has colic.' Chloe said this more calmly than she felt. 'Early evening is supposed to be the worst time for it.'

'Perhaps it's my fault?' A totally uncharacteristic look of guilt appeared in Zac's eyes. 'Maybe I held the bottle the wrong way.'

'Of course you didn't. Here, let me take her for a bit. You eat your meal. It's getting cold.'

'No, no. You eat first.'

Chloe shook her head. She couldn't possibly eat while Lucy was still so upset. 'Perhaps we should try changing her again...'

In the end, they ate their cooling and congealing dinner in shifts, while taking it in turns to pace the floor with the baby. Several times her crying calmed down and she began to look sleepy and their hopes soared.

Twice she nodded off and they actually placed her back in the cot, holding their breath and hoping she would stay asleep as they backed silently away on tiptoe. Both times, just when they thought all was well, Lucy suddenly threw up her hand and began to cry more lustily than ever.

She kept crying on and off until it was her feed time again. This time, when they changed her, they encountered their first dirty nappy and Zac rose another notch in Chloe's estimation when he didn't flinch, but gamely went to work with the wipes.

He insisted that Chloe be the one to feed Lucy this time. She made sure that the baby didn't guzzle and she stopped the feed halfway through for a little burping session—this time with results—and, to their infinite relief, when they tiptoed away from the cot, Lucy remained sleeping.

As the silence continued, they let out relieved sighs.

Bliss.

They shared tired smiles.

'I'm knackered,' Zac admitted with a sheepish smile. 'I was looking forward to kicking back with some more of that wine and cheese, but I'm not sure I have the strength.'

'Nor me,' agreed Chloe. 'Not if Lucy's going to wake again in three hours or so.'

She went back to her room to shower and to change into sleepwear and of course she chose the safety of a voluminous grey T-shirt and opaque black tights, but, when she came back, Zac was already in bed and he appeared to be sound asleep.

She smiled wearily. After making such an enormous fuss about the dangers of sleeping so close to Zac, the reality was going to be a non-event. All either of them wanted was the oblivion of deep sleep.

A small sound woke Chloe.

Drowsily, she rolled over without opening her eyes, then nestled back under the covers. No sound now. All was quiet again. Lovely. She didn't have to worry. The sound wasn't Lucy.

Zap!

Lucy? Shocked into wakefulness, Chloe shot up, heart thudding. The room was mostly in darkness, but there was enough light from a lamp in the corner for her to see that Zac was awake and sitting on the edge of his bed.

'I thought I heard something,' she whispered. 'Was it Lucy?'

'It's OK,' he whispered in answer. 'Go back to sleep.'

'But there was a noise. How is she?'

'She's fine. I've just fed her.'

'*You've* fed her?' Chloe stared at him in amazement. 'You mean you've done it all—changed her and fed her and burped her?'

'The whole deal.'

'So what's she doing now?'

'Sleeping again. Like a baby.'

Chloe gave a dazed shake of her head. 'Why didn't you wake me?'

'Didn't want to bother you.' Zac yawned. 'You were snoring your head off.' He yawned again. ''Night. See you in the morning.' And then he lay down with his back to her and pulled the covers high.

Chloe was too surprised to fall straight back to sleep. She was supposed to be moral support. She was sleeping in this room because Zac needed her help. Except he clearly hadn't needed her at all…and she wasn't sure how she felt about that…

She'd grown accustomed to him needing her…

Although perhaps she shouldn't be so surprised. She knew that Zac threw his whole weight into any project he undertook.

As she lay staring into the darkness, she thought again about the fuss she'd made this morning over sharing this room with him. She'd expected him to try to seduce her again. She'd imagined having to fend off his advances, even though she didn't really want to…

If she was brutally honest, she'd probably hoped he might try…

But, as Zac had promised, this was an entirely practical arrangement. He hadn't shown the slightest glimmer of sexual interest in her and now she felt a bit foolish about the way she'd made such a hue and cry.

Of course, it probably helped that she'd chosen to wear these gym clothes to bed rather than slinky pyjamas, but tonight she'd gained the impression that Zac would probably have ignored her even if she'd been wearing a transparent negligee. His focus was entirely on Lucy. And Chloe was delighted about that. She was. Really.

But she wasn't sure if she would get back to sleep.

CHAPTER EIGHT

AFTERWARDS, ZAC'S MEMORIES of Liv's funeral were fragmentary at best. He could recall the harrowing hollowness he felt on entering the small church lit with candles and Christmas brightness, and filled with a surprising number of people. But he remembered very little of the short eulogy he gave, although he did his best to give his sister's new friends a few cheering pictures of Liv's happy family life in Australia, and of the deep love he'd always felt for her.

He thanked everyone gathered there for offering his sister the welcoming warmth of their friendship and for coming today to honour Liv's memory. He thanked Father Tom...having earlier handed him an envelope with a cheque that he hoped would convey his immense gratitude.

Moving outside again was the worst moment—bidding farewell to Liv's coffin before it was driven away. Zac felt as if he couldn't breathe. His throat burned as if he'd swallowed a hot ember and his hand was shaking as he reached into his coat pocket and drew out a piece of coral, one of two pieces he'd found on a shelf in Liv's room.

Bleached white and bony, like miniature antlers, Zac had recognised them immediately as coral their mother had collected when they'd lived on the island, pieces that Liv had always kept with her.

Today he placed one slender branching cluster on her coffin.

'Bye, Liv,' he whispered. Then, blinded by tears, he wrapped his fingers around the other piece still in his pocket.

When he felt an arm slip through his, he turned to see Chloe, who offered him a markedly wobbly smile.

'You were wonderful,' she told him, and her eyes were shiny with tears as she picked up the tail of his scarf and tucked it back inside his coat, before lifting her face to press a warm kiss to his cheek.

Zac closed his eyes, more touched by the simple gesture than was possibly appropriate. He suspected that, while other memories might fade, this particular moment would stay with him for ever.

Even though it was Christmas Eve, Skye and Liv's other housemates insisted on inviting everyone back to the house. In no time the place was crammed with a huge range of young people, including Father Tom.

As mugs of mulled wine and savoury platters were passed around, Chloe was introduced to a fascinating crowd with a wide range of British accents, as well as the more distinctive voices of people who were clearly new arrivals, just as Liv had been.

She met a Brazilian man, a kitchen hand who was not only stunningly handsome but extremely polite and charming. Next, she was introduced to two Polish plumbers with shaved heads who looked fierce but were actually super-friendly. A large West Indian girl showered everyone with her beaming smile.

Of course, all of Liv's friends wanted to make a fuss of Lucy and, to Chloe's surprise, they'd even brought presents for the baby—so many gifts, in fact, that Zac was going to need another suitcase.

Zac was extremely tolerant as the baby was passed around,

and Chloe guessed that he was as touched as she was to discover how supportive Liv's community of friends had been. And, fortunately, Lucy seemed to enjoy all the attention.

'That went well,' Zac said quietly as a taxi took them back to the hotel. 'I had no idea what to expect, but it couldn't have been better, really.'

But he still looked sad...terribly sad...and Chloe's heart ached for him.

Almost as soon as they got back to the hotel, Zac made his excuses. 'There are one or two matters I need to see to,' he said enigmatically before disappearing.

Chloe knew he had to collect Lucy's passport, but she was also sure he needed a little time to himself. Actually, she was more than ready for some thinking space, too... There were one or two matters she needed to chew over...including the fact that the longer she was in close proximity to Zac Corrigan the more she liked him, the more she cared about him. Deeply. Maybe even *loved* him...

In the past few days her understanding of her boss had changed massively, especially since they'd begun caring for Lucy. There were times when Zac had looked at her with an emotion that went way deeper than teasing or desire. Moments when Chloe saw a kind of tenderness that made her heart tremble and hold its breath, as if...

Her more sensible self wanted to argue with this, of course, but Chloe was tired of her internal debates...or perhaps she was just plain tired. Lucy had been colicky again in the early hours...

Curled in the armchair, she must have nodded off, and she woke with a start when Zac returned.

'Sorry.' He sent her a smile as he tiptoed across the room to peek into the cot. 'I was trying not to wake you.'

'Doesn't matter. Is Lucy still asleep?'

'Out like a light.'

Chloe's limbs were stiff as she unfurled from her cramped

position and sat straighter. She rubbed at her eyes and blinked. No, she hadn't imagined it. Zac was not merely smiling; he was looking particularly pleased with himself.

She'd assumed he'd been walking around London's streets, sunk in his grief, but his smile was definitely triumphant as he tossed his coat onto the end of his bed before he sank comfortably into the other armchair. 'I've collected Lucy's passport and I've sorted out our Christmas,' he said.

'Sorted it how?' Despite the beautiful decorations and lights and the frenzy of shopping all around them, Chloe had almost stopped thinking about Christmas. 'I thought we'd have turkey and plum pudding here in the room.'

'No, Chloe, you deserve better than that.'

'I do?' she asked, frowning.

'Yes, you do, Chloe Meadows.' Zac smiled gently and she wished he wouldn't. 'You've given up your own plans for Christmas without a word of complaint and you deserve some fun.'

An edgy uncertainty launched her to her feet. What was Zac planning? That she should go off and celebrate Christmas on her own while he stayed here with Lucy? She couldn't imagine she'd enjoy that very much.

'Zac, I don't need a fancy Christmas. I've said all along that I'm happy to help with Lucy.'

'Don't worry about Lucy. I've organised a sitter.'

She stared at him in surprise. 'But you don't believe in babysitters.'

Zac frowned. 'I don't think I ever said that exactly.' Now he rose from his chair to stand beside her. 'I'm not keen on nannies, particularly if they're used as a mother substitute. But this is different. It's not fair to you to be locked up in here on Christmas Day with someone else's baby.'

His eyes sparkled. 'After all, I did promise you a flash London Christmas to make up for missing our office party.'

'So you did.' Chloe found that she was smiling too as she remembered what a big deal the office Christmas party had been for her. Only a few days ago. So much had changed since then. And now...the very fact that Zac had obviously been thinking about her, making plans in an effort to please her made her feel unexpectedly happy and glowing...

'Actually, I've also been thinking ahead,' Zac said. 'I've been thinking about when I get home. I've realised that I can't expect *any* woman to be tied to the baby around the clock. She'll have to have help.'

Any woman... He was referring to his future wife, of course, and a shiver skittered down Chloe, as if he'd dropped a cold key down the back of her shirt. How silly she'd been to imagine... to think that he might possibly...

'So,' she said stiffly as she tried to ignore the chilling slap of ridiculous, unwarranted disappointment. 'What do you have planned for tomorrow?'

'Are you all right, Chloe?'

'Yes, of course.' She was working hard now to ignore the confusion and tumult that seemed to have taken up residence in her head and her heart.

Turning away from him to the window, she stared out at the park with its huge bare trees. She saw children in woolly hats chasing each other, saw businessmen with newspapers and furled umbrellas. An elderly couple were walking their dogs. And then her vision blurred.

She certainly wasn't all right. She was very afraid that, against her better judgement, she'd fallen in love with her boss.

She was as foolish as all his other females. More foolish actually, because she'd always known that falling for Zac was dangerous.

Somehow, over the past few days, she'd been seduced by their moments of deep connectedness. She'd been charmed by those times when he'd looked at her with a true appreciation that went way deeper than the mere respect of a boss for a trusted employee.

Saturday night had been different—Chloe had found it difficult but at least possible to resist Zac when he'd so clearly set out to seduce her. After all, she knew that Zac Corrigan would try to seduce any young woman he dated. But this morning, outside the church, Zac had needed her emotional support. And her heart had never felt so full...

'Chloe, what is it? What's the matter?' Zac was standing close behind her now and at any minute he was going to discover her tears.

'I—I was just thinking about... Christmas,' she said, grasping at any excuse.

'I suppose you must be missing your parents.'

'Yes.' Across the street a young woman was running through the park. The woman wore a red coat and her blonde hair was flying behind her like a banner.

'Chloe.' She felt Zac's hand on her shoulder and she tried to keep her head averted. The girl in the park was running to meet a young man. The young man was hurrying too and at any moment they would fall into each other's arms.

'You're crying,' Zac said and he made a soft sound of despair. 'Come here.' With sure hands, he pulled her around to face him. 'Let me see you.'

Chloe shook her head, made her eyes extra wide in a desperate attempt to hold back the tears. *I'm being an idiot.*

Zac had positioned her in front of him now, a hand on each of her shoulders as he searched her face, his grey eyes mirrors of her sadness. 'Chloe, what's the matter?'

How could she tell him? She shook her head and she might have held up her hand to ward him off but, before she could, his arms were around her, drawing her against him.

'Oh, Chloe.'

Now she was clinging to him, pressing her damp face into the comforting wall of his chest, and his arms were around her, warm and strong, holding her close. She could smell a faint trace of his aftershave, could hear his ragged breathing, could feel his heart thudding against hers. Now she could feel his lips brushing a soft kiss to her brow...and that tiny intimacy was all it took.

In the next breath she was coming undone, wanted nothing more than for Zac to kiss her properly. On the lips. And if he kissed her, she would kiss him back. She would kiss him deeply, passionately, throw caution to the wind.

With him suddenly so close, her emotions were a fiercely rushing tide. Desire churned deep inside her, and she knew she had no choice but to ride the flood...rising, rising... She was gripped by a kind of desperation. It was now or never... If Zac kissed her, she would surrender. She would give herself to him completely. Nothing else mattered.

Oh, how she longed for him to kiss her.

Fortunately, he was a mind reader.

With a hand beneath her chin, he lifted her face and touched his lips to hers and everything went wild. Their kiss flared from hello to explosive in a heartbeat and Chloe wound her arms around his neck, pressing close, turning to fire.

Neither of them spoke. It was as if they both feared that words might break the spell. This coming together was all about emotion and longing and heat...as their mouths hungered and their hands turned feverish...as clothing fell silently onto white carpet...as they stumbled in a lip-locked tango to the nearest bed.

For a fleeting second, as they landed together on the mattress, Chloe's more sensible self tried to slam on the brakes. But Zac was gazing down at her and he had that look in his eyes—a look that was a mix of heartbreak and surprise and unmistakable desire. A look that melted her.

And now his hand was gliding over her skin and flames leapt to life wherever he touched. He lowered his lips to her breast and the longing inside Chloe bucked like a wild beast fighting to be free. All hope of resistance was lost...

* * *

Afterwards…the thrashing of their heartbeats gradually subsided as they lay side by side… And the silence continued…

Chloe couldn't find the right words. What did you say to your boss when you'd just shared blazing, uninhibited, mind-blowing sex with him? She had no idea, and it seemed Zac had been struck dumb as well.

Cautiously, she turned her face towards him. With equal caution, he turned to her and his eyes reflected the same shell-shock she felt.

They both knew this wasn't supposed to happen. They'd clarified on Saturday night that there were very valid reasons why this should never happen.

But now…their lovemaking had been so spontaneous, so flaming and passionate, it had taken them both by storm.

'Are—are you OK?' Zac asked gently, his words touching her skin and reaching into her heart, just as his kisses had, mere moments ago.

'Yes,' Chloe whispered.

He let out a huff of breath and a soft sound that might have been a sigh or the merest hint of a laugh. 'At least one of us is OK then.'

What did he mean? She knew she should ask, should at least say *something,* but she certainly wasn't willing to analyse the whys and wherefores of this, and she was still struggling to find the right words when Lucy woke with a lusty yell.

Grateful for the distraction, both Chloe and Zac rolled out of opposite sides of the bed and began to drag on clothes with the speed of commandos responding to an alarm.

'You can heat the formula,' Chloe said as she pulled her shirt over her head. Zac knew how to look after the formula now and he was quite expert at testing the temperature of the milk on the inside of his wrist. He was standing by with Lucy's bottle when Chloe had changed her nappy and re-dressed her.

'Why don't you feed her?' Chloe suggested, without quite

meeting his gaze. 'I'll make a cup of tea.' OK, so perhaps it was another ploy to avoid talking to him about what had just happened, but the tea making had also become part of their surprisingly domesticated routine. 'Then you can tell me what you have planned for Christmas,' she added.

'Christmas?' Zac gave a soft, self-deprecating laugh. 'Went clear out of my mind.'

'And remember, don't let her guzzle,' Chloe warned, desperately needing to remain businesslike and matter-of-fact, but her thoughts were churning as she went to fill the kettle.

Zac found it hard to concentrate on feeding the baby. He had too much to think about. He'd always believed he was reasonably knowledgeable when it came to women and seduction. He'd also thought he knew his PA quite well. He'd been wrong on both counts and to say that he was stunned was putting it mildly.

He cringed now when he recalled accusing Chloe of being an old maid. Clearly, she was far more worldly than he'd ever dreamed. He didn't want to start making comparisons, but something amazingly spontaneous and earth-shatteringly good had happened just now. Something way, *way* beyond random meaningless sex...

No doubt he'd stuffed up the very fine working relationship he had with his PA, however, and that was damn stupid. At this point, he had no idea where to take things from here, but one thing was certain—he would have to think this situation through very carefully before he made another move.

Perhaps his Christmas plans would be a useful diversion. He'd pulled off quite a coup, managing to wangle tickets for the hotel's sumptuous Christmas banquet. There was to be a six-course menu with every delicacy imaginable.

He reckoned the best news was that he'd secured a properly certified babysitter for the entire afternoon. Of course, he'd had to pay an exorbitant sum for a sitter on Christmas Day and at such late notice but, with the help of the concierge, it was all settled.

He'd been really looking forward to sharing this news with Chloe, but now...a Christmas feast paled into insignificance after what they'd just shared.

As Chloe poured boiling water over tea bags, her mind was spinning. Why hadn't she remembered that leaping into bed with Zac was simply *not* an option? Clearly her brain had snapped. She'd fallen into the oldest trap—giving in to lust and confusing it with love.

Surely she knew better than that? She was opening herself up to all kinds of pain.

Zac was never going to love her, so the outcome could only be painful. After all, she'd experienced what it was like to truly love someone and to be loved in return. And she knew Zac's attitude to love was light years away from her own. He was focused on finding a wife from a database, rather than searching his heart.

Her problem was that she'd spent too much time in his company. She'd become too caught up in his personal life and, for a short time, she'd totally lost her perspective.

Her only choice now was to accept that she'd made a very silly mistake and then to forgive herself. Forgive and forget. That was what Zac would expect her to do and, with luck, she would survive the emotional fallout.

OK. She felt marginally better now that she'd thought this through. It meant she simply had to put her feelings for her boss on ice until she got back to Australia and then she should be safe. She would come to her senses. Surely that was a workable plan?

Their lunch of toasted ham, cheese and tomato sandwiches with coffee was a strained and quiet affair.

'I guess we should talk about...you know,' Zac said as he

finished his second sandwich, but he still looked extremely uncomfortable.

Chloe drew a quick breath for courage. 'If you like...but I don't expect a post-mortem.'

'What about an apology?'

Shyly, she shook her head. They both knew this had been a two-sided affair.

'That's good,' Zac said. 'Because I wouldn't want to apologise for something so—'

He left the sentence unfinished, as if words were inadequate...or too revealing...

'Maybe it was inevitable,' Chloe said without looking at him. 'A guy and a girl in constant close proximity.'

When she looked up, she saw his puzzled smile. No doubt he'd expected tears and recrimination. That would have to wait till later when she was alone.

'Chloe, for the record, I'd like you to know that—' Zac hesitated again and his throat worked. 'It's so hard to express this properly, but you must know that kind of chemistry is pretty damn rare.'

Heat flooded her face. For her, their lovemaking had been astonishing, an outpouring of passion beyond anything she'd ever experienced—even with Sam—but she mustn't think about what that signified, or she'd end up with a broken heart. 'Maybe it's best if we don't say too much right now,' she said.

Zac nodded, a cautious smile still playing at the corner of his mouth as he picked up a final sandwich. 'A cooling-off period.'

'Yes.' She was too worried that she'd let her emotions show, that she'd burst into tears and make an awkward situation a thousand times worse.

'I'm sure that's probably wise,' Zac said, but he looked thoughtful, as if he was in the middle of a puzzle he hadn't quite solved. Then his expression lightened. 'Actually, to change the subject, I was wondering if we should brave the elements this afternoon and take Lucy for a walk.'

It was a brilliant idea. Chloe nodded enthusiastically. 'I think we're all in need of fresh air. If we put a little bonnet and mittens on her and bundle her in an extra warm blanket, she should be fine.'

Seemed they were both eager to hit the streets for a final Christmas shopping spree, and Chloe hoped fervently that the bustle of crowds and the dazzle of decorations would prove a very welcome distraction from her way too sexy employer.

'I'm keen to buy something for Lucy's first Christmas,' Zac said as they headed down Oxford Street. 'Any ideas?'

'I was thinking this morning, when Skye was madly taking photos, that it would be lovely to start an album for Lucy and to include shots of London.'

'Good thinking.' He didn't add *Ms Meadows* this time, but he was smiling again, almost back to the Zac of old. 'Lucy should have a record that begins right here with her very first Christmas.'

'I took photos of Skye and her friends with my phone. I'll email them to you, if you like.'

'Great. They should certainly be part of the record.' He definitely looked pleased. 'So an album's first on our list. What else? Liv already bought Lucy her first teddy bear.'

'Maybe you could buy her a gorgeous Christmas stocking while you're here, something that will become a tradition for her every year.'

'Yep, sounds good.' Zac trapped her with a private smile. 'Am I right in guessing you're a girl who likes traditions?'

'Possibly.'

For too long, they stood in the crowded and busy store, smiling goofily at each other until they realised they were blocking an aisle.

'And I think I'd like Lucy to have a little gold bracelet,' Zac said. 'I remember Liv used to wear one when she was a kid.'

'With a heart locket?' Chloe asked.

'Yes.'

She smiled. 'I had one of those too. I loved it, but I lost it once when my neighbours took me water-skiing.'

Zac's grey eyes shimmered and Chloe gulped. She was so susceptible to that look. 'What's the matter? Do I have a smut on my face?'

'I'm trying to picture you as a little girl.'

Her heart tumbled like a snowball on a very steep slope. 'Don't talk like that,' she said, almost begging him. 'Concentrate on the shopping.'

CHAPTER NINE

AT BREAKFAST ON Christmas morning, when Chloe announced that she would like to go to church, Zac surprised her by saying that he'd like to come too.

'Church two days in a row?' she queried.

'I've been reading about St Paul's Cathedral.' Apparently, Zac was fascinated by the cathedral's history. It was rebuilt after the Great Fire of London in 1666, and then later survived the Blitz in World War II when most of the surrounding buildings were flattened in bombing raids. 'It's become a symbol of resurrection and rebirth,' Zac said. 'And that seems rather fitting for Lucy's first Christmas.'

Considering the sad and miraculous circumstances of Lucy's birth such a few short days ago, Chloe had to agree.

'I don't think another outing will hurt her, do you?' he asked.

'She should be fine. She was actually better last night after all that shopping.'

While Zac checked the times of the services, Chloe rang her parents, who had almost finished their Christmas Day in Australia.

'It was wonderful,' they gushed. 'The loveliest Christmas, Chloe. The chauffeur took us to church and then brought us back here in time for lunch. And, my goodness, you should have seen the spread. We've never eaten so well. Please give our love to Zac.'

'My parents are probably your biggest fans,' she told Zac as she hung up, and she felt unexpectedly happy at the thought of going off with him and Lucy to celebrate Christmas in St Paul's.

OK, it might feel like the three of you are almost a proper family, but don't get ideas, girl.

'We've time for presents before we go,' Zac announced as they finished their simple breakfast of coffee and croissants, in lieu of the banquet to come. With a boyish grin, he crossed to the wardrobe and produced a small package.

'Hang on.' Chloe dived for the floor and rummaged under her bed. 'I have a little something for you, too.'

It was also a small gift, but the shop assistant had worked magic with a square of green and white striped paper and a bright red bow. Chloe set the gift on the table in front of Zac, rather than placing it in his hand. Probably an over-the-top precaution, but after yesterday's 'mistake', she was super-conscious of the dangers of any skin contact with this man.

Zac, however, had no qualms about kissing her cheek as he handed her his gift. 'Merry Christmas, Chloe,' he said warmly.

'Thank you.' She knew she couldn't refuse to return his kiss, but she did this so quickly she barely touched his cheek. 'And Merry Christmas to you.' She nodded towards the little green and white package.

'Thanks!' He looked so genuinely delighted that she wondered how he normally spent his Christmases. It was possible that, without close family, he was often quite lonely. The thought stabbed at her soft heart.

'Aren't you going to open it?' Zac had already freed the red ribbon and had started ripping into the paper.

'Yes, of course.' Her parcel was wrapped in pink and silver tissue and topped by a posy of tiny silk roses. 'But it's almost too pretty to open.'

Zac grinned. 'Go on, get stuck into it. I dare you.'

Chloe laughed. She was actually far more excited than she should have been, but a hand-selected gift from Zac was quite a novelty. Back in Brisbane, it was her job to order his corporate gifts for employees and business associates, as well as sending flowers and perfume to his girlfriends.

His gift to her usually came in the form of a Christmas bonus and, generous and welcome as this was, she couldn't help being curious about what he might buy when he made the selection entirely on his own.

There was a box inside the wrapping and it looked like a jewellery box. Chloe's heart fluttered and she shot a quick glance to see if Zac had opened his gift.

He was watching her and smiling. 'You go first.'

'All right.' She knew her cheeks were pink as she lifted the lid to find, nestling inside in a bed of cream silk, a solid gold chain bracelet with a heart-shaped locket. 'Oh, Zac, it's beautiful. It's just like Lucy's.'

'Hopefully, a grown-up version.'

'Yes, a *very* grown-up version.' Unlike the delicacy of the baby's bracelet, this one was solid and shiny gold and Chloe knew it had probably cost a small fortune.

'I almost bought you a necklace,' Zac said, 'but I knew you'd lost your bracelet when you were little.' He gave a self-conscious little smile and shrugged. 'I thought you might like a replacement.'

This was so much more than a replacement. It was a gift that mirrored the one Zac had bought for his niece. It wasn't only expensive, it was *personal*...

There was a good chance Chloe's blush deepened. 'I'll love wearing this. Thank you.' On her wrist it looked perfect. Toning beautifully with her skin, it made her feel mega glamorous.

She looked pointedly at the box in Zac's hand. 'Your turn.'

'Ah, yes...'

Chloe held her breath as he lifted the lid on the silver cufflinks she'd bought him. She watched his face, saw the flash in his grey eyes when he recognised the significance, and his face broke into a delighted grin. 'Sea turtles!' His grin broadened. 'You remembered from the other night.'

'I loved your story about living on the island and I thought these were incredibly stylish but cute,' Chloe said. 'But I also thought they might bring back happy memories.'

'They do. They will. They're wonderful.' He looked as if he might have hugged her, but perhaps he'd picked up on her caution. Perhaps he was as afraid as she was that they'd end up in bed again, ravishing each other...

'Thank you, Chloe,' he said instead, but his eyes had that look again, the one that told her he was remembering every detail of their passion, the look that made her head spin and her insides tremble.

'I feel dangerously virtuous after all that carol singing.' Zac was in high spirits as they came back into the hotel room. 'I'm certainly ready to eat, drink and be merry.'

Chloe knew what he meant. She'd felt wonderfully uplifted by the beautiful music in the magnificent cathedral and it seemed somehow perfect to follow up with her first slap-up Christmas dinner in a posh hotel.

Just the same, Zac's flippant comment about dangerous virtue sent her thoughts off once again in inappropriate directions, which was probably why she made herself busy writing notes for the babysitter, double-checking with room service for the delivery of the sitter's special Christmas dinner, and ensuring that everything Lucy might need was already laid out for her.

'At least we'll only be a few floors away, so the sitter can call us if she has any worries.'

Zac pulled a face. 'I wouldn't encourage her to call.'

'But we have to leave her a phone number, Zac.'

'Oh, if you insist.' His smile was teasing again as he walked to the cot. 'You go and get ready, while I have a quiet talk to this child. It's time I delivered her first lecture. She needs to understand that we expect nothing from her but her very best behaviour.'

For Chloe, entering the hotel's special banquet room was like walking into the dining room of a royal palace. There was so much to take in—the high ornate ceiling and stunning red walls with huge mirrors that reflected back the splendour, a tall Christmas tree covered in fairy lights in the corner, candles everywhere in glass holders, chandeliers overhead.

Down the middle of the room stretched long tables covered in red tartan and set with sparkling glassware, shining silver, starched white napkins. The guests were beautifully dressed and Chloe was more pleased than ever that she'd lashed out on her expensive red number.

With a glass of Yuletide punch in her hand, Zac's lovely bracelet on her wrist and his tall, dark and exceptionally handsome presence at her side, she'd never felt more glamorous and confident.

She had such a good time. They met a lovely Canadian couple who'd come to England to track down their family history, two genial elderly Scottish brothers who apparently spent Christmas at this hotel every year, a group of New Zealanders...

There was even a famous American author called Gloria Hart, who was accompanied by a much younger man whom she openly introduced as her lover. Chloe had read a few of her books, so meeting her was quite a fan girl moment.

Gloria made a beeline for Zac and although she kept her arm firmly linked with her young man's, she made sheep's eyes at him, and then she turned to Chloe with a coy smile. 'I do like your young man,' she said. 'I'm almost jealous.'

'Ah, but I'm taken,' Zac said gallantly as he slipped his arm around Chloe's shoulders and dropped a proprietorial kiss on her cheek.

Chloe hoped her smile held. Zac probably had no idea that his simple gesture gave her lightning bolts of both pleasure and pain.

Champagne was opened as they all took their seats and settled in for a truly sensational meal. White-coated waiters brought the most amazing dishes—Colchester rock oysters, shellfish platters, roast middle white pork with winter jelly, roast goose with Brussels sprouts and all the trimmings. These were followed by mince pies, Christmas pudding, Ayrshire cream and cider and chestnut syllabub.

Fortunately, there was plenty of time between courses, plenty of laughter and storytelling. Zac, as always, drew more than his share of feminine interest, but he got on well with the men, too, and he was attentive to Chloe throughout the afternoon.

Like Gloria Hart, everyone assumed they were a couple. Chloe almost set them straight, but then she caught Zac's eye and saw an ever so subtle warning smile, as if he was urging her to leave things be. She could almost hear him say, *What's the harm in a little pretence?*

She just wished she could feel happier about it, wished she didn't mind that it was only a charade...

Of course, when she explained that the occasional texts she sent were to their sitter, it was also assumed that she and Zac were Lucy's parents.

'You've regained your figure so quickly,' one woman commented.

Chloe smiled her thanks and this time she avoided catching Zac's eye. But she couldn't help silly thoughts that began with the fireworks of yesterday's unforgettable passion and ended with the bleak sadness of *if only*...

Give up now, Chloe. You know it's never going to happen... and you're not in love with him. You can't be. She didn't want to fall in love again, couldn't bear to risk that kind of heartbreak. And falling for Zac could bring nothing but heartbreak.

She knew him too well. *Just play the game. It's only for a few more hours and tomorrow you'll be on the plane, safely winging your way home.*

In the breaks between courses, people got up and moved about, mingling and chatting with other guests, going to the tall windows at the far end of the room to look out at the views across the park. Twice, Zac went back to the room to check on Lucy, which made Chloe smile.

The second time he left was just before their coffee arrived, and when he came back he hurried to Chloe and leaned close to her ear. 'Come with me,' he whispered.

Turning, she saw unmistakable excitement in his eyes and he nodded to the windows. 'I want to show you something.'

'What is it?'

His smile was the sort that made her ache inside. 'Come and see for yourself.'

Of course she was curious, so she excused herself from her neighbour and Zac grabbed her hand, hurrying her to the far end of the room.

'Look.'

Chloe looked and gasped.

Outside, it was dark, but the street lights and the lights of the buildings caught the dazzle of dancing, snowy white flakes. *Snow!* Real, no-doubt-about-it snow was falling silently, landing on tree branches, along railings and on the roofs of parked cars.

'Wow!' she exclaimed, gripping Zac's hand in her excitement. 'I've never seen snow before. Isn't it beautiful?'

'I thought you'd like it.'

'Oh, Zac, it's amazing. It's the perfect end to a perfect day.'

'I don't know how long it will last. I vote we skip coffee and go outside to dance about in it.'

'Yes, I'd love to. But we'll need to go back for our coats and gloves.'

'All sorted. I collected them while I was up checking on Lucy.'

Lucy. 'I forgot to ask. How is she?'

'She's fine, Chloe. The lecture I gave her paid off. She's a fast learner.' Zac slipped his arm through hers and gave a tug. 'Come on. Let's go.'

They made their farewells.

'It's snowing,' Chloe explained, which caused quite a stir. 'I'm afraid I've never seen snow before, so we're going outside. I want to catch the full experience.'

'Yes, off you go, lass,' one of the Scotsmen said. 'Although I should warn you that London doesn't have real snow.'

'Zac, make sure you keep Chloe warm,' called Gloria Hart.

They were laughing as they left amidst calls of 'Goodbye, lovely to meet you' and 'Merry Christmas'.

Chloe hadn't thought it was possible for her Christmas Day to get any better, but she was floating with happiness as Zac slipped his arm around her shoulders and they walked together along the paths in the park while the snow fell softly all around them.

'I'm going to wake up soon,' she said, holding out a red-gloved hand to catch a flurry of snowflakes. 'This is so magical. It's simply too good to be true.'

'It might not stay pretty, so I wanted you to enjoy it while it's fresh.'

She looked back to the hotel, where she could see the big window of the dining room, the twinkling lights of the Christmas tree and the chandeliers, and the silhouettes of people moving about inside.

'Thanks for dragging yourself away from the party and bringing me out here,' she said. 'I would have hated to miss this.'

'So would I,' Zac said with a mysterious shy smile.

Even though it was dark now, the park was well lit and the

space rang with the excited shouts and laughter of children and adults alike, making the most of the white Christmas. Chloe was zinging with excitement as she and Zac walked on, under bare-branched trees that now gathered white coats, and she loved the way he kept his arm securely around her...

They reached the far side of the park and were turning back when Zac said, 'Actually, while I'm in your good books, Chloe, I wonder if I could put a proposal to you.'

She frowned at this. Something about Zac's careful tone took the high gloss off her happiness. Thinking fast, she tried to guess what this proposal might be about. No doubt something to do with work, or with Lucy, or possibly with Marissa Johnson. She certainly hoped it wasn't Marissa. Not now. Not today.

'What kind of proposal?' she asked cautiously.

'Actually, I was thinking of a marriage proposal.'

Chloe's reaction was inevitable. Her silly heart toppled and crashed.

'Your proposal to Marissa?' She knew her shoulders drooped. She thought Zac had more tact than to bring this up now and spoil Christmas Day.

He gave a soft groan and came to a standstill. 'No, Chloe. This has nothing to do with Marissa.' He was standing in front of her now, blocking her path, as white flecks of snow floated onto his shiny black hair. 'I want to ask you to marry me.'

Chloe struggled to breathe as she stared at him and a cyclone of emotions whirled chaotically inside her, stirring all the longing she'd ever felt for him, along with the confusion and pain, the sympathy and tenderness.

For a giddy moment she allowed herself to picture being married to Zac and of course her silly brain zapped straight back to yesterday's lovemaking and she was instantly melting at the thought of a lifetime of fabulous sex.

And she thought about Lucy. The baby was now an inevitable part of the Zac Corrigan package, and Chloe knew she would adore taking care of the little girl and stepping into the role as her mother. And then there was Zac's business which Chloe knew inside out and was almost as passionate about as he was.

For so many reasons his proposal felt right. But, oh, dear heavens, she had to be careful. She had to remember that this gorgeous, kind and generous man was also the playboy she knew all too well. As far as she could tell, Zac had no real concept of being faithful. As for love...for crying out loud, until five minutes ago, he was planning to pick his prospective wife from a spreadsheet.

Chloe shivered inside her warm coat. 'Don't play games,' she said wearily. 'Not today, Zac. Please, don't be silly.'

He gave an angry shake of his head. 'Why do you always assume I'm playing games? I'm absolutely serious. Think about it, Chloe. It makes so much sense.'

'Sense?' Her eyes stung and it wasn't from the cold.

'I thought you liked to be sensible.'

Oh, give me a break, Zac. How many girls want to be sensible about romance?

But the question wasn't worth voicing. 'So why is this so sensible?' she demanded instead. 'Because I tick most of the boxes on your checklist?'

Zac looked surprised. '*Most* of the boxes? Chloe, you tick every single one of them. Actually, I'd have to add extra boxes for you. You're an amazing girl.'

'And I'm so good with Lucy,' she added flatly.

His smile wavered. 'Well, yes,' he said as if this was obvious.

Oh, Lord. Chloe couldn't hold back a heavy, shuddering sigh. *Please, please, don't let me cry.*

Zac stood very still now, watching her with troubled eyes. He wasn't wearing his scarf and she could see the movement of his throat as he swallowed uncomfortably. 'I've stuffed this up, haven't I?' he said quietly.

Fighting tears, Chloe gave a helpless flap of her hands.

'Maybe you got carried away after the luncheon today, when everyone assumed we were married.'

Now, with his hands plunged into his coat pockets, he tipped his head back and stared up at the dark sky. He sighed, releasing his breath in a soft white cloud. 'Give me some credit, Chloe.'

She could feel the weight of the gold bracelet around her wrist, reminding her of their happiness this morning when they went to church together and opened their presents. She hated that this had happened, hated that they were so tense now, on the raw edge of a fight, at the end of this beautiful, perfect day.

'Can I ask you a difficult question, Zac?'

He looked doubtful, but he nodded.

'Are you honestly in love with me?'

'Honestly?' he repeated, looking more worried than ever.

'There's no point in lying,' she said bravely. 'I know we've been pretending to others all day, but I need brutal honesty now.'

There was a long uncomfortable silence as Zac stood staring at her, his silver-grey eyes betraying a haunted uncertainty. He seemed to try for a smile and miss, then he said, 'I told you I don't really believe in "love".' He made air quotes around the word. 'And I'm afraid that's the truth. I think it's a dangerous illusion.'

Lifting his hands, palms up, as if protesting his innocence, he smiled. 'But I really like you, Chloe. As I said before, I think you're amazing. And you can't deny we have fabulous chemistry.'

A sad little laugh escaped her. Here she was in the perfect romantic setting for a marriage proposal, and instead she received a sensible, practical, *logical* proposal without a glimmer of romance.

Zac's eyes were shiny as he watched her. 'So... I take it that's a no then?'

Oh, Zac.

She had an eerie sense of time standing still. She felt so torn.

She knew this was her big chance to be reckless and brave and to grab a wonderful opportunity. She had no doubt she could give her heart to Zac and to Lucy, along with her loyalty to Zed-Cee Management Consultants.

But the big question was—what could she expect from Zac in return? A comfortable, entertaining, possibly exciting lifestyle…until his interest in her waned.

She was far too familiar with the pattern of Zac's love life. When it came to women, he had the attention span of a two-year-old, and if Chloe was ever going to risk love again, she needed certainty. She needed a man who could bring himself to say and mean those dreaded words: *I love you.*

'I'm sorry,' she said, fighting tears. 'I'm still an idealist. A romantic, I guess.'

'So you want an admission of true love *as well as* brutal honesty? *And* you want both from the same man?' Zac shook his head and it was clear he believed she was asking for the impossible.

Inevitably, the day ended on a low note.

There was no reassuring arm around Chloe's shoulders as they went back to the hotel, where they shook out their snowy coats and took the lift upstairs to find Lucy fast asleep and the sitter about to watch the Queen's Christmas message on TV.

So they watched the royal message with the sitter and then she left them with some reluctance, assuring them that she'd had a lovely day.

And Chloe left, too, going next door to remove her make-up and to change out of her red dress. She put the bracelet back in its box, and stowed it in her already packed suitcase. Then she added the dress, carefully folded between sheets of tissue paper.

Although she wanted to cry, she forced herself to be strong as she cleaned her teeth, creamed her face and brushed her hair.

A faint *'waa…'* from next door warned her that Lucy was

awake so, although she really didn't want to face Zac again this evening, she went back to his room to help with the evening feed, which was often the most difficult and colicky time.

However, the baby settled quickly, even before Zac and Chloe had drunk their ritual cuppas, but Chloe didn't join Zac in the armchairs for a cosy chat.

'I'll get on with Lucy's packing,' she said, knowing they would need to head for Heathrow soon after breakfast in the morning.

Taking up space in the middle of the room, Zac managed to look spectacularly manly and helpless. 'Anything I can do to help?'

'Probably better if I look after it,' Chloe muttered, ducking around him. 'I have a list.'

He smiled crookedly. 'Of course you do.'

She was so anxious and edgy and sad, she was glad of an excuse to keep busy, collecting scattered items like a baby sock from behind a cushion, a bib from beneath a pillow, and sorting out exactly what they'd need for Lucy on the journey. She packed a special carry-on bag with baby bottles, formula, nappies, wipes and several changes of clothes. Then she double-checked all their passports and travel documents.

'I've already checked those papers,' Zac said.

'Doesn't hurt to check again.'

Now that she'd rejected his marriage proposal and their final evening was ruined, she was extra keen to be on her way. If there was a hitch at the airport tomorrow—anything that meant they couldn't leave the UK—she was likely to have some kind of breakdown.

She wanted to be home. She needed to be caring for her boring sweet parents, needed to get her life back to normal as quickly as possible. Once she was safely home, she would put this London experience and everything that came with it behind her. Once again she would be nothing more than Zac Corrigan's

132   A VERY SPECIAL HOLIDAY GIFT

highly efficient and more or less invisible PA. As always, she would co-ordinate his private life as well as his business affairs, while she secretly turned up her nose at his *Foolish Females*.

CHAPTER TEN

ZAC WAS BEGINNING to suspect that Lucy could pick up on their vibes. Tonight he and Chloe were both as tense as tripwires, and Lucy was fussier than ever after her next feed. It was close to midnight before she settled back to sleep.

'We're going to have a hell of a trip home if she's like this tomorrow night,' Chloe commented tiredly.

'It will help if we make sure we're relaxed.'

'Relaxed?' The word snapped from Chloe like a rifle shot and, out of the corner of his eye, Zac saw the baby flinch.

He sighed. 'Look, I apologise if I've spoiled your Christmas. I know I've upset you.'

'Of course you haven't upset me. I'm fine.' Chloe's eyes were unnaturally wide as she said this and she promptly made an about-turn and headed for the door.

'Where are you going?'

She gave an impatient shrug. 'It's probably best if I sleep in my own room.'

'You really think that's going to help?'

'Help what?' she shot back with a scowling frown.

Was she being deliberately obtuse?

'Help *us*,' Zac said patiently. 'This walking on eggshells tension.' He had visions of a twenty-two-hour flight back to Australia without resolving whatever bugged her.

At least Chloe gave a faint nod, as if she acknowledged this, then she leaned her back against the door and folded her arms over her chest and speared him with her nut-brown gaze. 'So you're saying that you need to talk about our relationship—or rather our lack of a relationship?'

'Well, from my experience, talking things over is usually what girls want.'

She smiled. Damn, even when the smile was glum, she looked incredibly lovely when she smiled. Zac had to work hard to curb his impulse to cross the room and haul her into his arms. He wanted to relight those wild flames again. Taste her lips, her skin, feel her going wild with him. Hell, how could he ever forget that blazing encounter?

How could he forget how much he'd loved having her around on a twenty-four hour basis? He'd never met a girl he felt so comfortable with. Until he'd wrecked things with his clumsy proposal, sharing his personal life with Chloe had felt so unexpectedly *right*...as if their personalities slotted magically together like one of those Chinese puzzles...

'So what do you think we need to talk about?' Chloe asked.

'To be honest, I'm not totally sure, but it sure as hell can't happen if you're on the other side of that wall.'

Now she lifted her hands in a gesture of surrender. 'OK. No big deal. I'll stay here. I'm actually very tired, though.'

'The talk's not mandatory,' he said, feeling ridiculously relieved by this small victory.

Nevertheless, after they both got into their separate beds, he could see, via the faint glow of Lucy's night light, that Chloe remained, as he was, lying on her back with her hands beneath her head, staring up at the ceiling.

It wasn't long before her voice reached him through the darkness. 'So what do you want to talk about?'

There was no mistaking the distrust in her tone.

Zac couldn't help smiling to himself. 'I thought I was supposed to ask that question.'

'But I've already told you. I don't have any issues. I'm perfectly fine.'

This was patently not true. Since they'd arrived back from the park Chloe had been tearing about like a wound-up toy on top speed.

'But I must admit I don't understand *you*,' she said next.

Zac had heard this comment before from women. Had heard it with regular monotony, if he was honest.

'I mean,' Chloe went on in that earnest way of hers, 'I don't understand why you're so convinced that falling in love is nothing but a fairy tale.'

She wasn't going to let go of this. Clearly, it was at the heart of her tension.

'Well, OK,' he said smoothly. 'Convince me otherwise. I'm assuming you have a vast experience of falling in love?'

'I don't know about vast,' she said. 'But I was certainly in love with my fiancé.'

Whack.

Zac's smugness vanished as surprise juddered through him like a jack-hammer. How had he never known about her fiancé? More importantly, why hadn't Chloe said something about this guy when she so quickly and forcefully rejected his proposal?

Although he'd tried to make light of her rejection, her loud and clear *no* had stung. Zac had felt as if he was standing at the door of Aladdin's Cave, where the glittering riches and jewels represented a chance for a lifetime's happiness and contentment.

Heaven help him, he'd actually pictured a home with Chloe and Lucy and then, just when this dream was within his reach, the portcullis had slammed down, cutting him off from his vision of happiness.

Now, he said, 'I... I didn't realise you were engaged.'

'I'm not any more,' Chloe said softly. 'My fiancé died.'

Another shock. Despite the hotel's perfectly controlled heating, Zac was suddenly cold. 'Hell. I'm sorry. I had no idea.'

'I wouldn't expect you to know. It happened before I started working for you.'

'Right.' He swallowed uncomfortably as he absorbed this news.

Lying there in the dark beside her, it occurred to him that his assumptions about his PA had been entirely based on the image she presented at the office, but over the past few days that image had been crumbling and now it was blasted clear out of the water. 'Is it OK to ask what happened?'

After a small silence she said, 'Sam was a soldier—a Special Forces soldier. He was killed in Afghanistan.'

Zac swore and then quickly apologised. But this was almost one surprise too many. Special Forces soldiers were so damn tough and daring—the most highly skilled—which meant that Chloe had been about to marry a real life hero. 'I had no idea,' he said lamely.

'I don't like to talk about it.'

'No, I guess it must be hard.'

From the bed beside him, he heard a heavy sigh.

'I was a complete mess when it happened,' she said. 'That's why I came home to live with my parents. I didn't want to go out like other young people. I just wanted to hide away and... and grieve. I guess it wasn't exactly a healthy reaction.'

'But understandable.'

He heard the rustle of sheets as Chloe rolled to face him. 'Anyway, for what it's worth, I did love Sam. For me it was very real, an inescapable emotion. I suppose it was an attraction of opposites, but it worked for us. We were very happy and we had big plans for a family and everything.'

'That's...great...'

Zac had no idea what to say, but thinking about Chloe and her soldier made him feel inexplicably jealous...and depressed...

Inadequate, too. He understood now why Chloe had rejected him. She thought he merely wanted a mother for Lucy.

Damn it, he should have tried to express his feelings more truthfully but, chances were, anything he offered now would be a very poor second best to her true romance with her heroic soldier.

And if he tried to tell her how he really felt, how his days were always brighter when she was around, how, even at home in Brisbane, the weekends so often dragged and he couldn't wait till Monday mornings to see her again, it would sound crazy, as if he was in love...

'Are you asleep, Zac?' Chloe's voice dragged him back from his gloomy musings.

'Sorry. Were you saying something?'

'Now I've spilled my story, I was asking about you. Are you still going to insist that you've never fallen in love?'

His mind flashed to that one time in his past when he'd been young and deeply in love, with his head full of dreams and his heart full of hope. Until...

No. He never talked about that. He'd worked hard to put it all behind him and he wasn't going there now.

Chloe, however, was waiting for his answer.

'Well, yeah, sure I've been in love,' he told her with a joviality he didn't really feel. 'Hundreds of times.'

This was met by silence... It was ages before Chloe spoke and then she said quietly, 'That's exactly the answer I expected from you.'

After that she rolled away with her back to him. 'Goodnight, Zac.'

Her fed-up tone left him with the strong conviction that their conversation hadn't helped either of them and he knew he was going to have trouble getting to sleep.

Damn. The last thing he wanted was to lie awake remembering Rebecca...or what was now far worse—wrestling with regrets about Chloe...

***

The flight was scheduled for midday and both Chloe and Zac were nervous about how Lucy would behave during the long hours that stretched ahead of them.

To their relief, their fears were unfounded. When Lucy was awake the flight attendants seemed to love fussing over her, and when she slept the droning hum of the plane's engines seemed to soothe her into a deeper slumber.

'She's gorgeous and such a good baby,' several of the female passengers told Chloe. 'You're so lucky.' Chloe could tell from the way their eyes wandered that they considered Zac to be a major component of this luck.

Of course, Chloe thanked them and once again she didn't try to explain that she was neither Lucy's mother nor Zac's wife. But afterwards...she had to try to ignore the gnawing hollowness inside her, the annoying regret and second thoughts that had plagued her ever since she'd turned down Zac's proposal of marriage.

She knew she was going to miss Lucy terribly. In these few short days, she'd lost her heart to the baby. She'd grown to adore her, to love the feel and the smell of her, to love her bright curious eyes and hungry little mouth. When Zac wasn't looking, she'd even given Lucy little baby massages, following the instructions she'd read in one of the magazines.

As for Zac...despite the many strict lectures she'd delivered to herself, she felt desperately miserable whenever she thought about the end of this journey...when they went their separate ways. She'd grown so used to being with him twenty-four hours a day, to sharing meals with him, sharing middle of the night attempts to calm Lucy, listening to him in those quieter moments when he'd felt a need to talk a little more about Liv.

As for making love with him... Chloe's thoughts were seriously undisciplined when it came to *that* subject. She spent far too much time torturing herself by recalling every raunchy detail of going to bed with Zac…before firmly reminding herself it would never happen again.

'A penny for your thoughts.'

Chloe blushed. 'Excuse me?'

Zac leaned closer. 'You had your worried look, Ms Meadows. I wondered what was bothering you.'

She had no idea what to say. 'Um… I wasn't thinking about anything in particular.'

'Lucky you,' Zac murmured, leaning closer still.

'Why am I lucky?'

'You're not being tormented the way I am. I can't stop thinking about how much I want to kiss you.'

'Zac, don't be crazy. You can't start kissing on a plane.' Was he no longer bothered that she'd rejected his proposal?

'Why not?' he asked with that winning smile of his. 'They've dimmed the lights and no one's looking.'

So tempting…

'You want to, don't you?'

'No,' Chloe whispered, but she knew she didn't sound very convincing. No doubt because it wasn't the truth. She wanted nothing more.

When Zac leaned even closer and touched his lips to her cheek, she felt her whole body break into a smile. Instinctively, she closed her eyes and turned to him so her lips and his were almost touching. He needed no further invitation. His mouth brushed over hers in a teasing whisper-soft kiss that sent warm coils of pleasure spiralling deep. Chloe let her lips drift open and she welcomed the slide of his tongue.

'Mmm…' With a soft sound of longing, she moved as close to him as possible, kissing him harder…losing herself in the strength and the taste and the smell of him.

'I love you,' he whispered and wave after wave of happiness welled inside her. Everything was all right after all. It was OK to love Zac. There was no reason to hold back.

She slipped one hand behind his neck to anchor herself and

then she nudged her leg against his, as she was seized by a hot and feverish longing to climb into his lap.

'Chloe?'

Zac's questioning voice sounded quite loudly in her ear.

Chloe blinked. Her head was on Zac's shoulder. Her hand was curled around his nape. Her knee was hooked over his thigh. When she pulled back to check his face, he was staring at her with a strangely puzzled smile.

'What happened?' she asked.

'I think you fell asleep.'

Oh, my God. Had she been dreaming?

Cheeks burning with embarrassment, Chloe whipped her hand away and swerved back into her seat. 'I... I'm so sorry. I have no idea how that happened.' With a soft moan she sank her face into her hands.

'Hey, don't worry,' she heard him say. 'I'm already wishing I didn't wake you up.'

Chloe lowered her hands from her face. 'How long was I—?'

'Climbing all over me?'

She cringed. 'Yeah.'

'Only about ten minutes or so. I'd say there were only about a dozen people who walked past.'

She stared at him in horror. 'They saw me?'

But Zac was grinning hard now and she realised he was teasing her. She gave his arm a punch. 'You're a lying rat, Zac Corrigan.'

Her embarrassment lingered, however. Even if half the people in the cabin hadn't seen her draping herself all over Zac, *he* knew all about it. She thanked her lucky stars that he hadn't pushed her for a proper explanation. But what must he be thinking?

They were finally flying over Australian soil, although it would still be several hours before they touched down in Brisbane.

Chloe had just come back from the changing room with

Lucy, and Zac was waiting with the heated bottle the flight attendant had delivered.

'Do you want to do the honours?' Chloe asked him.

'Sure.' He held out his arms for the baby and Chloe's heart had a minor meltdown as she watched the tender way he smiled at his niece.

'You know,' he said, as he settled Lucy in his arms and carefully tipped the teat into her eager little mouth, 'I hate to think about trying to do this on my own when I get home. It won't be the same without your help.'

Chloe closed her eyes against the pang of dismay his comment aroused. She was going to miss this, too, more than she could possibly have imagined. When she opened her eyes again, the sight of Zac and Lucy together was beyond gorgeous.

In moments like this, the temptation to retract her rejection of Zac's proposal was huge...until she remembered that he only wanted her because she was good with Lucy...and possibly because their chemistry was undeniably hot. Was she crazy to believe these reasons weren't enough?

She thought about Sam and the way he'd made her feel and the many ways he'd showed her that he cared...just through little things like gifts or a surprise invitation, or the way he held her close. Of course, those gestures weren't all that different from Zac's behaviour, really. And the annoying thing was there were times when she felt even closer to Zac than she ever had with Sam.

Truth to tell, during the two years Chloe had known Sam, he'd spent a good proportion of the time on deployment in Afghanistan. So she was certainly better acquainted with Zac, with his good and bad habits, his strengths, hopes and fears. His belief that love was an illusion...

This thought sobered Chloe. 'You'll find some other woman to help you,' she said.

'Not straight away. That will take time to arrange.'

'Well, yes, I doubt that even you could manage to pull off

a wedding inside a week, Zac. You'll need to hire a sitter or a nanny for the interim.'

'And that won't be easy in the week between Christmas and New Year.'

Chloe slid him a sideways glance. 'You'll manage.'

'So you wouldn't consider it?' he asked, trapping her once again with his clear grey gaze.

'Consider what, exactly?'

'Helping me out for a few more days?'

She should have seen this coming, should have been prepared, but she'd thought, after her rejection, that Zac would back right off.

'Chloe?'

'I don't know,' she said. 'I'm thinking.'

'I've plenty of bedrooms,' he went on, offering one of his customary coaxing smiles. 'You could have your own room and we could put Lucy in the room next door to you.'

'Where would you be?'

'Just down the hall a bit.' Now he had the cheek to grin at her. 'Safely out of your way, but near enough to be on call to help with Lucy.'

If she thought about it rationally, without her silly emotions getting in the way, his request was probably reasonable. As long as this wasn't the thin end of the wedge...

'So what's your plan, Zac? You're still planning to...to...get married, aren't you?'

Chloe saw an unreadable flicker in his eyes, but his face was deadpan. 'I still think that's the preferable option.'

'And Marissa's the preferable candidate?'

'I guess so, yes.' His tone suggested that he still needed to give this serious thought. 'But I know I'll have important groundwork to do before I can convince her. At the moment, I don't even know if she's still available.'

'So it could take some time...'

Zac set the baby's bottle on the tray table while he gently

lifted Lucy onto his shoulder to help her to bring up her wind. 'I wouldn't expect you to stay at my place for too long, Chloe. Just for a night or two, till I get my bearings.'

'My parents might—'

'Your parents are welcome to stay on at the hotel, as long as they're enjoying it.'

'Oh, they're enjoying it all right.'

'Then, would you consider it?'

The last thing Chloe needed was more time in Zac's company. What she needed was distance. Time and space to regroup and to clear herself of her tangled thoughts and emotions. But then she looked at Lucy. Zac had shifted her onto his lap and she was curled over his big hand as he gently rubbed her back. She was such a dear little thing and she looked so cute now.

'I wonder if Marissa likes babies,' she found herself saying.

Zac lifted a dark eyebrow. 'I have no idea. I guess that's one of the many things I'll have to ask her.'

Chloe had never been to Zac's penthouse apartment, perched high in an inner city tower block. He'd project-managed its construction and it was a striking piece of architecture with views up and down the Brisbane River—all very shiny and modern with high gloss timber floors, large expanses of glass and a flashy granite and stainless steel kitchen.

By the time they'd emerged from Customs it was too late to try to go shopping for baby gear, so they went straight to Zac's place and made a snug nest for Lucy by pushing two black leather lounge chairs together and then lining the space with a quilt.

'She looks impossibly tiny, doesn't she?' Lucy said as they stood looking down at her.

'Yeah.' Zac reached down and softly stroked Lucy's dark hair. 'Welcome home, tiny girl.'

The love shining in his eyes brought a lump to Chloe's throat.

Then he straightened and his eyes were still shiny as he smiled at Chloe.

'There's a restaurant downstairs,' he said. 'I could send down for a takeaway meal.'

'I'm not especially hungry.' She would blame jet lag for her low mood, but from the moment she'd arrived she'd felt on the verge of tears.

'Maybe just one serving to share?' Zac suggested. 'Something light? They do great chilli prawns.'

Which was how they ended up on that first night, sitting on his balcony with a fresh breeze blowing up the river, eating chilli prawns and washing it down with a glass of white wine, while they enjoyed the city lights.

'You must love living here,' Chloe commented as she watched pretty ladders of light stretch across the smooth surface of the river.

'It's been great,' Zac admitted. 'At least it's been very handy for a bachelor.'

'Party Central?'

'At times, yes.' But Zac was frowning. 'I'm not sure I'd like to stay here with Lucy. She'll need a backyard with swings and other kids in her street to play with.'

'That safe suburban life you dream of,' Chloe suggested with a tired smile.

'Exactly.'

'Do you think you'll find it hard to adapt to that kind of life?'

'I guess that depends on who I can convince to come and live with us,' he said quietly and there was just enough light for Chloe to see the way his gaze flashed in her direction.

Without warning, her throat was choked and her eyes were stinging, spilling tears.

'Chloe.'

She threw up her hands. 'It's just jet lag. I need to hit the sack.' Already she was on her feet. 'Thanks for the prawns, Zac. They were delicious.'

'Don't get up when Lucy wakes,' he called after her. 'I'm not too tired. I'll be fine.'

'OK, thanks.' She kept her tear-stained face averted. 'See you in the morning. Goodnight.'

Of course, after that, Chloe took ages to get to sleep. She tossed and turned and agonised about Zac, but when she finally nodded off she slept deeply and soundly. She woke to find bright daylight streaming through the crack between her curtains and from below she could hear the sounds of city traffic.

Feeling guilty about spending an entire night without helping, she sprang out of bed and hurried to the lounge room, but the baby wasn't in her makeshift cot.

Chloe shot a hasty glance to the kitchen. An empty baby's bottle stood on the granite counter, but there was no other sign that Zac had been up and she couldn't hear any sounds from within the apartment. Quickly she dashed back to her room to check the time. It was only just coming up to six o'clock, much earlier than she'd expected, but of course the sun rose super-early in Brisbane in midsummer.

And where was Lucy?

She tiptoed down the hallway towards Zac's room, then stood listening for Lucy's snuffles and snorts.

Nothing.

She knew it was silly to panic, but where Lucy was concerned her imagination leapt into overdrive. Something had happened. Lucy was ill. Zac had rushed with her to a twenty-four-hour medical centre.

Having thoroughly alarmed herself, she dashed into Zac's bedroom. And came to a skidding halt.

He was sound asleep, lying on his back. And Lucy was in the bed beside him, while another empty baby's bottle stood on the bedside table.

Chloe found herself transfixed as she looked down at them— the great big man and the tiny baby girl. Zac had kicked the sheet off and he was only wearing a pair of black silk boxer shorts, which allowed her a perfect opportunity to admire his broad bare chest, his muscular arms and shoulders, the smattering of dark hair narrowing down to the waistband of his shorts.

She couldn't help reliving her amazing experience of being up close and personal with that toned and golden body.

'Morning.'

His deep voice startled her. She'd been so busy ogling him, she hadn't noticed that he'd woken.

'I... I was just checking to see where Lucy was,' she stammered.

Zac grinned sleepily. His eyes were mere silver slits, but she knew he'd caught her checking him out. Then he sat up, scrubbed a hand over his face and blinked at the baby beside him. 'I didn't mean to bring her back here, but with the jet lag and everything...' He frowned as he leaned closer to check the tiny sleeping girl. Her tummy was moving softly up and down as she breathed. 'Thank God I didn't roll on her.'

'When's she due for another feed?' Chloe was eager now to shoulder her share of the duties.

Zac squinted at the bedside clock. 'I'd say in about another hour.'

'You should go back to sleep then. If she wakes I'll deal with her.'

'Sounds great. Thanks.' He was smiling as he flopped back onto the bed.

As she left Zac's room, Chloe hoped he hadn't been keeping tabs on her recent 'lapses'. First there'd been her attempt to climb all over him in the plane, then her tears last night, and now this morning's ogling. Surely these added up to highly inappropriate behaviour from a girl who had flatly rejected him?

It was a difficult day. They had to drag themselves around while their body clocks readjusted, and between snatches of sleep they made phone calls. Chloe rang her parents and Zac rang Marissa. His phone call took ages. Chloe had no idea what transpired and her curiosity was killing her but Zac chose not to tell her, which was appropriate, of course, now that she was simply his PA again. In the afternoon they went shopping for the necessary baby gear.

They aimed for an early night and fortunately Lucy co-operated. While Chloe put through a load of washing, Zac cooked their dinner, making a fair fist of grilling steaks on the balcony barbecue. He served them with mushrooms and beans and they ate the meal outside again, enjoying the warm evening and the city lights.

'Wow,' said Chloe as she tucked in. 'This is delicious, Zac. You've put lemon and chilli on the beans, haven't you? And some kind of herb on the mushrooms?'

He ducked his head towards the attractive cluster of potted herbs on his balcony. 'I sprinkled a little thyme over them.'

'Hmm.' Chloe speared a succulent mushroom with her fork. 'I think I've uncovered a dark horse, Zachary Corrigan.'

'What makes you say that?'

'You're actually a closet chef.'

He lifted a gorgeous black eyebrow.

'You are, aren't you, Zac?'

This brought an embarrassed smile. 'Closet chef? That's a big statement to make after sampling one hasty meal.'

'Hasty or not, this meal is sensational.' Chloe sliced off a tender corner of steak. 'But I actually have further evidence. I checked out your pantry and fridge.'

'When?'

'While I was stowing away Lucy's formula.'

'So you've been spying on me?'

'I couldn't resist a little snooping. Sorry, it's a bad habit of mine, but I have a thing about fridges and pantries. You see, they tell so much about a person—in the kitchen, at least. And, well, I noticed you keep a French brand of Parmesan and an Italian brand of risotto, and you have all these bottles of Thai and Vietnamese sauces and about three different types of olive oil...'

'So?'

'Zac, you know very well that only a serious cook would bother.'

'I like to eat.' He shrugged. 'And cooking's actually relaxing...'

Relaxing? This was such a surprise Chloe laughed. 'And here I was, imagining that you ate out every night.'

'No way. Only every second night.'

They smiled at each other across the table. It was a smile of friendship and understanding and...something far deeper... which made Chloe feel all shivery and confused again.

'Do you like to cook?' Zac asked her.

'Well, I usually cook for my parents, but they only like very plain food like shepherd's pie or—' She stopped. This conversation was becoming far too intimate. It was making her feel closer to Zac when she was supposed to be stepping away.

CHAPTER ELEVEN

CHLOE WAS GIVING Lucy her bath when Zac left, shortly after breakfast.

'See you later,' he said, ducking his head around the bathroom doorway.

Unhappily guessing that he was heading off to see Marissa, Chloe forced brightness into her voice. 'You might heighten your luck if you take her flowers and chocolate.'

Zac frowned. 'I guess...'

'Marissa likes Oriental lilies and ginger chocolate.'

'How do you know these things?' he asked, but then he gave a soft humourless laugh. 'Don't tell me. It's all on a spreadsheet.'

'Naturally.' Chloe wished him luck but, as soon as she heard the apartment's front door close behind him, her face crumpled and she was overwhelmed by the most devastating, painful loss.

Zac was gone. She'd thrown away her very last opportunity and this was the end.

She felt cold all over as she scooped the baby out of the water and wrapped her in a fluffy bath towel.

'Oh, God, Lucy,' she whispered. 'You know what I've done, don't you? I've just thrown away the chance to be your mummy. And I've lost my very last opportunity to be with Zac.'

A terrible ache bloomed in her chest as she hugged Lucy to her and breathed in the scent of her clean baby skin. 'Honestly, Luce, I was only trying to be sensible. I can't marry a man who doesn't even know if he loves me.'

But how could I have known that being sensible and letting him go would still break my heart?

Misery washed through her, as cold and bleak as when she'd lost Sam. She carried Lucy through to the spare bedroom, now designated as the baby's nursery, and laid her gently on the new changing table, part of the furniture she and Zac had bought yesterday. Carefully, she patted the baby's skin dry and sprinkled and smoothed talcum powder into her creases. She picked up one of the tiny singlets and slipped it over Lucy's head, before angling her arms through the holes.

Luckily, she'd done this many times now because the entire time she worked her mind was miles away. With Zac. She was picturing his arrival at Marissa's, making his charming apologies or doing whatever was necessary to placate her, and then inviting her out. They would probably go to the beach. Chloe could imagine them walking hand in hand along the sand at the water's edge, or having a drink at a bar overlooking the sea. Zac would be at his alluring best as he explained the sad situation that had left him with Lucy. By the time he'd finished, Marissa would be putty in his hands.

Of course she would want to marry him.

And Chloe couldn't bear it. Couldn't bear to think that Zac would marry a woman he didn't love—and who probably didn't love him, simply to provide a mother for Lucy. How could he be such a fool?

She finished dressing the baby and took her through to the kitchen to collect a bottle of formula from the fridge. As she waited for it to heat, she paced restlessly, agonising over her own foolishness. And Zac's foolishness, too.

Surely he was deceiving himself when he claimed that he

didn't believe in love? For heaven's sake, she only had to think back over the past few days to see all kinds of evidence of Zac's love in action.

He'd gone above and beyond the call of mere duty for Liv and for Lucy, but he'd also gone out of his way for Chloe as well. Not just with lovely gifts like the bracelet and the Christmas banquet, although she knew these were more personal and special than the gifts Zac usually bestowed on his women—but, beyond that, he'd also been thoughtful and considerate and kind. And fun.

Both in and out of bed...

Chloe wondered now, too late, if she should have given Zac a chance to explain his vision of the marriage he'd proposed. She'd simply jumped to conclusions and assumed he would continue to play the field.

But if she thought about the past week, when she'd been with him day and night, she couldn't really fault his behaviour. Actually, if anyone had misbehaved, she had. She'd practically thrown herself into his arms on that day they'd made love.

Now, as she went back to the kitchen to collect the heated bottle, she was more depressed than ever. She couldn't believe she'd brought this pain on herself and she'd thrown everything away because she'd needed to hear three stupid words from Zac. Hadn't she known all along that words were easy? Actions carried so much more weight...and Zac's actions had said so much...but now she'd lost him and she had no one to blame but herself.

'I hope I don't weep all over you,' she told Lucy as she settled in an armchair to feed her. 'I don't want to upset you. Don't take any notice of me, will you, darling? I'll try to stop thinking about him.'

It was impossible to turn her thoughts off, of course. She figured that by now Zac would be well on his way to the Gold Coast—too far down the expressway for her to phone him with some weak excuse that would bring him back. She had tried to be sensible one time too many, and as a result she felt as bereft and as heartbroken as she had when she lost Sam.

And Lucy had already finished her bottle.

'Sorry!' Chloe felt all kinds of guilty as she set the bottle aside and lifted Lucy to her shoulder. She hadn't been paying attention and she'd let the baby feed too quickly. Now the poor darling would probably be in pain.

Chloe stood, hoping that a little walking up and down would do the trick, but she was only halfway across the lounge room when the doorbell rang.

'Who on earth could this be?' she complained, sounding scarily like her mother, and as she went to open the door she dashed a hand to her face and hoped it wasn't too obvious that she'd been crying.

A young woman stood on the doorstep—a very pretty young woman with long blonde hair and the kind of slender figure that came from living on lettuce leaves and very little else. She was wearing strong perfume, tight floral jeans and a tiny tight top that revealed a toned and tanned midriff, as well as a silver navel ring.

The girl's jaw dropped when she saw Chloe and Lucy. 'Who are you?' she demanded.

'Are you looking for Zac?' Chloe asked in response.

'Yes. What's happened to him?' The girl looked genuinely worried. 'He just took off and he's been away for the whole of Christmas.'

'There was a family emergency and he had to rush to London.' Chloe felt obliged to explain this, even though she had no idea who this girl was. She certainly wasn't one of Zac's regulars. 'Zac's sister died,' she said.

The girl frowned, clearly struggling to take this in. 'That's sad. So are you a relative then?'

'No, I'm Zac's PA and this is his little niece, Lucy.'

'His PA? I think you rang Zac last week. Yes, it was you, wasn't it? And then he went racing off.'

'Yes, it was all terribly sudden.' Chloe realised this had to be the girl who'd answered Zac's phone on that fateful Wednesday night. She'd pretended to be answering from a Chinese takeaway.

'I'm sorry to hear about his sister,' the girl said.

'It was terrible,' Chloe agreed just as Lucy pulled up her knees and began to wail loudly.

'I take it Zac's not here now?' The girl raised her voice to be heard above Lucy.

'No. I'm not sure when he'll be back.'

'I guess I'll just have to keep trying his mobile then.'

'I'm not sure that's a good idea,' Chloe responded hastily. 'Not today. He's...he's still very busy.'

The girl pouted. 'Well, can you at least tell him that Daisy called?'

'Of course I can, Daisy. I won't forget. Nice to meet you.'

Lucy was distraught as Chloe closed the door. 'Oh, sweetheart, I'm so sorry.' She began to pace, jiggling the baby gently. 'I'm afraid I know how you feel. I want to wail along with you.'

Back in the lounge room, she tried sitting with Lucy in her lap. Zac had perfected the art of burping her this way and Chloe willed herself to forget about her own woes and to concentrate on comforting the baby. She was rewarded by a massive burp.

'Oh, wow! Good girl. Aren't you clever?' She kissed the baby's downy head and cuddled her close and she sat there for a while, enjoying the warmth and snuggling closeness. But she was close to tears again as she took Lucy back to her brand new cot and tucked her in. She set the teddy bear that Liv had bought where Lucy could see it and then she tiptoed away.

From the doorway she looked back. 'I'm going to miss you so much.'

She waited for an answering wail, but the baby remained silent. When Chloe stole back into the room to double-check,

Lucy's eyes were already closed. Chloe went back to the lounge room and collected the empty bottle, took it through to the kitchen...

Now what?

Unfortunately, the answer came almost immediately. Her next task was to write her letter of resignation.

She gave an agonised groan as this thought hit home. But she had no choice. It had to be done. She couldn't continue as Zac's PA now that she'd become so intimately involved in his personal life. She cared too much about Lucy *and* about Zac and she would care too much about the personal choices Zac made in the future.

And how could she pretend that their blazing lovemaking wouldn't always be there between them? A teasing, haunting memory. How could she ever forget that amazing spontaneity and passion? Heavens, if she stayed in Zac's office, she might find herself hoping it could happen again.

For that reason alone, she had no choice but to leave. It would be untenable for her to continue working for Zac after he was married to Marissa.

She hoped he would see that, too.

She should act immediately, draft a resignation now and have it ready for when he returned. She could type it on her phone, could even email it straight to Zac. With luck, he would accept it without too much argument.

It was so hard, though... Chloe felt sick as she started to type.

She began with *Dear Mr Corrigan,* then deleted it and replaced it with *Dear Zac.* Her hands were shaking, her thumbs fumbling on the keys as she forced herself to continue.

It is with deep regret...

Again she stopped and deleted. She had to keep this businesslike.

I wish to advise that I am resigning from my position as Personal Assistant to the Managing Director of ZedCee Management Consultants.

The terms of my contract require two weeks' notice for the termination of employment from either party. I will make myself available to assist in a smooth transition for my replacement.

Chloe pressed her hand against the new ache that flared just beneath her ribs, then she continued to type...

I've enjoyed working at...

She stopped and let out another soft groan. What was the point of telling Zac that? He knew only too well how much she'd loved her job. Better to just ask him for a reference.

Did she want a reference? She supposed she should have one, but she hated the thought of having to hunt for another job...

As she began to type again she heard a noise... Once again, it was coming from the front door...

Another caller?

This time there was the unmistakable sound of a key turning in the lock...

Not another of Zac's girlfriends? Chloe wasn't sure she could face another of Zac's blonde beauties. And it seemed that this one had privileged status and her very own key.

Wincing as she set her half-written letter aside, Chloe got to her feet. Her *bare* feet.

She couldn't remember the last time she'd checked her appearance in a mirror and there was every chance she had baby dribble on her T-shirt, and if this woman had a key she was sure to be at least as glamorous as Daisy. Chloe was madly finger-combing her hair as she heard footsteps coming down the hallway. She braced herself for a vision of sexy high fashion.

She had the words ready. 'I'm sorry, but Zac isn't—'

The figure coming into the lounge room was tall and dark and exceptionally masculine. Chloe's heart almost stopped.

'Zac?'

'Hi.' He dropped his keys into a pottery dish on the low entertainment unit, and then he set down a pot of bright red double gerberas and a box of chocolates. He looked pale, almost unwell, and deep lines furrowed his brow and the sides of his mouth.

'What happened?' Chloe had visions of a highway smash. 'Is everything all right? Did you get as far as the Gold Coast?'

'No.' Zac stood in the middle of the room with his hands on his hips. His chest expanded as he drew a deep breath.

Something had clearly gone wrong. Had Marissa refused to see him?

'Is there anything I can do? A cup of—'

A faint sad smile briefly tilted a corner of his mouth. 'All I need is for you to listen, Chloe. There's—' his Adam's apple rippled as he swallowed '—there's something I need to tell you.'

The growing knots of anxiety in Chloe's stomach tightened as Zac turned, looked around his lounge room, almost as if he was seeing it for the first time. Then he took a seat in the chair opposite her, and he leaned back against the smooth leather upholstery as if this could somehow help him to relax.

He was wearing jeans and a white shirt, unbuttoned at the collar and with the sleeves rolled back. Despite the crackling tension, Chloe couldn't help admiring the way his dark hair and bronzed skin contrasted so gorgeously with the whiteness of his shirt.

'I hope you haven't had more bad news,' she said gently.

'No, just a painful revelation.' Again, he cracked the faintest glimmer of a smile, before he dropped his gaze and traced the arm of the chair with his fingertips, as if he was testing the texture of the leather.

Chloe tried not to notice how beautiful his hands were, so long-fingered and strong, and she struggled to banish unhelpful memories of his hands touching and caressing her, driving her to rapture.

'I didn't go to the Gold Coast,' he said. 'Actually, I have a confession. Almost as soon as I dialled Marissa's number yesterday, I knew that proposing to her would be a huge mistake, but then I had to spend the next hour coming up with a crazy explanation for why I'd rung her...and then more time trying to wriggle out of seeing her again.' He gave a wry smile as he shook his head. 'It was yet another of my famous stuff-ups.'

Chloe swallowed nervously, unsure what to say.

'I'm sorry I gave you the wrong impression, Chloe. I should have set you straight this morning when you mentioned the flowers, but I wasn't ready to explain.'

'It's not really my business.'

Zac smiled at her then. 'Of course, Ms Meadows.' Then his expression was serious once more as he said, 'Truth is, I've been walking the streets, trying to clear my head and think everything through.'

Chloe nodded. This was understandable. He'd had next to no privacy in the past few days.

'You asked me in London if I've ever been in love,' he said next, somewhat abruptly.

In an instant her skin turned to goosebumps. 'Yes, I did.'

'I said I hadn't, but I lied.'

Oh. Chloe couldn't think what to say, but her heart had begun to pound so loudly now that she was sure Zac must be able to hear it.

'I was in love once, a long time ago,' he went on quietly. 'It was in my first year at university.' His shoulders lifted in a shrug. 'I guess it was first love, or puppy love, or whatever, but it certainly felt real at the time.' He looked away to the far window and its views of the sunny city skyline. 'Her name was Rebecca and I was crazy about her.'

Chloe had no idea why Zac had come back with flowers or why he was telling her this, and she certainly couldn't risk trying to guess, but she was so tense now she thought she might snap in two.

'Of course, I had all these dreams,' he went on. 'Nothing flash. Just the usual—marriage, family, happy ever after...'

The things he no longer believed in.

'Then my parents disappeared,' he said. 'And my life changed overnight. I felt I had to give up university and get a job, and take on the responsibility of looking after Liv. I needed to be home for her on the weekends and in the evenings. I didn't have time for a social life, so I put my dreams on the back burner.'

'And you broke up with Rebecca,' Chloe guessed.

'Yes.' He gave another crookedly cynical smile. 'She soon took up with another guy and within two years she married him.'

Oh, dear.

Chloe could see it all so clearly... Zac's world had been turned upside down when his parents disappeared... He'd sacrificed his dreams, only to be rewarded by heartbreak...

But as she sat there, listening and watching him and not daring to analyse why he was telling her this, she realised something so surprising that she gasped and felt quite giddy...

Surely, Zac's whole playboy persona had been a reaction to this heartbreak? After he'd lost his parents and his first girlfriend—a girl he'd genuinely loved—he'd been desperate to save his little sister. But then Liv had proved rebellious and Zac had responded with his own form of rebellion—his never-ending procession of *Foolish Females*.

Playing the field had been Zac's way of escaping, of protecting himself from ever being hurt again...

Of course it was far safer to never fall in love. Chloe knew this only too well. She'd been doing the same thing in a different way. After Sam's death, she'd avoided a social life, with its accompanying risks and pain, by hiding away and caring for her parents.

Oh, Zac. Her heart ached for him as she watched him now, as he drew another deep, nervous breath and let it out with a sigh.

She wondered if his current dilemma was her fault somehow. Had he realised that Marissa would also expect a declaration of love...and that, for him, it was still a step too far...

'So does this mean...?' she began, but then she stopped, uncertain of how to voice her thoughts diplomatically.

Zac looked across at her, not quite smiling. 'The long-winded point that I'm trying to make is that I do know what it's like to love someone and to lose her.'

'Yes, but that shouldn't—'

Chloe stopped again as the silent message in Zac's eyes made her heart thump so loudly she was sure he must hear it. She was poised on the edge of her seat now and she held her breath, not daring to say anything more, not daring to wonder, even fearfully, where exactly this revelation was heading.

Without warning, Zac launched to his feet again.

'I walked over the bridge and into the city,' he said. 'One of my mates is a real estate agent and I was going to ask him to look out for a place for Lucy and me.'

Chloe nodded miserably. Zac had decided to take responsibility for Lucy after all—without 'using' one of his women. It was an important step forward for him and she knew she should be pleased.

He forced an edgy smile, then turned and picked up the pot of red gerberas. 'I didn't get as far as my mate's office. I walked past a florist's.' The flowers trembled in Zac's hand. He was shaking and Chloe couldn't bear it.

'There were all these lilies in the window. You'd told me to get lilies for Marissa, but I suddenly knew: if I bought flowers for anyone, it had to be for you.'

She could barely hear him now over the ridiculous thundering of her heartbeats and it was almost impossible to see him through her tears.

'But I had no idea which were your favourites,' Zac said. 'I don't have a spreadsheet for you, Chloe.' He gave her another of his gorgeous crooked, sad smiles. 'But these made me think of your red dress and...and I hope you like them. Anyway, I had no choice. I had to bring them back to *you*.'

She was shaking, pressing a hand to her mouth...

'I was hoping to...to have another shot at that proposal.'

Now Chloe was on the edge of her seat, so tense she could only bite her lip as tears filled her eyes.

'I... I think I might have given you the impression last time that I only asked you to marry me because you would make a good mother for Lucy. And you would—you'd be perfect, but that's not why I need you, Chloe. That's so, so wrong.'

She swiped at her stupid, blinding tears. She wanted to see him—*needed* to see him. Oh, dear Lord, he looked so worried.

'The truth is,' Zac said, 'I reckon I've probably been in love with you since you first arrived in the office. I guess I just wouldn't let myself admit it, but I love being around you, Chloe. I love seeing you, whether you're serious or happy, or telling me off. I love hearing your voice. I love asking your advice. I even love drinking your damn cups of tea... I know it sounds crazy, but I hurry to work each day, just to see you.'

She thought of all those mornings that she'd looked forward to, too... Zac almost always arrived early, around the same time that she did and they always shared a little harmless light conversation. He would crack a joke, talk about something he'd heard on the news as he was driving to work, share a little gossip about one of their competitors. Drink the tea that she made.

Those mornings, before the rest of the staff arrived, had been her favourite time of day and now she could feel the truth of his claim filling her with light. Golden light was flooding her from the toes up, filling her chest, her arms, her head.

'No, it doesn't sound crazy,' she told him.

Zac swallowed. 'No?'

'I've felt the same about you.'

His eyes widened. 'You have?'

She felt brave enough to tell him now. 'Hopelessly in love from Day One. Probably ever since my job interview.'

For a trembling moment they stared at each other while this astonishing truth sank in. Then Zac set down the flowers and held out his arms and at last—at *last*—Chloe flew to safety.

As she hurled herself against him, his arms came around her, holding her preciously close. 'Oh, Chloe, I do love you. So, so much.'

'I know, I know.' She pressed her face against his shoulder, loving that she now had the right to be there, in his arms, leaning in to his strength.

'But I need to apologise about the way I carried on with the rubbish about romance and delusions,' Zac persisted. 'I was deluding myself. I *know* love's real. It's how I feel about you. Standing outside that florist's, I couldn't breathe when I realised I was losing you. I love you so much.'

He pulled back to look into her eyes. 'You do believe me, don't you?'

'I do, Zac.'

'Honestly?'

'You've already shown me in so many ways.'

'Oh, God, I hope so.'

There were no more tears now as she kissed his jaw, his cheek.

'Oh, Chloe.' Framing her face with his hands, Zac touched his lips to hers and his kiss was so tender and lingering and loving, Chloe thought she might actually swoon with an excess of happiness.

It was some time before their kiss ended and she nestled her head against his shoulder again. 'You were right,' she said. 'We don't need the words.'

He gave a soft laugh. 'But I want to say them now. I'm not scared of them and it feels so good. I'm going to tell you every day that I love you.' With gentle fingers, he traced the line of her cheek. 'Isn't it incredible that we've both been waiting? Why did it take us so damn long to work this out?'

'We're both sticklers for office protocol?'

This brought one of Zac's beautifully devilish grins and, a beat later, he slipped one arm around Chloe's shoulders, then a hand beneath her knees as he literally swept her off her feet. 'Stuff the protocol, Ms Meadows.'

He was already halfway to the bedroom.

EPILOGUE

AT FIRST, when Chloe woke, she forgot what day it was. She lay very still with her eyes closed, enjoying the warm stream of the sunlight that filtered through the poinciana tree outside the bedroom window.

Then she rolled towards Zac, reaching for him...only to find an empty space in the bed. Her eyes flashed open and she saw their bedroom, bright with summer sunlight, saw the little silver tree on the dressing table, the red glass tumblers holding the tea light candles that she'd lit last night. She'd had so much fun decorating the house for Christmas.

Zap. She sat up with a jolt as she remembered. This was it. Christmas morning.

How on earth could she have slept in? She'd been looking forward to this day with an almost childish excitement.

Now there was no time to waste. She had to see if Lucy was awake and she needed to know what Zac was up to.

Throwing off the sheet, she smiled at her new Christmas pyjamas—a red T-shirt teamed with cotton pants decorated with bright green holly and red bows. Although Chloe had always loved Christmas, this year she'd probably gone a trifle overboard, with decorations in every room of the house as well as extra details like special tablecloths and napkins for their Christmas dinner. She'd even bought special festive coffee mugs. Luckily, Zac didn't seem to mind.

Now, she ducked into Lucy's room. 'Merry Christmas, baby g—'

The cot was empty and Chloe felt a stab of disappointment, but she quickly squashed it as the smell of coffee wafted from downstairs...and then, as she descended, she heard the deep rumbling voice that she knew so well...

'And this is a special ornament that Mummy bought last Christmas in Selfridges in London... You were there, too, you know, pumpkin. Such a teensy little thing you were then...and it was wintertime and cold, not sweltering and hot like today... And over here under the tree are all the lovely presents... No, no, hang on. You can't rip them to pieces just yet. We can't open them till Mummy wakes up...'

At the bottom of the stairs now, Chloe caught a glimpse through to the lounge room and she stopped to admire the view of Zac and Lucy together. Zac was balancing Lucy on his hip with the practised ease of an expert and the baby was chuckling and reaching up to grab at a bright decoration. When she couldn't reach, she tried to squeeze his nose instead.

In response, Zac ducked, then playfully pretended to nibble Lucy's hand, which made her squeal with delight.

Chloe grinned. She never tired of seeing these two together. Over the past year they had formed a very special bond that boded very well for the future.

Lucy had grown into such a cute little bundle of mischief. She was a sturdy and determined one-year-old, now, and her hair was a mass of glossy dark curls, her eyes a bright, vivid blue. And she was constantly breaking into the most wonderfully happy smiles.

In Zac's strong arms, however, she still looked small and vulnerable...but safe. So wonderfully safe.

'And up here is something incredibly important,' Zac told

the little girl as he pointed to a bunch of greenery in the doorway. 'This is a VIP plant that I have to show your mummy. It's called mistletoe and it's a tradition. Your mum's very fond of tradition...'

Chloe smiled again and felt a flush of pure, unfiltered joy. Soon it would all begin—the exchange of presents, the feasting, and sharing the day with her parents...

It would be quite a simple Christmas compared with last year's cathedral and banquet, but for Chloe this felt like the perfect end to a year that had been wonderful in so many ways—bringing happiness beyond her wildest dreams. At times it had seemed almost too good to be true and she'd had to pinch herself.

Of course, the three hundred and sixty-five days since their Christmas in London hadn't been a total bed of roses. In fact, the year had started off quite busily, and Chloe had spent most of January learning to balance caring for Lucy with helping a new PA to settle into her job.

Zac had been worried that Chloe might be bored with staying at home full-time and so they'd experimented with hiring a babysitter, who minded Lucy for one day a week while Chloe worked on the ZedCee files from her home office. It had worked well. Chloe loved being Lucy's mum, but she also found it rewarding to keep in touch with projects that had nothing to do with nappies or feeding schedules.

Then, in March, they'd moved out of the inner city apartment and into their contemporary two-storey home in the leafy suburb of Kenmore. They'd had a ton of fun house-hunting together, and they loved this house. With Zac's assistance, Chloe's parents were resettled two blocks away, in a lovely cottage in a retirement complex.

Chloe visited them almost every day, often walking there and taking Lucy for an outing in the pram. The little girl loved her Grammy and Gramps, and of course Hettie and Joe Meadows were utterly smitten by the baby, and they were completely shameless about their hero worship of Zac.

The wedding had been in June. Zac and Chloe had chosen a simple ceremony on the beach with a select group of friends and Chloe's misty-eyed parents. Afterwards, Zac and Chloe had flown north to Hamilton Island and, naturally, they'd taken Lucy with them. It was all quite magical.

There'd been tough days too, of course, times when Zac's grief for Liv had caught up with him, but it helped that Chloe had been through her own dark days of grief and she understood.

She'd been worried when Lucy's first birthday drew near, knowing that it coincided with a very sad anniversary. But six days ago the three of them had taken the ferry across to Stradbroke Island and there, while Lucy crawled on the sand and tried to chase tiny crabs, Chloe had watched as Zac paddled alone on a surfboard, out beyond the breakers. He'd taken a bunch of yellow roses and the small urn with Liv's ashes...

Afterwards, they'd stayed on the beach, playing with Lucy and talking quietly, remembering their journey to London... and Zac had shared one or two memories of Liv...

Eventually, Lucy had fallen asleep in Zac's arms and so they'd stayed there, sitting together on the warm sand and watching the distant horizon until the last of the daylight faded into the black of night...and the moon rose, bright and golden and full of new promise...

'I'd like to come here every year,' Zac had said. 'Liv loved this place...and...and I reckon it helps.'

'Yes, it's important,' Chloe had agreed. Somehow, the sea and the wind, the wide open sky and the reassuring crash and thump of the surf seemed to help to soothe Zac's pain. 'We should definitely make it a tradition.'

Now, Zac turned and caught sight of Chloe at the bottom of the stairs.

'Hey,' he cried, his face lighting up. 'Lucy, look who's awake!'

'Mumma!' the baby girl shouted as she held out her chubby arms.

Still holding Lucy, Zac hurried over and slipped an arm around Chloe and kissed her. 'Merry Christmas, my bright-eyed girl.'

'Merry Christmas.' Chloe couldn't resist stroking his lovely bare chest. 'I hear you've been educating Lucy about Christmas traditions.'

'Like mistletoe?'

'Uh-huh.'

His eyes shimmered with secret amusement as he smiled at her. 'If you'd been listening carefully, you would know that there are one or two other traditions I'm reserving just for you.'

Chloe grinned. It was a promise she would definitely hold him to.

* * * * *

Christmas Baby For The Billionaire
Donna Alward

Donna Alward lives on Canada's east coast with her family, which includes her husband, a couple of kids, a senior dog and two crazy cats. Her heartwarming stories of love, hope and homecoming have been translated into several languages, hit bestseller lists and won awards, but her favorite thing is hearing from readers! When she's not writing, she enjoys reading (of course), knitting, gardening, cooking…and she is a *Masterpiece* addict. You can visit her on the web at donnaalward.com and join her mailing list at donnaalward.com/newsletter.

Books by Donna Alward

Harlequin Romance

Destination Brides

Summer Escape with the Tycoon

Marrying a Millionaire

Best Man for the Wedding Planner
Secret Millionaire for the Surrogate

Holiday Miracles

Sleigh Ride with the Rancher

Heart to Heart

Hired: The Italian's Bride

Visit the Author Profile page
at millsandboon.com.au for more titles.

Dear Reader,

Welcome to a new trilogy—the South Shore Billionaires! I had so much fun writing this holiday story to kick it off. There are so many of my personal loves in this book, from favorite holiday movies to the scent of evergreens to Junior's pineapple cheesecake—introduced to me by Damon Suede and which I agreed was "life changing." Christmas in New York is magical!

I wrote this story during a time when I was facing a lot of emotional challenges. It's funny how life sometimes sends you multiple crises in a row and somehow you get through it. It's pretty appropriate, then, that the beach by the Sandpiper Resort is based on a place my husband and I visit each summer; a stunning, kilometer-long stretch of sand on Nova Scotia's South Shore. Why is it appropriate? Because as I was dealing with each crisis, my husband was right there with me, holding my hand and being my rock. Just like he has been for the past twenty-three years. (Yes, clearly I was a child bride!)

I hope you get swept away in Jeremy and Tori's story! And look for Bran's story, coming soon!

With love,

Donna

To Mum. The older I get, the more I admire your strength and your capacity for unconditional love. Your children and grandchildren have been incredibly blessed.

Praise for Donna Alward

"This is Donna Alward at her best.... Her stories are homey and comfy and gentle—this one is no different."

—*Goodreads* on *A Cowboy to Come Home To*

CHAPTER ONE

THERE WERE MORNINGS when a girl just didn't want to get out of bed, but she had to because a) she had to pee and b) she had to go to work because no one else was going to pay the bills.

Tori closed her eyes, gathered her get-up-and-go and threw off the covers. It wasn't that she didn't like her job; she loved it. The Sandpiper Resort was her life. She'd started there doing housekeeping as a teenager and had worked her way up to assistant general manager, overseeing many of the day-to-day operations. Stepping inside the doors each morning felt as much like being at home as entering her own small house, bought just last year.

So even though she was bone tired, despite having slept all night, she flipped on the light switch and turned on the shower. At least the morning sickness had been fleeting, lasting only a few weeks and consisting mostly of inconvenient nausea. Now in her second trimester, she simply got tired more easily. And was in the process of overhauling her wardrobe. Things didn't fit anymore now that her baby bump had made an appearance.

Thirty minutes later, hair blow-dried and makeup on, she left the house with her decaf coffee in a travel mug and made the five-minute drive to work. It had been mild for November, and she didn't have to scrape the frost off her windshield this morning, which was a plus. On arriving at the hotel, she stepped inside, inhaling the fresh scent of evergreens. Once Remembrance Day had passed, the Christmas decorations had come out, turning the resort into a fairyland of white twinkle lights and pungent pine and spruce boughs punctuated with gorgeous red and gold bows. She greeted the staff at the front desk with a smile, then stopped at the kitchen to ask for a toasted bagel and some fruit—her usual breakfast fare.

"You need some eggs for the little one, there?" Neil asked, his chef's hat bobbing. "Mamas need protein."

She grinned. "When are you gonna stop pampering me?" she asked, taking a sip of her coffee. For a few weeks, she'd been turned off the smell of the brew. Now she inhaled the richness of it and sighed.

"Never," he replied, his eyes crinkling at the corners. Neil had been working in this kitchen since before she'd started cleaning rooms. Pretty soon his granddaughter would be looking for a summer job.

Eggs did sound good this morning, so she smiled. "You know how I like them," she acquiesced. "Thanks, Neil. You're a gem."

"You betcha."

Ten minutes later one of the waitstaff brought her breakfast, as well as a glass of milk. "Neil says you need your calcium," Ellen said, and even though she was younger than Tori, her voice came across as motherly.

"Neil is being overprotective and I love it," she remarked, smiling up at the waitress who'd joined their team last May. "Thanks." She unrolled her cutlery from the napkin. "Everything going okay in the dining room?"

Ellen nodded. "Slower now that the leaves are gone and no one really comes for the beach."

"I know. I'm sorry about the cut hours."

"It's okay. It's a seasonal thing. We all get it."

"We've got some holiday events planned, so if you're up for working those, I'll make sure you're on the list for scheduling." The ticketed events always meant decent tips, and Ellen's eyes lit up.

"I'd appreciate that. Thanks, Tori."

"No problem. It helps a bit when regular hours are short and Christmas is coming." Besides, Ellen had proved herself to be competent and reliable. Throwing a few extra hours her way was small reward.

Once Ellen was gone, Tori dug into her breakfast. Neil had added cheese to her eggs, and a little parsley...delicious. There were two slices of honeydew and a little dish of fresh strawberries, plus a whole-grain bagel with her favorite topping—plain cream cheese sprinkled with cinnamon sugar.

They really were a family around here, taking care of each other. Which was good for Tori, because it was only her and her mom now. Her mom, Shelley, was a nurse and had taken a job at the hospital in Lunenburg. It wasn't far away, but after Tori's father had died of cancer, Shelley had moved into an apartment right in the town for convenience. It put her about fifty kilometers away—close enough for weekly visits.

Tori put her hand on the swell of her belly. Now she was going to have her own family. And she *was* happy, deep down. The question of whether or not to have the baby hadn't even been brought up. She didn't have much family, and now she'd have a baby to love, and he or she would love her in return. Her mother would have a grandchild. Circumstances weren't ideal, but Tori had started thinking of this pregnancy as a surprise blessing.

The bagel caught in her throat and she took a deep drink of the milk to wash it down along with the unease that kept nagging her when she thought of her decision not to tell the father— at least not yet. Every time she'd determined to say nothing, she heard her mother's voice telling her that Jeremy deserved to know. The problem was, she agreed with her mom. She wasn't going to be able to keep this from him forever. She just had to figure out the logistics. The right way.

Jeremy Fisher... What had she been thinking, getting caught

up with him last summer? It had been two weeks of sheer bliss, during which time she'd completely lost her head. They'd agreed it was a holiday romance, and boy, had they made the most of their time together. When it was over, he'd gone back to his life in New York and she'd been left behind in small-town Nova Scotia, in a tiny house on the water. And that had been exactly as she'd wanted it. She wasn't a fairy-tale kind of woman, with dreams of being whisked away to a lavish lifestyle and a happy ever after. Well, she had been, once. She'd been swept off her feet by a handsome man with tons of plans. Riley had seemed perfect on the surface. And she'd fallen for him, hard.

Until she realized he'd been living a double life. He'd showered her with gifts and affection, but behind it all was a history of defrauding people and going into debt. For a long time she'd blamed herself for being so stupid.

She bit into a strawberry and considered her summer affair. Perhaps her "relationship" with Jeremy had been different because from the start there had been no question that it would be anything other than a fling. Indeed, it had been quite out of character for her, considering he was a guest at the resort. But they'd been discreet. And after two years of hard work, losing her dad and feeling alone, she'd given herself permission to enjoy this one thing.

She hadn't thought there'd be these kinds of consequences.

The power dynamic hadn't mattered during those few weeks. But it mattered now. Jeremy was a rich, powerful man, and she was...well, not *nobody*. She had enough self-esteem to give herself that much. But she certainly didn't have the same clout and resources at her disposal, and it made for a very uneven balance between them.

She shook her head and pushed her plate aside, eager to get to work. The hotel manager, Thomas, was on vacation this week, so it was up to Tori to steer the ship. She spent the morning at her desk, then met with the housekeeping manager and the catering manager about requirements for a holiday function scheduled for mid-December. There was a Christmas wedding planned for the weekend before the twenty-fifth, and another on New Year's Eve, where the ceremony would actually begin just before midnight so the bride and groom would be the first married couple of the new year. They were making a number of special accommodations for that event, from late checkout the next day to food service at one in the morning. The couple was willing to pay, so the hotel was willing to take their business.

It was mid-afternoon when she got up to do a walk-around, to get out of her office and to talk to staff and see what was happening. It was her favorite time of the day, actually, chatting with the staff, wandering through her second home, caring for it with love and affection. She made a note of a ding in a corner wall that would need to be touched up with paint, and gave a mental check mark to whoever had cleaned the public bathrooms on the lobby level. They sparkled and smelled like the hotel's custom lemongrass-and-ginger scent. She greeted staff by name and made a few more notes about additional Christmas decorations that could be added to the dining room and small on-site gift shop. Maybe business was slower this time of year, but for those who did arrive for an escape or a special dinner, the hotel would show to best advantage.

She was just returning to the administration offices when the front door blew open, bringing in a smattering of brown leaves and rain; a man was propelled in with them, shaking his arms to rid his coat of water droplets.

She turned to the sound...and froze.

"Tori?"

She'd never known that a person could feel blood rush out of their face, but she felt it now.

No.

No, no, no, no, no.

He couldn't be here. This was all wrong.

"Jeremy."

He grinned widely, his thousand-watt smile hitting her right in the solar plexus. Why did he have to be so handsome? "I hoped you'd be here. What's it been? Four months?"

Four months, three weeks, and five days, she wanted to answer, but nothing came out of her mouth. What was he doing here? And could she escape without him noticing the obvious?

No such luck. At her silence, his gaze swept down, then back up, and his eyes were filled with questions and confusion. Of course, she'd chosen today to unveil her new maternity wardrobe. Her *condition* was perfectly plain for all to see.

"Why don't you step into my office?" she asked, pulling herself together. "We can catch up. What brings you back to the Sandpiper?" Her voice came out smooth and steady, thankfully. It wouldn't do for him to see her discomposed.

She turned her back and started toward the offices, her body trembling. Not just because of the lie of omission he'd caught her in, but because just the sight of him still had the power to turn her knees to jelly.

It had been a very good few weeks, after all. Too good.

She heard his steps behind her and once they were in her office, she shut the door. Staff might be family, but they didn't need to hear every conversation, and no one here knew the identity of her baby's father. She and Jeremy had tried to be discreet.

Her office was small, and felt smaller still with him in it. She turned around and faced him, finally, attempting to put up an emotional wall so she could maintain her objectivity. It was harder than she'd imagined. Jeremy had a presence about him that was magnetic. Today he was dressed in a charcoal-gray suit with a precisely knotted tie, and an overcoat that protected him from the cold Atlantic wind. His hair was tousled, as though the ocean breeze had fingers it had run through the strands, making them seem carelessly styled, and tiny drops of rain sparkled on the top. And his eyes... Right now his eyes were the same steel gray as the white-capped waves along the shore. Cold and unhappy. Her tummy turned over with anxiety.

"What brings you back to the area?" she asked, feigning a

smile, skirting around him to sit behind her desk. Her tummy was hidden that way...

"Real estate. And I thought I'd look you up again while I was here. I didn't expect to find you pregnant."

The blunt statement hit her like a slap. So much for the hope of him not cluing in. It had been a long shot but she'd held out a smidgen of hope that her top might have camouflaged her bump.

She shrugged. "To be honest, it was a surprise to me, too."

"Is it mine?"

Her stomach plummeted. There was no beating around the bush with him. Never had been. Right from the start, he'd been up front about his attraction to her. He'd been staying in their best suite and she'd checked in on him on the first day to make sure everything was okay. They'd ended up chatting for a long time, about the area and about how different it was from his life in the Big Apple. When he'd invited her out for a drink she'd said yes, and it had been over a pomegranate martini that he'd told her she had the most intriguing eyes of anyone he'd ever met. She'd been charmed...and wooed.

She'd admired his confidence and honesty then, though she wasn't such a big fan of it at this moment.

For the briefest time, she considered saying no. It would solve a lot. But that simple answer was complicated by the small matter of her conscience. She had already been struggling with the fact that she hadn't yet told him about the pregnancy. Then there was a certain amount of integrity at stake. There had been no one else. He'd been the only one.

"Of course it is. I don't...make a habit of what happened between us."

He regarded her dispassionately. "How was I to know that? And were you ever going to tell me?"

Curse her and her honesty. She held his gaze, determined not to cower. "Eventually. And thanks for that wonderful endorsement of my character. It's always pleasant to be shamed by your baby's father."

He let out a breath and turned away for a moment, before turning back again. His gray eyes were contrite. "I'm sorry. That was uncalled for. It's just… This is a hell of a surprise, Tori."

"Yes," she said, "I'm sure it is."

"When…how…?"

Tori picked up a pen and played with it, resolving to keep up her appearance of strength. "We both know the answer to that question. Early July, and presumably one of the times we had sex."

She did not call it making love, though it had certainly felt like that at the time. Her cheeks heated as a memory swept through her. As hokey as it sounded, she had a feeling that she knew exactly when it had happened. They'd spent the day at the beach, splashing about in the water and having a picnic on the sand. And then in the late afternoon they'd gone back to her place and had finished off the day by taking their sweet time with each other.

He'd been a fantastic lover. Gentle, attentive, passionate.

Now, with him standing in her office, at the very least unhappy and very likely angry, those sweet memories were somehow tarnished.

He let out a huge breath. "May I sit?"

She held out a hand. "Of course." She wasn't exactly in a position to deny him anything right now, was she? The fears she'd had about him knowing about the baby were all crammed into her brain and she fought hard to ignore them. Perhaps she could put him off somehow, so she could prepare what she wanted to say to him.

He pulled out the guest chair, then shrugged out of his coat and laid it over the back before sitting. He leaned forward onto his knees, resting on his elbows. Tori bit down on her lip. It wasn't fair that he was so handsome. His brown hair and strong chin were reminiscent of JFK Jr., to her mind, but instead of his eyes being a rich brown, they were gray and heavily lashed.

And right now they were looking at her with something like accusation and disappointment in their depths.

"I'm going to be a father," he said, his voice rough. "You're halfway through your pregnancy... When were you going to tell me?"

Her hands shook so she folded them on top of her desk. "I don't know. I was waiting for the right time, and I've been going back and forth about it every day." She figured honesty was the best policy here; Jeremy would see through any attempt to mollify or placate him, and he'd definitely sense a lie.

His voice hardened. "I have a right to know."

This was the hard part. Just this morning she'd come to work like any other day. There was comfort in that. More than anything, Jeremy transported her out of her comfort zone and she struggled to find her feet in order to deal with this conversation.

She met his gaze again. "Our circumstances are a bit unique, you know. We had a fling. We live far apart, in two very different worlds. And I have no idea how to structure a co-parenting arrangement with someone who is, in many ways, a stranger." She took a breath. "You have resources I don't and I would lose in any sort of power struggle if you made a play for custody." There. She'd said it. No sense beating around the bush.

He sat back then, the questions in his eyes replaced by... Could it be? He was hurt by her last statement. Or at least offended. Her pulse was hammering so hard right now she couldn't quite trust her observations.

"Do you really think I'd do such a thing?"

She sat up straighter. "As I said, we don't really know each other, do we? It wasn't a chance I was willing to take. I'd die before letting someone take my baby away."

Jeremy tried to breathe through the cramping in his chest. He'd been looking forward to surprising Tori today. Work had brought him back to the area on behalf of a client and he'd imagined reigniting the flame that had raged between them last summer. Truthfully, he hadn't been able to get her out of his head, and this work trip on Branson's behalf had given him the perfect excuse to get her out of his system once and for all.

Instead he'd found her carrying his baby. The pregnancy shook him to the core, but the veiled accusation he'd just heard... that was a real gut punch.

He was a straight shooter and liked to think he was a good man. But right now he held back the words forming in his brain and those already stuck in his throat. Because he was confused, and angry, and another emotion he couldn't quite place. Hurt was part of it. And maybe disappointed. It was just a mess.

With his child stuck in the middle.

This was his worst nightmare. A family, kids—a wife, even—were not on his agenda.

"We used protection," he said numbly.

"Which isn't a hundred percent reliable. We were pretty careful, but..." Her hazel eyes met his. "Not careful enough, I guess. Believe me, this was not planned."

His suit jacket felt too tight, and his tie strangled his throat. But he kept his hands firm on the arms of the chair. His gaze stole to her midsection again, though most of it was hidden behind the desk.

His child. With a woman he barely knew, someone with whom he had simply enjoyed a few weeks during a summer trip. And he'd come here with the sole objective of hooking up with her again. He ran his hand over his face.

He should have known that someday his behavior was going to land him in trouble. That eventually his casual approach to relationships would come back to bite him. No words of *I love you*, no commitments, no strings. That was how he liked it. And even though he'd enjoyed his time here, a few states and an international border had made Tori Sharpe seem like a perfectly safe...distraction.

He wasn't really a player, but he'd classify his approach to romance as...cavalier. His best friend Cole called him a serial dater. Branson had silently agreed with the assessment. He hadn't had a relationship that had lasted over a month since college.

He let out a breath and tried to relax his shoulders. "Okay. So the news is out now, like it or not." He pinned her with his gaze. "And I have no idea what to do."

The lines in her face softened. "That's okay. I do. I don't expect anything from you, Jeremy. I'm not going to come after you for exorbitant amounts of child support or anything. I'm going to raise this baby right here. I have tons of friends I can count on, and my mom is here, and we'll be as happy as anything. I'll even sign papers if you want."

No child support? No contact? And raising the baby in this small town that was nearly dead in the off-season?

"Anything but that," he replied.

CHAPTER TWO

AFTER JEREMY'S LAST STATEMENT, tensions had ratcheted up again. Tori had asserted that nothing was going to be decided that afternoon and perhaps they could pick up the discussion later after they'd both had time to think. He hadn't looked happy, but Tori knew they could have gone around in circles indefinitely. It was going to take time to sort out, and she needed time to decide what she really wanted and how best to present it to Jeremy. Being caught on the fly had only made her panic, though she'd tried to cover it up as best she could.

She could compromise on a lot of things, but not on the basics. The baby would live here, with her. As far as his involvement went, that was negotiable. Now that he knew, she could hardly shut him out of everything and pretend he didn't exist if that wasn't what he wanted.

If she tried to cut him out of the baby's life, she had the suspicious feeling he'd start throwing his weight around. And he had the money and connections to make things difficult. The fantasy bubble in which she'd held the memories of their time together was truly popped. It was like her mom said—if it seemed too good to be true, it probably was.

What a tightrope she was going to have to walk. Hopefully he was in town for only a few days.

He'd gone to check in to his room and she logged in to the reservations system to get the details of his stay. To her dismay, she discovered he'd booked twelve days. That took them well into December. And it was more than enough time for things to go seriously wrong. She tapped her fingers on her desk. How the heck was she supposed to navigate this?

She thought back to earlier, when she'd admitted flat out that she'd lose in a power struggle. His gray eyes had looked so shocked that she'd even think such a thing. He'd run his fingers through his hair, and his throat had bobbed as he swallowed. Her words had left their mark, and it boded well as far as being able to reach him. He wasn't a cold and calculating monster, though she knew he was a tough negotiator when pushed. Watching him work closing deals last summer had shown her that, and she'd admired him for it at the time.

His wounded expression had also touched something in her heart she wished didn't exist. She cared about him. Two weeks together in the summer had been more than enough time for her to develop feelings. Not love, certainly, but definitely affection. It hadn't all been sexual. He'd been charming, and funny, and smart. In fact, he'd been nearly perfect. Even if she'd been absolutely fine knowing their time together would be no more than a whirlwind fling, it was hard to erase all of those memories and see him dispassionately as the father of her unborn child. He wasn't just a sperm donor.

One morning they'd basked in the sunlight streaming through the bedroom window and he'd told her about why he loved real estate. It wasn't just about the bargaining or the money. As his fingers had traced down her arm, he'd said it was about finding homes for people, places where they belonged and could be happy. And when he'd realized he'd let her in, he'd immediately backtracked and said it was just a big bonus that his clients were all stinkin' rich.

But it had been a defense mechanism, she was sure. And she'd liked that glimpse into the man, and not just the fantasy.

Perhaps the best way to reach him was to approach the situation on a very human level. She could do that and still keep her other feelings locked away, right?

She put her hand on her tummy, wondering when she was going to start feeling the baby move. So far she had the bump but she hadn't really felt much. A few times she wondered if she might be feeling flutterings of movement, but she'd been told they were probably just gas.

Either way, she'd do what she had to in order to make sure her baby was loved and secure.

Whatever it took. Even being super nice to Jeremy Fisher.

The mile-long beach in front of the Sandpiper Resort was beautiful, even in late November. The waves were now more gray than blue, and the wind was raw, but there was a wildness to it that Jeremy loved, and the sound of the waves soothed his troubled mind.

Because he was, indeed, very troubled.

He'd left his running shoes on, meaning he'd have to shake them out later as the sand, even in the November chill, was still soft and thick. The wind whipped his hair around and made his jacket billow out behind him. Just a few months ago he'd walked this very beach with Tori. She'd worn a red bikini and had left her hair down, damp with seawater. They'd had so much fun; fun that had been missing in his life for too long. For those two weeks he'd put his troubles aside and let himself go. She had, too, or at least he'd thought so. They'd shared a blanket on the beach and soaked in the sun's rays; nibbled at a picnic prepared by the hotel kitchen; plucked seashells out of the damp sand that she said she was going to keep in her bathroom.

And then she'd taken him to her house and they'd spent hours exploring each other.

Just the memory made his body react, and he briefly considered jumping into the ocean, fully clothed, to cool off.

It had been easy being with her, because he'd known all

along that he'd be leaving again. She wasn't his usual type of woman; his family and his money generally ensured that his dates were not of the small-town, girl-next-door variety, and being with her had been utterly refreshing. Now he'd be tied to her forever, because she was having his kid and there was no way on earth he would abandon his own child. He'd never planned to have any children, but he had to deal with the reality that he was going to be a father, and he was determined to be a better one than his own had been.

But how could he demand that Tori uproot her life? That wasn't fair either, and as much as Jeremy was used to getting what he wanted, he was a fair man. Or at least he wanted to think so.

He needed a plan. He was having a hard time formulating one because he was still stuck on the idea that he was going to be a dad.

The idea was terrifying.

The raw wind bit through his jacket right to his bones as he carried on down the beach. His own parents had divorced when he was two, and he barely remembered his dad. Too often he'd been a pawn in battles between his parents, to the point where he'd often felt like a commodity rather than a son. His mother had remarried when he was four, and his siblings had been much older than him. By the time he'd started high school, his sister had been eighteen and starting college, and his brother, ten years his senior, had already been working in Silicon Valley. Jeremy had gone to prep school, away from home.

From the outside he'd certainly looked like a child of great privilege. There had always been money. There hadn't been a lot of love or warm fuzzies.

He stopped and stared out into the white-topped waves. Yesterday he'd watched as Tori cradled her gently swelling tummy and he'd seen the beatific expression on her face. That sort of maternal affection was completely foreign to him.

No matter what, he wouldn't take this baby away from her.

And he or she would never be a pawn in some battle. Not if he could help it.

He started the mile-long walk back to the resort, his thoughts still churning. It would be different if Tori forced his hand. What if she tried to shut him out? He wouldn't try to shut her out, but he wasn't about to let her keep him from being a part of the baby's life. He didn't want his child growing up feeling unloved, or that he didn't care. The situation had to be handled with delicacy, that was for sure.

When he was almost to the resort, he looked up and saw a figure moving around the deck that in the summer had been a patio restaurant. The woman wore a heavy coat and a headband covered her ears, a dark ponytail keeping her hair tamed and out of her face in the brisk wind. The swirl of tension in his gut told him that it was Tori, even though her back was to him. On closer examination, he saw that she was stringing lights along the railing.

He jogged up to the main resort building and climbed the steps leading from the beach to the deck. "That's a cold job," he called out, and her head snapped up, the strands of lights forgotten in her fingers.

"Sorry," he apologized. "I didn't mean to startle you."

"I didn't hear you over the wind and waves."

He opened the gate and stepped onto the deck. He had gloves on his hands, but her fingers were bare and red. "You should be wearing gloves."

"They make my fingers too clunky," she answered, going back to the string of lights.

Jeremy moved forward and took them from her, then removed his gloves, tucked them beneath his arm, and took her hands in his. They were icy cold, and he chafed his fingers over hers to warm them. "Here. Put these on."

"Jeremy, I'm—"

"Shh. They're warm." He tugged the gloves over her fingers.

They were too big, but she flexed her hands and he knew the material still held some of his heat.

Moments ago he'd been ready to take her on if she decided to play hardball. Now he was giving her gloves for her cold fingers. For a moment he wondered if he was a weak man, but then he reminded himself that being on good terms would only help matters in the end.

"Let me do a few of these. You show me how you want them."

"I'm just looping them on each post, see?" She held out a hand full of tie wraps. "Putting these on them, and snipping the ends with cutters."

Unease slipped through him. She was looping them, certainly, but he went back and saw how she did it and tried to re-create the same positioning of the string, though it took a few tries. And the tie wrap... He figured out that one end went through the other and he had to pull it tight, but it was a foreign sensation. He was not a handy kind of guy, in any sense. Someone had always done that sort of thing at home. He had many talents. Being handy was not one of them.

Ugh. He really was a spoiled brat, wasn't he?

She reached into her pocket for her cutters, then tightened his wrap a bit more and snipped the end. "Have you never hung Christmas lights?" she asked.

"First time," he admitted, pulling on the strand until it was taut again. His fingers were already getting cold; how had she managed to put this many up without getting frostbite? But he pushed on because he didn't want her to think he was a wimp or completely inept. Together they positioned, fastened and clipped the lights into place. Once they traded gloves so he could warm his hands, too, and then he put the lights up and over the arched entrance to the deck. "Will anyone even come out here?" he asked, trying hard not to shiver. He was pretty sure he couldn't feel his ears anymore.

"No. But we always put the lights up and a lit tree out here. It looks nice from the beach and also from the dining room."

He clapped his hands together for warmth. "You mean we still have to do a tree?"

"What's the matter, not used to the cold?"

New York got plenty cold in the winter, but the icy wind off the ocean was going right through him today. When he didn't answer right away, she laughed—a soft, musical sound that suddenly made him feel lighter. "Your ears are pink. We'd better get you inside. Don't worry, we set up the tree inside and then move it out. Thanks for your help, though. My fingers appreciate it."

"You're welcome." Despite the cold, it had been kind of fun.

She looked at her watch. "It's nearly noon. Do you want to come in for some lunch? Or do you have appointments?"

He shrugged. "I don't have an appointment until two, so I have an hour to spare."

She opened the door that led from the deck to the dining room. "Our chef, Neil, does a curried carrot and ginger soup that is amazing. Definitely cold-weather comfort food."

They went inside and he watched as Tori went to the bar and spoke to the server behind the counter. When she came back, she led them to a table near the fireplace and hung her jacket over a chair. "Phew," she said, sitting down. "I'm not going to lie, that fire feels wonderful."

There were a handful of guests in the dining room, but it was otherwise quiet. "Not your busy time of year, huh?"

She shook her head as he took the chair opposite her. "No. The weekends are busier. People out for dinner, and our Sunday brunch is amazing." She looked up, and he got caught in her eyes again. Today her hazel eyes looked more green than brown, and her thick lashes made them seem bigger. He wondered if their baby would have her eyes.

"I'll have to try it while I'm here."

He sat back when the waitress came over with a basket of warm rolls and pats of butter. "Your lunch will be right out, Ms. Sharpe."

"Thank you, Ellen."

Tori looked up at him, a smile on her lips. "You warming up yet? Your ears aren't quite so pink."

He chuckled a little, his gaze stuck on her lips. Just his luck he couldn't quite forget kissing them. There could be none of that now. "The fire is helping. The wind is so bitter today."

"So why were you walking the beach?" she asked, picking up a roll and breaking it in half.

"Thinking," he replied, meeting her gaze. "I had a lot to think about."

"And did you come to any conclusions?"

Her voice was calm, but he could see a tightening around her mouth. She was nervous about this, too. It gave him a little comfort. The lives they'd both built—separately—were about to be disrupted.

"A few," he admitted. "But I'm not sure you're ready to hear them."

CHAPTER THREE

UNEASE SETTLED THROUGH HER, making her limbs feel heavy and her breath short. This was never going to be easy, but despite all the thinking she'd been doing the last twenty-four hours, she felt ill-prepared for whatever was going to come out of his mouth next.

She nibbled on a corner of the roll, though her appetite was diminishing rapidly. "Oh?" she asked, keeping her voice deceptively light.

He met her gaze and held it. "One thing is for sure, Tori—I can't go back to New York and pretend that this isn't happening. I'm going to be a father. I'm not going to abandon you or my child."

Tears stung her eyes and she looked down at the napkin in her lap. It was lovely to know that he accepted the pregnancy and wanted to be a part of their baby's life. But it stung that they were no more than an obligation to him; that he was tied to them out of duty and DNA and not affection.

"Thank you," she whispered.

"And whatever you need, you only have to ask. You need to know I'm willing and able to support you financially."

Financially. She clenched her fingers into fists under the table.

"Tori?"

She'd been silent so long he reached over and touched her arm, prompting her to look up. She took a deep breath, met his gaze and said quite clearly, "Thank you, Jeremy. But I'm quite able to provide for us."

His expression grew puzzled as his brows knit together. "Then what do you want from me?"

"Honestly? I don't know. Time, I suppose. To figure this out."

He looked at her tummy and then back to her face, and a hint of a smile quirked at the corner of his lips. "Well, we are on a bit of a ticking clock, don't you think? And it's halfway to midnight."

She raised her eyebrow in response. "I'm hardly Cinderella. Or a damsel in distress that needs rescuing."

At that moment their lunch was served; piping-hot bowls of soup along with bacon-and-avocado paninis that seemed to satisfy some sort of craving of Tori's right now.

"This smells delicious."

"It is. I'm kind of addicted to these sandwiches. I'm not sure if it's the avocado or the bacon that the baby likes so much, but it's my favorite."

They ate in silence for a few moments, and then Jeremy spoke again. "This feels so weird. Last summer…"

His voice trailed away and Tori's cheeks heated. Last summer she'd felt about ten years younger and stupidly carefree. Days on the beach, toes in the sand, love in the middle of the day. She'd told herself she deserved a bit of fun, but she'd been careless. They both had.

"Last summer was just…what it was." She wiped her lips with her napkin and tried to calm the rapid beat of her heart. "We got carried away. We were impulsive, and now there are consequences. We can't be impulsive this time, Jeremy. We have to make the right decisions."

"I know."

She thought of her mom, who was both dismayed at how

the pregnancy had occurred and ecstatic about being a grandmother. There were just the two of them now. She was an only child, a bit of a miracle baby, really, since her mother had been told she'd probably never conceive. Her grandparents lived in Newfoundland and she rarely saw them. Her father had died two years earlier. Tori felt a certain responsibility to be there for her mom. Without Tori, Shelley had no family.

She looked at Jeremy. "Do you have brothers and sisters?"

"One of each."

The topic had never come up during their few weeks of bliss. Now that Tori thought back to those sun-soaked days, she realized that anytime she had gotten close to talking about his family, he'd changed the subject. Even now, he didn't offer any explanations. Just "one of each."

"And your parents? Are they both back in New York?"

"My mother is in Connecticut. My father lives in the Virgin Islands. They divorced when I was little."

He picked up his sandwich and took a bite, but his face was set in a grim expression even as he chewed. Her heart sank a bit. It would be a shame if he wasn't close with his family. What would that mean for their child?

"Cousins? Favorite aunts and uncles?"

He swallowed and wiped his fingers on his napkin. "What's the point of this family tree examination?"

All the warmth from earlier was gone from his voice, and she withdrew a little bit. "We just...don't know much about each other, that's all. And it seems strange under the circumstances. Besides..." She lifted her chin a bit. "These people are going to be our baby's family, too. Isn't it right I know more about them?"

He took a drink of water and put down his glass, then placed his napkin on the table as he rose. "I'm sorry, but I really should head out to my appointment. Thank you for lunch."

He took a step to pass the table and she reached out to put a hand on his arm. "Is your family so bad you won't even talk about them?"

He looked down at her, and she couldn't read his eyes at all. They were flinty gray and shuttered, keeping her from seeing anything too personal. "It's not something to discuss over lunch."

"Then later?"

He moved his arm out from beneath her hand. "I've got to go, Tori."

The way he said her name at the end told her he wasn't as closed off as he appeared. Perhaps what they really needed was some time away from prying eyes to discuss properly what the pregnancy meant—to both of them.

"Drive carefully," she replied and shifted in her seat, letting him off the hook.

When he was gone she tried to finish her sandwich, but her appetite had gone with him.

The hot shower was exactly what Jeremy needed after the long day. This afternoon he'd visited three different properties along the South Shore, looking for the perfect home for his client, Branson Black, who was also a former classmate and one of his closest friends. Black was nearly as rich as Jeremy, but he wanted little to do with the money, which Jeremy couldn't quite understand. His instructions were to find a property with a view of the ocean and away from just about everything else. Jeremy was all about giving the client what he or she wanted, but he worried that Bran was trying to hide away from life and not just recover from recent trauma.

Still, he'd found one that he felt was perfect, and under three million. It even came with its own lighthouse, which, of course, was defunct but still lent the property an air of history and uniqueness. He had appointments to see several others during the week, though, before narrowing the choices down to send to Bran.

Being next to the ocean all day, walking the properties, had chilled him to the bone. He'd warmed himself during walk-throughs and by cranking the heat in the car, but the hot shower and warm hotel were more than welcome once he returned.

The hotel might be cozy, but Jeremy's thoughts were not.

He kept messing things up with Tori. He should have known that she'd start asking questions about his family. She was that type. Girl-next-door, nurturing, home-and-family type. He'd always been able to spot them because theirs had been so very different from his own upbringing. Last summer she'd talked about her mom a lot, and missing her dad, and Jeremy had always changed the subject. She didn't need to know that his dad had walked out when he was a little boy and that his mother hadn't been much of a mother at all; she'd left that to the nannies—plural, because his mother tended to hire young women looking to gain some "adventure" by working for rich families for a year or two and then moving on. Some had been nice. Some had been tolerable, more excited about the money and their days off. The last one had had an affair with his stepfather, and that had been the end of the nannies and the beginning of the talk about boarding school. His stepdad had stayed. Jeremy had been sent away.

But it had been a blessing, really. When he'd finished middle school, he'd been sent to out-of-the-way Merrick Hall. And there he'd found his family—of sorts. Including Branson.

He tugged on a warm sweater and called down to room service for dinner. When it was delivered forty minutes later, he opened the door to find Tori's soft face behind the cart.

"Room service," she said softly, and offered a timid smile.

He couldn't find it in himself to stay irritated. He opened the door wide and let her in, watching her hips sway as she moved the cart into the room. He swallowed thickly. Tori Sharpe was no less attractive now than she'd been five months ago. There was a subtle sexuality about her that was alluring. And when she turned around and the gentle swell of her tummy was visible, his heart gave a little thump. That was his child in there.

He had no idea what to do but he knew for sure he wanted to be a better dad than his own had been.

"It's late. I didn't think you'd still be working," he said, then realized how critical he must sound right now. "Thank you for bringing it," he added, trying to be less of a jerk. After all, he'd walked out of their lunch like a coward.

"I waited for you to come back," she admitted, her dark eyes troubled. "I didn't like how we left things at lunch, and I wanted to say I was sorry for prying."

"You had a right to ask those questions. It's not your fault I don't like answering them."

She folded her hands in front of her. "You should eat while it's hot. Let me set this up for you."

He watched as she set a place at the small table and chair by the window of the suite, poured his beer into a glass and whisked the cover off his entrée to reveal a glistening steak surrounded by roasted potatoes, grilled asparagus and button mushrooms in garlic butter. It smelled heavenly, and his stomach growled in response.

"Have you eaten?"

"I have," she said. "So please, sit down. I'll leave you to it."

She turned to go and was almost to the door when he said, "Tori? Stay."

The moment she paused seemed filled with…well, surely not possibility? There was a change though, somehow. As if the invitation marked a willing step toward discussion. Intention, rather than dancing around the topic or taking the temperature of the situation.

And when she turned back around and faced him, his stomach quivered. He didn't let himself get too personally involved with anyone, but he was going to have to with her, wasn't he? At least if he wanted more of a relationship with his kid than sending a support check every month.

"Are you sure?"

He nodded. "I was rude this afternoon. I'm sorry about that."

She took a single step toward him. "Neither of us knows how to navigate this. It's an unusual situation."

He gestured to the seat across the table from his food. "Come sit. Do you want some tea? Or anything else sent up?"

"There's water on the cart. I'll grab one of your glasses and have some. That's all I need."

He waited until she had her water and then they sat together. It felt wrong, eating while she wasn't, but the food was delicious and by her own admission she'd had dinner already. The asparagus was done to perfection and the steak mouthwateringly medium, just as he'd requested.

"Your chef is very good," he said. "This is delicious."

"Tastes here aren't terribly adventurous, so he does simple things well and adds a bit of flair when he can. But no one leaves hungry." She smiled. "Neil has been here a long time, and the rest of the kitchen staff have trained under him. It makes for a consistent culinary experience."

The resort wasn't as glamorous as some he'd stayed in, but he had no complaints.

"And you've been here a long time, too."

She lifted her water glass. "Since I was in high school. I started in housekeeping. Then moved to waitressing when I was legal age. Front desk for a while, too."

"You trained yourself to know the different departments," he observed, and her cheeks colored a little.

"I wanted to be in administration. For a while I was the events manager, in charge of special functions. Then when the assistant manager retired, I applied for the job and got it. This week, I'm acting manager since Tom is away on vacation. Saint Lucia, lucky thing!"

"And your mom is here. You have strong ties."

"The strongest. My mom doesn't have anyone else, really. As far as family goes, that is. Of course, she has friends."

"As do you."

Her brow furrowed. "Well, yes."

"And so you probably wouldn't consider moving."

Her hand stilled halfway to the table, the glass trembling in her fingers. "Moving? As in..."

"Nearer to me. So our baby could be close to both parents."

"Not *with* you."

His eyes widened. Did she think he was going to ask her to move in with him? Or "do the right thing" and propose? Their affair had been amazing, but there wasn't love between them.

"This isn't the fifties. We don't have to get married to parent this child. But I did wonder if you'd consider moving somewhere closer to, well, me. Of course, I'd look after everything financially."

Her throat worked for several seconds while she studied her fingers, then looked up. Her eyes were clear and there was no censure on her face, either. "It's a generous offer, Jeremy. But my life is here, as you just heard. I'm truly glad you want to be a part of his or her life, but I'm not prepared to completely uproot mine to make that happen, any more than you're willing to uproot yours."

She was right. If the shoe were on the other foot, he'd never agree to leaving his life behind and moving to small-town Nova Scotia. They were from totally different worlds.

"I respect that," he said, putting down his knife and fork. "I really do. But I thought I should at least put the possibility on the table."

"Of course."

"We don't have to decide right away, right? You've got a few more months to go."

She nodded. Then her expression softened. "About today... I'm sorry if I picked at a sore spot. Was your childhood awful? Is that why you don't talk about your family?"

He sliced into the steak and considered. She was going to find out at some point, wasn't she? All she had to do was get on the internet and do a bit of digging and she'd find out who he was. "My older sister works on Wall Street. And my big brother moved to California straight out of MIT. He worked for a few start-ups right out of college and then started his own. Now he's CEO of a Fortune 500 tech company."

"Wow."

"Yeah. Being in property, I'm kind of the underachiever of the family."

"But property is a huge investment," she contradicted, and he was amused and a bit flattered that she jumped to his defense. "And you don't sell average houses. Your clientele are all rich, right?"

"Yeah. Dropping a few mil on a house is no big deal for them." He realized she had no idea exactly how wealthy he was, and it both amused and pleased him.

"It's a whole other world."

He looked at her and held her gaze. "They're people, just like anyone else. They have their own pressures, insecurities, heartache. It's true that money can't buy happiness, you know."

"But it sure can help take some of the stress off," she remarked, leaning back in her chair. "So how much are you worth, Jeremy?"

She said it lightly, teasing even, but he figured now was the time to be honest.

"One point two billion," he replied.

She burst out laughing, then stopped abruptly as he merely kept watching her. He knew it was a crazy sum of money. Some days he didn't believe it himself.

"Wait. You're not joking."

"No, I'm not."

"You've made that much money in realty?" Her lips dropped open in disbelief.

"Hardly." He pushed his plate away, leaving a few little potatoes, and reached for the beer. "But I had a big trust fund—the one thing my dad left me. And I have a sister on Wall Street who manages my money for me. Add all my assets together... and you get that number."

She breathed out a couple of curse words that made him grin. "I always knew you had money, but...holy—"

"Our child won't have to worry about a thing, and neither will you." On impulse, he leaned over and took her hand. "I don't know what this is going to look like, but I do know this. I promise that I will never abandon you or our kid. If that means we're just friendly and we co-parent, then that's how it'll be. But if you need anything at all, you just have to pick up the phone. I'll be there for you."

He meant every word. He also knew that what he'd just said had essentially tied him to her for the rest of his life.

What had he just done?

CHAPTER FOUR

TORI TRIED TO quell the thrill that slid through her as Jeremy took her hand and promised to be there for her and their child. He was a tough man to resist at any time, but right now, with her hand in his, and the knowledge that he was a freaking billionaire swimming through her brain, she was quite overwhelmed.

She didn't care that he had bags of money. It wasn't that. It was just that she'd never met anyone quite this rich before. She certainly hadn't known last summer. It shouldn't change him in her eyes, but it did. He was so out of her league.

Not as a person; she knew that money and character were two very different things. But in worldly ways, he was on a whole other plane of existence.

"I don't know what to say," she responded, biting down on her lip. "I had no idea that... Well, Jeremy." She let out a big breath. "I'll make you a promise in return. I promise that I will never exploit the fact that you have money. I don't want us to use money against each other, you know? Either how much we have or the lack of it."

"Me, either. I want us to figure this out in a way that's best for our baby."

"You really do believe everything, don't you? About it being yours and everything?"

He let out a sigh. "I didn't react so well when I saw you were pregnant. But yes, I believe you."

"When the baby is born we can do a DNA test. I wasn't going to do an amnio if I could avoid it. The idea freaks me out."

"A what?"

"An amniocentesis. It's a test where they insert this needle and withdraw a bit of the amniotic fluid—"

He shuddered. "Ouch, and gross."

She laughed. "Yeah. And there are some risks involved. I didn't want to take any chances."

"So you really do want the baby."

She nodded. "I do. It wasn't planned, but I... I don't have much family. And I like children, a lot."

Her clock hadn't really begun ticking yet, not at twenty-eight, but she couldn't lie. She'd been starting to think about a family the last few years. This pregnancy was inconvenient and a shock, yes. But also a blessing.

"I'm not close to mine, as you might have gathered." He took a long pull of his beer and pursed his lips. "I'm closest to my sister, and we both live in New York so we see each other most of anyone. But my brother... He's on his third marriage already and does his own thing."

"And your mom?"

"She's still at the family home in Connecticut. Married to my stepfather. Socializing with the right people, that sort of thing. My dad left and she got the house. Not much else, but we all had our trust funds and she married again within a few years. She made sure she was looked after."

There was a bitterness in his voice he couldn't disguise, and Tori wondered about the little boy he must have been. "I take it she wasn't the nurturing type?"

He laughed—a short, mocking sound. "Not an ounce," he replied, then drained his beer glass. He got up, went to the minibar, and took out a bottle of Cape Breton whiskey, adding a significant splash to a highball glass. He swirled it for a moment before turning and looking at her. "My mom was a social climber. I didn't know it then, but I know it now. I see the type. And when Dad left, she lost her ticket. She would have had to sell the house and finish bringing us up on her own. Instead she married Bruce, and since she came with the house, he brought the rest of his money and status was restored. Some investments on her part paid for our college. Bruce, apparently, was more than happy to pay my four years of tuition to boarding school. I wasn't really home after I finished eighth grade."

He downed the whiskey in one gulp, and poured another.

She sat quietly. First of all, clearly the topic was painful to him, because he was fortifying himself with alcohol. And secondly, as much as his words were delivered in a factual, who-gives-a-care way, she could tell that the lack of affection had left its mark on him.

Tori couldn't imagine not loving your own child, or considering them in the way. Or sending them away, at such a difficult age.

"Where did you go?"

"Merrick Hall, an all-boys school in Connecticut. Very *Dead Poets Society* with old buildings and rituals and dormitories. Top-notch learning, though." He must have seen her alarmed look because he attempted a smile and went to her. "It was fine, really," he assured her. "I belonged there. I met my best friends there. And despite my cold family, I do have some really great friends."

Tori let out a breath. "Oh, of course you do. But now I understand your reluctance. Do you still see your mother? Your stepfather?"

He nodded. "Now and again. Despite everything, she *is* my mother."

Tori was glad. Estrangement could be such a horrible thing.

"So now you know what I didn't want to talk about over lunch." He sipped at his drink this time, to her relief. "I don't know what kind of father I'll make. But I promise to try. Any kid of mine is going to feel wanted and loved. Not in the way."

He said it with such finality that Tori's heart broke just a little. She'd been brought up in a home with so much love. It was incomprehensible to think of a parent being so careless and dismissive, but she knew it happened.

She looked up at Jeremy, at his dark hair and stormy eyes and cheeks, slightly flushed from the day's wind and the warm whiskey. She wanted to reach up and brush the errant curl off his forehead, to smooth the creases on his forehead, to see his lips curve in a smile again. But she kept her hands to herself, knowing that touching him, kissing him, would only make matters more complicated than they already were.

"Then we're going to be fine," she whispered, twisting her fingers together to keep from reaching out. "Because that's what I want, too. And we'll figure out the rest of the details somehow."

Their gazes held for a few seconds, and then a few seconds more, long enough for something to stir between them. Her body remembered what his felt like and ached to feel it pressed against her again. She remembered how he tasted, the way he angled his head to kiss her, and how he nibbled at her lower lip before taking a kiss deeper.

She stepped back, unwilling to cross that line again. "I should go. It's getting late and I'm on shift again tomorrow."

"When do you get a day off?"

"On Thursday, when Tom is back from his holiday."

"I'll have narrowed down some properties by then. Why don't you come along for some second walk-throughs? Some of these places are really stunning. You can tell me where we should eat lunch and we can make a day of it."

She frowned. "Are you sure that's a good idea?"

"How are we going to manage to parent together if we can't get through a day in each other's company?"

He made sense, even though Tori knew it was simplifying

the matter. "Well, all right. If the weather is good. And as long as nothing comes up here."

"Of course."

She began to clear his plate and dinner mess and put it back on the room service cart. "You don't have to do that," he said.

She laughed. "Sure I do. I work here, remember? I'll drop it off at the kitchen and then go home."

He opened the door for her and she wheeled the cart out into the hall. Then she looked back at him. "Thanks for telling me about your family, Jeremy," she said. "I know you didn't want to."

"It's out there now," he replied, leaning on the door. "Just please...don't judge me on the basis of my relatives. I've tried very hard to be...different."

"I judge a person on what I see them do," she answered, and gave him a smile. "So far you're in the clear."

He smiled back then, a sexy sideways little slice of amusement. "I'll see you soon." Then with a little laugh, he backed up and shut the door.

She wheeled the cart down the hallway to the elevator while trying to calm her thrumming pulse. Amity was better than enmity, for sure, but how was she going to deal with a smiling Jeremy? Because she still found him incredibly attractive. Still got that light feeling in her chest when he smiled at her. And with their baby on the way, she couldn't afford to let her head get into the clouds.

Life wasn't made of fairy tales. It just had reality, and this was hers. She'd better figure it out.

Thursday dawned bright and clear, and after a brief meeting with Tom to bring him up to speed, Tori bundled up in her warm parka and gloves. Her knee-high boots and leggings were comfortable and warmer than she would have been in a skirt. The jacket was a bit snug around the waist, and she tugged on the zipper to get it over her growing bump. She supposed a new coat would be on the shopping list, but she hated spending the money on something she'd wear for only one winter.

Jeremy was waiting in the lounge sipping on coffee when she emerged from her office. To be honest, she was looking forward to the morning. There were worse things than wandering through luxury homes. She loved flipping through magazines and seeing the fancy decor. Now she could see some in person. Maybe even get some ideas for the hotel.

"Hi there."

Jeremy turned around and she tried not to stare. He was in suit pants and shoes, with a soft wool coat and plaid scarf around his neck. His hair was finger-combed back from his face, making it seem groomed but carelessly so.

"Hi, yourself. Do you want a tea for the road? Something hot?"

"No, I'm fine. I had a decaf in the office with Tom this morning. You're ready?"

"Just let me get this in a travel cup and I will be." He flashed her a smile—another jolt to her heart—and beckoned for the waitress to grab him a cup. Within seconds he had his hand at the base of Tori's spine, solicitously leading her out to his rental.

It was a freaking Jaguar.

He held the door and she slid into the sleek interior, the soft leather cradling her like it was shaped to her bottom. It was cold, but in moments he had the heater turned up and her heated seat on. A map on the console flashed and he hit a preset for one of the properties, and then they were on the road, heading toward Bridgewater.

"Where are we going first?"

He tapped the wheel along with the satellite radio station that was playing. "A house in the Pleasantville area. On the LaHave River."

"I know the area."

"Branson's looking for a place to...well, regroup, I guess. He's had a rough year."

"Branson?"

"My client. And my friend."

"How has his year been rough?"

Jeremy frowned. "It's not really my place to say, you know? He's a private guy, and I respect that. But if he wants to be invisible, I'm going to help him get what he needs and make sure it's a good investment. I don't think he'll live here full-time, at least not after a while." He looked over at Tori. "As his friend, my hope is he'll put himself back together, and use this place as a summer home. Get back to throwing parties and having fun. He needs to smile again."

Tori wondered what could be so awful that Jeremy couldn't talk about it, but she respected his desire to protect his friend's privacy. "He's one of your Merrick friends?"

Jeremy nodded. "Yep."

The drive to Pleasantville wasn't long, and Jeremy had just finished his coffee when they pulled through iron gates into a long drive.

At the top was a gorgeous gray-shingled house with a three-car garage attached. Tori's breath caught—it was so cozy looking despite its size. "How much did you say this was?" she asked, scanning the yard, which was covered with a thin layer of snow.

"One point four."

"It doesn't seem quite that grand."

He chuckled. "You wait. It's three acres on the water, and the bottom floor is a walkout. It looks much bigger from the back than the front."

He led her to the front door and then opened the lockbox, giving them entry. She stepped inside and gasped. It was so airy and light and beautiful!

She took off her boots and left them on the rug at the door, then stepped onto the silky hardwood. "Okay, so you're right. It's bigger inside than it looks from the outside."

He took her on a walk-through. The kitchen walls were a pale yellow, with white cupboards and woodwork, and granite countertop along the counters and the center island. Stainless steel appliances gleamed in the morning sun, and Tori couldn't stop herself from oohing over the double wall ovens. Their footsteps echoed through the rest of the downstairs rooms, and then they went up the curved staircase to the next level, where several of the rooms had windows overlooking the water. Even the en suite bathroom was perfectly situated so that one could soak in the oversize tub and look out at the river and a huge tree standing sentinel by a small dock.

"A dock for a boat."

"Yes. And a short sail down the river to the ocean. What do you think?"

She laughed. "It's beautiful and ginormous. You've seen my cottage. What would I ever do with this much room?"

She could feel his gaze on her as she wandered to the windows of the master bedroom again. "But it is lovely. Truly. And despite the size, it feels like a home. That's nice."

They put their shoes back on and wandered around the outside for a bit, and Tori discovered he was right. The house's most impressive aspect was from the river, looking in. Three stories of large windows shone in the sunlight.

"Kids could play here," she mused. "It's just a gentle slope to the water. And gardens. Are there gardens in the summer?"

"Yes, though, of course, we can't see them now."

"Wow. Is this the kind of place you always show, Jeremy?"

He laughed. "Yes and no. This type of property would cost a lot more in other areas. And some of the properties in Manhattan would stop your heart."

"Like yours?"

He shrugged. "I live on the Upper East Side. It's not known for being cheap."

She put her hands in her pockets and squinted up at him. "How much was your place?"

He met her gaze. "Just over four."

"Million?"

He nodded. "It's pretty modest. I didn't need someplace huge and empty, you know?"

"Oh, my—"

He burst out laughing then and she joined in, just because it all seemed so incredulous and the sound of his laughter filled her with some sort of strange joy.

"Come on," he said, holding out his hand. "Let's go see the next one."

They left the house behind and journeyed a short way to a property that was more isolated and right on the ocean. A small cliff separated the property from the sea, and at once Tori was taken with it.

"If the last one was homey, this one is wild," she said, stepping out of the car. The wind off the water whipped her hair off her face and she turned into it, loving the feel even though it wrapped around her with icy-cold fingers. "It's incredible here!"

She had to shout to be heard, but she could see the look of admiration on Jeremy's face and knew this was a favorite of his, too. She rounded the hood of the car and met him on the crushed walkway to the house. "You love it, don't you?" she asked, tucking a swath of hair behind her ear.

"I do. And you'll see why in a minute."

When they got inside, he swept out an arm. "Now do you see?"

Past the foyer was a center area with a small table in the middle, holding a bouquet of flowers. And to the left was the beginning of a circular staircase that climbed up…and up…and up. Tori went to the middle and looked up. There was a skylight at the top, so that a perfect column of light fell from the roof right to the spot where the table sat, and the column was framed by the dark wood of the railings and the creamy white of the steps' risers.

"That," she said definitively, "is a conversation piece. Amazing."

"Isn't it? And there's a sauna downstairs, and an exercise room…"

"No private beach?"

"There is, but it's not direct access because of the cliffs. I'd show you, but I'm afraid it's a bit icy and I don't want you to fall."

There was a room on the side that was rounded, like a hexagon, windows all around to provide a 270-degree view. A stone fireplace was in one "corner," with granite along the bottom of the wall, giving it a rustic feel.

"Can you imagine," she said, unable to keep the awe out of her voice, "sitting here with the fire blazing and a storm outside, with a glass of wine and a book?"

"Yeah," he said softly. "I can."

Their eyes met. This house was not for them. They weren't even a *thing*. But walking through it together was…intimate in a way she hadn't expected. She cleared her throat. "Come on, show me the rest, then."

On top of the porch was a railed deck, with French doors leading from the master bedroom. Tori had never seen such luxury in her life. Even with the furniture moved out, the rooms were commanding in their size and the views were incomparable. Two more huge bedrooms, each with their own bath, finished the upstairs.

"You want to recommend this one, don't you?" she asked. "You like it a lot."

He nodded. "I think it suits Branson, but it's pretty isolated. And did I mention the best part? It has its own lighthouse at the edge of the property. Look."

He pointed southeast, where the land jutted out into the ocean. It wasn't huge, but sure enough, a red-and-white lighthouse stood sentinel, looking a little worse for wear. "Is it still active?"

"No," he replied, sounding disappointed. "But the owner

assures me it's still in working order. Solid as the cliff it's built on."

It was undeniably romantic. Who wouldn't want to have their own lighthouse?

"Can we see it?"

He shook his head. "It's a different key, and I don't have access to it."

"Oh."

They wandered through some more, and Tori was quite taken with it all. When he told her the price tag, she laughed and said a girl could dream, but then laughed again and asked what she'd ever do with all that space. It needed people to fill it up. It needed not only priceless views but life and laughter.

They headed back toward Liverpool, went past the exit and on to a third house that was on Jeremy's short list. She didn't like it nearly as well, though. It was in the same price range as the others, but was a little too avant-garde for her in its design. The house itself looked like a giant block dropped on the sand, and inside it was nearly as austere.

"You don't like it," he said as they walked through.

"It has every amenity a person could want," she remarked, "but I feel off balance. I don't feel at home here. And I know it sounds weird, but I feel like it could just tip over into the Atlantic."

He laughed. "Fair enough."

She put her hands on the cold railing of the stairs and said, "It's the kind of place that people call 'innovative' and 'remarkable' but there's not a lot of comfort here."

"So let's take it off the list."

She looked at him with some alarm. "Oh, gosh, don't take anything I say into account! I have no idea about real estate."

He came over and stood next to her, his hand on the railing close to hers. "But you do know what goes into making people feel comfortable and at home. It's part of why the Sandpiper is such a success. That's what my friend needs right now."

Her heart stuttered a bit. He was a surprise for sure. "Which one gets you the biggest commission?"

He laughed. "This one, actually. But it's never about that."

"It's not?"

"I don't need the money. But I like finding people places to live. I like to imagine them happy there."

"You surprise me, Jeremy."

"Why?"

She put her hand on his chest. "Because in there is the heart of a man who is looking for a home."

His face closed off immediately and he stood back. "That's just you being sentimental."

She'd touched a nerve; it didn't take a genius to figure that out. She dropped her hand. "Oh, maybe. I still think it's nice that you think about what suits the person and not just the biggest payoff."

He lifted his chin, gesturing toward the front door. "Should we find some lunch?"

Her stomach had been growling for an hour, so she readily agreed. "I know just the place."

He followed her outside, and she waited while he locked up. All the while Tori realized she was getting a better glimpse of what made Jeremy Fisher tick. And so far, what she saw made her heart soften. He could deny it all he wanted, but she'd been right. He was looking for home.

She'd always known what home meant. She'd always been wanted and nurtured and valued. What must it be like to have to search for those things?

CHAPTER FIVE

JEREMY WAS STILL shaken by Tori's observation back at the house. Was she right? Did everything come down to wanting to find a place he could call home? He'd done that, hadn't he? He loved his place, with the view of Central Park and the bustle of New York all around him. He was in the middle of it all. Work, restaurants, theater, museums.

But still, there was something missing. And how astute of Tori to realize it.

He buckled his seat belt and turned to her. "Okay, so where are we going?"

She took him to a little hole-in-the-wall restaurant with scarred wood tables and plastic tablecloths, and ordered them both fish and chips. "It's the house specialty," she insisted, and when the food came he goggled at the size of the platter. The whole plate was covered in crispy fries, with two pieces of battered fish on top, a paper cup of tartar sauce and a dish of coleslaw on the side.

"Vinegar?" the waitress asked, as she put down the steaming plates.

"Oh, yes, please."

Jeremy watched as Tori liberally shook vinegar on her fish

and fries. "Come on," she said, grabbing her paper napkin and putting it on her knees. "Dig in."

He cut a piece of fish off with his fork and popped it in his mouth. Delicious. Light batter, perfectly crispy and flaky haddock inside. "Mmm."

"See?" She grinned at him as she speared a fry and dipped it in some ketchup.

He took another bite, then ate a fry and then tried some of the tangy coleslaw. Everything was amazing. He was glad he'd had only a fruit cup at breakfast with his coffee. The portions were huge.

"Why didn't we come here last summer?" he asked. It was close to her place, close to the Sandpiper.

"Because you can't get in the door here in the summertime. It's packed." She grinned up at him and let out a breath. "I need to slow down."

"Don't do it on my account." Truthfully, her love of food amused him. The last few dates he'd been on, the women had barely tasted their food and then insisted they were full. It had never made sense to him. People needed to eat to survive. It was also an experience to be enjoyed. Seeing Tori's grin as she bit down on a french fry made him happy for some reason.

"You're probably used to nicer restaurants," she said, pausing to take a drink of water. "Honestly, last summer I had no idea you were so rich. I would have recommended a few places. Particularly in Halifax."

He met her gaze. "At the time I was happy with whatever filled my hunger."

Her cheeks colored as she interpreted a double meaning he hadn't intended. But it was true. He'd been hungry for her. He still was, if he were being honest with himself. Knowing she was carrying his child only made her more beautiful, if that were possible. He had no trouble remembering the taste of her lips or the softness of her skin, the scent of sunscreen filling the air and the tangle of her hair in his hands. It was what had driven him to come back here in the first place. Branson's request had simply given him the excuse.

He shifted in his chair and dug into the fillet once more. Then he changed the conversation to safer topics, like the houses they'd already looked at. "You're going to recommend the one on the bluff, aren't you?" she asked.

"I think so, yes. I'll show him all three and give him my impressions, but overall I think that's what he'll pick."

"It was my favorite. I love how the ocean is so wild there, right on the point."

They'd made it through their fish and half the fries when Tori pushed her plate back. "Okay, I really have to stop if I'm going to have dessert."

He gawped. "Dessert?"

She laughed. "Yes. Because they make all their pies on-site and the coconut cream is my favorite."

He wasn't sure where he was going to put it, and he wouldn't have to eat for the rest of the day, but when the waitress came back, they ordered pie—the coconut cream for her and butterscotch for him, something he'd never had before. He had another coffee and she ordered a decaf, and they lingered a long time, sipping and picking at their dessert.

"This was nice," she said, absently fluffing her fork through some of the cream on top of her pie. "I think it bodes well for us getting along."

"Me, too. Though we didn't really talk about the future."

Her face turned troubled, with her lips tightening and her lashes cast down. He wondered why she did that, because he'd noticed it a few times now when there was the potential for conflict.

"Hey," he said softly, making her look up at him. "We'll get there. I've got more time here. Another week, anyway. I've got to go up to Halifax for a few days, too. You can take some time, and I will, too, to see if we can come up with a plan."

She nodded. "I know. It's fine, really. I just realized that this really wasn't how I'd planned to start a family. With his or her parents living in different countries."

"It's not ideal, but it's the reality we have to work with." At her downcast expression, he put his hand over hers. "Hey. Look on the bright side. I have the means to come visit, or have you come to New York. That sounds okay, right? We won't have to stress over money."

Her eyes brightened. "You mean you'd be okay with us staying here?"

He hadn't meant to agree to that so readily. Truthfully, he'd thought about how great it would be to have her move to New York so he could see his kid whenever he wanted. But he didn't want to get into that now, and mar the great day they'd been having. "There are a lot of options," he deflected, pulling his hand away and reaching for the last of his coffee. "So maybe what we need to do is think about what we each want and then sit down and have a discussion about it. See if we can find some middle ground."

"That sounds fair," she agreed. "I mean, so far we've managed not to argue about anything, and that's quite an achievement, considering."

He nodded, but something felt a little bit off. Like they hadn't argued…yet. And that something was going to come along and cause some friction, and he really didn't want that to happen. He didn't want to argue with her at all. Quite the contrary.

Jeremy frowned as he picked up the check. That was part of the problem, wasn't it? He still desired her, and now that they were spending more time together, he was discovering he still liked her, too. The woman he'd met last summer was the real Tori—smiling and easygoing, easy to be with, and a knack for making him smile. He'd been drawn to her charm and easy laugh, and had felt like he could simply be himself.

The combination made her more dangerous than she could imagine. Because the last thing he wanted was a ready-made family. He didn't know the first thing about how real families worked. His had always been dysfunctional. His most normal relationship had been with the gardener who had come around twice a week to look after the grounds and cut the grass.

Lord, what would Mr. Adley have to say about this predicament?

He'd tell him to do the right thing. The only trouble was, Jeremy had no idea what the right thing might be. It certainly wasn't a slapped-together marriage for the sake of a baby. For a marriage, there needed to be love, and Jeremy was relatively certain that he wasn't capable of that particular emotion.

They got in the car and headed back toward the hotel, where Tori would be able to pick up her car and head home. When they were maybe five minutes away, Tori sat up straight in her seat and pointed. "Slow down…there." She looked over at him and then pointed again, right at a small for-sale sign on a stake at the roadside. "Turn in here, Jeremy. Please!"

She said it with such urgency that he immediately braked and turned into the side road. "What are you looking for?"

"There was a for-sale sign, and there are only a few houses in here. I'm curious."

They'd finished their viewings, and it was still early, so he figured he might as well indulge her. "It's definitely off the beaten path."

"And straight down to the beach. Not the one by the inn, but a kilometer or so down the coast. It's not as big, but it's lovely. And it's on private property."

They found the for-sale sign close to the end of the lane, but the gate was closed. Tori looked so disappointed that he picked up his cell and dialed the number for the agent.

Then he turned to Tori with a smile. "He can be here in twenty minutes. It's vacant—do you want to get out and walk the property?"

"I could stand to walk off some lunch," she replied, her eyes brightening again. "I'm gonna confess, Jeremy. I've always wanted to see this property. I've seen it from the water. I had no idea it was for sale, though."

"Then let's go."

He parked the car along the side of the lane, then took Tori's arm as they navigated their way around the small gate that was more for show than security. The drive was about a hundred and fifty yards long through a stand of trees, but then it opened up to a cleared yard and a property that was smaller and less grand than the others they'd seen, but impressive just the same.

"Oh, wow," Tori breathed, letting go of his arm as she moved forward. "Look at that."

The outside of the house was done in gray siding with white trim, with an oversize front door and stone steps and a stone walkway leading toward the drive. He'd seen and dismissed this property listing earlier in the week; at under three thousand square feet and a price tag below a million, it was less than what Branson was looking for. That didn't detract in any way from its charm. Under the film of snow, they saw stone gardens dotted with evergreen shrubs, and other areas that would no doubt sprout into a profusion of perennials come spring. The back of the house faced the water, and a path that ended in a set of steps led to the white-sand beach below. A quick assessment told Jeremy that the property probably included about three hundred feet or more of shoreline.

Tucked away in a corner was another smaller building, what Jeremy would have assumed was a converted boathouse. It too was gray, but with shaker shingles and a charming red front door. He was acutely aware of Tori at his side, eyes wide, falling in love with the place.

Her current house was about the size of the boathouse, certainly under a thousand square feet. Charm galore, but tiny.

"Oh, isn't this lovely?" She peeked into the front window. "It could be a guesthouse, or…" She turned to him, her eyes bright. "Something the owners could rent out or something. I mean, it's nicer than renting a room or basement. Guests would have their own space. I wonder if there's a little kitchen. It's cute as anything."

She was beautiful like this, so animated and with her eyes full of possibilities. It was what made her sweet, what made her entirely suited for her job at the Sandpiper. As she circled the little house, he realized with a sinking heart that she belonged here. She wasn't the kind to be happy in the city, was she? She loved the ocean, the open spaces, the wildness. It was as different from New York as sun from rain.

And he couldn't live here. Oh, financially he didn't need to work another day in his life if he didn't want to. But he'd be miserable otherwise. He needed a purpose. A challenge.

By the time she'd finished examining the lot, the Realtor arrived and was ready to show them the house. Inside was just as stunning as he'd imagined, with surprises in some of the detail, such as the iron-and-glass doors to a hidden patio. The iron was in the pattern of lilies, scrolling up through the glass. It was one of the nicest custom-made pieces he'd seen, and that was saying something. There were three large bedrooms upstairs, sweeping views, a chef's delight of a kitchen, and a garden with a stone firepit in the back.

"Oh, look. That's so pretty! And you could put chairs around it and have fires and roast marshmallows in the summer. And hear the ocean." Tori stood at the window, her face nearly touching the glass. "I know you said it wasn't on your list, but this is my favorite one yet."

"It's a bit small for the client. But you're right. It's a wonderful property. How long has it been on the market?"

The Realtor, who'd been wisely letting the house speak for itself, stepped forward. "Since September."

"Really." Jeremy lifted an eyebrow.

"It's not really a seller's market at the moment, as I'm sure you know." There was no harm in saying it, Jeremy knew exactly what the market was like and the other man knew it. "But the owners don't want to sell it for less than it's worth."

Of course not. And in truth, they could have added a good fifty-to-one-hundred thousand to the price and it would still be a good deal.

"I'll keep it in mind for other clients," Jeremy said, offering his hand. "Thanks for coming out today."

"My pleasure."

They stepped outside the house again and walked down the lane to where they'd parked the car. Tori lifted her hand in a friendly wave as the Realtor passed them on the way by. He smiled to himself; it was such a small-town thing to do.

They settled back into his car and started on the short drive back to the hotel. Tori sank into the seat and let out a sigh, resting her hand on her tummy. It was such a maternal gesture that his heart wrenched a little. She was going to be a good mother. There was genuine warmth and gentleness to her and he was at least thankful that his child would be in a happy, nurturing environment.

He cast his eyes back onto the road again. He was already thinking in terms of his child living with her as if everything was already settled. Was that really what he wanted? To just back off and leave his kid here, while he returned to his previously scheduled life, with occasional visits so his son or daughter at least knew what he looked like?

He thought back to his upbringing, and his gut twisted. He actually couldn't remember what his father looked like, and it had taken many, many years for him to stop hoping that one day Brett Fisher would show up for his birthday or for Christmas, and take him away from the cold, lonely life he led. He refused to let any kid of his feel that way—always looking out the window, wondering if his father would come, disappointed when he didn't, only to have his hopes raised and dashed again and again.

What was the alternative?

They arrived back at the hotel and he got out and opened Tori's door before she had a chance to. She smiled up at him and his stomach twisted again, this time not out of pain but out of confusion. In some ways Tori was a stranger. They'd spent a few weeks having some fun, and now a few days talking. But in other ways, she was more than that. His feelings were complicated by desire and concern and, he realized, a bit of fear.

Because he liked her, dammit. And wanted her. And the baby they'd made would join them together forever.

"What's wrong?" she asked, putting her hand on his arm, concern etching her face. "You're frowning."

"Just thinking," he replied, but consciously relaxed his features. "I should probably go up and put my thoughts together for Branson, and give him a call."

"Right. I keep forgetting today was work for you." She smiled, then looped her arm through his as they walked toward the lobby doors. "It was fun for me."

He tried to ignore how good her arm felt around his, her body pressed close to his side. "It was for me, too. Not every day is like this, though."

"Do you think your friend will put in an offer?"

"Perhaps."

"Why Nova Scotia, instead of somewhere else? I mean, there's Cape Cod. Or the Maine coast. What about the Hamptons? Don't all the richest people live in the Hamptons?"

She was so sweet and artless. She was looking up at him with a playful smile and he fought the urge to simply turn her into his arms and kiss her lips. "I think there's a family connection somehow," he replied, swallowing against the urge to make a move. And that was all he'd say about Branson's connection to Nova Scotia. The rest would require explaining about events of recent months, and he valued Bran's privacy too much.

They stepped into the lobby, straight into warmth and hospitality and holiday cheer. A new addition—a ten-foot Christmas tree—was front and center, with sparkling white lights and blue plaid ribbon wrapped around its evergreen fullness. Clear, silver and blue ornaments shone from the tiny lights.

"The Nova Scotia tartan," he murmured, nodding at the tree. "The ribbon. Whose idea?"

"Every year a different department gets to decorate the tree. This year it was housekeeping." She let go of his arm and walked to the tree, then plucked off an ornament and shook her head. "Oh, look at these," she said, holding it out in her hand.

He took it from her palm and turned it over in his fingers. The ball was white but transparent, and in silver paint was the word *Dream*.

There were others, they discovered. Some said *Rest*. Others *Relax* and *Indulge*. "I bet Miriam made these," Tori murmured, hanging one back on the tree. "She's amazing."

His mother would die before having handmade ornaments on her tree, and yet here he was in a luxury hotel and it was celebrated, not discouraged. The ornaments were as nice as any he'd seen, simple but elegant. At the top of each one was a perfect bow made from the same tartan pattern.

"You have some talented staff." He ran his fingertips over the sharp needles of the tree. "And you let them thrive."

"Everyone brings talents to the table. What kind of place would we be if we didn't take their ideas into account? Some of them are very, very good."

"You're incredible," he murmured, standing way too close to her. As if they suddenly realized it, he took a step back and Tori shifted away. But then the distance gave him a chance to see what was above her head. A large sprig of fresh mistletoe hung from the archway, and Tori was directly beneath it.

Before he could talk himself out of it, he stepped up to her and put his hand on the nape of her neck.

Alarmed eyes met with his. "What are you doing?" she whispered.

And then he pointed up, to the mistletoe above their heads. And when she looked back at him again, the confusion was gone and her face reflected back to him what he was feeling. Longing and fear together.

He leaned forward and touched his lips to hers, softly, testing. She was stiff, as if holding her breath, but the moment he paused and slid his fingers an inch through her hair, she relaxed and her lips opened a little. Just a bit, but enough that their mouths fitted together with a sweetness that shook him to the soles of his feet.

This woman. This moment. Carrying his child.

His head said he should not be kissing her. But to his heart it felt...right.

He didn't let the kiss linger too long; he slid his fingers over the curve of her neck and moved away, a few inches at a time, marveling at the quick beat of his heart from such an innocent bit of contact. Her cheeks were flushed and her lips pink and plump, open as if in surprise.

"I couldn't let perfectly good mistletoe go to waste," he murmured, and he ran his tongue over his bottom lip. It was a mistake, because the taste of her lingered there. He'd be a liar if he said he didn't want more.

"Then I think we should just say Merry Christmas and goodnight," she replied, taking a shaky breath.

"It's not even dinnertime yet."

"Then...goodbye, then. I mean... Damn. I said *then* twice. I just mean..."

Her stammer was adorable, and told him she was just as affected as he was.

"I'll see you later. *Then.*" He added the last word and smiled, and before he could change his mind, walked to the stairs that would take him to his suite.

What she did for the rest of the evening was none of his business. None at all.

CHAPTER SIX

SATURDAY AFTERNOON TEA had become a weekly ritual, as long as Tori's mom wasn't on shift at the hospital. This weekend was no different from any other, except that Tori was anxious about telling her mom that Jeremy was in town. While Shelley was supportive, she wasn't a fan of how the pregnancy had happened, during a summer fling. Neither was Tori, to be honest. It would be different if it was an accident in an actual relationship based on love and not just…lust. But they had both agreed that since nothing could be changed, it was about looking to the future.

Now she was sitting in her mom's living room, nibbling on a gingersnap as her mom brought in a teapot and a little jug of milk, no sugar. Neither of them liked it in their tea.

Tori poured a cup and handed it to her mom, then poured one for herself. She took a sip of the hot brew and felt her muscles relax. There was nothing like a cup of tea to settle her thoughts.

"You're feeling okay?" Shelley said, looking over the rim of her mug with worried eyes. "You look a little pale. Is your iron low?"

"A little tired, maybe. I've had a lot on my mind lately. But everything's fine. I go for my ultrasound in a few days."

"When?"

"Tuesday."

"I'm on day shift. I can see if someone will switch if you want company."

Her mom's eyes lit up when she said it, and Tori got the idea she was looking for an invitation. But Tori wasn't sure she wanted company. She almost thought she wanted to go alone and have some time with the baby. It didn't really make sense; the baby wasn't even born yet, and she was "alone" with him or her all the time. Maybe it was just because she was overwhelmed.

"That's okay. I'll get pictures and everything and show you, okay?"

"Okay. If that's what you want." Shelley smiled and reached for a cookie, but before she could take a bite, Tori blurted out the truth.

"Jeremy's in town."

Shelley dropped the cookie. It hit the coffee table and sugar sprinkled everywhere.

"*The* Jeremy? The father?"

She nodded and focused on her cup. "Yeah. He came on business and thought he'd look me up. And found me like this." She pointed to her stomach.

Shelley sat back on the sofa. "Oh, honey. Well, at least now he knows."

Tori looked up at her mom and grimaced. "Yeah. That decision was taken out of my hands."

"Maybe it's for the best. I know it's awkward, but I always thought he should know."

"I know. And me too, really. I'm just…scared."

"Scared that he'll what? Leave you alone? Not be supportive?"

On the contrary. Tori took another fortifying drink of tea. The other day, looking at houses, that kiss… All it had done was remind Tori of how much she'd enjoyed being with Jeremy in the first place. Yes, their relationship had been mostly physical over the summer. But she'd *liked* him…a lot. While she hadn't fostered any dreams of being whisked away to a fairy-tale ending, she had cherished their time together and had tucked the memories away as something very special. Her biggest fear was how to negotiate parenthood without letting her heart get involved. He was a good guy, underneath. He could have made things difficult for her, and instead he was taking his time, not making any demands. But for how long?

She was sure that at some point there was going to be a price to pay.

"You're quiet, so I guess there's more going on here than you want to talk to your mom about." Shelley's eyebrow lifted in a wry expression, but it wasn't condemning. They were close, but Tori had never really shared all the details with her mom.

"He's rich, Mom. Like lots-of-zeroes rich. And if he wanted to, he could make things really difficult."

"Do you think he would?" Concern overtook Shelley's face and her eyes darkened.

"I don't want to think so. He's nice. Caring, really. He hasn't made any demands. We're just…talking."

"Talking is good."

"He wants to be a part of the baby's life."

"That's good, isn't it? It shows he wants to step up. Be responsible."

"It also means I'll have to see him. And I wonder if he'll change his mind about how much custody he wants. If he decides that, I can't afford to challenge him. I'm scared, Mama." Her lips quivered a little on the last word; she rarely called her mom "Mama." "I love this baby already."

"Oh, honey, of course you do." Shelley moved over to the love seat where Tori sat. "You have to have faith, you know? You say he's a good man. I'm sure, then, that you can work this out."

"He is. We spent the day together on Thursday. It was fun. He said if we are going to co-parent, we need to be able to spend time together."

"He's not wrong." Shelley looked at Tori a little more closely.

"But is there more? I mean, there's a reason why you got pregnant. Is that still a factor?"

"I don't know." She let the words out on a breath. "Yeah, I still find him attractive, and there's still...something. At least for me. And I think for him, too. He..."

She halted. Swallowed against a lump in her throat. That kiss had been...something. More destructive to her defenses in its sweetness than any passionate overture might have been.

"He what, honey?"

"He kissed me under the lobby mistletoe."

Shelley laughed lightly. "Sweetie, you could do worse than kissing a good-looking millionaire in the lobby."

"Billionaire," she corrected. "Jeremy Fisher is a billionaire, thanks to his trust fund, his business, and apparently a sister who is a genius with stocks."

Shelley's mouth fell open. "Well."

"How do I prepare myself for this, Mom? I couldn't care less about his money, but it does change things. We live in different countries and are from different worlds. And we're having a kid together. It's such a mess."

Shelley reached for her hand and squeezed it. "You get through it just like you get through anything else. One day at a time, making the best decisions you know how. And then you trust everything will work out."

"You have a lot more faith than I do."

"I don't think so. Just keep an open mind. And if you do everything for the right reasons, chances are it's gonna be fine in the end." She let go of Tori's hand. "Now, have another cookie and drink your tea. Do you want to stay for dinner?"

"Of course I do."

"Good. Then I can send you home with potpie leftovers."

Jeremy switched the phone to the other ear as he sat at the table in his suite, his laptop open in front of him. "So it's down to the one on the river, or the one with the lighthouse, yeah?"

Branson's voice came over the line loud and clear. "I trust you, Jer. You know what I need right now."

His friend needed time and space. "I'm worried you'll become a long-haired, shaggy-bearded hermit who yells at kids to get off his lawn."

A rare, rusty laugh from Branson came over the line. "I don't like beards."

Which was true. But still, Jeremy worried. "You're sure there's no place closer to the city? Or south, somewhere warm?"

"No one knows me up there. No one will recognize me. I need that for a while. And when the house outlives its purpose, I'll sell it again. No big."

"Then the lighthouse one. It's a better value, and to be honest, the location is spectacular enough it should move on resale within a reasonable time frame."

"Put in an offer. I'll pay the asking price. And a quick close."

"You're going to move north during the winter. Are you nuts?"

"I need to get out of here. The house is too full of ghosts."

Which was fair enough.

"Hey, Bran? Can I unload something on you for a minute?"

There was a pause. "Yeah, of course. I owe you a ton in therapy minutes."

They both chuckled a little. It wasn't like they kept score.

"So, remember the girl I told you about? From last summer?"

"Yeah, the fling. You said you were going to look her up again. How'd you make out?"

"She's pregnant."

When he said it all the air rushed out of his lungs. It was almost like until this moment it wasn't really official. He hadn't told anyone until now. Because sometimes you needed your best buddy to give your head a whack.

"Nice work, Romeo. And she didn't tell you?"

"It's complicated."

"Well, duh." There was a pause. "So what now?"

"I don't know. I won't ignore my kid, you know? I can't do that."

"Of course not. And you're a good catch, you know. The electric bill will always be paid on time."

"I'm not sure she's ready for New York. And I'd be bored here within a month."

"So you split your time."

"I guess."

"Your mom know yet?"

"Hell, no."

"Well, my one piece of advice is if you consider making a play for this girl, you be up front with what your family is like before it's all settled. Don't blindside her with it after you've brokered a deal."

"Parenting isn't like buying a house."

Bran laughed again. "Good, I'm glad you came to that conclusion all on your own. Feel better?"

"Yes and no. But thank you. I'll be in touch about the offer."

"Just send me what I need to sign. I trust you."

They ended the call and Jeremy rested his forehead on his hands for a few moments. Bran was right. He needed Tori to meet his family. And he wanted to meet her mom, too.

What an unholy mess.

He made another call and verbally made an offer on the property. Considering he was offering asking price, he was relatively sure that it would be a simple transaction. Once that was done, he ventured down to the business center to take care of the necessary paperwork. As he was sending it off, he realized this meant he no longer had to be at the Sandpiper for more than a few more days. He could pack his things and head back to Manhattan. Get ready for Christmas.

It seemed odd and empty to think about now.

"So, did your friend decide on a house?"

He startled, jumping in his seat as her voice came from behind him.

"Sorry. I didn't mean to scare you."

"I was just thinking." He clicked his mouse and then looked up at her. She was glowing, dressed in black leggings and heels that accentuated her long legs, and a maternity top in a blue that matched the tartan on the Christmas tree. "You look good. Feeling well?"

"I slept a lot on the weekend and read a good book. It was heavenly."

She'd slept and he'd been doing some business in Halifax. They hadn't seen each other at all over the weekend. "I'm glad. And yes. Unless something falls through, it's the house in Kingsburg."

"The one with the lighthouse!" Her eyes lit up. "Oh, that's great. It's so impressive." Then she looked at him thoughtfully. "It does mean that you'll have a good friend in the area."

He hadn't actually considered that before. It was true. At least for a while, Bran would be here. She would be here, and their baby. He had ties to the South Shore without ever intending to.

"It also means I'll be leaving to go back to New York in a few days."

"I suppose it does."

Did she look disappointed? He almost hoped so. Plus they hadn't really come to any conclusions.

He wasn't sure quite what to say when her face changed and her hand went to the swell of her belly. "Whoa."

Alarm skittered through his veins as he shot up from the chair. "Are you all right? What's wrong?"

"Nothing." She looked up at him with wide eyes. "I think the baby just moved."

He guided her to the chair. "Really? What did it feel like?"

"I don't know. Like butterflies, kind of, but running in a line down my belly. I've felt similar things lately, but not this strong. Oh, my, maybe the baby has been moving and I didn't know it!" Her face broke into a smile. "Oh, there it is again."

She reached for his hand and put it on her top, pressed against the solid curve. He didn't have time to react or hesitate; one moment he was standing there and the next he was crouched by her side, palm pressed against her navel. He waited, holding his breath, and then felt the tiniest flutter against his hand. "Is that it?"

She grinned and nodded. "You can feel it? I wasn't sure it would be strong enough."

It was. His child was in there, moving around, and his mother looked like a flipping angel, a perfect picture of motherhood. Something joyful and expansive filled his chest, while a balancing cold trickle of fear ran down his spine. This was amazing! And absolutely terrifying.

He waited, but there was no more movement, so he reluctantly took his hand away and stood again. She let out a huge breath, and then looked up into his face. "You okay? You've got a bit of a deer-in-the-headlights look about you."

"I'm all right. Terrified, but all right."

"I know. It takes some getting used to."

"It just got really real today, I think. I told my friend Branson, too."

She stood and went to him, putting her hand on his shoulder. "I've had a few months of pregnancy so I'm past the surreal part. You've got some catching up to do."

She'd gone through finding out and dealing with the first weeks alone, and an internet search had quickly told him what she'd probably gone through. He'd found out just yesterday that the baby was probably roughly the size of a banana now.

"Jeremy?" She called him back out of his thoughts. "I'm a bit late having my ultrasound, but it's scheduled for tomorrow afternoon. Do you want to go with me?"

Pictures of his baby. His! He felt as if he were being thrown into the deep end so very quickly, but he also knew there was really no other way. "I'd like that. A lot."

"It's in Bridgewater. Kind of close to that first house we saw last week."

"That's fine. You just tell me when we need to leave and I'll be ready."

"Okay." She reached down and took his hand. "It's going to be okay, you know. We'll figure everything out. My mom told me this weekend to have faith, and that's what I'm going to do."

Faith. Jeremy smiled but his heart wasn't in it. He didn't have faith. Not in anything, or really anyone. And Tori was making a mistake if she was placing her faith in him. He could try to live up to it, but chances were he'd fail. There was a reason that he was still single at thirty-six, and never been married. The women who liked him, he didn't like in return. And the ones he liked, he didn't trust. The guys were right. He was a serial dater. It kept him from being lonely, without the messiness of emotions and expectations.

He liked Tori, liked her too much. And he wanted to trust her. But faith? That was just asking for trouble.

Tori had thought what she wanted was to go to the ultrasound alone, but as she sat in the waiting room with Jeremy, she was glad she wasn't alone. And that he was there. He was the baby's father, after all. It seemed right that they share this moment together.

"Are you nervous?"

She looked over at him. His knee bounced up and down. "I think you're the nervous one."

He stopped bouncing his knee and smiled sheepishly. "It feels weird. I never imagined I'd be a father."

"Really? You never wanted a family?" She appreciated how well he'd accepted the situation, and his promises to be there, but it worried her that he might not have seen this role as part of his future.

"It wasn't so much wanting or not wanting," he revealed. "It's more... I just didn't have a great example to follow, and believe it or not, dating is hard with my money."

She gave the obligatory laugh, but then put her hand on his

knee. "It must be hard to figure out who's genuine and who's after your bank account. I don't have that problem." And then she laughed again. And hoped he realized she didn't care about his money, either.

"Yeah, there's that. Some women want the status. But I have my own issues. I don't trust easily. Other people, or my own intuition. When it comes to relationships, anyway."

"Then this situation must be driving you crazy," she said, jostling his shoulder. "Because now there's a baby mama in the mix."

"You're being awfully chill about this."

She shrugged. "I am what I am. I can't make you believe that I'm genuine, that I don't want your money or that I'm out for anything. All I can do is tell you my truth. You're the father. I can and will do this by myself if you bail. I can support me and my child, and I'll be okay. So there's no pressure from me on your bank account. Just room for you to be a father."

She turned sideways in her chair and met his gaze squarely. "My only demand is that if you choose to be involved, you're consistent and honest. I don't want our kid always to be wondering if you're ever coming back or if you care."

To her surprise, his eyes softened. "I *was* that kid, Tori. I won't do that to my own." He swallowed and his throat bobbed with the effort. "I promise you I will not be that dad."

"Then we will figure everything else out."

The door across from them opened. "Victoria? We're ready for you now."

They went in together. Jeremy waited to the side while Tori got on the bed with the paper sheet beneath her. The room was warm, thankfully, and in a few moments they'd adjusted her clothing so that her shirt was up and the waistbands of her leggings and underwear were rolled down right to her pubic bone. She looked over at Jeremy and realized his eyes had widened, looking at her belly. He hadn't seen it before, not like this. She smiled up at him, reassuringly. "You gonna be okay, Dad?" she asked lightly.

He nodded. "Yeah. Yeah."

"Okay, then," the technician said. "Let's get started." She squirted gel on Tori's belly, then began, the pressure from the probe firm. Tori couldn't see the screen, though she wouldn't know what she was looking at anyway. The tech made clicks here and there, saying that she was taking measurements first. Then she turned the screen around. "Okay, are you ready to see?"

During Tori's first scan, at only eight weeks, there'd been very little to see. This time, however, was different. The image shifted, but she could make out the head, and the ridge that was the spine, and appendages. "Look at the little toes," she whispered, tears forming in the corners of her eyes.

She tore her gaze away to look at Jeremy, who was staring at the screen in wonder. "That's our baby. My kid." His fingers flexed and unflexed. "I just... I can't..."

"Do you want to know what you're having? I can't tell you today, but the report will go to your doctor."

Tori looked up at him. "I don't mind it being a surprise. Gender's not important to me anyway." Her only concern was that the baby be healthy. Besides, she didn't go into all the pink and blue stuff and gender-reveal things. She'd already started decorating her tiny second bedroom with a Beatrix Potter theme, something neutral. Peter Rabbit and Squirrel Nutkin were way too cute.

"If you want it to be a surprise, then that's fine with me," he said.

"You're sure?"

"Whatever you want." A smile broke out over his face. "Wow. That's our kid in there."

It was the genuine smile that did it. He'd moved past the looks of alarm and panic to that of... Well, looking at him right now all she could see was joy. Relief swamped her heart as well as a feeling of...happiness? Was that possible? Their relationship was still something they didn't talk about. Nothing had been decided about how they were going to make this work. But she remembered what her mom had said only a few days earlier. One day at a time. And today she was going to enjoy this lovely moment.

"Do you want to see the heartbeat?" the tech asked.

"Yes." There was no hesitation from Jeremy and Tori laughed.

She pointed to a spot on the screen where the *ba-bump, ba-bump* flash flickered in a little heart.

Jeremy went around to the foot of the bed and sat, covering his mouth with a hand. Tori watched him as he stared at the monitor, feeling her heart slipping bit by bit. He said he didn't trust. He'd had a loveless childhood, from the sounds of it. And yet he was capable of so much feeling. He was good, underneath it all. She truly believed that. Could she keep her feelings for him under wraps? Wait it out until they faded? Wasn't it natural to have feelings about the father of her baby?

Even if they weren't returned...or couldn't lead anywhere?

She looked back at the monitor again, and the form of her unborn child there. Every decision she made had to be for the good of her baby. They were the most important thing now.

"Okay, give me a few minutes and I'll take some pictures for you." The tech started moving the wand again, then held it in position and hit a few keys. She tried again and started to chuckle. "Your baby's moving around in there and won't sit still. So much for napping."

It took another few minutes but then it was done and the tech gave her a towel to wipe away the gel as the pictures printed. "I'll give you a few minutes to put yourself back together." She handed the pictures to Jeremy. "Congratulations."

Tori wiped off the gel and adjusted her clothing, then got up from the bed and dropped the cloth in the used bin. When she returned, she stopped in front of Jeremy. "Are you okay?"

He nodded. "I think so." He reached out and pulled her closer, so his hand was on her hip and his face was just below her breasts. He cradled her bump and then, to her surprise, placed a kiss on it. Tears stung her eyes at the tender gesture.

"Are you real?" she asked softly, putting her hands on each side of his head. He looked up and into her eyes. "You could have run the moment you found out. You could have offered to buy me off. You could have made demands. But you haven't, and I don't understand, and I'm... I'm afraid that someday soon there's going to be a price I need to pay and I don't know what it is."

He sighed, a heavy, weighted sigh that sounded so weary she wasn't quite sure what to say.

"I'm trying to do the right thing," he finally said. "I'm as responsible for this as you are. There is no blame and if there is, we share it equally. The truth is, that's my child in there. I saw them on the screen and saw their heart beating. It's humbling, Tori. I have no idea how to do this but I want us to try."

"Us," she said, a bit numb from what she thought he might mean.

"We're going to be parents together. We like each other. For God's sake, we kissed the other day."

"You kissed me," she clarified, though her heart thumped against her ribs.

He stood then, so she had to look up the tiniest bit. "If you tell me there's nothing between us at all, I'll drop the subject right now. But if there is, don't we owe it to our baby to try?"

"If we blow it, the stakes are really high," she responded. And yet he was so close she could smell his cologne and feel his warmth. She couldn't lie and say there was nothing between them because there was. Both the attraction from the summer, and the depth of character he'd shown since his return. He'd been far more understanding than a lot of men might have been.

"Look. Look at this picture and tell me this little nugget doesn't deserve us to try at the very least."

She hesitated but couldn't take her eyes off the ultrasound

picture. And he'd called him or her a nugget. It was an adorable little name.

Jeremy cupped her cheek, then kissed her forehead. "Let me take you home. Maybe we can talk it over."

Her home. Where she had, in all likelihood, conceived their child. Where they'd spent lazy evenings after a day at the beach. And lazy morning-afters, watching the sunrise.

"Okay," she replied. "Let's go home. And talk."

Because she was really unsure about this step, and they needed to set some solid boundaries.

CHAPTER SEVEN

SHE WAS VERY aware of how small her house was when they stepped in it again, Jeremy for the first time since last July. Just under a thousand square feet meant two bedrooms, a small kitchen with dining area to the side, a modest living room and a bathroom that was smaller than the closet in his suite at the Sandpiper. Still, it suited her well. It was cozy, and it was hers.

He didn't seem to mind as he removed his coat and draped it over the back of her sofa. He slipped off his shoes, too, and left them by the door, stepping inside in his socks. Today he'd worn jeans and a simple sweater, and the look of him in casual clothing, so approachable, made her want to slip into his arms. But she couldn't. Not with what he'd suggested hovering between them.

Could they be more than simple co-parents? More than... friends?

"You're nervous," he said quietly, moving toward her. "Don't be."

"How can I not?" She turned around, folding her hands in front of her. "What you said... It would change everything. I was thinking we could just be friends. Work together as a team. But not..."

Her voice trailed off.

"Not lovers?" he answered, reaching out and putting his hand along her upper arm, rubbing gently.

"Yes, that," she answered, trying hard to keep her breath even. Right now, despite the thread of desire winding its way through her body, she couldn't imagine having sex with him. Her body had changed. Heck, everything had changed. It certainly wouldn't be a summer fling.

He gazed into her eyes for a long moment, then leaned closer, slowly, giving her lots of time to move away, or put a hand on his chest to stop him, or say no. But she couldn't, because the truth was she wanted him to kiss her. Wanted to feel his lips on hers again. His arms around her without mistletoe overhead or staff meters away.

He touched his lips to hers, and she let out a breath. More of a sigh, really, as his arms came around her and pulled her close. Her mouth opened beneath his and she let him guide her, softly, seductively, no rush. Like they had all the time in the world.

She melted against his chest and tilted her head up a bit, hungry for more. Her wordless request was rewarded with a deeper kiss, more urgency, and the desire that had been a slow burn began to blaze brighter.

This was what had gotten them into this mess in the first place. Not that her baby would ever be a "mess," but the situation was certainly complicated.

She pulled back a bit, startled by her response to him, needing space to breathe and think.

"I, uh..." That was as far as she got. Actual words weren't making it from her brain to her mouth.

"I know. It's not what we expected. Well, actually, it is what I expected when I came back. That we could go out again, have some fun. I think it's clear that the attraction is still alive and well. We can't ignore it, you know? Because it'll crop up from time to time."

"I can't deny that, after what just happened." She moved another step backward. His unflinching tendency to state the obvious was at times refreshing and other times vastly uncomfortable. He liked to deal with problems head-on. She did, too, or so she had thought. Still, highlighting the fact that there was still sexual attraction simmering between them threw her off balance. It wasn't something they could compartmentalize in a little box, isolated from the situation.

The sad bit of it was, she wanted him to kiss her again, and again, until her head was swimming with it, and the scent of his cologne, and the feel of his hands on her... Being pregnant hadn't eradicated her libido. Actually, in this moment, she wondered if it hadn't increased. She crossed her arms in front of her and tried to ignore the sensations running through her body.

"We're having a child," she said, and wondered how many times over the last week she'd said those words. "Where do you see this going? Because we're going to be tied together for life, do you understand that? If this goes sideways, it could be a disaster."

But if it didn't...

A secret want bubbled up in her. What would it be like for them to be a family? The two of them together, their child... more children? She gave herself a mental shake. How would that even work? Once again she reminded herself they were from two very different worlds. That the fairy tale had never been in the equation.

"You think we need to set boundaries. Figure out the what-ifs."

"Yes," she said, letting out a huge breath of relief. "That's it exactly."

He went to her, took her hand and led her to the sofa. "Come, sit down. I don't like the idea of us staring each other down like we're in a negotiation."

She followed him and sank into the sofa, the cushions cradling her lower back, which had started to bother her a little after the long day.

"You want to know what happens if we try this and one of us

walks away. From a romantic relationship," he clarified. "Not parenthood. We both agree we're in that for the long haul."

"Yes. And there are a lot of things to figure out. I live here. You live in New York. How would it work?"

"I actually have an idea about that," he said, reaching for her hand. He turned on the sofa a bit and tucked his left ankle under his right leg, so he was facing her. "Come to New York with me for a week."

Her stomach plummeted. "A week? In December? Before Christmas?"

He nodded, undaunted. "Yeah. Christmas in New York is amazing. I can show you the sights… Have you ever been?"

She shook her head. She really hadn't traveled much of anywhere. One year, in high school, they'd taken the CAT ferry from Yarmouth to Bar Harbor and gone to Old Orchard Beach. The rest of her travel had been east of Toronto.

Jeremy squeezed her fingers. "I'll take some time off. We can spend it together, figuring things out. With no one interfering."

So this wasn't a ploy to convince her to move there, but to give them time away to evaluate? She sighed. "I don't know…" She pulled away a bit, feeling incredibly overwhelmed with it all. "Jeremy, a week ago I hadn't even decided how and when to tell you, and now you're here, and we're trying to sort out how we're going to do this, and you've kissed me…twice…"

"And you kissed me back," he said firmly. "If it's boundaries you're worried about, then let me put it plainly for you. If for any reason something…more…comes of this, but then either one of us wants to pull the plug, then we can. With the important thing being we do so amicably with the well-being of the baby first and foremost."

It sounded so simple and logical when he put it that way. Could it really be that easy?

Her heart—and her head—said no.

And yet the man sitting next to her, with the earnest eyes and seriously kissable lips, made her believe yes. The idea of a whole week in New York was enticing. She'd only ever seen videos and pictures of things like the giant Christmas tree in Rockefeller Square, the shops on Fifth Avenue...

"I don't know, Jeremy," she whispered. "This—all of this—is so crazy and scary. Everything about my life is changing. Now, talking about going away for a week, together..." She bit down on her lip. "I'm finding it hard to keep up."

He lifted his hand and put it along her cheek. "Don't worry. We'll use it as get-to-know-each-other time. No pressure. No decisions. You're right about one thing. Last summer was so fast, and now we're being thrust into parenthood. If we stand any chance of doing this together, we have to know each other better. Develop trust. I know where you live and your world. But you don't know mine."

It all sounded perfect, which was exactly why Tori was so uneasy. Nothing was ever perfect.

"I'll have to ask for the time off first," she said, surprised she was actually considering it.

"We can go whenever you like. I can work my schedule around you, though I do have a series of meetings on the nineteenth and twentieth I can't miss."

"So I'd be back here for Christmas."

"I'm sure you'll want to be with your mom, won't you?"

She nodded. "Okay. I'll go."

A wide smile lit up his face. "That's great!" He gathered her hands in his and kissed her knuckles. "We're going to be fine. Just wait and see."

Jeremy watched as Tori's eyes widened at the sight of the private jet sitting on the tarmac at Halifax's airport. The option for a direct flight would have taken them only to Newark, with all the other flights requiring a stop. Why would he do that when he could charter something and leave on his own schedule?

Plus he wasn't above trying to impress her a little bit. The woman deserved a bit of pampering and glamour. She worked hard and didn't have a lot to show for it. A cozy little house, sure, and a close-knit work family. But there was a big world out there and he wanted to show her a little bit of it.

"Is this yours?"

He laughed. "No. I chartered it."

Her face relaxed. "Oh. I was having a moment thinking you had your own plane and I was… I don't know."

"I thought about it, and went back and forth about whether I wanted to own one, but in the end, I keep coming back to using charters. It seemed simpler than worrying about where to keep it, having a pilot on call, maintenance… This way I pick up the phone, my assistant books me a charter and I show up." He took her arm as they got to the steps leading to the door. "I like to keep things simple, believe it or not."

It was her turn to laugh. "Jeremy, there is nothing simple about you."

He wasn't sure if that was a compliment or a criticism, but her voice was easy and a smile was on her lips so he was going to take it as a compliment.

She climbed the stairs ahead of him. He watched the gentle sway of her hips, thinking how pretty she looked in jeans and ankle boots with her jacket bundled up around her. She turned and flashed a smile at him when she reached the door and he realized he loved how young and energetic she looked with her hair back in a simple perky ponytail and the minimal makeup she wore, which made her skin look fresh and dewy. Or maybe that was her pregnant glow. It was then that he noticed how snug the jacket was around her tummy. She was only going to get bigger, and the winter was barely begun.

A shopping trip would definitely be on the itinerary.

Once inside, an attendant named Gerry took their coats and got them settled in soft leather seats. The more Tori looked around, the happier Jeremy was that he'd booked the flight. Her lips were open in what he thought was amazement and her eyes flitted over every seat, table and detail of decor in the Gulfstream.

They took off, and her face was fairly stuck to the window as they raced down the runway and left solid ground beneath them.

"This is maybe the coolest thing I've ever done," she said, turning away and smiling up at him. "Is this normal for you? I don't know how I'd ever get used to it."

"It wasn't always. For a while I usually booked first class." He grinned at her. "And some of the commuter jets don't even have a first class." He shuddered for effect, making her laugh.

"I'd be disappointed if I thought you meant that," she replied, sitting back against the comfortable seat. "But you aren't the pretentious type. At least, I don't think you are."

He frowned a little. "That's one of the reasons I suggested the week, Tori. So we could get to know each other better. But I'm relieved you don't think I'm a stuck-up snob."

"Stuck up, no. Used to the finer things? Definitely."

At that moment, Gerry returned. "Are you ready for your breakfast, sir?"

"Breakfast?" Tori parroted, looking from Jeremy to Gerry and back again.

"You didn't think I wasn't going to feed you, did you? It's only ten. If you ate at all this morning, it was hours ago." It was true, because it was over two hours to the airport, and they'd had to return his rental to the agency, then clear security and then customs before boarding.

The meal smelled delicious, and Gerry whisked the cover away to reveal scrambled eggs, a bagel with butter and jam, and heaps of fresh strawberries and raspberries. "Would you like something to drink, ma'am?" he asked.

"Oh, goodness." The low rumble of her stomach was audible, and Jeremy hid a smile. "Maybe some orange juice? Or even just iced water would be lovely."

He took Jeremy's lid as well and Jeremy said, "Water is fine for me, thank you, Gerry."

"This is too much," she said when Gerry had disappeared.

"It's scrambled eggs," Jeremy laughed. "I mean, it's not like it's eggs Benedict or anything elaborate. But I do know that you like eggs in the morning."

Her eyes widened. "You do?"

"You mentioned it one morning when I first arrived. You said Neil made them just the way you liked."

He watched as she took a bite and then turned her amazed gaze to him. "With a bit of cheese and some parsley. I can't believe you remembered that."

The approval in her gaze made him go all warm inside. "Well, I'll confess I asked Neil. Because I get the feeling that you'll just go along with anything rather than voice any preferences."

She put her fork down and her face sobered, her lips turning downward. "What's wrong? Did I say something?" he asked.

"You're half right. I probably would be happy to just go along with things. But maybe I pick my battles. Scrambled eggs, no big deal. Our child's future…big deal."

She wasn't going to be a pushover. Good. Not that he didn't want to get his way, but he admired strength. "Of course."

Gerry returned with orange juice and water for Tori and water for Jeremy, and left quietly. They ate their breakfast in companionable silence, until Tori sat back with a satisfied sigh. "Okay, so you were right. That was delicious and I needed the protein. Thank you."

"You're most welcome. What would you like to do today? We'll be at my place before noon."

"I have no idea." She laughed. "I guess I figured you'd have an itinerary."

"Sometimes the best vacations don't have itineraries," he replied, and cocked an eyebrow.

She blushed prettily. The last "vacation" for both of them had been those magical days in the summer, when they'd soaked up the sun and each other, with no schedule whatsoever. "Jeremy, if you're expecting..." She swallowed and her blush deepened.

"I have no expectations beyond wanting to show you my town," he replied, then reached over to take her hand. His heart hammered in his chest. There was no denying that the attraction to her hadn't gone away. But it was something he wanted to work with, not against. To acknowledge, not ignore. "You're a beautiful woman, Tori. I'm not going to lie and say that what I'm feeling is totally platonic. But I'm not going to push."

Her eyes delved into his. "Me, too," she breathed. "And I shouldn't have admitted that, I suppose. I'm not good at holding my cards close to my chest."

"This isn't poker, or some business merger. It's okay. I'm glad you're being honest."

"Me, too. About you, I mean."

The statement left him somewhat uncomfortable, because he hadn't been completely honest with her about what he really wanted. He was more...hoping she'd come around to the same way of thinking without him having to say so. He wanted her to love his place, love New York and to want to be closer. Hell, he'd even consider living somewhere else and commuting. He was saved from saying more as Gerry returned to take their plates away, bring Jeremy fresh coffee and put a tiny pot of steaming water and a cup in front of Tori.

She looked up in confusion and he smiled at her. "Mint tea, ma'am. Mr. Fisher said you preferred it."

"Thank you, Gerry."

She looked over at Jeremy and raised an eyebrow. "Well, aren't you one for anticipating my needs," she said, a hint of sarcasm in her voice.

"Too much?" he asked, sitting back in his seat. He loved it when she had a hint of sass, and his lips twitched.

"I could tell you it's a bit obvious. Or perhaps heavy-handed. But it smells heavenly." She poured from the pot into her cup and the refreshing scent of mint filled the air. "So I should probably just say thank you."

He leaned forward, determined to be honest, at least in the moment. "No, thank you. For coming on this trip. For being so open-minded and for not pushing back when I said I wanted to be a part of our baby's life."

"You're the father," she said simply.

"Yes, but I know you didn't have to tell me, and considered not doing so. I arrived and took that decision out of your hands, and I'm not sorry. But I know it's been difficult and I appreciate you meeting me in the middle."

More than that. He wanted to treat her well because seeing her walk through those grand houses had made him see that he wanted to be able to convince her to be closer. He didn't want to have to fly every few months to see his kid. He couldn't run his business from Back-End-of-Nowhere, Nova Scotia, either. Dictating his desires would accomplish nothing; the right way was to make her want this for herself. His wonderful home in Manhattan. Top schools and opportunities. Weekends away, and no financial stress. In exchange, he'd be there for his kid—the one thing in the world he wanted most. He would never be an absentee father like his own dad had been. His child would never have to wonder if he was loved or if his father even cared at all.

Seeing the ultrasound picture that now lay tucked in his wallet, remembering the steady flicker of the heartbeat on the monitor as they watched... That had changed everything. As had feeling him or her kick against his hand. It had turned an idea into something utterly tangible.

"Likewise," she responded, her gaze soft. "You've been so understanding. Way more than I gave you credit for. I should have told you from the beginning."

"It doesn't matter. It really doesn't. Let's just keep looking forward."

"Deal." She took a sip of tea, then looked out the window for a few moments before turning back to him. "And what about... well...us?"

It was a tough question. He couldn't lie and say he was in love with her. He wasn't. They got along well and enjoyed being together, didn't they? And there was attraction on both sides. There was certainly more warmth between them than had ever been between his parents, obviously, or his mom and stepdad. He wasn't sure he even believed in a burning passion that lasted forever. Hell, his brother was an aficionado of everlasting love and had believed in it so strongly he'd tried it...three times.

So he was as honest as he dared to be. "Tori, you're beautiful, and smart, and you make me laugh. You have this way of lifting one eyebrow that literally makes me hear you say 'Really, Jeremy?' in my mind. You light up when you talk about the baby. Your staff loves you and you love them... And that doesn't often happen with management. It wasn't an accident we connected last summer. And all the things I liked about you then I still like about you now."

She twisted her hands in her lap, as if his declaration made her uncomfortable. She gave an odd laugh and shrugged. "The things you liked about me then? I'm afraid I definitely don't look as good in a bikini as I did last summer."

He remembered, all right. She'd had a red one that seemed to be held together by strings, and then a black one that tied around her neck and made her breasts look—

He clenched his jaw. The image that flooded his brain now was of her in that same bikini, only with the gentle swell of their child curving her stomach. It was no less sexy in his mind.

"I'm not sure about that."

"Oh, I am. My boobs are bigger and wouldn't even fit in those cups—"

"I'm not seeing the problem here."

She stared at him, and then started to giggle. "Oh, I suppose not. But thanks for the laugh."

He wasn't exactly laughing. In fact, he had to shift in his seat to be a little more comfortable.

Gerry reappeared. "Sir, we're going to start our descent soon. In another five minutes or so, you'll need to fasten your seat belts."

"So soon?" Tori looked up with a smile. "Thank you. I think I'll freshen up before I have to get buckled in."

She rose from her seat and made her way to the bathroom. Jeremy ran his finger over his lower lip and tried to get the image of Tori in her bikini out of his mind, but he couldn't.

They'd shared a few relatively chaste kisses in the last week, but clearly the summer had been a lot more heated; the pregnancy was evidence enough of that. He had to admit to himself, at least, that he'd wondered about a sexual relationship with her again. They'd been incredibly compatible...

The more he thought about it, the more he realized that she was near perfect for him. Kind, funny, sexually compatible, she'd be a great mother. Smart and intuitive...there really wasn't anything he didn't like about her.

She checked all his boxes, and a few he hadn't realized he had.

When she returned from the bathroom, he smiled and waited for her to resume her seat and get buckled in. Then, as they approached, he pointed out landmarks through the window, half watching the view and half watching her.

That was it. He'd pull out all the stops. And make her see how perfect their life could be. Her, him and, most important of all, their baby.

CHAPTER EIGHT

TORI'S FIRST IMPRESSION of New York was of noise and traffic. She'd never seen anything like it, and on the drive from La Guardia to the Upper East Side, she'd basically kept her nose pressed against the window of the luxury car that had been waiting for them when they arrived. Not a stretch limo or anything, thank goodness, but a bona fide car service and driver. *Surreal* didn't even begin to cover what she'd already experienced today.

They were dropped off outside Jeremy's building. It didn't look like anything overly special from the outside, but inside was a different story. They took an elevator to his floor, and when he opened the door to his home, she nearly gasped.

What she did immediately was remove her leather boots and place them by the door. There was no way she would track on these floors.

The floor of the foyer gleamed like glass, and just beyond was a kitchen to the left. White cupboards, stainless state-of-the-art appliances, a slate-gray butcher block in the center and an enormous bouquet of fresh flowers made it look more like one of his real estate showings than a home. The concept was open, but a partial wall separated the working part of the kitchen—which looked as if it had never been used—from a dining room. A long table with upholstered chairs was the centerpiece of the space, with a long, silver runner down the middle and a bowl of more flowers sitting in its center. The table had seating for eight, and Tori could almost imagine a dinner party around such a table, with the clink of silverware and tinkle of crystal.

Yep. Definitely out of her league.

"Over here is the living room," Jeremy said from behind her, and she turned to see him holding out an arm. She followed close behind and was bathed in sunlight from the windows. "You can see the park from here," he offered, taking her hand and pulling her forward. She looked out the window... Indeed, there was lots of city around them, but also the huge expanse of Central Park, now covered with an inch of snow, looking cold but a little magical, too.

She was no Realtor but she knew that location was everything. And that he had paid a lot of money for this particular location. She'd looked up his address on the internet, looked at a street view. He was close to the Met, to Central Park, Broadway...

It was nearly overwhelming.

"What do you think?"

She turned to face him and found his face expectant. She glanced around at the impeccably decorated living room. To be honest, it was beautiful but it was missing something. It seriously felt like one of his listings, staged for a potential buyer, made to look wonderful without revealing the personality of the person who lived within.

There wasn't much of Jeremy here. But clearly he was proud of it, so she smiled. "It's gorgeous."

His answering grin made her glad she'd answered as she did. "Come on, let me show you the rest."

The rest included a powder room, plus two more full bathrooms—one main bathroom between two bedrooms and then a luxurious en suite bathroom off the master. The guest rooms were impeccable, of course, and the master bedroom housed a king-size bed with a black leather headboard and a thick silver duvet. The top was turned down to reveal the ends of the sheets beneath, and they were black silk. Chrome-and-black bedside tables held a docking station for electronics and a lamp, and he pulled the drapes aside to reveal another breathtaking view.

He looked at her and smiled again. Were they going to smile their way through the next week? "Whichever bedroom you'd like as yours is fine. The other bathroom is yours, as well."

At least he didn't assume they'd be sharing a room. Not that she'd expected that, but she'd gotten a little nervous on the plane after his bikini comment. As much as the idea of him still finding her attractive was exciting, she needed space and time to figure out if they truly could move forward as a couple. It felt like they kept taking steps that way, and then retreated into the safety of a relationship of utility and co-parenting.

Neither bedroom was overly welcoming. Beautiful, yes, but not...warm. That was it. The grayscale was trendy and definitely classy and elegant, but it was missing warmth.

"The one across the hall will be fine." She knew it had a queen-size bed and the bedding looked thicker and softer there. Like something she could curl up in.

"Great." He clapped his hands together. "I'll put your bag in your room so you can unpack. And then maybe we can go for a walk in the park."

A walk in the park was the perfect way to spend the afternoon. The air was crisp without being frigid, the sky a clear blue, and Jeremy reached down and held her hand as they wandered along. When she said she wanted a hot dog from a street vendor, he obliged, and they sat on a cold bench with cold noses, biting into hot dogs with sweet ketchup and sharp mustard. They wound their way around the paths and he showed her The Plaza, and she told him about one of her favorite children's book characters, Eloise. They had coffee in a little shop to warm their toes and fingers, and then when she looked longingly at the horse-drawn carriages, he obliged and they went on a carriage ride, which he said was eye-rollingly touristy but didn't complain when she got cold and leaned against him, prompting him to put his arm around her and cuddle her close.

The afternoon darkened and it was time to go home. It had been a marvelous first introduction to the Big Apple, and when Jeremy suggested she take a nap before dinner, she didn't put up any fight. She'd been up since five and the fresh air and walking had done its work.

After an hour he woke her and said that dinner was ready. He didn't let her in the kitchen, but seated her at the dining table, where he'd put two place settings at corners to each other, and lit a couple of candles. "Did you have a good nap?"

"The best. I woke up and forgot where I was."

He chuckled. "It's the fresh air. Plus you were up super early this morning."

"And I nap very easily these days," she admitted. "This growing-another-human thing takes some energy."

He disappeared into the kitchen and returned with a plate. "Which is why you need this. You've only had a hot dog and a latte since this morning."

The meal was simple. Chicken, asparagus and pasta were tossed in a white sauce, with a green salad on the side. But it was delicious and Tori ate up every bite on her plate.

"You're a decent cook. Where did you learn?"

"I can't take the credit. I eat out a lot and I have a housekeeper come in once a week. She also brings in a variety of meals and puts them in the fridge with instructions for reheating. I literally just had to put this in the oven, and voilà."

"Oh. Well, my compliments to the chef, whoever she may be." Jeremy was not the domestic type. It was more and more obvious as the day wore on. His apartment...condo...whatever barely looked lived in. There certainly weren't bits that jumped out as being "Jeremy." But he'd fed her and it had been scrumptious, so she patted her belly and said, "There. The baby's happy."

"Is he?" Jeremy's gaze met hers and held. "Is he happy?"

"Maybe it's a she."

"Of course. How about...are they happy?"

"I think so. At least it seems as if they're doing a jig in there."

His gaze deepened, and she thought she caught a glimpse of vulnerability. "May I feel?"

It was sweet of him to ask, lovely of him to want to. "Of course," she replied. She pushed her chair out a little, and so did he, and then slid to the edge of his seat so they bumped knees. He put his hand on her belly, his palm wide and warm. But the ripple of feeling was in a different spot, so she put her hand on his wrist and guided him to the left a little. Whether it was arms or legs or somersaults, it didn't take long and the movement thudded against his hand, little taps and rolls.

"Wow," he breathed, staring at his hand, then up at her. "I can't get over that. How does it feel, you know, on the inside?"

She knew he meant the actual sensation rather than her response, but all she could say was, "Wonderful."

He didn't move his hand. But he leaned forward and pressed his forehead to hers. Not kissing, just...connecting. Tears stung her eyes. Maybe this was what had drawn her to him in the first place. Connection. She'd had friends, coworkers. Her mom. But not this kind of connection with another human. Not for a very long time, because she'd always backed away, not trusting that she wouldn't be hurt or duped in the end, as she had been before.

And she'd never had a connection of this depth, because this time they shared a child. His DNA and hers had come together to create a whole other person. It was a huge and sobering thought.

"Jeremy," she whispered. Her throat swelled with unshed tears.

He leaned back and took his hand from her belly and rested it on her cheek. "I don't understand," he whispered back. "You already love this baby so much, and it isn't even born yet. And I don't—" His voice broke off, and he cleared his throat. "Damn,

I'm not a little kid. I don't know why this gets to me. I just don't ever remember feeling this much warmth in my home."

Her heart broke a little. "Were there never any fun times? Laughter?"

He shrugged. "I suppose there must have been, but I don't really remember them much. Mom and Dad divorced before I really formed any solid memories. When we were little Mom and Bruce took us to Disney once. And we went to summer camps and that was fun. But I can't remember a single other family vacation that we took together. Mom and Bruce would take off for a weekend in the city, see a show, dinner, hotel. They definitely traveled while we were in school. But never with us."

It was impossible to fathom. "But who cared for you?"

His hand slipped away. "We had staff."

"Shut up! Are you serious?"

She looked so disgusted a smile turned up the corners of his mouth. "It wasn't so bad. Some of the nannies were okay, and I really got along with the gardener who came twice a week."

He had to have been so lonely...and felt so unloved. Her heart ached for the kind of boy he must have been. "That's horrible. And I'm amazed you turned out to be a decent human being, which I know you are, because you've been nothing but kind and understanding throughout this whole thing."

"If I am, it's only because of Merrick. I met my best friends there. Teachers who, for the most part, cared enough to turn us from spoiled, scared brats into actual humans. Not that it always worked, mind you." He chuckled softly. "As a group we were a rich, entitled bunch."

"Materially, maybe."

"I can't complain, Tori. I have had advantages that most people only dream of."

She was glad he realized it, but deep down she knew all the money in the world couldn't buy real affection and love. She thought of all the summers she'd gone camping with her parents to any of the provincial parks. They'd always allowed her to take a friend. There'd been swimming and playgrounds and campfires with roasted marshmallows that scalded the roof of her mouth. Christmases watching movies and drinking hot chocolate. They hadn't had a lot of money but they'd gone on a walk every Thanksgiving Day since she was a little girl, enjoying the fall weather and colors. There had been story time at night before bed, and when she was sick, her dad carrying her to her room and tucking her into bed. There hadn't always been a lot of money, but she wouldn't trade a single moment of it.

Jeremy didn't know anything about any of those things. Not through any fault of his own, but she wondered how he was going to handle a different kind of parenthood.

It worried her, but she wasn't about to deny him the opportunity to try.

She squeezed his fingers in hers. "It's gonna be okay. I'll help you. I had a great dad." Grief at his loss welled up, but gratitude, too, that he'd been a wonderful father. "I'll share him with you, tell you all about him and the stuff he used to do with me. You don't have to wait for the baby to be born to be a good father, Jeremy. You're doing it already."

His gaze snapped up to hers. "How come you are so great? Why aren't you scared? Freaking out about what's to come?"

"You think I'm not scared? Of course I am. But deep down I believe everything is going to be okay. It has to be."

Faith. It seemed she had some after all.

He squeezed her fingers back. "Okay. I'm going to trust you. At least for now." Clearing his throat, he gave her fingers a final squeeze and then sat up straight. "What do you say we clean up these dishes and then watch a movie or something?"

"That sounds amazing."

The sky was dark but lit by the millions of city lights. After they loaded the dishwasher, Jeremy put down the blinds over the windows while Tori sank into the couch. It wasn't just for looks; the cushions were super comfortable and Jeremy came back with a soft throw blanket from a closet somewhere. "Okay, so regular movie or Christmas movie?"

She was in Manhattan in December. "Christmas, and *Miracle on 34th Street*."

He laughed. "When in Rome... So, original or remake?" He handed her the blanket and reached for his phone. She shook her head. He could control everything from that thing.

"I know I should say the original...but the remake. Because Richard Attenborough *is* Santa Claus."

"Yes, but Natalie Wood..."

"I know. So my pick tonight, yours tomorrow?"

"Sounds fair."

He scrolled through a streaming app until he found the movie, and then it was on, complete with Thanksgiving Day parade, a drunk parade Santa and Mara Wilson looking adorable. Halfway through he disappeared to make her a cup of tea—apparently said housekeeper had stocked up on a few things before their arrival—and after sipping at the comforting brew, Tori found herself blinking slowly.

She shouldn't be tired. She'd had a wonderful nap before dinner.

Jeremy shifted on the sofa. "Here. Lean against me. You'll be more comfortable and have some support for your neck."

He lifted his arm and she curled in against his side, the soft blanket covering her from waist to toes. He was so warm and stable, and her belly rested against his hip as if it were perfectly suited for the angle. And oh, he smelled good. Like clean clothes and the expensive cologne he always wore. She closed her eyes and inhaled.

On the screen, Dylan McDermott was proposing to Elizabeth Perkins, a huge ring in a red box. Tori opened her eyes and sighed.

"What?"

"I never understand why she's so mean to Bryan in this moment."

"Well, she's afraid."

"I know that. But it makes her stupid."

Jeremy chuckled, low in his chest. "Then there's the fact that there's still a lot of movie to get through and the happy ending. Why would people keep watching if she said yes?"

She looked up at him. "To see if Kris Kringle is real, of course."

He shook his head. "Uh-uh. You know as well as I do that the love story is the main attraction here. And the question of whether or not Susan gets her house and a dad and a baby brother for Christmas."

"I hate it when you're right," she mumbled, but curled up against his shoulder again, where it was warm and inviting.

CHAPTER NINE

JEREMY WATCHED THE end credits roll and leaned his head back against the sofa. He could shut off the TV right now but he didn't want to disturb Tori, who had finally drifted off just before the courtroom verdict in the movie. She'd missed the happy ending, the perfect house and family and a new brother on the way. Emotion clogged his throat for a moment as he turned his head an inch and looked down at her, lashes against her cheeks, warm belly pressed against his hip.

She would be so easy to love, if he were capable of it.

As it was, he definitely had feelings for her. She was the purest person he'd ever known. Always seemed to find a bright side, a positive angle. Cared about people.

Cared about him.

At least she made him believe she did. And she was snuggled up to him right now, trusting.

He felt pretty damned unworthy of that.

The credits ended and the app went to a home screen with "suggested for you" thumbnails of other holiday movies. It wasn't late, but it was late enough, and clearly she was exhausted. She'd been working long hours for days, and carrying the baby, too.

As carefully as he could, he shifted his hips so that her head was cradled in his elbow, then turned so that he was off the sofa, leaning over her. With as much gentleness as he could muster, he slipped an arm beneath her legs and the other beneath her shoulders, keeping her head snug against him. He lifted her in his arms and adjusted her weight as her lashes fluttered.

"Jeremy?"

"Shh... You fell asleep. I'm taking you to bed."

He got halfway down the hall before she actually lifted her head. "You really are carrying me. You're going to give yourself a hernia."

He couldn't stop the burst of laughter that started in his chest. Lord, but she made him laugh sometimes at the most unexpected moments.

"I'm pretty sure I can handle it," he replied.

He nudged open the door to her room and laid her down on the bed, but she was awake now and scooted up so that she was sitting. "That was very sweet of you."

"I was hoping I wouldn't wake you. You looked so peaceful."

"I was comfortable." She smiled, the edges of it soft from sleep. "You're kind of warm and cozy."

Jeremy went to the bed and sat on the edge. "Honestly? I don't think I've ever been called that before."

"Well, you are. And I need to be awake anyway, because I need to pee and brush my teeth." She put her hand on his forearm. "It was a really nice night. A nice day, when all is said and done. Thank you."

He reached over to pat her hand and ended up taking her fingers in his instead, twining them together, linking them in a way that frightened him just a bit. Still, this was what he'd suggested, wasn't it? Acknowledgment of their attraction for each other? Desire? Affection? His thumb rubbed over the top of her hand, and he met her gaze, saying nothing. The air between them grew heavy with words unspoken, possibilities unrealized.

"You're going to kiss me, aren't you?" she murmured, but

instead of looking away, as she had a tendency to do, she held his gaze.

"Only if you want me to."

She said nothing for a few seconds that felt like an eternity, and he waited, trying to be patient. Wanting to leave this decision in her hands.

"You want me to say it." She bit down on her lip, another thing he realized she did when she was nervous.

"Yeah," he replied, his voice rough. "I do."

Another long moment, and then she said it, her voice barely above a whisper. "Kiss me, Jeremy. Please."

She didn't have to ask twice, or even add the sweet-sounding "please" to the end. "Kiss me" was enough. He squeezed her fingers tighter and leaned forward. "No mistletoe in here," he murmured, only an inch away from her lips.

"We don't need it," she answered, and he closed the remaining distance between them.

Nothing in the world could be as soft as her lips. They opened beneath his, sweet and willing, and an expansive feeling rushed through him as he drank her in. He inched closer, close enough that if he moved his arm at all it would be around her and pulling her close, but tonight she was in charge. She set the pace. He'd kissed her twice already. Tonight he wanted—needed—to know that she wanted him as much as he wanted her.

As the kiss deepened, she leaned forward, moving to get closer to him, and before they lost their balance he put out his left hand and braced it on the bed. Tori curled her hand up around his neck and exerted a little pressure, pulling him closer to her, then shifting so that she was slowly inching downward with him leaning over her from above. Desire surged; last summer hadn't been a fluke, and she still had the power to make him weak and strong at the same time. Their chemistry couldn't be ignored as she made a little sound in the back of her throat. He slid his mouth off hers and pressed his lips to the sensitive spot on her neck where her pulse drummed.

"Oh," she breathed, arching her neck. "Jeremy... That feels so nice."

"Damn right," he growled, fighting to keep his hands gentle.

"Jeremy, I—" Another sigh stopped her midsentence, but she picked up again, undaunted. "Can we just kiss tonight?"

She had to know what she was asking. He wanted to touch her everywhere. Feel her warm, smooth skin against his. But he'd promised himself that she could take the lead and so he dutifully answered, "Of course."

"You're a good kisser."

"Mmm... Likewise."

"You've got SKL. Do you know what that is?"

"Uh-uh." He licked at her earlobe and goose bumps erupted on her shoulders as he slid his fingers along the skin revealed by the slouchy sweater's neckline. It had a V-neck, and with it pulled a bit sideways, a generous slice of cleavage and the swell of her full breast were visible before the rest was concealed by her bra.

"Seriously kissable lips. Not too full, not too thin, really nice and soft. With that little dip in the middle, right here." She slid her hand from his hair down his jaw, then dotted the dip in his upper lip with a fingertip.

"Tori?"

"Yeah?"

"You talk too much."

And then he went to work shutting her up. Because if she wanted to be kissed—and that was all she wanted—he'd give her what she asked for. And he'd do it right.

Tori rolled over in bed the next morning and stared at the ceiling. The events of last night were crammed in her brain, one on top of the other, until everything was clouded with Jeremy.

She'd intended to be cautious. Said she only wanted kissing. But she'd been mistaken if she'd thought kissing him gave her any sort of protection. Instead, Jeremy Fisher and his clever mouth had sneaked past all her defenses.

It was a good thing that he had no idea how close she'd been to inviting him to stay in her bed. Just when she'd reached the point where she was ready to ask for more, he'd pulled back, kissed the tip of her nose, and wished her good-night.

She supposed she had to add honorable to his list of qualities, too. Instead of being comforted, the thought set her on edge. It couldn't be this simple. There was something about him that had to be flawed, something that was going to go wrong. She wished she had some idea what it was so she could prepare herself for it. She definitely didn't want to be blindsided again.

She got up and went to the bathroom for a refreshing shower, then dressed in tights and a swing-type dress from her "before pregnant" wardrobe that accommodated her growing tummy nicely, at least at this stage. The neckline looked a bit bare, so she found an infinity scarf and wound it around her neck, then put her hair up in a messy bun. She looked in the mirror with a critical eye. Back home this would be dressing up. But here... It was a different atmosphere. Different expectations, too.

Jeremy was in the kitchen, pouring cereal into a bowl. "Good morning. There's decaf if you want it."

Her outfit would be completed with her black boots, but inside she was in her stockinged feet and felt a little vulnerable. She tried a smile, wondering how he could act so normal while inside she was still stuck on last night's kisses and him carrying her to the bedroom.

"I'd like that."

"I'll get it. Help yourself to what you want for breakfast. There's bread for toast, or cereal, and fresh eggs. Or smoothies. I keep stuff on hand for shakes. It's what I normally eat, though today I felt like cereal."

He was quite the conversationalist in the morning, she thought, accepting the mug of coffee he handed over, fixed the way she liked—how had he remembered that?

"You look nice today," he added, touching her arm on his way past her with his cereal bowl. Instead of eating at the dining room table, he perched on a bar stool at a high counter. It was far more comfortable than the huge table and formal setting.

She stuck her head in the refrigerator so he wouldn't see her blush. "Thanks. And there are berries! Excellent."

She turned around and saw Jeremy's eyes flit up to her face. He'd been staring at her backside as she looked in the fridge.

"Sorry," he said, without sounding too sorry at all. "I got distracted by your butt."

Her lips twitched. "You really don't beat around the bush, do you?"

"I try not to."

"Well, then, stop looking at my butt and tell me what's on the agenda today."

She sat next to him on a high stool and arranged berries and melon on a plate. Took a sip of coffee and put the mug down, tried to pretend this was as normal as could be.

"Well, I thought you might like to do some shopping."

"You don't have to buy me things, you know. I have clothes."

"Sure, but how often do you get to shop on Fifth Avenue? Come on, surely there are stores you'd like to go into. Besides, you actually need a few things. Like a coat. Your regular winter one is getting snug already. You're not going to make it through to March or April and still be able to zip it up."

He was right about the coat; she'd already realized it. "Well, I can get one back home."

"And you can get one here. Let me spoil you a little. Besides, I need a new tie."

"Sure you do."

He wiggled his eyebrows. "So, I probably don't. But I can't in all conscience bring you here for a week and not take you shopping. We can walk. And this afternoon I have a surprise for you."

She paused, a piece of honeydew on her fork. "What kind of a surprise?"

"Nope. Not going to get it out of me that easily."

"I don't know, Jeremy. This makes me uncomfortable. I can't ever possibly pay you back."

He frowned. "Why would I want you to do that? Look, Tori. I have more money than I know what to do with, frankly, and rarely have anyone to spend it on. This is a treat for me to do this for you, okay? A gift, nothing more."

"Well, I can't reciprocate, either."

"I don't need you to. Buying you a few clothes, taking you to see a few new things… If I promise not to shower you with jewels, are we okay?"

What could she say? He was right. A day's shopping was a drop in the bucket to him, so why should it bother her so much?

Because it made her feel as if she owed him something.

And she couldn't say that to him without insulting him. Especially when he'd been so very nice to her already. Never pushing. Not once had he given her any indication he had a hidden agenda or was trying to manipulate her or the situation. She was the one coming up with that scenario, purely out of fear.

Maybe it was as her mom said. Sometimes you had to have a little faith.

By the time early afternoon arrived, Tori was laden with bags, most of which contained what she'd been wearing that morning. Her boots were in a boot box and new ones cradled her feet and calves; she wore the same swing dress and tights of the morning but the scarf was replaced with a new checked one of wool and silk. Instead of her everyday jacket, which was now tucked in another box in a huge bag, she wore a cashmere cape and gloves that Jeremy had insisted he buy her. Add in the sunglasses and she was pretty sure today's ensemble came to more than she'd spent on the down payment for her house.

She felt both glamorous and a fraud, beautiful and a bit not-quite-herself, but today's shopping had been an experience. Brands she'd only ever seen online or in magazines were now on her body.

Jeremy had also insisted she buy some maternity clothes, so he'd taken her into Saks, where he'd slapped down his credit card for two pairs of pants, three tops and two dresses—one that she could wear for any occasion, and the other a cocktail dress. When she protested that one, he'd insisted that sometime over Christmas she might like to dress up. She'd countered by saying she'd be overdressed in something so expensive, and then he'd raised an eyebrow at her and she'd given up. Maybe she would have fought harder if she didn't absolutely love the navy dress, but from the moment she'd put it on, it had been perfect. Then it was off to buy shoes. She'd reached her limit when he came around a corner with a plump, plush penguin in his hand. "And something for the baby, too," he'd said, flashing her a smile.

He carried most of the bags while she held the ones containing the penguin and the dresses. They'd started walking back toward the park—at least that was what she thought if her sense of direction was right—when he stopped and lifted his chin at something over his shoulder.

She turned around and looked. It was the same spot they'd been the day before, just steps away from The Plaza.

"Tea?"

Her mouth dropped open. "Are you serious?"

He nodded. "I got us in for three o'clock, and since we didn't stop for lunch, you must be famished. Today you can be Eloise and have high tea at The Plaza."

"Jeremy."

He laughed at her tone of voice. "Yes?"

"I do not know how you pulled this off. Do people really live like this? I don't believe it."

His eyes shone at her. "Every day? No. Once in a while? Everyone should. Just once in their lifetime, I think."

"I'm afraid I'll get something on me. Seriously." She knew

the cape had cost far too much. Right now wasn't life, it was pretending. But she couldn't help it. She'd pretend for a little while longer, because it was amazing.

"Come on. It's ten to three, and we'll get there just in time. You can even freshen up a bit before we're seated."

When they walked in the door, her head nearly swiveled all the way around. The lobby was stunning in and of itself, but when Jeremy led her to The Palm Court, she had to catch her breath.

Light. And elegance. And green palms and the most amazing ceiling...the iconic stained glass dome. She couldn't believe she was here.

"Tori? Tori." Jeremy was at her side, touching her elbow. "It's going to be a few minutes. Come on, we can leave our bags with the concierge and pick them up when we're done. I'll show you where the powder room is."

She tore herself away from the sight and followed him, her boots clicking on the floor. In the powder room she tidied her hair and refreshed her lipstick. There were roses in her cheeks; partly from the fresh, cold air and partly because of excitement, she was sure. She found Jeremy again and he solicitously took her cape, draping it over his arm for the time being.

When they were led to their table, she looked around at all the other people having tea. Some were dressed more casually than she. Others were dressed impeccably from head to toe, without a hair out of place. At her seat, she placed a hand on her tummy as she sat, tucking the skirt of her dress beneath her.

"So. Surprised?"

"Very," she responded, unable to stop staring. "Oh, look at this place. And how did you ever get a table on such short notice? I've always heard that it takes weeks or months to get in for tea."

"I pulled some strings," he admitted. "While you were asleep yesterday."

Of course he had.

"Look at the menu," he suggested. "I'll say everything's good, but you should make your selections based on what you like. Especially if there's something the baby doesn't like, or you can't eat while you're pregnant."

She lifted her gaze to his. "Has someone been doing some reading?"

"Maybe. When I sent the grocery list to my housekeeper—Melissa, by the way—I wanted to get some things you like and...well, healthy things."

She pointed to the list of sweets on the tea menu. "These are not healthy, and I am going to enjoy several."

He laughed. "Good."

He ordered a plain black tea for himself, while Tori went for a more aromatic Earl Grey. All around them was the clink of silverware on china, the hum of conversations. Tea arrived, and their tray of delights—finger sandwiches of cucumber, salmon, and turkey, perfect scones with Devonshire cream and lemon curd, and a selection of pastries and sweets that nearly made her teeth ache just looking at them. The entire hour, eating and chatting and people watching, was a dream come true. No matter what happened in their future, she'd always have this day to remember.

She'd told him once she wasn't Cinderella, but she was surely feeling like it now. She was in the hotel business, was assistant manager to an upscale resort, but the Sandpiper and all its wonderful amenities paled in comparison to this.

It was like a mansion being compared to a palace.

"Have the last scone," Jeremy suggested. "I can tell you love the cream with the preserves."

They were a bit of heaven for sure. She didn't argue, didn't protest, just reached for the light-as-air scone and smeared it with strawberry, then topped it with cream and popped it in her mouth.

"I love watching you eat," he said, a smile lighting his face.

She nearly choked on a crumb. "Er...what?"

"I just mean you like food. You don't pretend not to."

Oh, goodness. He was probably used to stick women who starved themselves or something. Or perhaps her manners were lacking. How mortifying.

"Don't worry, it's a compliment. You're real, Tori. It's one of the things I like about you."

"Are you sure? Because I'm pretty confident I have scone crumbs on my dress now and sadly when we get home and I take these boots off my ankles are probably going to swell from all the walking and stuff we did today."

"Real," he repeated. "Flesh and blood. No pretending to be someone you're not, no putting on airs to try to impress me. You are who you are and you're comfortable with it. That kind of confidence is rare."

She didn't know what to say. She was very aware that she'd gained a few pounds with the baby and some of it was due to potato chips. And until now, she hadn't really cared. She understood he was paying her a compliment. But she hadn't considered confidence before. "I mean, I guess I just am who I am. I'm not sure I can change for anyone, or be a chameleon."

"I would hope not." He leaned forward. "Because you're normal, you see? And when I'm with you, I feel normal, too."

"Are you lonely, Jeremy?"

"Sometimes. I have my friends and all, and my sister and I are semi close, but it's not the same as being…"

This time his voice drifted off, and he looked away for a moment.

"Intimate with someone?"

His gaze came back to hers. "Yeah. And not just physically, though that's not a problem with you either, it seems."

The baby must have enjoyed the tea as well, because it was moving around fairly consistently. She absently rubbed a hand over the curve, mindlessly soothing. But Jeremy noticed, and his face softened.

"I want us to be a family somehow. You should know that."

Nerves quivered in her stomach. "We will be. No matter what we decide to do. Because we're going to raise this baby together. Okay?"

He nodded.

When their tea was cleared away, he helped her put her cape back on, tenderly buttoning the top button. She picked up her new wristlet containing her phone and cards, and as Jeremy placed his hand along the small of her back, she caught a glimpse of a woman, probably in her fifties, watching them with a soft smile on her face. Tori smiled back shyly and as they passed the woman's table, she said, "Congratulations."

"Oh! Thank you," she answered, pressing her hand on her belly as a reflex.

Right now she felt as if they *were* a family. But the day was pretend. Wasn't it?

CHAPTER TEN

THE WEEK TURNED into a whirlwind, and Jeremy tried to hit every iconic New York experience he could think of.

One evening he took her to the Christmas Spectacular with the Rockettes at Radio City Music Hall, and they watched them kick their way through a dance routine that would have had him winded in about thirty seconds. Tori's eyes had shone as she focused on the stage, her smile bright as she turned to him time and again throughout the show.

Then there were the frenetic lights and sounds of Times Square, filled with tourists. It wasn't his favorite spot, but she'd wanted to see where the ball would drop on New Year's Eve. He showed her, and vowed to himself that one day he'd bring her here on December 31 so she could see it for real.

Of course, no trip to Times Square could be enjoyed without a piece of cheesecake from Junior's, and he bought her pineapple because he thought it was the best. He hadn't been wrong, it seemed, because she'd savored every bite, laughingly proclaiming that it was for the baby.

There'd been pizza one night, sitting on the carpet and finally watching the original *Miracle on 34th Street*, and slow but sweet kisses stolen here and there. A trip up the Empire State

Building, where she'd held his hand as she looked out over the city, and a more sobering visit to the 9/11 Memorial.

Alas, he couldn't avoid work altogether, and he'd been sneaking the odd hour here and there to look after things that couldn't wait. He had to go into his office, though, so he left her the keys and told her to have a relaxing day, wherever that might take her. She'd made noises about wanting to visit the park again, or maybe go to the Met. Both were practically on his doorstep, so he left with no worries about how she'd spend the day.

At one o'clock, he realized he hadn't eaten lunch, so he decided to pop down to the bottom floor and the restaurant onsite. Before he could get out of the office door, however, two familiar faces came toward him down the hall.

"The two of you here together? Something big must be up."

Cole Abbott flashed a grin. "Well, Bran said he was coming to see you, and I was going to be in the city, so I thought I'd tag along."

They exchanged backslapping hugs, then Jeremy turned back around toward his office. "It's good to see you two."

"Bran said you had some news. Wouldn't tell me what it is, though."

Cole scowled at his companion. Bran was smiling, but it didn't quite reach his eyes, and his cheeks still looked hollow from grief. Jeremy knew exactly what had brought Cole to the city. Worry for their friend.

"Bran's bought a house in Nova Scotia. Did he tell you that?"

"Yes, so I know that's not the news. What's up?"

Jeremy took a moment to look out his office window. He had a great view of the Hudson. He had just about everything a man could want.

He faced the men again and let out a breath. "Well, I'm going to be a father."

Branson stared at Cole, who sat heavily in a chair in front of Jeremy's desk. He let out a curse word and ran his hand over his face. "For real?"

Jeremy laughed. "Yeah. Needless to say, it was a surprise for me, too."

"Who is she? When? How did it happen?"

"Tori, last summer, and the usual way."

Branson laughed, the sound rusty. "Oh, man. Your face, Cole. This is why I didn't tell you."

Jeremy chuckled. "It's not the end of the world, dude."

"Are you sure?"

"We're all nearly thirty-six years old. It was bound to happen to one of us eventually."

Silence fell. Jeremy suddenly wished he could cut out his tongue. It had happened—to Bran. And then it had been ripped away. All his happiness.

"Oh, Bran, I'm sorry. That was thoughtless."

Bran waved a hand. "Forget it."

"I can't. I'm so, so—"

Bran looked him dead in the eye. "It's okay, Jeremy. Really. I can't pretend it didn't happen, and you guys can't tap-dance around it for the rest of your lives. So shut up and tell us what's happening. Because last I heard you were in Canada finding out the news and freaking out a bit."

Jeremy perched on the edge of the desk as the tension in the room dissipated a bit. "Well, she's here, actually. I brought her here for a week so we could talk about what we want to do."

"Are you guys a thing?"

"I don't know. Yes? But no. I mean, we haven't slept together."

"Clearly you did…"

"I mean since I found out." He aimed a "smart aleck" look at Cole. "But I like her, a lot. And she likes me. And we've kissed…"

Bran nudged Cole. "This is nearly as bad as when we were freshmen and he was telling us about the girl he'd left behind… What was her name? Jill? Jane? Though I think he said he'd felt her up once."

"Again, shut up. I don't know why we're still friends." But

a smile curved up his cheek. This was exactly why they were friends, and had been for over twenty years.

"So what, you brought her here? Is she going to move here to be with you? So you can bring the baby up together?"

"We haven't really talked about it."

"But that's what you want, right?" Bran always got to the heart of the matter.

"Yeah." He let out a breath. "I just can't see us living in two different countries and trying to parent. I'm kind of hoping that she'll like it here enough to consider moving."

"Wow." Cole sat back in the chair. "So then what? Marriage? Are you thinking of staying in your place, or buying elsewhere? Your place isn't really one where I can picture kids running around."

Jeremy frowned. "I can always redecorate. And there's room. Plus it's close to everything."

"I don't know, man. It's a lot to ask of a woman. To pack up and leave everything behind." This from Bran.

Cole scoffed. "Yeah, leave behind what? Jeremy's loaded. She's landed herself in clover."

Jeremy pushed away from the desk. "It's not like that. She doesn't care about money. And don't roll your eyes," he said in response to Cole's facial expression. "It's true. If anyone has any ulterior motives here, it's me." He sighed. "Mom and Bruce are having a party in a few days. I'm going to take her. If we do this, she's got to have her eyes wide open." He nodded at Bran. "That was your advice, and I think you're right."

"You're springing the Wicked Witch of the West on her?"

Again, Jeremy couldn't help but laugh at Cole. "Yeah, I am. But Sarah's going, too." He was thrilled his sister had agreed. He hadn't told her about Tori either, but she'd be an ally.

"Damn, brother."

"I know."

There was quiet for a moment, and then Cole said, with a bit of wonder in his voice, "You're gonna be a dad."

"Seems like it."

He got up and clapped Jeremy on the back. "Congratulations, man. You're gonna nail this."

Nope, he wasn't going to cry over this unexpected gesture. Cole was not the touchy-feely type. So he chuckled instead. "You think? Because I had a crappy example."

"Didn't we all? So just do the exact opposite of what your mom and stepdad did and you'll be great."

Bran stood up. "And if the city thing doesn't work out, maybe we'll be neighbors, Jeremy."

Cole looked at them both.

"His new house is less than an hour away from Tori," Jeremy confirmed. "Have you seen it?" He went to his computer and brought the pics up on the monitor. "Look at that. Lighthouse and everything."

Cole tapped his lips. "How much?"

"Just under three."

"You're joking."

"Nope. You looking for an investment property?"

"I might. I've been floating a few ideas around for something. We can talk in the new year."

"Sure."

Bran coughed. "I don't know about you ladies, but I came for lunch. Let's go get a steak somewhere."

"Okay, but I can't be late getting home. I left Tori on her own today."

Bran laughed and clapped him on the shoulder. "And so it begins, bro. And so it begins."

Jeremy took the teasing with a smile. Yeah, they were right and they were ribbing him about it. But it occurred to him that he really didn't mind at all.

Tori had spent the day walking in the park, having a sandwich in a small shop somewhere and then window-shopping. She'd found this little store in Midtown that had an appealing array of housewares in the window, and inside was even better. Now, as she waited for Jeremy to come home, she looked at the items she'd bought and fought against nerves. What if he didn't like the changes? What if he resented her stepping in and doing anything to his space?

She had receipts. She could take it all back.

The kitchen smelled good, too. She'd stopped at a market and bought the groceries required to make her curried chicken and broccoli casserole. She'd made a salad, too.

The casserole was almost ready and she was watching another holiday movie on TV when Jeremy came through the door. "Wow, something smells great in here," he said from the foyer.

Score one. She got up from the sofa and went to the foyer to greet him as he hung up his coat.

"Hi. I made dinner. Not that Melissa isn't a great cook, but I like to cook and since I was at loose ends today..."

"No explanation required. I'm glad you got out today."

"I did! I had fun."

He stepped into the main living area and stopped short. "What the—? You decorated."

"Only a little." She folded her hands in front of her. "You didn't have anything up for Christmas, and it felt a little... monochrome in here."

He unbuttoned his suit jacket and loosened his tie, staying quiet long enough that her nerves bubbled up again. "I think that was the decorator's objective," he said. "To let the space speak for itself."

"Oh." His lukewarm response let all the air out of her joy balloon. She'd wanted it to be a lovely surprise. To see his face light up. Now she was just let down.

He pulled off his tie and stuffed it into his pants pocket while she stood there, unsure of what to do next. She rather liked the little three-foot tree she'd bought, decorated with white lights and red and silver bows. The poinsettia centerpiece she'd had delivered from the florist graced the center of the dining table.

The air smelled of pine boughs and cones from the candle arrangement on the glass coffee table. A small gift bag sat on the table, too, and her eyes stung. He didn't like it.

She wouldn't be so obvious as to move his present right away. She'd wait until he moved somewhere else and sneak it away to her room, or perhaps in the drawer of the table. She could return it tomorrow. Return everything.

"I have receipts," she whispered.

"What?"

"Receipts. To take everything back. I know it was presumptuous of me. This is your home. I just thought...it could use some Christmas spirit in here."

He looked at her strangely, then turned his back and went to the kitchen. She rushed over to the table, grabbed the gift bag and tucked it into the drawer where he kept his remotes and magazines.

"There's a rooster in my kitchen!"

Tori froze. Oh, God, was he angry? She pressed her hand to her chest and pursed her lips, letting out a slow breath. Up until now, he'd been so easygoing. It was one of the things she liked about him. But his living space... It didn't fit with the Jeremy she had spent time with so far. It was colorless and without humor. Without life. She puckered her eyebrows. That made no sense. How could decor have a sense of humor? But it was how she felt just the same. He was larger than life. His apartment was...prescriptive.

She went into the kitchen and prepared herself for, at the very least, an annoyed Jeremy.

He was staring at the ceramic rooster she'd bought, sitting in the middle of the counter. She suddenly felt a wave of irritation sweep over her. All she'd done was add a few holiday decorations and buy a stupid knickknack. He didn't have to be so...cold. It wasn't like him, or at least the Jeremy she knew.

Maybe the problem was she didn't know him at all.

"Your place is boring, Jeremy. You needed a conversation piece, and I got you one." She put her hands on her hips.

His head swiveled and he stared at her for a long moment, and then the most surprising thing happened. He started laughing. A low chuckle, almost despite himself, and her lips twitched. Then harder, and she tried really hard not to laugh back. But when he let loose and bent over, laughing himself silly, she couldn't help it. She started laughing, too, until they were both breathless.

"A…a…conversation piece," he choked out, still laughing. "A rooster. Oh, my God."

Oh, goodness. He was too adorable right now. And not mad. She didn't know what he was feeling, not really, but he wasn't mad at her, and her relief was great.

The oven timer dinged and she took a deep breath. "I have to stop laughing so I can take that out of the oven."

"What is it?"

She looked at the rooster, looked at Jeremy and said, deadpan, "Chicken."

That set them off again.

It wasn't that funny. Maybe the stress of the last few weeks was getting to them.

She got the casserole out of the oven and put it on the stove to cool. Jeremy had finally stopped laughing and leaned over her shoulder to look at the dish. "Hmm. Not familiar. But it smells good."

"It is good. You wait and see." She slid off the oven mitts and turned around. He was close to her, so close her heart started a pitter-patter that she both loved and hated. "Do you really hate the decorations?" She wanted the truth now that the awkwardness had passed.

He shook his head, his gaze sobering. "No, I don't. I just wasn't prepared."

"For what? Christmas?"

"For it to look like home."

The pitter-patter turned to solid thumping. "Why? Why shouldn't your home look like a home?"

"I don't know. And this... Look, Tori. I'm just overwhelmed. I came home to you today. To an apartment with holiday decorations and a woman pregnant with my child and a home-cooked meal. I have no idea what to do with that."

How cold had his life been?

"You must have had Christmas trees."

"Not like this. Not...for me. You did this for me, didn't you?"

She nodded slightly.

Ignoring the hot casserole dish behind her, he put his hands on the edge of the cold stove and leaned in to kiss her. Really kiss her, with not only skill but with enough emotion that she turned to mush. Could they make this work? He hadn't responded because he was overwhelmed. Because he'd been floored by the idea that someone had done that for him... Her heart broke a little for the lonely boy he must have been. And now he was kissing her as if she'd given him the moon. She'd spent no more than he'd spent on tea yesterday, but she felt as if she'd given him the world.

It would be so easy to fall in love with this Jeremy. Not just the man who'd been a fantastic lover in the summer sun, or the guy who'd treated her like a princess yesterday, but this man, who let her glimpse his heart. Who could be absolutely tender with her when she needed it most.

His body fit so perfectly against hers, even with the baby between them. Over the last week she'd seen a difference in her bump, and the recent snug waistlines had given way to full-on showing. With Jeremy kissing her like she was something precious, and his baby growing within her, she felt both incredibly feminine and extraordinarily powerful in such a beautiful, natural way.

He'd given that to her. And it was worth more than some artificial tree with a few lights and bows.

And when he broke the kiss and hugged her, she felt herself slipping further under his spell.

"Thank you. I'm sorry I didn't say it before. I love that you thought of me and wanted to do this for me. I don't think I've ever really had that before."

"Then I'm glad I did it because everyone deserves to feel seen and important," she answered, holding on to his shoulders. She slid her fingers into his hair. "You're a lot of things, Jeremy, but you're also a man, and you're human."

He kissed her again, long and slow, and she gave herself over to the emotion of the moment. He'd asked her here so they could see where they were in their relationship. What if this could work somehow? What if there really was a happy ending? She tried not to worry about logistics. Those weren't really what concerned her at this point. It was Jeremy, and whether they could parent together, if they could be together. A couple *and* a family.

Right now, all the signs pointed to yes, because he was threading his hands through her hair and she was reaching for the buttons on his shirt.

She was halfway down his chest when he put his hand over hers. "You sure?" he asked, a little hint of sexy gravel in his voice. "You have to be sure."

"I'm sure." She lifted her chin. "I want you. All of you."

Including his heart. And maybe that wouldn't happen today. But she hoped it would someday, because his was a heart worth cherishing.

CHAPTER ELEVEN

JEREMY HAD NEVER once been scared before making love to a woman, but he was scared tonight.

There was a lot at stake. A ton of possibility that could be the best thing ever to happen to him—or he could blow it and they'd be back to square one, just like they were in her office the day he'd discovered she was pregnant.

But more than that, he'd never before made love to a woman where his heart was involved, and it was with Tori. As much as he tried to deny it, she touched something inside him he usually kept locked away. And he'd let her get a glimpse of it. He didn't like being that vulnerable.

She was standing in his room now, facing him, the soft light of a pair of lamps illuminating her pale skin. He moved forward, wanting to undress her, as scared as he'd been his very first time. Her gaze locked with his, her eyes warmed and her lips curved up in a small smile.

"Don't be scared," she said, as if she could read his thoughts.

"I want to see you." His heart clubbed against his ribs as he reached for her sweater, bunching it up in his hands until it went past her waist, over her breasts, over her head. When her hair was free she shook it out, and he dropped the sweater. Her full breasts were cupped by a plain black satin bra, and her leggings came up over her bump. Holding his gaze, she pushed the waistband down until she was standing before him in the bra and matching underwear, the bikini elastic sitting low below where her tummy began to curve.

She was so beautiful. He could stare at her forever, marveling at how gorgeous she was and the awesomeness of her carrying their child.

"Are you going to touch me?" she asked, tilting her head.

He reached out and put his hand on her hip, pulling her closer, and lifted his other hand to her ribs, skimming over her thickened waist, his thumb roving toward her breast. Dammit, his hands were shaking.

She put her fingers on his face, guiding him to look her in the eyes. "I need to know, Jeremy. Need to know that this is still good and real. We have a lot to figure out, but most of all we need to decide how we feel about each other."

"You think I have a choice? That I can decide?"

He was already a goner.

"Maybe *decide* is the wrong word. Maybe *acknowledge*." Her fingers traced over his jaw, the fingernail scraping his stubble a little bit. "Me, here with you, like this... I'm acknowledging that I feel something for you."

"I don't take this lightly," he murmured.

"Nor do I. So when you touch me...when you take me... know that I've made this choice tonight. Knowing the risks and wanting you anyway."

He was afraid. Humbled. He almost considered not going through with it, and then she moved toward him, pressing her lips to the hollow between his shoulder and collarbone. He shuddered and closed his eyes, drinking in the sensation, the tenderness, the heat of it. Their time together in the summer had been nothing short of spectacular. With the news of the baby and walking on eggshells, he'd nearly forgotten. But not now.

Not with her so close to him with his shirt spread open and their skin touching, warm and soft.

He let out a shaky sigh, then gathered her against him and shut out the world.

Tori rolled over and felt the sheets gathered beneath her armpits. They were silk, black silk, and caressed her body as she shifted to face Jeremy.

He was still sleeping on his back, his lips relaxed and his lashes resting peacefully.

She was wearing nothing but her bikini panties again, which she vaguely remembered pulling on before sliding back into bed and into his arms, falling into sleep.

That had been two hours ago, around eight o'clock. Right now, her belly rumbled and the baby kicked all at the same time. They hadn't eaten dinner.

"Someone's hungry."

Her breath caught at the sound of his amused voice. His eyes were still closed, but the corners of his mouth twitched.

"I am. And so's your kid. Besides, that casserole is cold now and we should eat it and then put the leftovers in the fridge."

"But you're warm and snuggly."

Snuggly wasn't the word she'd use. Her breasts were heavier now and more sensitive with the pregnancy, and the slippery sheets felt almost like a caress. She was nearly naked in bed with him; that was distraction enough. But she was also starving. And truthfully, she was still reeling from what had happened between them. She needed some distance to make sense of her thoughts.

It had been good between them before. Tonight had been... better. Because it wasn't just a fling anymore. Their connection had been transcendent.

She shook her head and figured that kind of thinking was going to get her into trouble. They still had to figure out this parenting thing with clear heads. Regretfully, she slipped out of the sheets and went searching for her bra.

"Here." He got out of bed and, fully naked, went to the closet and took out a soft robe. "Put this on if you don't want to get all dressed up again."

It was charcoal gray and thick and soft, and she wrapped it around her body while his scent rose from the fabric. "Thanks," she murmured.

And tried not to look at his butt when he went back to the closet, but she failed. It was a rather spectacular backside.

He returned wearing a pair of plaid sleep pants and a sweatshirt. It shouldn't have been attractive, but it made her want to crawl inside his embrace again.

They went to the kitchen and Tori scooped up servings of casserole and put them in the microwave. While they were heating, she put the rest in containers and put them in the fridge, next to the salad that had never been touched. Jeremy filled water glasses, and within moments they were seated at the counter again, chowing down on the chicken, broccoli and rice with creamy sauce.

"This is delicious."

"It's my mom's recipe. I don't know where she got it, but she used to make it now and again, especially for potlucks."

He took a sip of water. "Potlucks?"

She laughed. "Okay, so not everyone in the world caters their functions. A potluck is where you have a gathering of some kind and everyone brings a dish. It's awesome because you get this amazing variety of food. Some people just stop at the grocery store and get platters of veggies and stuff, you know? But then other people bring amazing dishes. We had a neighbor who always made meatballs. A guy from church who came with a ton of hot chicken wings. And don't get me started on the salads and cheeses and appetizers..."

He laughed, scooping up more food. "It sounds fun."

"It is. And if it's a kitchen party, then you also bring your own alcohol and someone is likely to bring a guitar and it gets fun and rowdy."

His face took on a faraway expression. "What?" she asked.

"I don't think I've ever had that in my life."

She patted his hand. "Where I come from, few people are rolling in cash. Everyone chips in, good times had by all. It's what happens in a community."

"In my community, people decorate and cater and send out invitations and try to impress each other."

"Sounds dreadful."

Now his face was downright pensive. "I'm sorry to hear that, because my mom is holding something quite similar to that on Saturday, at our house in Connecticut. I want you to come."

All the warmth that had been flooding through her body froze. "Oh, no. Meet the parents? Not likely."

He pushed his plate aside, and she did, too. She didn't have much appetite left.

"Tori, after tonight, I think we need to start talking about what we plan to do. I mean, really talk about it. This whole week has been amazing and fun. But the point was also to be alone together, to decide what we want to do about us and the baby. We haven't even talked about that at all."

She nodded, looking down at the smears of sauce on her plate. "I know. I've been avoiding it because everything is going to change."

He put his hand over hers. "Would you consider moving here?"

Panic slid down her body. She was still vulnerable from the hours spent in his arms, and her hopes warred with caution. "I don't know. I don't want to say no right off the bat, but while I've enjoyed my week here, I'm not sure I'm the kind of person who can live in the middle of a huge city. Let alone Manhattan."

"We could keep this place and stay here when we want to come into the city. And I'd be willing to look at properties elsewhere that you might like better."

"Like Connecticut?"

He laughed a little. "And be that close to my family? Hell, no. Maybe more like Long Island. There are some particularly good places for young families there." He squeezed her hand. "This is my job, you know. I can find us a place, if you'll consider moving."

Was she really considering it? The idea took her breath away. "You're assuming that I'm okay with picking up and leaving my life. But I like my life. And I like working. I know I wouldn't have to provide an income for us to live off. But the Sandpiper has been my home away from home for years now. I've helped build it into the hotel it is today. It's asking a lot, to leave the life I've built behind."

"I know." He let out a sigh. "But you can work anywhere, right? Especially if it's not about the money. You could find something that you really like."

She thought about it. A big house, their baby, a job she could work at to give her purpose…never any worries about bills. She wasn't sure she trusted a future that seemed so perfect. "After what you said about your mom, I thought you'd want me to be home to look after the baby all the time."

He snorted. "My mom was home all the time and never spent a second with us. Being a good parent isn't decided on who gets to stay home and who works. Even I know that."

She smiled. "Okay, fair enough." She looked over at him. "And you're sure you don't want to come to Nova Scotia?"

"Don't get me wrong. I love the province. It's beautiful. But the market is so much smaller. I'd be bored out of my mind. And that has nothing to do with you, and everything to do with me not wanting to fall into the trap of the 'idle rich.' I need a purpose, too."

She got that. She truly did.

"There's immigration stuff to worry about. I'm not a US citizen." Especially if a marriage wasn't in the picture.

"We can get a lawyer for that."

"I suppose." She slid her hand out from beneath his. "And problems do go away easier when you can throw money at them."

It was quiet for a few moments, before Jeremy spoke up again, his eyes telegraphing his disappointment. "That's the first time you've thrown money in my face. Are you upset?"

She felt badly, even though what she'd said was true. Solutions to problems came easier when there was lots of money to look after them. Truthfully, though, she was scared. Not angry. Just overwhelmed.

This gorgeous man, sitting in his robe, eating leftovers after making love... She was petrified of making a wrong decision. Because right now the truth was she could envision their life together and it seemed so perfect. She was pretty sure she was falling in love with him, and after what had happened earlier tonight, she thought it might be a possibility that he'd fall for her, too. He'd confided in her. And then they'd been intimate. There had been a moment when their eyes had met and it had felt as if everything clicked into place.

She just had to be brave enough.

"There's a lot of personal risk for me," she said quietly, and swiveled on her stool so she was facing him. Their knees barely touched. "Yes, it would mean both of us being there to parent our child. And yes, this week has been really promising with regards to...us. It's still a leap and a half to think about quitting my job, leaving my country and moving in with you with no guarantees." She patted his knee. "Please don't think I'm looking for guarantees. I'm not. It's much too soon for that."

"We can lay out any terms you want," he replied. His gaze held hers. "You can go home whenever. You know that, right? It's not just about business for me, either, Tori. The opportunities here for him or her... They're huge. I want our kid to have the best of both worlds—the opportunities I had with the love and support I didn't. But I think you did."

Would living here be so bad? Especially if there was money—

which there would be—for her mom to fly here, or for her to fly home? It was a fairly short direct flight, after all. And it wasn't as if she hated his apartment; she had loved her week here and all the things New York offered. "You'd really look at moving outside the city and commuting in?"

He shrugged. "Lots of people do it. Besides, I'm not always in the city anyway. We could get a place near the water. Have a boat. Hell, we could travel up the coast to visit your mom if you wanted."

Because money was no object. Except it was all his money, and she knew she shouldn't feel guilty but did anyway.

"I'd want some sort of agreement drawn up," she said firmly. "Something stating that if this doesn't work out, I can't go after your money. I'm not a gold digger, Jeremy."

His lips dropped open. "I know that."

"I want it in writing just the same."

"Whatever makes you happy." He slid forward on his bar stool a bit. "Tori, I know I'm asking a lot of you. In return I promise to do whatever I can to make sure you're happy and content. If that means you look for a job, so be it. If you want to stay home with the baby, that's fine, too." He put his hand on her belly. "I like you a lot, and I think you like me." That flirty smile was back on his lips. "At least the last few hours give me that impression. I have to do better than my own father did with me, you know? And if that means giving our relationship a try, then what do we have to lose? If it doesn't work, we figure out a new arrangement. But there's so much to gain, sweetheart. So much."

Damn. He'd hit her right in her vulnerable spots. She knew how much his father's abandonment had affected him. And he'd called her *sweetheart*—to her mind, the first endearment to leave his lips.

It wasn't the normal progression for a relationship, but what did that matter? He'd been wonderful from the start. Yes, they had their differences—financially, geographically—but did that mean they couldn't have a future together? Of course not.

"Well, I'm willing to look at some options. No guarantees, but I'm not saying no."

A brilliant smile broke over his lips. "It's a *maybe*, which is way better than *no*. I'll take it. And I can show you some examples of nice properties for us."

She also wanted to ask him about citizenship for the baby, because she couldn't imagine having her baby outside Canada. But that didn't have to be decided tonight. The fact that they'd come up with the beginnings of a plan was huge.

That she'd be facing a lot of changes meant she had a lot to think over. Work, for example, and how long she'd stay at the hotel before the baby was born. Living arrangements. Possibly listing her own house, if she decided to move.

He got up and took their plates into the kitchen, stopping to load them in the dishwasher. "Come on," he said, once they were out of sight. "Come to bed and get some sleep. We have Mom's on Saturday, but tomorrow I have another surprise for you. Something I haven't done since I was a kid."

"Oh?" Her interest piqued, she lifted her head and peered around the corner at him. "What's that?"

He came back and held out his hand. She took it. "If I told you, it wouldn't be a surprise." He tugged on her hand, and she slipped off the stool. "But I promise you'll like it."

"You haven't steered me wrong yet," she admitted, and let herself be pulled closer, so that his arm was around her as they made their way back down the hall.

At the junction to their bedrooms, he stopped and looked into her eyes. "If you want to sleep in your own bed, I understand, but if you want to stay with me, I'd like that, too. It's your choice."

Spending the night seemed like a big deal, but then, if they were really going to give this a shot, she couldn't keep shying away from intimacy. At some point she had to trust that he was as good as he seemed.

"Your room is fine," she said, butterflies settling in her stomach at this new step in their relationship. "But I'd like to get my pajamas first, if that's okay."

"If it makes you more comfortable," he answered, tapping a fingertip on her nose and smiling. "Don't do it on my account."

Heat crept up her cheeks, but she tried to enjoy it. Sharing a child made the stakes high, but there was no reason why this couldn't turn out to be a good, healthy relationship. Why it couldn't be a real future. It was a dizzying and sobering thought.

She scurried away to get her comfy boxer shorts and top. Tonight they were sharing his room. Tomorrow, some sort of surprise. And then night after that, she was meeting his family.

If that didn't sound like a guy who was serious about moving forward, she wasn't sure what did.

CHAPTER TWELVE

Jeremy knelt before Tori and tightened up the laces on her skate. "Is this too tight?"

"No, it feels just right."

He gave the ends another tug, then tied the knot and bow. "Okay, then. Give me your other foot."

Skating at Rockefeller Center was something he'd done as a kid. While his mom had come to the city to shop, their nanny at the time would take them skating and then off to some other adventure—and lunch—since dragging three kids around had cramped his mom's style, and his brother and sister weren't old enough to be left to their own devices. There had always been a trip to see Santa Claus, too. He'd loved that at first; his siblings had been much older and had rolled their eyes. Some years he couldn't remember; he'd been too young. Another, though, he'd asked for some video game system while sitting on Santa's lap.

Christmas morning arrived. No gaming console. His mother had been quite put out at him when he'd complained, and said how was she to know he wanted it? Maybe because he'd mentioned it only a million times and put it in his letter to Santa.

Despite that unfortunate memory, today actually brought back a lot of good ones, including lacing up skates and the hot chocolate that was to follow. Besides, as a kid, the last thing he would have wanted was to be dragged from store to store.

"Jeremy? You okay?"

He lifted his head and met her gaze. "Yeah, sorry. Just got caught up in a memory and forgot to keep tying."

"I hope it was a good one."

He smiled and tugged on the laces. "It was. I came here a lot as a kid." He gave the bow a final jerk and sat back. "There you go. All set."

She waited as he put on his own skates. "I did not expect this for a surprise today."

"It's not Christmas without the tree here and skating. And hot chocolate."

Tori pulled on thick mittens. Today she wore the older jacket that zipped up in front, which was better for skating. But she wore a new hat, he realized, and grinned. It had a hole in the top, and her dark ponytail came out and trailed down the back of her head to her neck.

Adorable was the best word to describe her right now.

"You all set?"

She nodded and held out a hand. "Let's do it."

The ice was smooth and the air crisp as they took their first gliding steps. "Be careful," he warned. "I don't want you falling down."

She laughed. "I've been skating since I was three years old. Don't worry about me." Then she twisted a little and pretended to look at her bottom. "And besides, I have lots of cushioning at the moment."

She didn't. She had curves and perhaps her figure had softened since last summer, but he found it even more alluring. Last night he'd marveled at the feel of her against him, around him. The softness of her skin and her sighs. He was in serious danger here. Thank goodness she was considering moving, because he wasn't sure what he would have said if she'd flat out refused. It wasn't just the baby, now. He wanted her with him.

She was right. The apartment was monochrome. His life was monochrome. Until she'd arrived and brought all the color and life with her.

He gave her hand a small tug, and she did a little flip so that she was skating backward and now facing him. But he held on firmly, slowing them until they were stopped. And then he slid the few inches needed to have her puffy jacket pressed against his.

"Jeremy?"

He kissed her then, on her cold, soft lips, absorbing the taste of her, the scent of her skin, the gentle pressure of her belly against him. He wasn't into showy PDA, so he let her go after a few seconds, but her eyes glittered and her cheeks were rosy.

"What was that for?"

"For being you. For agreeing to come here. For putting decorations in my apartment. For everything."

Goodness, he was feeling all sentimental and mushy, but he wouldn't always be able to hide his feelings, would he? He was sure she wasn't in love with him. She hadn't exactly leaped at the idea of moving here to be with him. But she cared, and he knew she would do whatever she thought was best for their baby. And that made her damn near perfect in his eyes.

"You're welcome. Not that I did anything."

"You've done more than you know, sweetheart."

"Come on. Let's skate. We're just standing here like idiots."

He laughed and took her hand again, and they skated around the rink, enjoying the winter air and the holiday energy and the benefit of physical exertion. They took a break for a bit and Tori took pictures of the giant Christmas tree and the statue of Prometheus.

"It's amazing at night, all lit up," he said, one arm around her waist as she leaned back against him. "But on a Friday night? Busy." He gave her a small squeeze. "Maybe next year we can come back, at night. And bring the baby, too."

The moment he said it something huge opened up inside him.

Next year at this time, they would have a seven-month-old baby. They'd be a *family*. He thought about what Tori would look like, their child in her arms, breath cloudy in the frosty air, and his heart turned over. This was the right thing. He was sure of it.

"Oh, Jeremy." She sighed and leaned against him. "Are we gonna be okay? Can we really do this?"

He turned her around and looked her square in the eye. "Of course we can, and we will. Because we both know what's really important."

Her eyes shone, and she gave a sniff. "I'm falling for you, Jeremy. And scared to death because of it. I don't want to screw up the future for our baby and I don't want to set myself up for heartbreak. I'm terrified."

He didn't want to examine his own feelings too closely. Love wasn't something he did or really wanted. Love was what really hurt, and he wanted to be happy with Tori. But he could offer other assurances, couldn't he, without getting himself in too deep? "You can count on me, I promise," he said, and pulled her to him in a hug. "I've never done this before, you know. But I'm going to give you my best."

"That's all anyone can give," she said, her voice muffled against his jacket. "And I'll do the same. And we'll rely on each other, won't we?"

"Yes, sweetheart, we will."

She nodded against him and he closed his eyes as he rested his cheek along her thick hat. She was so honest and kind and willing to think the best of people. He never wanted to do anything to break the trust they had. He'd do anything to protect her and the baby. They were the most important thing now.

She gave a mighty sniff and pulled back. "Oh, I'm such an emotional wreck," she laughed, looking slightly embarrassed.

"No, you're not. If you didn't care so much, I wouldn't l... like you so much."

He'd almost said *love*. It had been right there, on the tip of his tongue, and he could tell by her wide eyes that she'd caught the slip. He couldn't say it, he couldn't give her false hope for something he wasn't capable of giving. What was most important was not repeating his parents' mistakes.

Which reminded him of the following night. The one thing he had left to do was take Bran's advice and take her to Connecticut. He didn't really want to; these days his interaction with his mother was only at special occasions. Still, if Tori was going to understand him, and his feelings about parenting, and if he wanted to have a future with her as well as his child, she had to know what she was becoming part of. Anything else wouldn't be fair.

"Let's skate some more," she suggested, and he shook off his thoughts and smiled at her. Her face was so alight with childish enthusiasm he couldn't resist.

"Okay, but I'm skating backward so you can skate forward and hold on to my hands."

"Overprotective much?"

"Indulge me."

She wiggled her eyebrows. "Okay. Maybe I'll indulge you later, too."

Now that she was starting to drop her guard, he was in even more emotional danger.

They started to circle the ice. Once, he nearly freaked because Tori let go of one hand, then did a half turn so they were both skating backward. It almost felt as if they were...dancing! Then with a laugh, she turned again, faced him, gave a push forward and slid under his arm.

"What the heck are you doing?"

She giggled. "Dancing with you!"

"Be careful."

"I'm always careful!"

In the end, though, it was Jeremy who caught an edge and felt himself go. He was holding her hand and forgot to let go; as he tumbled to the ice, he took her with him. He landed on his hip and he heard her breath leave her body with an *"oof."*

"Oh, God! Are you okay?"

She was sprawled on top of him, and she started to laugh. "Other than having the air knocked out of me? I'm fine."

He scowled. "Don't laugh! You scared me."

Her face grew tender as she looked down at him. "You gave me a soft place to fall," she whispered, and he was a goner.

If he had his way, he would always be her soft place to fall.

After skating, they had hot chocolate and cookies, and then they walked back to his apartment. His hip hurt a bit, but he was more worried about Tori. "I'm just tired," she insisted, but he wasn't so sure. Skating had probably been a bad idea. What if she'd fallen on her belly? What would have happened to the baby?

"Do you have any cramping? Any pain anywhere?"

They reached his building. "Stop fussing. Seriously, I just need a nap. I'm fine, and so is the baby."

He wasn't convinced, but he wasn't going to take chances. Once inside, he tucked her into his bed and called a doctor.

When the doctor arrived, he went in to wake Tori. She was lying on her side, her lips open, a little bit of drool clinging to the side of her mouth. She'd taken out her ponytail and her hair lay in a dark tangle on his pillowcase. Had she been right? Was she just tired? Still, it never hurt to make sure everything was okay.

"Tori?"

"Hmm?" She squeezed her eyes shut tight, and then opened them a little. "What time is it? How long did I sleep?"

"About an hour and a half. I called a doctor to come see you."

She rolled over to her back and frowned. "You called a doctor? And he's here?"

"She's here, and yes. I was worried. You got so quiet. You did have a fall, you know."

"Oh, Jeremy, you didn't have to do that. If I'd had any cramping or anything I would have said."

"Will you let her check you out anyway? It'll make me feel better."

She sighed. "Since she's already here, sure." She pushed herself up to sitting. "Let me put myself together first."

He handed her the elastic from the bedside table and watched as she deftly put her hair up again. Then he handed her a tissue. "You might have drooled a little."

"So attractive," she grumbled. "Okay, send her in. I still can't believe you got someone to make a house call."

What was the sense of having money if he couldn't use it to help the mother of his baby?

He waited outside while the doctor spoke to Tori; he'd made the decision to call but he did respect her privacy. He paced the hallway instead, wondering if there were dangers to the baby that Tori couldn't feel, chastising himself once again for taking her skating in the first place, not thinking of the dangers. Instead he'd been arrogant, thinking he'd keep her from falling when he'd been the one to take the tumble.

If anything was wrong, it was his fault.

Ten minutes after she went in, the doctor came out again. "Mr. Fisher, would you like to come in?"

Oh, no.

Tori was sitting up on the bed, a smile on her face. "I told you," she said triumphantly. "Nothing wrong."

The doctor gave her an amused look. "You still have to watch for anything abnormal, okay? And call if you start cramping or spotting."

"I will. Promise."

"So you're okay? The baby's okay?"

"If you don't trust me, will you trust her?" Tori nodded at the doctor, who was looking rather amused at the whole situation.

"She's had no cramping, no bleeding, heartbeat's steady, and she's felt the baby move. Everything seems fine. But it's always better to be safe than sorry." The doc smiled. "She said you broke her fall."

"We wouldn't have fallen if I hadn't tripped," he admitted. "I'm so sorry."

"Oh, heavens," Tori said. "It's not your fault. You can't keep me in Bubble Wrap for the next four months."

"Are you sure?"

She patted the bed. "Come sit here and listen."

He sat on one side of the bed while Tori scooted down. She'd taken off her sweatpants before sliding under the covers for her nap, so she just had to pull her shirt up as the doctor reached for a handheld machine.

"It's a portable Doppler," Tori explained. "So you can actually hear the heartbeat this time."

His own pulse took a jump. He'd calmed a bit when he'd been assured everything was okay, but now anticipation had his heartbeat accelerating. He still had the ultrasound picture tucked away in his wallet. And he'd seen the little heartbeat on the monitor before, but hearing it...

It took only seconds for the doctor to find the beat and turn up the volume, and a rapid thumping sound touched his ears.

"That's it?"

"That's it, Dad." The doctor turned the unit around so he could see. The number was 137 and the sound coming from it was his baby's tiny heart, beating inside its mother.

Tears stung his eyes and he blinked rapidly. He wouldn't cry at this moment. But he wanted to, his relief was so great. "That's the best sound in the world."

"Yup." After a few more seconds, the doctor removed the tiny wand and Tori used a cloth to wipe away the blob of gel.

The sound was gone, but he could still hear it in his head.

"Now, I've told Tori to take it easy for a day or so, just as a precaution, and the fact that it'll make you happy."

She was right it would. "Forget about my mom's tomorrow. We don't have to go."

Tori sighed. "I'm perfectly capable of going to a stuffy cocktail party for a few hours. And to be honest, I'd rather get this over with."

He couldn't blame her.

"Don't back out using me as an excuse, Jeremy."

"Fine."

The doctor merely chuckled in the background as she packed up her things.

"I'll walk you to the door," Jeremy said, erasing the scowl from his face. Besides, Tori was right.

It would be good to get it over with.

CHAPTER THIRTEEN

TORI DIDN'T KNOW why she hadn't thought to ask if Jeremy had a car. Of course he did. And the next night they left the city and headed to Connecticut, to his family home and the party that would be waiting for them.

She was dressed in the cocktail dress he'd bought her that first day of shopping, and new shoes, and the cape. She carried a little clutch and felt more than ever like Cinderella going to the ball, only this time it felt as if the host wasn't a prince but the evil stepmother.

By the time they left it was dark, so Tori couldn't even focus on the scenery. Instead, nerves bubbled up inside her. Jeremy had said that she had to know what she was getting herself into, and that didn't bode well. She had enough anxiety for the both of them; she didn't need to be absorbing any of Jeremy's. His hands gripped the steering wheel and his jaw was set. He wasn't looking forward to this holiday party, either.

"Just remember that it doesn't matter what my mother thinks of you, okay? Or Bruce, either."

"So why is it so important for me to meet them? I mean, I don't want to say that I think being estranged is a good thing, but I'm just..." She took a breath and let out what she was really thinking. "Are you hoping that it'll scare me off?"

"What? No!" He took his eyes off the road for a moment. "Of course not!"

Then he sighed, a heavy, weary sigh. "I talked to my friend Bran when we were still back in Nova Scotia. He told me I shouldn't blindside you with my family. That you should know what you're getting into. He's right. And maybe there's a part of me that thinks that maybe it'll help you understand me a little better, too." He looked over again, a grim smile on his lips. "Warts and all."

She tried a small smile. "Kissing frogs who turn into princes?"

"I'm no prince." He smiled back, though it was edged with tension. "Also, a holiday cocktail party means Mom will be on her best behavior, or at least I hope so. Tomorrow morning we'll drive back and it'll be over and done with."

They still hadn't talked about when she'd be returning home, but she did have to be back by Thursday of the following week. She couldn't take unlimited vacation and leave Tom in the lurch with the hotel.

She supposed that meant in the new year she'd be talking to him about resigning and creating an exit plan.

The thought made her sad, and a bit lonely, but she was moving on to big things. And it would have to be done, regardless, because her maternity leave was scheduled to start at the beginning of April.

It was nearly eight when a gate swung open and they pulled into a large, circular drive. The lane leading up to the property was heavily treed, so Tori only saw darkness out the passenger side window. A number of cars were already parked. The party had begun, apparently.

"Cocktails now, dinner at eight thirty," he murmured, turning off the engine. "Phew. Are you ready?"

"No. You're making me nervous."

"I'm sorry." He ran his hand through his hair, a clear sign he was agitated. "I'm being a coward."

She turned in her seat. "Listen, we don't have to go in. If

you're this upset, that tells me all I need to know. Don't do this because of me."

He relaxed a little. "I think it's like ripping off a Band-Aid. Once it's done, I'll feel better. And then I won't have to worry about it again."

"Well, then, let's get ripping. It's going to get cold out here in about thirty seconds." A light snow had started to fall.

He got out and then went around the car to open her door, and held her elbow firmly as they walked to the entrance of the grand home.

At first glance, Tori thought the house was simply a large colonial style—gorgeous but not the imposing mansion she'd been expecting. But as they stepped up to the oversize oak door, she realized that tucked back behind the main house were expansive wings, afforded privacy by the large, sheltering trees to each side of the main building. "Oh," she whispered.

"Nine thousand square feet, give or take," he offered, knocking on the door.

Way larger than even the nicest house they'd looked at back home. And, if she could guess, well over twice the cost, especially when considering currency exchange.

She gripped her clutch even tighter.

The door opened and they were ushered in and divested of their outerwear; they walked only five feet when they were offered a cocktail. Jeremy accepted one while Tori said a quiet, "No, thank you."

Instead of leaving it there, though, Jeremy asked for them to bring her a club soda and lime.

"How did you know what I'd like?"

He leaned closer. "You've been drinking it all week at my place."

He noticed the most mundane things, and she couldn't help but be pleased.

Now they were at the door to a large room, and conversations hummed from inside. His mother was in there. Probably his sister. Stepfather. Their social circle. She was a small-town nobody from Nova Scotia. She couldn't be more out of place if she tried.

She was about to ask him for more time, but then a woman appeared at the door, carrying a glass of red wine, and smiled widely. "About time you got here! I wondered if you'd fed me to the wolves."

"Hey, Sarah." He gave her a hug, but it was more polite than overt affection. "I'd like you to meet Tori."

"Hello, Tori. Nice of you to…"

She'd just noticed Tori's baby bump. "Oh. *Oh*. Well. Congratulations."

Tori placed her hand protectively over the baby. "Thank you."

Sarah looked at Jeremy. "Does Mom know?"

"Of course not."

"Wow, Jeremy, you're going to make her a grandmother. She won't be able to lie about her age anymore."

"Well, cheers to that." The siblings touched glasses.

Sarah relaxed a little. "Seriously, though, congratulations. I'm surprised as hell, but one of us deserves to be happy. When's the due date?"

"April fourteenth," Tori supplied.

"Well, you might as well come in. You can't stay in the doorway all night."

Tori's club soda arrived, so her hands were full of purse and drink as they entered a room that she was sure was nearly as big as her whole house.

The men wore black tie, the same as Jeremy, creating a striking look. The women were dressed in conservative cocktail dresses, with nary a bared shoulder or plunging neckline in sight. Except for one woman, Tori noticed. She had on a little black dress that dipped to the waist in the back, and came to mid-thigh. When she turned around, it was like looking at Sarah all over again, only twenty-five years older and with three times the amount of makeup.

Unless Tori was sadly mistaken, she'd also had substantial work done. Her face had a pinched look that wasn't quite natural.

The woman spied Jeremy and smiled, then her gaze lit on Tori, drifted down to her belly and moved back up with both surprise and distaste in their depths. *Here we go.*

At least the front of the dress was more appropriate than the back. She excused herself and came to stand in front of Jeremy, as if Tori wasn't there at all.

"So good of you to come, Jeremy."

"Mother." He leaned forward and kissed her cheek. Tori wasn't sure the kiss had even made contact with skin. "Merry Christmas. I'd like to introduce you to Victoria Sharpe."

Tori put down her drink and held out her hand. "Hello, Mrs...."

It struck her suddenly. Jeremy never mentioned his mother by her first name, and since she'd remarried her last name wouldn't be Fisher any longer. It would be something else. Something Tori didn't know. She wanted to sink through the floor, especially when the other woman made no move to reduce Tori's embarrassment. She didn't even shake her hand. Tori dropped her hand to her side, feeling sick to her stomach.

"Oh, I'm sorry, Tori. Mom is now Carol Heppner. I can't believe I forgot to mention that."

"Yes really, Jeremy, it's like you don't care who I am at all," his mother chided, but instead of being hurt she just looked... disinterested.

"Oh, wait." Tori tried a smile and pried open the catch on her purse. "Mrs. Heppner, I brought you something. Just to say thank-you for having me tonight."

She took out the robin's-egg-blue bag and held it out. When she'd been shopping for Jeremy's decorations, she'd seen it and had thought maybe it would be fancy enough for his mother. She hadn't wanted to arrive empty-handed.

Jeremy looked uncomfortable and Carol stared at the bag for a moment before taking it. "Thank you."

She moved to hand it off to a servant when Jeremy's brittle voice came from beside her.

"Aren't you going to open it, Mother?"

With a sigh, Carol opened the bag, then the box inside, and the pouch inside that. She removed the delicate snowman on the red ribbon that Tori had thought so cute and that had taken a substantial chunk of her bank account.

"Isn't that...charming."

She stared at Tori's belly again, then looked at Jeremy and said, "I do hope you enjoy the party. Have you seen Sarah? She's here."

"We saw her on the way in." With a defiant set to his jaw, he added, "She wanted to congratulate us on the baby."

A weak smile touched his mother's lips. "Odd, how you wait until a party to tell your own mother. Oh, well. Let me add my congratulations, then. But excuse me. I do have other guests to attend to."

She walked away. Tori watched as she handed off the ornament to a staff member as if it were nothing at all.

"You got her a hostess gift? Tori, that's ballsy."

"Yeah, well, she didn't look impressed."

"Of course not. She's never impressed." His gaze softened. "I knew she'd have...exacting tastes. I know it was small. And a snowman... I'm an idiot."

He put his arm around her. "No, you're not. You're incredibly sweet and have better manners than my mother. Come on, let's find Sarah. She's as emotionally stunted as the rest of us, but she tries. And she's an ally."

Tori tried not to laugh but couldn't help it. Emotionally stunted? She didn't think Jeremy was. She thought he covered a lot with smiles and charm, but the last week he'd revealed a lot about himself.

"All right. Could I have another club soda, though? I feel like I need to have something in my hand."

"Of course. And dinner will be soon."

They mingled their way through the room in search of Sarah, whom they found in a corner drinking a glass of wine and holding an animated conversation with a man who looked perhaps thirty. As they drew closer, Tori could tell the conversation was centered on financial stuff she didn't understand. Sarah was clearly schooling the younger man, who was openly flirting back. What was it like to have that kind of confidence?"

"Excuse me," Sarah said. "I'm going to chat with my brother for a few minutes."

She extricated herself from the conversation and turned to Tori and Jeremy. "Oh, my goodness. They get younger every time I turn around. Thanks for the rescue."

"One good turn deserves another. We saw Mom."

"That must have been entertaining. I'm sorry I missed it." She took a big sip of wine. "What did she say?"

Tori looked up. "She said congratulations."

Sarah snorted. "She did not. And if she did, it wasn't in that sweet way that you just did. By the way, I can't place your accent. Where are you from?"

"Nova Scotia."

Sarah looked at Jeremy. "Last summer's trip."

He grinned. "Surprise." Then he leaned over and kissed Tori's cheek. "It wasn't quite what we planned on happening, but life doesn't always go according to plan."

They chatted a while longer and Tori started to relax. Once everyone was seated at dinner, she let out a long breath. "Okay. I think I'm doing okay."

"You are. I told you not to pay any attention to my mom. Everyone else loves you."

Well, everyone except Jeremy's stepdad. The best that could be said of him was that he was utterly ambivalent.

Tori and Jeremy sat together during the meal, which included foods that Tori had never even seen before but bravely tried. She avoided the pâté and soft cheese, but enjoyed whatever the poultry dish was—perhaps duck?—and some sort of fancy potato. And the dessert was delightful, a tarte tatin with cream. Not too exotic, but extra special. Something she'd love to have at the Sandpiper...

Except she wasn't going to be there anymore, was she? Her heart gave a little pang at the thought. Saying goodbye was going to be so very hard. She'd put her heart and soul into the resort.

As the sounds of clinking silverware and crystal glasses slowed, she wondered if this kind of thing would become her life. It was nice for a visit, but she wouldn't want to live like this. Then again, Jeremy didn't live like this. His place was extravagant but his mood was relaxed, his tastes plainer. Like eating casserole two hours late, or ordering in a pizza from his favorite pizza joint. Cheesecake at ten o'clock at night.

She understood now why he'd wanted her to come. This was where he'd come from, but it wasn't where he wanted to be. He'd always be connected to his family, but this wasn't the life he had chosen for himself.

Or for his child.

She leaned over. "This was delicious, but I think I get it now."

"Get what?"

"What you said about me needing to see it. Promise me we won't end up like this. I want backyard barbecues and kitchen parties and people feeling welcomed."

He looked into her eyes. "Of course you do. It's what you've always known."

"I'm sorry you haven't."

"I survived." He flashed her a smile. "Come on, let's go back to the drawing room, as Mother likes to call it. It makes her feel aristocratic."

She laughed and they rose from the table. Now that dinner was over, the mood was even more relaxed in the large room.

More wine was poured, and brandy. Tori realized that Jeremy had had his cocktail upon entering and one glass of wine at dinner, but that was it. When she mentioned as much, he shrugged. "I know we said we'd stay the night and go back tomorrow morning, but now I'm thinking we can drive back tonight. If that's okay with you."

She had no desire to stay any longer than she had to. She was a fish out of water here. "Whatever you want to do."

"I'm going to find Mom and let her know. We don't have to stay much longer if you're tired."

He left her with Sarah, who was definitely staying as she'd now switched to gin and tonic. "I know, I shouldn't," she said. "But I am staying the night, and it's the only way these parties are bearable."

"Then why come?" Tori asked. She'd given up club soda and was now drinking straight-up water.

"I don't know. Because it's expected. Because we get the 'you only visit your mother twice a year' guilt trip. And because we can't stand each other, but a few times a year we pretend to and it makes us feel better about our stupid dysfunctional family."

Tori snorted. Sarah didn't have much of a filter after a few drinks.

"But you and Jeremy...you get along okay."

"We muddle through. Out of the whole family, we're probably the closest."

"I'm glad. He talks about you a lot."

Sarah looked pleased at that. "I think you're good for him, if tonight hasn't scared you off."

"We're trying to figure it out." She put her hand on her stomach and sighed. "Can you tell me where the powder room is? I haven't gone all night and the baby's sitting right in a good spot." She smiled at Sarah.

"Outside the door, go right, down the hall. There's a door on the left just across from Bruce's office." She turned up her nose. "He likes to go in there for a cigar after dinner. Gross."

"Thanks. If Jeremy comes back, tell him I won't be long."

She made her way down the hall, away from the noise. The house truly was gorgeous, a real showpiece with creamy walls, white trim and a gorgeous iron railing on the staircase leading to the next floor, which was now bedecked with boughs and ribbon. There wasn't a speck of dust or a thing out of place. No personal knickknacks or photos; just perfectly placed flower arrangements—holiday themed, of course—and pieces of art on the walls. Each one was perfectly level, as if it wouldn't dare be a little bit crooked.

Beautiful, and perfect. But there was no personality, no sense of the people who lived there.

She caught sight of an open door—presumably the powder room—when she heard voices coming from the room across the hall.

Jeremy's voice. And his mother's in reply.

She went to the door, staying slightly behind. There'd been a strident reply to something from Jeremy, but she hadn't been able to make out the words. Now she strained to hear. She hoped he wasn't getting a lot of grief from his mother. They could just stay over if it was going to be a big deal for them to leave early.

"Why didn't I tell you before? When was the last time you called me, Mother? Asked how I was? I mean, do you even care?"

"Of course I care, Jeremy." Her voice was cold. "I'm going to be a grandmother."

"I highly doubt it. You weren't mother material, you sure as hell aren't cut out to be a grandmother."

Ouch.

"You're so cruel," she replied. "And finding out tonight, in a room full of guests? It was embarrassing. Or was that your intention?"

He didn't answer, so his mother continued in her patronizing voice. "Look, she's probably nice enough, in her way. But really, Jeremy? She's not our kind of people. She's plain, and… uncultured."

"And you know that after sneering at her for two minutes?"

"Seriously. The way you're acting, you'd think you were in love with the girl. You aren't, are you?"

Tori held her breath. Her pride stung from his mother's assessment, but she was angry on Jeremy's behalf. No wonder he stayed away. What a horrible creature.

Jeremy hesitated. Then he said the words: "Of course I'm not. Don't be ridiculous."

Tori's heart plummeted to her feet. The way he'd kissed her. Held her hand. Made love…

It couldn't all have been an act.

She refused to believe it.

"I'm not going to ask you how she got pregnant. We both know that and I don't need the details. What are you going to do about it now?"

"She's here, isn't she?" he snapped, and Tori blinked back tears. He sounded so…harsh. "Look. No kid of mine is going to wonder where the hell his father is. You and Dad…you should never have procreated. He left and you wanted nothing to do with us. And here's what you need to know. I will do anything—*anything*—to make sure I do a better job of parenting my kid than you ever did."

Silence dropped for a moment. Then his mother spoke quietly. "Even pretend to love its mother?"

"Even that. Whatever it takes."

"So you're not in love with her. I knew it."

"Mother, please."

Tori stepped backward from the door, reeling from the pure derision laced in his voice. She hurried back down the hall, determined he not see her. She came across one of the waitstaff and asked where she could find another bathroom. Once she'd located it, she went inside, shut the door and sat on the closed toilet for thirty seconds while she tried to sort out her thoughts. Her feelings.

She'd been played.

Mother, please.

Those words replayed over and over in her head. She'd really fallen for it, hadn't she? All the expensive outings and private flights and sweet words... He'd used his money after all, to get her to do what he wanted. He didn't even have to get a lawyer involved. He'd used her emotions instead, and played her like a violin.

She got off the toilet, turned around and opened the lid. Though she hadn't thrown up for weeks now, her dinner came back up and left her gasping.

Then she flushed the toilet, washed her hands, and patted her face as best she could. She wouldn't cry, not now. But she was more than ready to go home and lick her wounds. And once she'd done that, she'd start making plans to raise her baby.

Hurt threatened to pierce her heart, but she steeled herself and kept it away by sheer force of will. She'd gone along with every single thing he'd suggested, and she'd fallen in love with him. Except it wasn't really him; just a show he'd put on to get what he wanted. And what made her the angriest was that he was planning on working out his childhood issues by using his own child as...what? Therapy? That was no way to bring a baby into the world. Not to solve your own problems.

She still had her clutch with her, and she took out her phone, turned on the data and booked a flight back to Halifax for the next day, on a commercial flight, which left approximately seventy-two dollars of available credit on her card. A knock sounded on the bathroom door just as she was getting the confirmation email. "Tori? Are you okay?"

"I'm fine," she replied, lifting her chin and staring at herself in the mirror. Right now she hated this dress. It wasn't her. It was someone she thought she could be. It was a lie, just like everything he'd said had been a lie.

"Are you sick?"

"I'll be right out." She squared her shoulders and opened the door, unprepared for the shaft of pain she felt upon seeing his concerned face. He wanted her baby, not her. And she rather wished he'd just been honest about that from the beginning, rather than manipulating her.

"Sorry. Turns out dinner didn't agree with me after all. I think I'd like to go…" She hesitated before saying home. "Back to the apartment."

He didn't say much, just watched her with an odd expression as she passed him on her way out the door and led the way to the stairs.

"If that's what you want, I'll get our coats."

It was a long drive back to the city. She didn't relish the idea of being in the car with him for that long, because she wasn't ready to talk about this yet. But it was her only way back to New York. It wasn't like she could ask Sarah. She'd been drinking all night. And Tori refused to cause a scene here.

She didn't bother saying goodbye to Sarah and she certainly didn't say goodbye to the hosts, who hadn't wanted her there to begin with. The snow flurries had stopped, thankfully, and at least they wouldn't be driving back in a heavier snowfall.

She got in the car and he turned on the heater while he cleared off the half inch or so of snow that had fallen earlier.

"Are you sure you're all right? You look flushed."

"I'm fine. Tired." Her heightened color was because she was agitated. Her heart ached and yet she felt outrage. At him, at herself for being so willing to fall for him and his pretty stories of what their life could be together.

She'd been a fool.

And yet she didn't know how to navigate the conversation that needed to happen, so she leaned her head against the car window and stared outside at the darkness. After a few minutes, she closed her eyes and pretended to sleep.

Her thoughts were anything but quiet.

Her heart was broken. Her trust was broken. Her faith was broken. She'd believed him when he'd said he cared for her. When he'd promised not to use his money to fight for his advantage. But he'd used it anyway, in a method far more ruthless.

He'd never said he loved her. He'd used the words *like* and *care*. But never *love*. It was as though his conscience wouldn't let him go that far.

Tears leaked from the corners of her eyes and she fought the urge to wipe them away.

Most of all she was angry with herself, for buying into it all so willingly.

He didn't say anything until they were in the city. "Tori, wake up. We're almost home."

She'd never been asleep but she pretended to perk up, sitting up in the seat and stretching. Her neck was cramped from leaning at an angle on the car door, and her heart felt raw and empty. Now she was minutes away from the conversation she didn't want to have. But she wouldn't run with her tail between her legs as if she had done something wrong.

"Feeling any better?"

"A little," she lied.

"The food was a little rich. Maybe it was just too much."

She didn't reply until they'd reached his building, gone up in the elevator and he was opening the door.

"It wasn't the food that made me sick." She peeled off the cape and put it on a chair in the foyer. She wouldn't take it with her. It was too expensive. A symbol of everything that was wrong with their relationship. She'd take only the things she'd brought with her in the first place. They were good enough for home.

"What was it?" Concern etched the corners of his eyes and she wanted to scream at him to stop pretending he cared.

"I was upset."

"I know it was a hard night—"

"I was upset at you." She kicked off her heels. "I heard you talking to your mother. And just so you know, I'm booked on a flight back home tomorrow morning. Leaving from Newark." It was the only direct flight she could manage, and she did not want to spend two hours in Toronto going through customs and sitting around waiting for another flight.

His face blanked, and a flush crept up his neck. "I don't know what you think you heard…"

Her anger flared now, hot and bright. "Please, do me the courtesy of not lying to my face again. I'm not mistaken. I have excellent hearing."

"My mother doesn't bring out my best qualities."

"Oh, you mean like finding out you're a liar? That you did exactly what you promised you wouldn't do?"

"I don't understand. Why are you yelling at me?"

Because you don't love me, she wanted to scream, but she could hardly do that. It sounded pitiful and she wasn't going to beg.

"It's okay that you're not in love with me. And yeah, we haven't known each other long, despite the fact that we're having a baby together. But you used me, and you pretended to care, because you'd do anything to ensure you show your mother what a horrible parent she was. Even pretend to love me. And those are your words, not mine."

His mouth fell open.

She waited.

"You weren't supposed to hear that," he said, his voice quiet and rough.

"Clearly. But I did hear it, and I'm glad. Because you manipulated me. Tell me, Jeremy, if you manipulate the mother of your child, are you going to manipulate the baby, too? Use him or her to work out all your own mommy and daddy issues?"

His cheeks reddened. "This is so easy for you to say, when you had two parents growing up who clearly loved and cared for you."

Tori took a step forward. "You are a grown man. Do not

blame your poor decision-making on your mother. You had the chance to act with integrity. This is on you, and not anyone else." Tears burned in her eyes. "You used my emotions. But more than that, you've lost my respect. And that hurts almost as much as knowing you played me."

His face twisted in pain, and he turned away for a moment. She saw his shoulders rise and fall with a deep breath. Then he turned back. She didn't want to be moved by the look in his eyes. He looked tortured, but she steeled her spine. If he was, it was because he was dealing with the consequences of his actions.

"You've got it all wrong."

"How do I have it wrong? I heard you. Clear as day."

"I lied."

Her traitorous heart kicked a little bit when he said it, but she quickly replaced the momentary elation with doubt. "You lied...to whom? To me? To your mother? How am I supposed to believe you?"

Jeremy ran his hand through his hair, a gesture she now knew he used when he was agitated. "To my mother. Do you seriously think that I would admit my feelings for you to her?"

"Why not? What would happen if you did? It's not like you have a great relationship with her anyway."

"I just... I keep my feelings locked away there. Anytime I tried to talk to her as a kid I was told to get over it or I got a laundry list of all the advantages I had and how I was ungrateful for complaining. It's what I do, on instinct. So does Sarah. We all do." He lowered his voice. "I don't... I mean, it's a vulnerability thing."

She could understand that, but it didn't excuse his behavior. "Again, Jeremy, you're a grown man. You're educated, successful. Powerful. And you can't stand up to your mom? That says a lot to me."

"I don't want her to know how I feel. I don't want her to see any weakness. My feelings for you—"

"What, make you weak?" Hardly a compliment. "When people care about each other, it's supposed to make them *more*, not *less*. And somehow you've got it in your brain that weakness, vulnerability, is a bad thing. It's not."

"It's never been a good thing," he bit back. "For Pete's sake, I don't even think I know how to love anyone. This whole situation terrifies me."

Everything was falling apart. Even if it was true that he'd lied to his mom, that he really did care about her, he considered that a chink in his armor.

She wanted to believe his feelings for her were real. But even if they were, tonight had cast serious doubts on their future. If he was incapable of loving, if he considered that a weakness, how could he possibly love their baby? For all his good intentions, she never wanted her child to feel rejected by its father. Or to have to beg for affection.

"Let me tell you about weakness," she said quietly. "And vulnerability. From the moment I discovered I was pregnant, I knew I was vulnerable because of the power imbalance in our situations. I wouldn't have the resources to fight you for custody of our child if you decided to take me to court. Then you showed up and I was forced to tell you the truth. I figured if we could be on good terms, we could work through something together. You reminded me of the man I met in the summer. You were kind. I started to care for you again. You asked me to come here, and I did. You asked me to uproot my life and I was willing to consider it, even though the job I love and my family and friends are all back in Nova Scotia. I trusted you. I believed in you. And I'm not afraid to say it, even though you are. I fell in love with you."

"Tori—"

"No." She held up a hand. "Just no. I fell in love with the person I thought Jeremy Fisher was. Tonight I discovered he is someone else. He did a great job of faking it, but I don't know you. You wanted me to go tonight so I knew what I was getting into, and boy do I ever. So I'm going home. And after a while, we'll discuss custody and visitation like rational adults, I hope. Financial situation or not, I will fight back if you choose to get lawyers involved. I hope it doesn't come to that."

His eyes dulled and he looked utterly bereft. She didn't want to be affected by his forlorn look, but she was.

"Everything before tonight... It was true. I swear it."

Her insides trembled. "I don't know how to believe you. I don't know which Jeremy is the real one. And that's not something I'm willing to bet my life or my baby's happiness on. I'm sorry, Jeremy."

She moved past him and down the hall to her room, where she started to pack her bags. He came to stand in the doorway. "Please, Tori. I'm trying here." He ran his hand through his hair. "My mom brings out the worst in me, and I'm so sorry. I should have been stronger. Should have been honest."

She looked up at him. "The thing is, I think you were honest. I think your number one priority is to show your mother that you can be better than her. It's not me, and it's not love that's driving that decision. I won't uproot my whole life on that sort of gamble."

For a moment, she thought she saw tears glimmer in his eyes, and her resolve wavered. Then he swallowed and said, "What time is your flight tomorrow?"

"Ten."

"Get some sleep, then. I'll get you to the airport in lots of time."

She opened a drawer and took out some sweaters.

"Tori, I'm sorry. I handled everything badly. I know I messed this up. Wait, and let's try to work through it."

"I just need to go home," she said, not looking at him.

She sensed when he left her doorway, and she braced her hands on her suitcase as her head drooped. Was she overreacting? His explanations made sense, but the fact remained that even if he'd lied to his mother, he hadn't stood up for Tori. And even though he'd said he'd lied, he hadn't said that he loved her, either. Even after she'd admitted her feelings first.

She texted her mom, asking if she could pick her up at the airport the next afternoon, then finished packing. She sat up the rest of the night, unable to sleep.

When six thirty rolled around, she ordered a taxi and quietly made her way out of his apartment and to the bottom floor. She couldn't handle saying goodbye; her feelings were too raw. She didn't want to sit through another ride to the airport, either. When the cab arrived, the driver put her suitcase and carry bag in the trunk and they were off to New Jersey.

She was going home. Alone.

CHAPTER FOURTEEN

She was gone.

Jeremy stared at the spare room with disbelief. She'd run. Granted, last night had been a disaster. But he would have taken her to the airport. He'd hoped that they'd get up this morning and be able to talk about what had happened without the high emotions of last night. Maybe even change her mind.

But she was gone.

He wandered to the main living area, his heart sore. The flower arrangement she'd bought was still on the dining table; the evergreen centerpiece in the living room, along with that silly little tree. A few dishes remained in the sink from where they'd had a cup of coffee yesterday afternoon before heading to Connecticut.

She was still here, whether he wanted her to be or not.

Jeremy wandered to the windows and looked out over the snowy city. She'd been right about pretty much everything. He should have stood up to his mother. Why not? It wasn't as if they had a relationship to speak of anyway. But that house... Anytime he was inside he was back to being that little boy again. Protecting himself and his feelings against ridicule and neglect. Poor little rich boy.

He knew very well that rich people could be miserable, too.

It was eight o'clock now. She'd be boarding in an hour, heading back to Nova Scotia and the family and job she loved. After yesterday, he had no right to take her away from that. No matter how much he'd really wanted to try for the life they'd begun to plan.

And his baby... He sank onto the sofa and put his head in his hands. No matter what she thought of him, he wouldn't put either of them through a legal battle. And there was no way he'd take the baby from her. She was going to be a damned good mother.

He wandered through the day aimlessly. Sarah called on her way back from Connecticut and he put her off. Cole texted and he didn't reply. Right now he was licking his wounds.

If only she hadn't heard him in Bruce's office. He could have kept his mom at arm's length and then gone on with his plans. And yet, deep down, he knew that was a coward's reasoning.

He'd been fighting his feelings all week. He'd kept telling himself that he wasn't capable of love. That it wasn't on his agenda. That it wasn't necessary for them to make this work.

But he'd been lying to himself. He did love her. Maybe he had from the beginning, when their connection had been so strong it had knocked him off his feet. When he'd looked for a reason to go back and see her again. Bringing her here to New York.

Making love.

It had been love, too. Not just sex. He just hadn't wanted to admit it because it scared the hell out of him. Love was a weakness that could be exploited.

Except Tori would never do that. He knew that in his heart, and he'd lied to himself until it was too late and she had walked away.

And he could tell her all of that, but she was right. She didn't know which version was true, and she couldn't uproot her life for someone she didn't trust.

She'd loved him. She'd said it. And he'd messed it up by denying what was right in front of his face.

He sat on the sofa until the light turned dark again.

Arrivals seemed to take forever. First, she was seated at the very back of the plane, which meant she was last to get off. Then there was the long walk to customs, and the line to get through. Then waiting for luggage. Finally she cleared the secure area and walked through the doors to see her mom waiting, a smile on her face.

Tori started to cry.

"Oh, honey!" Shelley came forward and gave her a big, reassuring hug while Tori's hand clung to the handle of her suitcase. "Come on. Let's get you to the car and you can tell me what happened."

She had never been so glad to see someone in her whole life.

It took only a few minutes to reach the car in the parking garage and head out onto the highway that would take them first into Halifax, and then down to the South Shore. For the first few minutes, Shelley simply reached over and patted Tori's hand, as if to say, *It's going to be okay.* She kept quiet for ten minutes or so, and then simply said, "So what went wrong?"

Tori sighed. "I don't know where to start."

"Then let's stop somewhere to eat. Neither of us has had lunch. Did you even have breakfast?"

She shrugged. "I had a yogurt at the airport."

"Where do you want to go?"

"I don't care."

Shelley quieted again, and then turned off the highway and drove to a diner in Bedford. "Quieter here than Cora's on a Sunday," she said. "And breakfast all day. Come on."

She wasn't feeling very hungry, but she ordered a breakfast

skillet anyway, to make her mom happy. And orange juice, because it was her favorite.

Once they'd placed their orders, Shelley looked at her with a "tell your mom about it" expression. "Okay. So you came back a few days early, looking like a whipped puppy. What happened?"

She told her mom everything. By the time she finished, their meals had been placed in front of them and Shelley had gotten a refill of her coffee.

"Baby girl," she said, on a sigh. "You're right. You deserve a man who will stand up for you, and for your family. Who will do the right thing."

"I thought he was that man, you know? That's what hurts so much." She picked at a chunk of hash-browned potato in her skillet.

"You think he was pretending the whole time?"

Her fork kept moving the piece of potato around and around. "I did when I first heard what he said. And then... Oh, Mom. I don't know. It's hard to believe that it wasn't real. The whole week was actually pretty magical. And when he heard the baby's heartbeat..."

"You wonder how he could be such a good actor?"

"I...yeah. And I get mad at myself for wanting to believe him. But he never said he loves me. I keep coming back to that. And the fact that I don't know if I could believe him even if he did say it."

She sniffled. Put down her fork. "He had a rotten childhood. He never had a solid family unit like I had with you and Dad."

"Does that excuse his behavior?"

She shook her head. "But it makes me understand it. I know he wants to be a good father, but what if he just doesn't have the ability to let himself love someone? I thought I could go through with it. We were getting along so well. I could see our relationship growing so that someday maybe it would be...whole."

"But..."

"But it would never be what you had with Dad. And I don't want to settle for anything less."

Shelley reached for her napkin and dabbed her eyes and her nose. "Well, I guess your dad and I did something right."

"I miss him."

"Me, too, honey. Every day."

They picked at their food. Tori was hungry, and the more she ate, the better she felt. Even though she couldn't finish the large portion, she'd needed the nutrition. So did the baby.

Shelley looked up at her. "You said before that you thought you could go through with it. Don't hate me for asking, but is there a chance you're using what happened as a way out?"

She wanted to say yes without hesitation, but she couldn't.

"You hesitated, which means you're thinking about it. I just think maybe Jeremy isn't the villain he's been made out to be. Yes, he made a mistake and you absolutely deserve better. You shouldn't settle for less. But you need to be clear on your own motives too, sweetie. Picking up and moving countries to be with a man you care about but who might not love you in return is a big risk."

The meal she'd just eaten churned in her stomach. "And he gave me a way out without me having to take any responsibility." Ugh, had she really done that? Used his weakness to justify her own behavior, her own fears?

"I'm not saying you should have stayed. I think I'm saying this is a big mess, and the only way through it is for both of you to be completely honest with each other. You reacted and you left. But now there are a lot of feelings to sort through. I think you should take the time to do it." Then Shelley smiled. "And you can spend Christmas with your mama while you're sorting things out."

"I love you, Mom."

Shelley reached for the bill. "Well, duh. Of course you do. Look, kiddo, since your dad died, I've watched you be afraid. It made you grow up in a hurry. You haven't had a lot of relationships since Riley broke your trust, and I think that trust is your deal breaker. Have you told Jeremy that?"

"Not really."

"Look, your dad set a wonderful example and standard, but you were also hurt when he left."

"He didn't leave us. Not like Jeremy's dad did."

"Not in the same way, but he left just the same. Don't be afraid to love someone, honey. Jeremy lied to his mom. He didn't stand up for you. But that doesn't mean he doesn't love you."

"He didn't say it."

"I know. Just give it some thought, and when you're ready, you and Jeremy need to talk. Even if it's just to decide what's going to happen with visitation."

They got up and Shelley paid the bill, and then they got on the road again. As they merged onto the highway, Tori sighed. "I keep telling myself I'm afraid he'll use his money and power to take the baby. I feel like I need to protect myself and prepare for that possibility. And then my heart says he would never do such a thing. And I think I'm being a fool, again."

Shelley didn't answer, but Tori knew exactly what she would say. Sit on it. Think about it and sort through her feelings. And then talk to Jeremy.

The bar was crowded and noisy, and Jeremy could tell Bran was only going through the motions. Cole, on the other hand, was flirting with their waitress and being his charming self. And Jeremy was running around with his tail between his legs.

Still. He couldn't mope around his apartment forever, and Bran needed to get out now and again. His possession date for the new house was the first of February; then the three of them hanging out would be a rare occasion.

Of course, Bran was going to be close to Tori. And that irritated Jeremy like a scratchy tag on the back of his neck.

"Beer, whiskey, and a rum and coke." The waitress put their drinks on the table. "Can I get you anything else?"

"We're good for now," Cole said, flashing her a million-dollar smile.

She smiled back and was gone with a twitch of her hip.

"Stop that," Bran said, scowling. "You're not twenty-five anymore, Cole."

"What? The day I stop flirting is the day I die."

Bran shook his head. "Yeah, but you have no follow-through. You work too much."

Jeremy shook his head. "Listen, you two, I came out for drinks and a good time."

Cole sipped on his rum and coke. "No, you didn't. You came out because you're being a sad sack since Tori went back to Canada. We don't need to tell you how you messed that up, Jer."

He took a big pull of his beer. "Yeah, sure. I know that."

Bran looked at him. "When we saw you in your office that day, you looked pretty happy. She thinks you were faking it, right? That she was manipulated? But was she?"

The beer didn't quite settle in his stomach. "Of course not. I mean, I wanted to bring her around, but damn, you know?" He scowled. "The way I sounded at my mom's... It was like she wasn't worth loving. I don't blame her for being furious. Or walking away."

Cole saluted with his glass. "Well done, dumbass."

Bran rolled his eyes. "Jer, let me ask you this. What was the moment you first knew?"

"First knew what?"

"That you loved her."

The table went silent.

Bran took a drink of his whiskey and pushed back his shaggy hair. "Look, when I met Becca, I didn't love her at first. But there was a moment. It wasn't even a big moment. She was in my place and she looked over her shoulder at me and laughed and it was just there. *Bam, I love her.* And I'm guessing you had that moment, because you've been dragging yourself around for the last five days, beating yourself up and thinking about nothing but the fact she's gone. So when was it?"

Jeremy's throat tightened. "When we were skating. She did this turn thing and faced me, holding my hands, and she laughed and had this weird hat on with her ponytail out the top, and it was like someone opened my heart and poured in a ray of sunshine."

Cole swore and shook his head.

Bran wagged a finger at him. "Look, he-man. Don't be like that just because it hasn't happened to you."

Then Bran turned to Jeremy. "Dude, I'm telling you right now. You've got to go make this right. I won't have another chance with Becca. She's gone, but Tori isn't. She needs to know how you feel. You've got to lay it on the line, brother. You'll regret it forever if you don't. And she's having your kid. If you want to have a relationship with him or her, if you want to do better than your own father did, you've got to step up."

"She doesn't want to see me."

"Bull. I'm telling you right now, there's no room for pride at this point. You might have to beg. But if you love her…"

"Of course I do. And my kid, too. Hearing that heartbeat…"

"Then fight for her. You didn't do that when you had the chance, don't you see? And if she loves you, too, that had to break her heart."

Cole took a long drink. "As much as it pains me to say it, I agree with Dear Abby here. We were with you at school. We know you almost as well as you know yourself. You would do anything to not be your dad, and that's great. So stop acting like him. Man, every time you go to that house you act like… I don't know. Like she has some kind of say over your life. You're a grown man."

Jeremy chuckled despite the sting he felt at Cole's words. "That's what Tori said."

"So quit running away and stand up to your mom instead of

all that polite-distance kind of thing. And go talk to Tori. Tell her how you feel."

"Sometimes manning up means laying your heart on the line, rather than being 'strong,' you know?" Bran finished his whiskey. "I'm telling you guys, I'm a freaking mess, but I wouldn't trade any of the time I had with Bec."

"We know, man." Jeremy put his hand on Bran's shoulder. "And you're right. I just... I don't know how to do this."

Cole leaned forward. "I think the correct word is *beg*. Or maybe *grovel*."

"Helpful," Jeremy muttered. "I guess...family means everything to Tori. She loves her mom so much, and her dad died a couple years ago, and... I feel like a horrible human, not feeling that kind of connection or loyalty to my own family. Sarah excluded."

"Hey." Bran looked him dead in the eye. "Family is more than genetics. We learned that at Merrick."

"Go Monarchs," Cole and Jeremy said, lifting their glasses.

Jeremy settled back into his chair, while Cole signaled for another round. "Yeah, you're right. You guys are my brothers."

"And it's our job to kick you when you're being an idiot. So get yourself together and figure out how you're going to get her back. It's Christmas. A good present should come with the groveling."

The next round of drinks appeared, and Jeremy perked up. He at least had to try. He'd been miserable the last few days. The apartment was cold and empty. He couldn't focus. He stared endlessly at the ultrasound picture. He'd let the best thing in his life get away, because he couldn't deal with his feelings.

And as Bran and Cole started to discuss ordering some snacks, Jeremy got the first inklings of a plan. Starting tomorrow, he'd have to get himself in gear in order to have it all set for Christmas.

CHAPTER FIFTEEN

CHRISTMAS MORNING DAWNED bright and clear, with a pristine blue sky and a new dusting of snow that made everything look fresh and white but didn't play havoc with road conditions. Tori had slept at her mom's, and would stop in at the Sandpiper later. They kept a very light staff on Christmas Day and Boxing Day, and they had minimal bookings, too. Still, essential staff were away from their loved ones on Christmas morning, so she'd arranged for them all to have breakfast midmorning. The crew would have breakfast meats and eggs cooked by Neil and his sous chefs, and she'd brought in pastries from a local bakery. She'd even made a huge bowl of fruit salad herself and left it in the massive fridge.

Now, though, at barely eight o'clock, she sat beside her mother's decorated spruce tree, looking at the arrangement of presents beneath it.

She had a lot to be thankful for. She was healthy, her baby was healthy, she had a job she loved and a mother who doted on her. And yet the holiday felt lusterless and underwhelming. All because she couldn't get the father of her child off her mind.

"I made you tea," Shelley said, coming in from the kitchen. They were both dressed in fuzzy new pajamas; getting new ones on Christmas Eve had been a tradition for her when she was a kid, and in the past few years they'd taken to buying them for each other. She handed Tori the cup and sat down on a footstool nearby, cradling her own cup of coffee. "So. Have you opened your stocking?"

"I was waiting for you."

"Let me turn on some Christmas music first."

With the sound of carols in the background and the lights on the tree turned on, Tori reached for her stocking. Inside was her favorite chocolate, a three-pack of maternity underwear, some soft and fuzzy socks and the usual toiletries—body wash, deodorant, shampoo. There were some treats, too, like a new kind of tea and a little box of mini-facials. "Mom, this was too much."

"Don't be silly." Shelley was opening her own stocking, with her favorite treats and beauty brands, as well.

There were only a few presents under the tree. Two for each of them from each other, and there was one from the staff for Tori and one from the other nurses on Shelley's unit. Tori oohed over a new maternity outfit in the first box, and then watched as her mom opened her new pressure cooker she'd asked for. Her second gift contained a gorgeous lemon-yellow crocheted blanket.

"Oh, Mom."

"I haven't crocheted in years, but I figured this was as good a time as any to get out the old hook and take it up again. Do you like it?"

Tori ran her hand over the soft, fine yarn. "I love it. The baby will love it, too, because Grandma made it."

"Merry Christmas, sweetie."

"Open your last one, Mom."

She handed the gift bag to her mom. Shelley reached inside and took out a small box, then opened the box and withdrew the Christmas ornament. It was a glass ball with white and gold and the word *Grandma* painted on it with glitter.

"Where in the world did you find this?"

"In a little shop in New York." She had a similar ornament

still tucked away in a drawer in her room. The one she'd bought for Jeremy but had forgotten to give him. She'd grabbed it at the last minute and put it in her luggage, hoping it would make the trip without breaking.

She'd been so excited that day. And that night, she and Jeremy had slept together.

"Are you okay?"

"I'm fine." She put on a smile. "Really. We're both fine." She put her hand on her tummy. "And hungry."

They'd picked up the paper from their gifts and were just heading to the kitchen when there was a knock on the door.

"You expecting someone?" Tori called, as she opened the fridge door and got out eggs and ham for omelets.

When there was no answer right away, she straightened and poked her head out of the kitchen. "Who is it?"

Jeremy stepped into the entryway. "It's me."

She shouldn't be so glad to see him. But she was. He was here. In Nova Scotia. In her mother's hall. On Christmas morning.

"Hi," she said, belatedly realizing she was dressed in penguin pajamas with slippers on her feet and her hair in a messy ponytail.

"Merry Christmas."

It was incredibly awkward and emotionally charged. Shelley took a step back and murmured, "I'll just go start breakfast," while Tori and Jeremy stared at each other for a long, painful moment.

"You look wonderful," he said, his voice soft, and she wanted to believe him so badly it hurt.

"What are you doing here?"

"I came to ask for your forgiveness." He stepped forward but only to the edge of the mat; a film of snow was on his shoes. She went to him instead, not necessarily for intimacy but more for privacy. Her mother's house wasn't large, and conversations were easily overheard. She laughed a little as Shelley made an inordinate amount of noise with frying pans.

"You look like your mom," he said gently. "She frowns like you, too. Told me I'd better get it right this time."

Tori's cheeks heated. "Mom doesn't mince words."

"Neither does her daughter. And I've recently discovered that both of you are pretty much right."

She didn't want to hope. But it was Christmas. And he looked so handsome in perfectly fitted jeans and his peacoat, his hair slightly mussed and his gray eyes focused on her so intently.

His gaze swept down to her belly and back up. "You're feeling okay?"

She nodded, her throat tightening. "Yeah, we're both okay. The baby's been moving around a lot."

"That's good."

"Yeah."

"Tori—" His voice broke off, and then he took a breath and squared his shoulders. "I went to see my mother. And I told her what I should have told her the night of the party. I told her that I love you, and I love this baby, and that I want to do right by both of you. And I owe you such a huge apology, Tori. I never showed my emotions. Not in that house, not with any of my relationships, because every time I did I got punished for it. But you invited me to. You gave me a safe place with no judgment and I used that gift to hurt you. I'm so sorry, Tori. More than you know."

She stood there dumbly, not knowing what to say or do. It scared her how much she wanted to believe him. She'd had time to think over the past several days, and really look at what had happened. He'd hurt her terribly at the party, while she'd still been stinging from his mother's cold reception. And she'd felt incredibly out of her depth. And no, he hadn't told her that he loved her, but he had tried to explain and she hadn't let him.

Because she, too, was scared. And she'd run.

"You love me?" she asked. "And the baby? Not just so that we won't be in separate countries or living in separate homes?"

He swallowed. "I loved this baby from the moment I saw that picture on the ultrasound machine. And I think I loved you all along. But Tori, your family is here. Your job is here. I won't ask you to leave that behind, not if you don't want to."

"And I will stay here, and you'll stay…"

His gray eyes softened. "In New York. We'll work this out on your terms, Tori. I can't force you to forgive me, or love me. But you're going to be a wonderful mother, and I think the best way for me to be a good dad is to make sure you're happy."

Her eyes stung as tears sprang into them. "But you said you love me."

He nodded, and his eyes were bright, too. "I do. Enough to let you go, if that's what you want."

She caught her breath, and it sounded almost like a sob, but she wouldn't let that happen. She wouldn't cry today. "What if that's not what I want?"

The air between them stilled. "Then come over here and put me out of my misery."

She took three halting steps and then threw herself into his arms. His tightened around her, holding her close, the baby sandwiched between them. "You feel good," he whispered in her ear. "I was sure you'd tell me to walk out. Thank you for not doing that."

She nodded against his coat and sniffed. "It's partly my fault, too. I was overwhelmed and feeling like someone's poor cousin, and I wanted you to stand up for me. When you didn't… I just wanted to go home, where it was familiar. I used your mistake as an excuse, rather than talking it out. And I ran away."

"You had good reason. But, sweetheart…" His breath was warm against her ear. "I made a mistake. I didn't stop loving you. I just was too afraid to say it. Loving people has always made me weak, so I told myself I was incapable of it." He pushed back a little so he could look into her eyes. "Until now."

And then he kissed her, a wild welcoming that seemed to put everything right that had gone wrong. It wasn't the kiss of a coward or a pretender; it was the kiss of a man claiming the woman he loved. And when his hand cradled her baby bump, she closed her eyes and let the bit of gratitude that had been missing this morning trickle in.

"I hate to break up this happy reunion, but I have ham and cheese omelets and home fries for anyone who's hungry. That includes you, Jeremy."

He looked into Tori's eyes. "I don't deserve that kind of welcome," he whispered.

"Don't be silly. This is how family works." She clasped his hand. "We mess up and we forgive each other. I was awfully lonely this morning, Jeremy. Wishing you were here. Wondering if I should call you and what I should say. I'd forgiven you for what happened at the party, but I was still afraid, you see."

"You were gone about ten minutes before I started missing you," he murmured, kissing her forehead. "And my real brothers—Cole and Bran—told me I was an idiot for blowing it. It has to be love," he continued, squeezing her fingers. "Nothing else could ever hurt me this much."

Considering the pain he'd been through as a boy, that was saying something. And what was more, she believed him. Because the Jeremy at the party wasn't the real Jeremy. She'd had time to think about that and realize that she'd let one five-minute conversation negate everything else between them. The Jeremy in all the other moments was the real man. And he was something special.

"Let's have breakfast, then."

"Okay. And then I want you to get dressed, because I have something to show you."

"You do?"

"A surprise."

"You and your surprises," she said, making a *tsk* sound. But as they walked to the kitchen, Christmas was suddenly very merry indeed.

While Tori was having a quick shower and getting dressed, Jeremy grabbed a dish towel and started drying dishes for Shelley.

"Mrs. Sharpe?"

She looked up at him, her hands in the dishwater. "You'd better call me Shelley, don't you think?"

"Maybe another time. Right now... Well, since Tori's dad isn't here, I'm going to ask you."

She reached for the dish towel in his hands and dried hers off, then looked up at him. "Ask me what?"

His stomach quivered. This emotional nakedness was all new to him, and he was terrified he was going to get a lecture once he said what he needed to say. But it was the right thing to do.

"Ask you for permission to marry your daughter."

Her gaze bored into him, and he couldn't tell what she was thinking. After what had happened, he rather expected he was being measured and coming up short.

"My girl can make up her own mind."

He nodded. "Yes, she can. But your family is different from mine, and your approval means a lot. So I'm asking anyway."

Her expression softened. "If Tori says yes, I certainly won't stand in her way."

He sagged with relief. "Okay. Phew. Thanks for not giving me the third degree."

She touched his arm. "Look. Clearly I don't have to worry about her materially, her or the baby. My biggest concern is for her heart. I saw her face when she realized it was you at the door, and I saw yours, too. There's far more between you than just a baby. So I'll leave you two to work out whatever future fits."

"Even if I take her away?"

She nodded. "Even then."

"Mrs. Sharpe?"

"Shelley. And yes?"

"I wish I'd had a mom like you."

To his surprise, she handed him back the dish towel and patted his arm. "Well, now you do."

She went back to washing dishes as if she hadn't just turned his world on its end.

When Tori came back to the kitchen, he and Shelley were talking about Sharpe Christmas traditions. He broke off mid-sentence when Tori appeared in the doorway. She wore a new outfit of navy leggings and a soft gray sweater that molded to her shape and made her look so beautiful and maternal he thought his heart might burst. "Look at you," he said, putting down the towel.

"It's new. From Mom, for Christmas." She turned in a circle. "See, Mom? Fits perfectly."

"You look lovely." Shelley let the water out of the sink. "Now go on. Jeremy has a surprise for you. I'll expect you back for dinner at five."

"We'll be back before then," Jeremy assured her. "You shouldn't have to cook a whole Christmas dinner yourself."

"Take your time," she said with a laugh. "The prep's done. I'm going to put the bird in the oven and have a nap. Maybe read one of the books I got from the girls at work."

He held Tori's coat for her—still the parka that needed replacing—and then took her hand, leading her to his rented car. "Did you stay at the inn?" she asked, waiting as he opened the door for her.

"No, here in Lunenburg. I didn't want you to know I was in town yet."

"Oh."

"Come on. I've got something to show you."

They drove past Liverpool and toward the Sandpiper, and then past it. He looked over at her face as he turned up the lane leading to the house on the beach, the one they'd looked at after their feed of fish and chips. Her eyes widened.

"What are we doing here?"

"You'll see."

The gate was open, and they drove through, up the drive to the house. A huge wreath was on the front door, and just like at her mom's, a light dusting of snow made everything postcard perfect. He parked and got out of the car, patted his pocket, and went around to open her door. She put her hand in his and got out.

"Jeremy?"

"Come on."

He led her to the bluff overlooking the private stretch of beach. The wind was brisk off the water, but not bitter. The caps were white and the faint sound of the breakers touched his ears. This had been the right choice. No question.

"Tori?"

"Yes?"

"Remember the night we watched *Miracle on 34th Street*?"

She nodded.

"And there was the scene, at the end of the date, where Bryan proposes and she turns him down?"

Tori's eyes widened as she turned away from the ocean and stared up at him. "What?"

It was now or never. "You said to me, I don't know why she's so mean to Bryan. And I said, because she's scared. Plus they had to work to get to their happy ending."

She nodded, just barely, and he reached inside his pocket. "I know you're scared. I'm scared. But we shouldn't let that stop us from being happy. Not if we can be scared together. I'm ready to work toward that happy ending if you are."

And he held out the red ring box, identical to the one in the movie, and opened it.

Tori stared at the ring. It was possibly the most gorgeous thing she'd ever seen, nestled in velvet, winking in the winter sunlight. "You're proposing?"

"I am. I even asked your mom for permission."

She choked out a laugh, imagining how that conversation must have gone. "Oh, you didn't."

"I did. Because while my family is a hot mess, yours isn't. I thought it would mean a lot to you."

She sighed. "It does."

"Tori?"

She couldn't stop staring at the ring. "Hmm?"

"Will you marry me?"

She looked up at him, all gray stormy eyes and wild hair and sexy vulnerability. It was hard to believe that a chance affair months earlier had led to this moment, but it had, and he was standing before her, asking her to be his wife.

And she knew now, without a doubt, that he'd lied to his mom and he'd been honest every step of the way. The proof was in his smiles, in his tender gestures, in the way he made her laugh. In the way they made love. He wasn't perfect. And neither was she. But he was hers, and she was his, and it was time she had a little faith.

So she nodded, said yes, and told him to put it on her finger.

When he slid it over her knuckle, she started to cry. It was beautiful, but what it meant was more so. They'd stopped being afraid and had started facing things together.

He kissed her softly, his lips cold from the wind. "So that's not the only surprise," he said against her mouth.

"It's not?"

"Don't you wonder why I brought you here?"

She looked around. The for-sale sign was gone from the yard. There was a wreath on the door. "I don't know, but don't you think the owners will wonder why we're standing out here on their bluff?"

He reached into his pocket again, and this time he took out a key and placed it in her palm.

She lifted startled eyes to his.

"I doubt it, since I'm the new owner."

"You... What?"

He grinned at her now, excitement flashing through his smile. "You love it here. I love it here. I don't necessarily want to relocate, but can you think of a better summer home? You can be close to your mom whenever you want. We can spend summer days building sandcastles with our kids on the beach. We can put a boat in here and sail down the coast. Have bonfires in the back. Marrying me shouldn't have to mean you leave home behind. Not when we can manage to have you here. And if you want to keep up with your innkeeper roots..." He swept his arm to the other side of the property. "The guesthouse is there. You're right. You could turn it into a vacation rental with no trouble at all. If you want to."

She couldn't believe it. "You bought me...a house? For Christmas?"

He nodded.

She started to laugh. And then she laughed more and more until the sound of it echoed through the winter air.

"What's so funny?" His brows pulled together.

"Just that when we were looking at houses, you said this one wasn't large enough to suit. And now it's yours."

"I said it wasn't suited for Bran. Me? Well, I realized that it's not the house but the love inside it that matters." He spread his arms wide. "I came from a huge mansion with every advantage, but little love. Honey, let me tell you, this house is plenty big enough, as long as you're inside it."

She wrapped her arms around him and hugged him tight. She wasn't sure if fate was a thing, or serendipity, or what, but something had brought him here last summer and turned her world upside down. It was wonderful.

"Let's go inside," she suggested.

"You've got the key."

She went up the walk and turned the lock easily. Inside smelled like pine cones and cinnamon. There was no furniture, but in the corner of the living room, by the fireplace, was a huge decorated tree.

"Merry Christmas, sweetheart," he said from behind her.

She spun in a circle. "It really is. And now is the perfect time to give you your present."

She loved the look on his face right now. He'd thought he'd been in charge of all the surprises today, but she had one more.

"But you didn't even know you were going to see me."

She reached into her handbag and took out the little gift bag she'd hidden in his apartment. The one that had made it through without getting crushed in her luggage, despite being hastily shoved inside without soft packing to keep it safe. And before this Christmas tree was the perfect moment. She handed it to him and smiled. "Merry Christmas, Jeremy."

She stood back while he removed the tissue, then reached inside. The little box was the same as her mom's had been, but what was inside was even more special.

He opened the lid and took out the ornament she'd bought.

It was white, too, but in pink glitter it spelled out "Daddy's Girl" in swooping cursive.

His gaze shot up to hers. "Daddy's girl... We're having a girl?"

She nodded, tears clogging her throat. The look on his face right now... It was almost the same as when she'd first told him about the baby. Terror and surprise but now with an added ingredient: joy.

"I found out a bit by accident, just before we left for New York. I was going to tell you the night I'd decorated your apartment, but then we kind of fought and then we made up and it wasn't the right moment. But now...now it's right. We're having a baby girl, and you can hang that ornament on our very first Christmas tree."

Instead he came to her and crushed her in a hug. "I am not sure what I ever did to deserve you, but thank you. For rocking my world. For loving me. And for giving me a second chance. I'm not going to let you down, Tori. Or our baby."

And when he'd hung the ornament on the tree, they stepped back, held hands and moved into a new future as a family.

* * * * *

The Rancher's Christmas Promise

Allison Leigh

Though her name is frequently on bestseller lists, **Allison Leigh**'s high point as a writer is hearing from readers that they laughed, cried or lost sleep while reading her books. She credits her family with great patience for the time she's parked at her computer, and for blessing her with the kind of love she wants her readers to share with the characters living in the pages of her books. Contact her at allisonleigh.com.

Books by Allison Leigh

Harlequin Special Edition

Return to the Double C

Show Me a Hero
Yuletide Baby Bargain
A Child Under His Tree
The BFF Bride
One Night in Weaver...
A Weaver Christmas Gift
A Weaver Beginning
A Weaver Vow

The Fortunes of Texas: The Rulebreakers

Fortune's Homecoming

The Fortunes of Texas: The Secret Fortunes

Wild West Fortune

The Fortunes of Texas: All Fortune's Children

Fortune's Secret Heir

Visit the Author Profile page
at millsandboon.com.au for more titles.

Dear Reader,

I've always been a big fan of the Harlequin series books, and Special Edition is a personal favorite. In recognition of this wonderful program, I'll be recommending one Special Edition per month to encourage readers to discover the charm and appeal of these compelling contemporary romances. Many of these books feature Western settings, handsome cowboys, gutsy women and beautiful babies. The heroes and heroines are dynamic and relatable, trying their best to resist their attraction to each other while resolving the conflict that keeps them apart. But the undeniable chemistry that simmers between them cannot be denied. These books will pull you in and take you on an emotional and satisfying journey. Each story ends with a marriage proposal or wedding—delivering the happily-ever-after, because the love and security of family is the ultimate promise of Special Edition.

I'm proud to present the first author in this promotion, *New York Times* and *USA TODAY* bestselling author Allison Leigh. Allison has written more than fifty romances, and has received high praise for her authentic and engaging plots. Her latest release, *The Rancher's Christmas Promise*, is the story of a single rancher, Ryder Wilson, who is suddenly given the responsibility of taking care of a baby from his ex-wife. Although Ryder is unsure of the baby's paternity, he wants the child to have a great home. Greer Templeton steps in to help out when it's obvious Ryder is having a tough time balancing the duties of the ranch and caring for the baby. This memorable holiday tale will surely leave a lasting impression on you.

Please take me up on this invitation to read a Special Edition and indulge in a heartwarming story. I do hope you enjoy the reading experience and will be back next month for another exciting book.

All the best,

Paula Eykel Miller

For my family.

PROLOGUE

"YOU'VE GOT TO be kidding me."

Ryder Wilson stared at the people on his porch. Even before they introduced themselves, he'd known the short, skinny woman was a cop thanks to the Braden Police Department badge she was wearing. But the two men with her? He'd never seen them before.

And after the load of crap they'd just spewed, he'd like to never see them again.

"We're not kidding, Mr. Wilson." That came from the serious-looking bald guy. The one who looked like he was a walking heart attack, considering the way he kept mopping the sweat off his face even though it was freezing outside. March had roared in like a lion this year, bringing with it a major snowstorm. Ryder hadn't lived there that long—it was only his second winter there—but people around town said they hadn't seen anything like it in Braden for more than a decade.

All he knew was that the snow was piled three feet high, making his life these days even more challenging. Making him wonder why he'd ever chosen Wyoming over New Mexico in the first place. Yeah, they got snow in Taos. But not like this.

"We believe that the infant girl who's been under our protection since she was abandoned three months ago is your daughter." The man tried to look past Ryder's shoulder. "Perhaps we could discuss this inside?"

Ryder had no desire to invite them in. But one of them *was* a cop. He hadn't crossed purposes with the law before and he wasn't real anxious to do so now. Didn't mean he had to like it, though.

His aunt hadn't raised him to be slob. She'd be horrified if she ever knew strangers were seeing the house in its current state.

He slapped his leather gloves together. He had chores waiting for him. But he supposed a few minutes wouldn't make much difference. "Don't think there's much to discuss," he warned as he stepped out of the doorway. He folded his arms across his chest, standing pretty much in their way so they had to crowd together in the small space where he dumped his boots. Back home, his aunt Adelaide would call the space a *vestibule*. Here, it wasn't so formal; he'd carved out his home from a converted barn. "I appreciate your concern for an abandoned baby, but whoever's making claims I fathered a child is out of their mind." Once burned, twice shy. Another thing his aunt was fond of saying.

The cop's brown eyes looked pained. "Ryder—may I call you Ryder?" She didn't wait for his permission, but plowed right on, anyway. "I'm sorry we have to be the bearer of bad news, but we believe your wife was the baby's mother, and—"

At the word *wife*, what had been Ryder's already-thin patience went by the wayside. "My *wife* ran out on me a year ago. Whatever she's done since is her prob—"

"Not anymore," the dark-haired guy said.

"What'd you say your name was?" Ryder met the other man's gaze head-on, knowing perfectly well he hadn't said his name. The pretty cop's role there was obviously official. Same with the sweaty bald guy—he had to be from social services. But the third intruder? The guy who was watching him as though he'd already formed an opinion—a bad one?

"Grant Cooper." The man's voice was flat. "Karen's my sister."

"There's your problem," Ryder responded just as flatly. "My so-called *wife's* name was Daisy. Daisy Miranda. You've got the wrong guy." He pointedly reached around them for the door to show them out. "So if you'll excuse me, I've got ice to break so my animals can get at their water."

"This is Karen." Only because she was a little slip of a thing, the cop succeeded in maneuvering between him and the door. She held a wallet-sized photo up in front of his face.

Ryder's nerves tightened even more than when he'd first opened the door to find these people on his front porch.

He didn't want to touch the photograph or examine it. He didn't need to. He recognized his own face just fine. In the picture, he'd been kissing the wedding ring he'd just put on Daisy's finger. The wedding had been a whirlwind sort of thing, like everything else about their relationship. Three months start to finish, from the moment they met outside the bar where she'd just quit her job until the day she'd walked out on him two weeks after their wedding. That's how long it had taken to meet, get hitched and get unhitched.

Though the unhitching part was still a work in progress. Not that he'd been holding on to hope that she'd return. But he'd had other things more important keeping him occupied than getting a formal divorce. Namely the Diamond-L ranch, which he'd purchased only a few months before meeting her. His only regret was that he hadn't kept his attention entirely on the ranch all along. It would have saved him some grief.

"Where'd you get that?"

The cop asked her own question. "Can you confirm this is you and your wife in this picture?"

His jaw felt tight. "Yeah." Unfortunately. The Las Vegas wedding chapel had given them a cheap set of pictures. Ryder had tossed all of them in the fireplace, save the one the cop was holding now. He'd mailed that one to Daisy in response to a stupid postcard he'd gotten from her six months after she'd left him. A postcard on which she'd written only the words *I'm sorry.*

He still wasn't sure what she'd meant. Sorry for leaving him without a word or warning? Or sorry she'd ever married him in the first place?

"You wrote this?" The cop had turned the photo over, revealing his handwriting on the back. *So much for vows.*

Ryder was actually a little surprised that it was so legible, considering how drunk he'd been at the time he'd sent the photo. He nodded once.

The cop looked sympathetic. "I'm sorry to say that she died in a car accident over New Year's."

He waited as the words sank in. Expecting to feel something. Was he supposed to feel bad? Maybe he did. He wasn't sure. He'd known Daisy was a handful from the get-go. So when she took a powder the way she had, it shouldn't have been as much of a shock as it had been.

But one thing was certain. Everything that Daisy had told him had been a lie. From start to finish.

He might be an uncomplicated guy, but he understood the bottom line facing him now. "And you want to pawn off her baby on me." He looked the dark-haired guy in the face again. "Or do you just want money?" He lifted his arm, gesturing with the worn leather gloves. "Look around. All I've got is what you see. And it'll be a cold day in hell before I let a couple strangers making claims like yours get one finger on it."

Grant's eyes looked like flint. "As usual, my sister's taste in men was worse than—"

"Gentlemen." The other man mopped his forehead again, giving both Ryder and Grant wary looks even as he took a step between them. "Let's keep our cool. The baby is our focus."

Ryder ignored him. He pointed at Grant. "My wife never even told me she had a brother."

"My sister never told me she had a husband."

"The situation is complicated enough," the cop interrupted,

"without the two of you taking potshots at each other." Her expression was troubled, but her voice was calm. And Ryder couldn't miss the way she'd wrapped her hand familiarly around Grant's arm. "Ray is right. What's important here is the baby."

"Yes. The baby under our protection." Ray was obviously hoping to maintain control over the discussion. "There is no local record of the baby's birth. Our only way left to establish who the child's parents are is through you, Mr. Wilson. We've expended every other option."

"You don't even *know* the baby was hers?"

Ray looked pained. Grant looked like he wanted to punch something. Hell, maybe even Ryder. The cop just looked worried.

"The assumption is that your wife was the person to have left the baby at the home her former employer, Jaxon Swift, shared with his brother, Lincoln," she said.

"Now, that *does* sound like Daisy." Ryder knew he sounded bitter. "I only knew her a few months, but it was still long enough to learn she's good at running out on people."

Maybe he did feel a little bad about Daisy. He hadn't gotten around to divorcing his absent wife. Now, if what these people said were true, he wouldn't need to. Instead of being a man with a runaway wife, he was a man with a deceased one. There was probably something wrong with him for not feeling like his world had just been rocked. "But maybe you're wrong. She wasn't pregnant when she left me," he said bluntly. He couldn't let himself believe otherwise.

"Would you agree to a paternity test?"

"The court can compel you, Mr. Wilson," Ray added when Ryder didn't answer right away.

It was the wrong tack for Ray to take. Ryder had been down the whole paternity-accusation path before. He hadn't taken kindly to it then, and he wasn't inclined to now. "Daisy was my wife, loose as that term is in this case. A baby born to her during our marriage makes me the presumed father, whether there's a test or not. But you don't know that the baby was actually hers. You just admitted it. Which tells me the court probably isn't on your side as much as you're implying. Unless I say otherwise, and without you knowing who this baby's mother is, I'm just a guy in a picture."

"We should have brought Greer," Grant said impatiently to the cop. "She's used to guys like him."

But the cop wasn't listening to Grant. She was looking at Ryder with an earnest expression. "You aren't just a guy in a picture. You're our best hope for preventing the child we believe is Grant's niece from being adopted by strangers."

That's when Ryder saw that she'd reached out to clasp Grant's hand, their fingers entwined. So, she had a dog in this race.

He thought about pointing out that he was a stranger to them, too, no matter what sort of guy Grant had deemed Ryder to be. "And if I cooperated and the test confirms I'm *not* this baby's father, you still wouldn't have proof that Daisy is—" *dammit* "—*was* the baby's mother."

"If the test is positive, then we know she was," Ray said. "Without your cooperation, the proof of Karen's maternity is circumstantial. We admit that. But you were her husband. There's no putative father. If you even suspected she'd become pregnant during your marriage, your very existence is enough to establish legal paternity, DNA proof or not."

The cop looked even more earnest. "And the court can't proceed with an adoption set in motion by Layla's abandonment."

The name startled him. *"Layla!"*

The three stared at him with varying degrees of surprise and expectation.

"Layla was my mother's name." His voice sounded gruff, even to his own ears. Whatever it was that Daisy had done with her child, using that name was a sure way of making sure he'd get involved. After only a few months together, she'd learned enough about him to know that.

He exhaled roughly. Slapped his leather gloves together. Then he stepped out of the way so he wasn't blocking them from the rest of his home. "You'd better come inside and sit." He felt weary all of a sudden. As if everything he'd accomplished in his thirty-four years was for nothing. What was that song? "There Goes My Life."

"I expect this is gonna take a while to work out." He glanced at the disheveled room, with its leather couch and oversize, wall-mounted television. That's what happened when a man spent more time tending cows than he did anything else. He'd even tended some of them in this very room.

Fortunately, his aunt Adelaide would never need to know.

"You'll have to excuse the mess, though."

CHAPTER ONE

Five months later.

THE AUGUST HEAT was unbearable.

The forecasters kept saying the end of the heat wave was near, but Greer Templeton had lost faith in them. She twisted in her seat, trying to find the right position that allowed her to feel the cold air from the car vents on more than two square inches of her body. It wasn't as if she could pull up her skirt so the air could blow straight up her thighs or pull down her blouse so the air could get at the rest of her.

She'd tried that once, only to find herself the object of interest of a leering truck driver with a clear view down into her car. If she'd never seen or heard from the truck driver again, it wouldn't have been so bad. Instead, she'd had the displeasure of serving as the driver's public defender not two days later when he was charged with littering.

"I hate August!" she yelled, utterly frustrated.

Nobody heard.

The other vehicles crawling along the narrow, curving stretch of highway between Weaver—where she'd just come from a frustrating visit with a new client in jail—and Braden all had their windows closed against the oppressive heat, the same way she did.

It was thirty miles, give or take, between Braden and Weaver, and she drove it several times every week. Sometimes more than once in a single day. She knew the highway like the back of her hand. Where the infrequent passing zones were, where the dips filled with ice in the winter and where the shoulder was treacherous. She knew that mile marker 12 had the best view into Braden and mile marker 3 was the spot you were most likely to get a speeding ticket.

The worst, though, was grinding up and down the hills, going around the curves at a crawl because she was stuck behind a too-wide truck hogging the roadway with a too-tall load of hay.

Impatience raged inside her and she pushed her fingers against one of the car vents, feeling the air blast against her palm. It didn't provide much relief, because it was barely cool.

Probably because her car was close to overheating, she realized.

Even as she turned off the AC and rolled down the windows, a cloud billowed from beneath the front hood of her car.

She wanted to scream.

Instead, she coasted onto the weedy shoulder. It was barely wide enough.

The car behind her laid on its horn as it swerved around her.

"I hate August!" she yelled after it while her vehicle burped out steam into the already-miserable air.

So much for getting to Maddie's surprise baby shower early.

Ali was never going to forgive Greer. Unlike their sister, Maddie, the soul of patience she was not. Just that morning Ali had called to remind Greer of her tasks where the shower was concerned. It had been the fifth such call in as many days.

Marrying Grant hadn't softened Ali's annoying side at all.

Greer wasn't going to chance exiting through the driver's side because of the traffic, so she hitched up her skirt enough to climb over the console and out the passenger-side door.

In just the few minutes it took to get out of the car and open up the hood, Greer's silk blouse was glued to her skin by the perspiration sliding down her spine.

The engine had stopped spewing steam. But despite her father's best efforts to teach the triplets the fundamentals of car care when she and her sisters were growing up, what lived beneath the hood of Greer's car was still a mystery.

She knew from experience there was no point in checking her cell phone for a signal. There were about four points on the thirty-mile stretch where a signal reliably reached, and this spot wasn't one of them. If a Good Samaritan didn't happen to stop, she knew the schedules of both the Braden Police Department and the Weaver Sheriff's Department. Even if her disabled vehicle wasn't reported by someone passing by, officers from one or the other agency routinely traveled the roadway even on a hot August Saturday. She didn't expect it would be too long before she had some help.

She popped the trunk a few inches so the heat wouldn't build up any more than it already had and left the windows down. Then she walked along the shoulder until she reached an outcrop of rock that afforded a little shade from the sun and toed off her shoes, not even caring that she was probably ruining her silk blouse by leaning against the jagged stone.

Sorry, Ali.

Ryder saw the slender figure in white before he saw the car. It almost made him do a double take, the way sailors did when they spotted a mermaid sunning herself on a rock. A second look reassured him that lack of sleep hadn't caused him to start hallucinating.

Not yet, anyway.

She was on the opposite side of the road, and there was no place for him to pull his rig around to get to her. So he kept on driving until he reached his original destination—the turnoff to the Diamond-L. As soon as he did, he turned around and pulled back out onto the highway to head back to her.

It was only a matter of fifteen minutes.

The disabled foreign car was still sitting there, like a strange out-of-place insect among the pickup trucks rumbling by every few minutes. He parked behind it, but let his engine idle and kept the air-conditioning on. He propped his arm over the steering column and thumbed back his hat as he studied the woman.

She'd noticed him and was picking her way through the rough weeds back toward her car.

He'd recognized her easily enough.

Greer Templeton. One of the identical triplets who'd turned his life upside down. Starting with the cop, Ali, who'd come to his door five months ago.

It wasn't entirely their fault.

They weren't responsible for abandoning Layla. That was his late wife.

Now Layla was going through nannies like there was a revolving door on the nursery. Currently, the role was filled by Tina Lewis. She'd lasted two weeks but was already making dissatisfied noises.

He blew out a breath and checked the road before pushing open his door and getting out of the truck. "Looks like you've got a problem."

"Ryder?"

He spread his hands. "'Fraid so." Any minute she'd ask about the baby and he wasn't real sure what he would say.

For nearly five months—ever since Judge Stokes had officially made Layla his responsibility—the Templeton triplets had tiptoed around him. He'd quickly learned how attached they'd become to the baby, caring for her after Daisy dumped her on a "friend's" porch.

Supposedly, his wife hadn't been sleeping with that friend but Ryder still had his doubts. DNA might have ruled out Jaxon Swift as Layla's father, but the man owned Magic Jax, the bar where Daisy had briefly worked as a cocktail waitress before they'd met. He would never understand why she hadn't just come to *him* if she'd needed help. He had been her husband, for God's sake. Not her onetime boss. Unless she'd been more involved with Jax than they all had admitted.

As for the identity of Layla's real father, everyone had been happy as hell to stop wondering as soon as Ryder gave proof that he and Daisy had been married.

Didn't mean Ryder hadn't wondered, though.

But doing a DNA test at this point wouldn't change anything where he was concerned. It would prove Layla was his by blood. Or it wouldn't.

Either way, he believed she was his wife's child.

Which made Layla his responsibility. Period.

The questions about Daisy, though? Every time he looked at Layla, they bubbled up inside him.

For now, though, he focused on Greer.

It was no particular hardship.

The Templeton triplets scored pretty high in the looks department. He could tell Greer apart from her twins because she always looked a little more sophisticated. Maddie—the social worker who'd been Layla's foster mother—had long hair reaching halfway down her back. Ali—the cop who'd shown up on his doorstep—had blond streaks. And he'd never seen her dressed in anything besides her police uniform.

Greer, though?

Her dark hair barely reached her shoulders and not a single strand was ever out of place. She was a lawyer and dressed the part in skinny skirts with expensive-looking jackets and high heels that looked more big-city than Wyoming dirt. She'd been the one who'd ushered him through all the legalities with the baby. And she was the only one of her sisters who hadn't been openly crying when they'd brought Layla and all of her stuff out to his ranch to turn her over to his care. But there'd been no denying the emotion in her eyes. She just hadn't allowed herself the relief of tears.

For some reason, that had seemed worse.

Ryder had been uncomfortable as hell with so much female emotion. Greer's most of all.

He'd rather have to deal with the general animosity Daisy's brother clearly felt for him. That, at least, was straightforward and simple. Grant's sister was dead. Whether he'd voiced it outright or not, he blamed Ryder.

Since Ryder was already shouldering the blame, it didn't make any difference to him.

Now Greer was shading her eyes with one hand and holding her hair off her neck with the other. Instead of asking about Layla first thing, though, she stopped near the front bumper of her car. "It overheated. I saw steam coming out from the hood and pulled off as soon as I could."

He joined her in front of the car. He knew the basics when it came to engines—enough to keep the machinery on his ranch running without too much outside help—but he was a lot more comfortable with the anatomy of horses and cows. "How long have you been sitting out here?"

"Too long." She plucked the front of her blouse away from her throat and glanced at the watch circling her narrow wrist. "I thought someone would stop sooner than this. Ali'll think I'm deliberately late."

The only heat from the engine came from the sun glaring down on it. He checked a few of the hoses and looked underneath for signs of leaking coolant, but the ground beneath the car was dry. "Why's that?"

"We're throwing a surprise baby shower for Maddie today. I'm supposed to help set up."

"Didn't know she was pregnant." He straightened. It was impossible to miss the sharpness in Greer's brown eyes.

"Why would you, when you've been avoiding all of us since March?"

"Some law that says I needed to do otherwise?" He hadn't been avoiding them entirely. Just...mostly.

It had been easy, considering he had a ranch to run.

She pursed her bow-shaped lips. "You know my family has a vested interest in Layla. At the very least, you could try accepting an invitation or two when they're extended."

"Maybe I'm too busy to accept invitations." He waited a beat. "I am a single father, you know."

If he wasn't mistaken, her eye actually twitched.

She'd always struck him as the one most tightly wound.

It was too bad that he also couldn't look at her without wondering just what it would take to *un*wind her.

He closed the hood of her car with a firm hand. "You want to try starting her up? See what happens with the temperature gauge?"

He thought she might argue—if only for the sake of it—but she opened the passenger door. Then he had to choke back a laugh when she climbed across and into the driver's seat, where she started the engine. Her focus was clearly on her dashboard and he could tell the gauge was rising just by the frown on her face.

She shut off the engine again and looked through the windshield. "Needle went straight to the red." She climbed back out the passenger side.

"Something wrong with the driver's-side door?"

She was looking down at herself as she got out, tweaking that white skirt hugging her slender hips until it hung smooth and straight. "No, but I don't want it getting hit by a passing vehicle if I open it."

He eyed the distance between the edge of the road and where she'd pulled off on the shoulder. "Real cautious of you."

"I'm a lawyer. I'm always cautious."

"Overly so, I'd say." Not that he hadn't enjoyed the show. She was a little skinny for his taste, but he couldn't deny she was a looker. He pulled off his cowboy hat long enough to swipe his arm across his forehead. "I can drive you into town, or I can send a tow out for you." He didn't have time to do both, because he had to be back at the ranch before the nanny left or his housekeeper, Mrs. Pyle, would have kittens. "What's your choice?"

Greer swallowed her frustration. Considering Ryder Wilson's standoffishness since they'd met, she was a little surprised that he'd stopped to assist at all.

As soon as she'd realized who was driving the enormous pickup truck pulling up behind her car, she'd been torn between anticipation and the desire to cry *what next?*

It was entirely annoying that the brawny, blue-eyed rancher was the first man to make her hormones sit up and take notice in too long a while.

Annoying and impossible to act on, considering the strange nature of their acquaintance.

All she wanted to do was ask Ryder how Layla was doing. But Maddie had been insistent that none of them intrude on him too soon.

They'd all been wrapped around Layla's tiny little finger and none more than Maddie, who'd been caring for her nearly the whole while before Ali discovered Ryder's existence. Yet it was Maddie who'd urged them to give Ryder time. To adjust. To adapt. They knew Ryder was taking decent care of the baby he'd claimed, because Maddie's boss, Raymond Marx, checked up on him for a while at first, so he could report back to the courts. Give Ryder time, Maddie insisted, and eventually he would see the benefit of letting them past his walls.

Didn't mean that it had been easy.

Didn't mean it was easy now, not dashing over to the truck to see Layla.

She didn't know if it was that prospect that made her feel so shaky inside, or if it was because of Layla's brown-haired daddy. She wasn't sure she even liked Ryder all that much.

Yes, he'd been legally named Layla's father and yes, he'd

taken responsibility for her. But there was an edge to him that had rubbed Greer wrong from the very first time they met. She just hadn't been able to pinpoint why.

"If you don't mind driving me into town," she managed, "I'd be grateful."

The brim of his hat dipped briefly. "Probably should lock her up." He started for his big truck parked behind the car.

She watched him walk away. He was wearing blue jeans and a checked shirt with the sleeves rolled up to his elbows. Except for when he'd briefly swiped an arm over his forehead, he appeared unaffected by the sweltering day.

"Probably should lock her up," she parroted childishly under her breath. As if she didn't have the sense to know that without being told.

She retrieved her purse and briefcase from the back seat, looping the long straps over her shoulder, then warily lifted the trunk lid higher. The shower cake that she'd nestled carefully between two boxes full of work from the office amazingly didn't look too much the worse for wear. It was a delightful amalgam of block and ball shapes, frosted in white, yellow and blue. How Tabby Clay had balanced them all together like that was a mystery to Greer.

She was just glad to see that the creation hadn't melted into a puddle of goo while she'd waited on the side of the road.

She carefully lifted the white board with the heavy cake on top out of the trunk and gingerly carried it toward Ryder's truck. Her heart was beating so hard, she could hear it inside her head. The last time she'd seen Layla had been at Shop-World in Weaver, when she'd taken a client shopping for an affordable set of clothes to wear for trial, and Ryder had been in the next checkout line over, buying diapers, coffee and whiskey.

Layla had been asleep in the cart. Greer had noticed that her blond curls had gotten a reddish cast, but the stuffed pony she'd clutched was the same one Greer had given her for Valentine's Day.

It had been all she could do not to pluck the baby out of the cart and cuddle her close. Instead, after a stilted exchange with Ryder, she'd hustled her client through the checkout so fast that he'd wondered out loud if she'd slid through without paying for something. *No. That's what* you *like to do,* she'd told him as she'd rushed him out the door.

But now, when she got close enough to Ryder's truck to see inside, her feet dragged to a halt.

There was no car seat.

Definitely no Layla.

The disappointment that swamped her was so searing, it put the hot afternoon sun to shame. Her eyes stung and she blinked hard, quickening her pace once more only to feel her heel slide on the loose gravel. The heavy cake started tipping one way and she leveled the board, even as her shoulder banged against the side of his truck.

She froze, holding her breath as she held the cake board aloft.

"What the hell are you doing over here?"

She was hot. Sweaty. And brokenhearted that she wasn't getting a chance to see sweet Layla.

"What do you care?" she snapped back. She was still holding the cake straight out from her body, and the weight of it was considerable. "Just open the door, would you please? If I don't deliver this thing in one piece, Ali's going to skin me alive."

He gave her a wide berth as he reached around her to open the door of the truck. "Let me take it." His hands covered hers where she held the board, and she jerked as if he'd prodded her with a live wire.

Her face went hot. "I don't need your help."

He let go and held his hands up in the air. "Whatever." He backed away.

Nobody liked to feel self-conscious. Not even her.

She turned away from him to set the cake board inside the truck, but it was too big to fit on the floor, which meant she'd have to hold it on her lap.

Greer heaved out a breath and looked at Ryder. He wordlessly took the cake long enough for her to dump her briefcase and purse on the floor, and climb up on the high seat.

"All settled now?" His voice was mild.

For some reason, it annoyed her more than if he'd made some snarky comment.

Unfortunately, that's when she realized that she'd left her trunk open and the car unlocked.

She slid off the seat again, mentally cursing ranchers and their too-big trucks as she jumped out onto the ground. Ignoring the amused glint in his dark blue eyes, she strode past him, grinding her teeth when her heel again slid on the loose gravel.

She'd have landed on her butt if not for the quick hand he shot out to steady her.

She shrugged off his touch as if she'd been burned but managed a grudging "thank you." It figured that he could manage to hold on to the heavy cake and still keep her from landing on her butt.

She finally made it to her car without further mishap and secured it. The passenger door of his truck was still open and waiting for her when she returned.

She climbed inside and fastened the safety belt. Then he settled the enormous, heavy cake on her lap, taking an inordinate amount of time before sliding his big, warm hands away.

As soon as he did, she yanked the door closed.

The cool air flowed from the air-conditioning vents.

It was the only bright spot, and gave a suitable reason for the shivers that skipped down her spine.

She wrapped her hands firmly around the edge of the cake board to hold it in place while Ryder circled the front of the truck and got in behind the wheel.

His blue eyes skated over and she shivered again. Despite the heat. Despite the perspiration soaking her blouse.

Annoyance swelled inside her.

"I hope you have someone decent watching Layla."

His expression turned chilly. "I've got plenty of things I needed to be doing besides stopping to help you out. You really want to go there?"

She pressed her lips together. If Maddie ever found out she'd been rude to Ryder, her sister would never forgive her.

"Just drive," she said ungraciously.

He lifted an eyebrow slightly.

God. She really hated feeling self-conscious.

"Please," she added.

He waited a beat. "Better." Then he put the truck in gear.

CHAPTER TWO

"I KNEW YOU'D be late."

Greer ignored Ali's greeting as she entered the stately old mansion that Maddie shared with her husband, Lincoln Swift. She kicked the heavy front door closed, blocking out the sound of Ryder's departing truck. Passing the round table in the foyer loaded down with fancifully wrapped gifts and the grand wooden staircase, she headed into the dining room with the cake.

The sight of a cheerfully decorated sheet cake already sitting in the middle of the table shredded her last nerve.

She stared over her shoulder at Ali. Her sister looked uncommonly pretty in a bright yellow sundress. More damningly, Ali was as cool and fresh as the daisy she'd stuck in her messy ponytail. "You have a *backup* cake?"

"Of course I have a backup cake." Ali waved her hands, and the big diamond rock that Grant had put on her ring finger a few months earlier glinted in the sunlight shining through the mullioned windows. "Because I knew you would be late! You're always late, because you're always working for that slave driver over at the dark side."

"Well, I wouldn't have *been* late, if I hadn't broken down on the way back from Weaver! Now would you move that stupid cake so I can put this one down where it belongs?"

"Girls!" Their mother, Meredith, dashed into the dining room, accompanied by the usual tinkle of tiny bells on the ankle bracelet she wore. "This is supposed to be a party." She tsked. "You're thirty years old and you still sound as if you're bickering ten-year-olds." She whisked the offending backup cake off the table. "Ali, put this in the kitchen."

Ali took the sheet cake from their mother and crossed her eyes at Greer behind their mother's back while Greer set Tabby's masterpiece in its place.

"It's just beautiful," Meredith exclaimed, clasping her hands together. Despite her chastisement, her eyes were sparkling. "Maddie's going to love it." As she turned away, the dark hair she'd passed on to her daughters danced in corkscrew curls nearly to the small of her back. "It's just too bad that Tabby wasn't able to come to the party."

"If Gracie weren't running a fever, she'd have brought the cake herself." Greer glanced around. "Obviously Ali didn't have a problem decorating without me. It looks like the baby-shower fairy threw up in here." The raindrop theme was in full force. Silver and white balloons hovered above the table in a cluster of "clouds" from which shimmering crystal raindrops hung down, drifting slightly in the cool room. It was sweet and subtly chic and just like Maddie. Altogether perfect, really.

As usual, Ali hadn't really needed Greer at all.

Meredith squeezed her arm as if she'd read her mind. "Stop sweating the details, Greer. You had a hand in the planning of this, whether you were here to help pull it together this afternoon or not. Now—" she eyed Greer more closely "—what's this about your car breaking down?"

It was a timely reminder that she probably looked as bedraggled as she felt. A glance at her watch told her the guests would be arriving in a matter of minutes. Linc was supposed to be delivering Maddie—hopefully still in the dark about the surprise—shortly after that.

"The car overheated. I left it locked up on the side of the road."

"How'd you get here?"

She felt reluctant to say, knowing the mention of Ryder would only remind them all of how much they missed Layla. "Someone stopped and gave me a ride to town. I'll arrange a tow after the shower." She dashed her hand down the front of her outfit and headed for the stairs. "I need to put on something less wrinkled and sweaty. Hopefully there's more than just maternity clothes in Maddie's closet." She hadn't made it halfway up the staircase before the doorbell rang and she could hear Ali greeting the new arrivals.

She darted up the rest of the stairs.

Even after more than half a year, it was hard to get used to the fact that Maddie lived in this grand old house with Linc. The place had belonged to his and Jax's grandmother Ernestine. When the triplets were children, Meredith had cleaned house for Ernestine. Greer and her sisters had often accompanied her. Now, Jax no longer shared the house with Linc. Maddie did.

She entered the big walk-in closet, mentally sending an apology to her brother-in-law for the intrusion. She knew that Maddie wouldn't mind. Not surprisingly, most of the clothes hanging on the rods were designed for a woman who looked about a hundred months pregnant.

She could hear the doorbell chime again downstairs and quickly flipped through the hangers, finally pulling out a colorful dress she remembered Maddie wearing for Easter, when she'd had just a small baby bump. The dress had a stretchy waist that was a little loose on Greer, but it would do.

She changed and flipped her hair up into a clip. If there'd been blond streaks in her hair, she'd look just like Ali. Tousled and carefree.

But Greer hadn't felt carefree in what was starting to feel like forever.

She stared at her reflection and plucked at the loose waist of the dress. Maddie was pregnant. Now Ali and Grant were married. Considering how the two couldn't keep their hands off each other, it was only a matter of time before they were starting a family, too.

But Greer?

The last date she'd had that had gotten even remotely physical was more than two years ago, so if she wanted a baby, she was going to need either a serious miracle or big-time artificial intervention. As it was, the little birth control implant she had in her arm was pretty much pointless.

From downstairs, she heard a peal of laughter. Turning away from her reflection, she headed down to join them. She might not feel carefree, but she *was* thrilled about Maddie's coming baby. So she would put on a party face for that reason alone.

And she would try to forget that Ali had gotten a damn backup cake.

Ryder stared at Doreen Pyle. "What do you mean, you're quitting?"

"Just that, Ryder." Mrs. Pyle continued scooping mushy green food into Layla's mouth, even though the little girl kept twisting her head away. "When you hired me, it was to be your housekeeper. Not your nanny."

"That's because I *had* a nanny." His voice was tight. "Look, I'm sorry that Tina took a hike this afternoon with no warning." At least the others who'd come before her had given him some notice. "I'll start looking again first thing tomorrow."

"It won't matter, Ryder. Nobody wants to live all the way out here." She finally gave up on the green mush and glanced at him. The look in her lined eyes was more sympathetic than her tone had been. "You need to give up the idea of a live-in nanny, Ryder. Or else give up the idea of a housekeeper. You can't afford both."

He could, if he were willing to dip into his savings. But he wasn't willing. Any more than he was willing to take Adelaide's money. She'd made her way on her own, and he was doing the same. On his own. But if he were going to continue growing this small ranch, he couldn't be carting a growing baby around everywhere while he worked. "I'll give you another raise." He'd already given her one. "Stay on and take care of Layla. You're good with her. I'll hire someone to help with the housekeeping."

"I don't want to live out here, either." She pushed off her chair, wincing a little as she straightened. "The only difference between me and Tina is that I won't take off while your back is turned." She grabbed a cloth and started wiping up Layla's face. The baby squirmed, trying to avoid the cloth just like she'd tried to avoid the green muck. But Mrs. Pyle prevailed and then tossed the cloth aside. "You don't need a nanny around the clock, anyway. You're here at night." She lifted the baby out of the high chair. "You can take care of her yourself. Then just get some help during the day. Preferably someone who doesn't have to drive farther than from Braden, or once the winter comes, you're going to have problems all over again." She plopped Layla into his arms and hustled to the sink where she wet another cloth. "But it won't be me. I have my own family I need to look out for, too. My grandson—" She broke off, grimacing. She squeezed out the moisture and waved the rag at him. "I won't apologize for not wanting to be tied down to a baby all over again. Not at my age." She sounded defensive.

"I don't need an apology, Mrs. Pyle. I need someone to take care of Layla!"

The baby lightly slapped his face with her hands and laughed.

Mrs. Pyle's expression softened. She chucked Layla lightly under the chin. "Maybe instead of looking for a nanny, you should start looking for a mama for this little girl."

Ryder grimaced.

"There are plenty of other fish in the sea. All you need to do is cast your line. You're a good-looking cuss when you clean yourself up. Someone'll come biting before you know it."

"I don't think so." One foray into so-called wedded bliss was one disaster enough.

The look in Doreen's eyes got even more sympathetic. "I know what it's like to lose a spouse, hon. Single parents might be all the rage these days, but I'm here to tell you it's easier when two people are committed to their family. You're still young. You don't want to spend the rest of your life alone. I'm sure your poor wife wouldn't have wanted that, either. She'd surely want this little mite to have a proper mama. Someone who won't toss aside caring for Layla on some flighty whim the way Tina just did."

He managed a tight smile. His "poor wife" had been exactly that. A poor wife. But not in the way Doreen Pyle meant. Abandoning Layla had been a helluva way to show off her maternal nature. Tina's quitting out of the blue was a lot more forgivable. "Would you at least stay until I find someone new?" He had to finish getting the hay in before the weather turned. And then he and his closest neighbor to the east were helping each other through roundup. Then he'd be sorting and shipping and—

"I'll stay another week," she said, interrupting the litany of tasks running through his mind. "But that's it, Ryder."

Layla grinned up at him with her six teeth and smacked his face again with her hand.

He looked back at his housekeeper. "A week."

"That's all the time I can give you, Ryder. I'm sorry."

A week was better than nothing.

And it was damn sure more than Tina had given him.

"I don't suppose you could stay and watch Layla for another few hours or so?" As his housekeeper began shaking her head no, he grabbed the refrigerator door and stuck his head inside, so he could pretend he didn't see. "Got a friend—" big overstatement there "—who needs help towing her car back to town. Broke down up near Devil's Crossing." He grabbed the bottle of ketchup that Layla latched onto and stuck it back on the refrigerator shelf. She immediately reached for something else and he quickly shut the door and gave Mrs. Pyle a hopeful look. The same one he'd mastered by the time he was ten and living with Adelaide.

Instead of looking resigned and accepting, though, Mrs. Pyle was giving him an eyebrows-in-the-hairline look. "*Her* car? Is this female friend single?"

Warning alarms went off inside his head. "Yeah."

She lifted Layla out of his arms. "Well, go rescue your lady friend. And give my suggestion about a wife some thought."

He let her remark slide. "Thank you, Mrs. Pyle."

"Not going to change my leaving in a week," she warned as she carried the baby out of the kitchen. "And you might think about washing some of the day off yourself, as well, before you go out playing Dudley Do-Right."

He hadn't showered, but he *had* washed up and pulled on fresh clothes. And he still felt pretty stupid about it.

It wasn't as if he wanted to impress Greer Templeton. Not with a clean shirt or anything else. And it damn sure wasn't as if he was giving Mrs. Pyle's suggestion any consideration.

Marrying someone just for Layla's sake?

He pushed the idea straight out of his mind and shifted into Park at the top of the hill as he stared out at the worn-looking Victorian house.

The white paint on the fancy trim was peeling and the dove-gray paint on the siding was fading. The shingle roof needed repair, if not replacement, and the brick chimney looked as if it were related to the Leaning Tower of Pisa. But the yard around the house was green and neat.

Not exactly what he would have expected of the lady lawyer. But then again, she worked for the public defender's office, where the pay was reportedly abysmal and most of her clients were supposedly the dregs of society.

He turned off the engine and got out of the truck, walking around to the trailer he'd used to haul Greer's little car. He checked the chains holding it in place and then headed up the front walk to the door.

The street was quiet, and his boots clumped loudly as he went up the steps and crossed the porch to knock on the door. The heavy brass door knocker was shaped like a dragonfly.

If he could ever get Adelaide to come and visit Braden, she'd love the place.

When no one came to the door, he went back down the porch steps. There was an elderly woman across the street making a production of sweeping the sidewalk, though it seemed obvious she was more interested in giving him the once-over.

He tipped the brim of his hat toward her before he started unchaining Greer's car. "Evenin'."

The woman clutched her broom tightly and started across the street. A little black poodle trotted after her. "That's Greer's car," the woman said suspiciously.

He didn't stop what he was doing. "Yes, ma'am."

"What're you doing with it?"

"Unloading it."

She stopped several feet away, still holding the broom handle as if she was prepared to use it on him if need be. "I don't know you."

"No, ma'am." He fit the wheel ramps in place and hopped up onto the trailer. "I assure you that Greer does." He opened the car door and folded himself down inside it.

Maybe Greer—who was probably all of five two or three without those high heels she was always wearing—could fit comfortably into the car, but he couldn't. Not for any length of time, anyway.

He started the car, backed down the ramp and turned into the driveway. Then he shut off the engine, crawled out from behind the wheel and locked it up again before sticking the key back into the magnetic box he'd found tucked inside the wheel well.

The woman was still standing in the middle of the street.

He secured the ramps back up onto the trailer and gave her another nod. "If you see her, tell her she's got a thermostat problem."

"Tell her yourself." The woman pointed her broom handle at an expensive black SUV that had just crested the top of the hill. "Bet that's her now."

He bit back an oath. He still didn't know what had possessed him to haul Greer's car into town for her, particularly without her knowledge. And his chance of a clean escape had just disappeared.

The SUV pulled to a stop in front of Greer's house. The windows were tinted, so he couldn't see who was behind the wheel, but he definitely could see the shapely leg that emerged when the passenger-side door opened.

It belonged to Greer, looking very un-Greer-like in a flowy sort of dress patterned in vibrant swirls of color that could have rivaled one of his aunt's paintings. Half her hair was untidily pulled up and held by a glittery pink clip.

He still knew it was her, though, and not one of her sisters. No question, considering the sharp look she gave him as she closed the SUV door and approached him. "*You* hauled my car here?"

"I suppose there's no point in denying the obvious." He watched the big SUV pull around in the cul-de-sac and head back down the hill. The identity of the driver was none of his business. He wondered, anyway. "Boyfriend?"

She frowned. "Grant. And why did you haul it?"

No wonder the SUV had turned around and left. "You'd rather have it still sitting out on the side of the highway?"

"Of course not, but—" She broke off, looking consternated, and only then seemed to notice that they had an audience. "How are you doing, Mrs. Gunderson?" She leaned down to pet the little round dog. Ryder wasn't enough of a gentleman to look away when the stretchy, ruffled neckline of Greer's dress revealed more than it should have.

"Just fine, dearie. Oh, Mignon, don't jump!"

Mrs. Gunderson's admonishment was too late, though, because the dog had already bounced up and into Greer's arms.

He was actually a little impressed that the fat Mignon could jump.

But he was more impressed by the way Greer caught him and laughed.

He had never heard her laugh before. Not her or her sisters. Her chocolate-colored eyes sparkled and her face practically glowed.

And damned if he didn't feel something warm streak down his spine.

"You probably need a new thermostat," he said abruptly.

The dog was licking the bottom of her chin even though she was trying to avoid his tongue, but she didn't put Mignon down. "How do you know?"

"Because I checked everything else that would cause your overheating before I towed it back here." He stepped around the two women. "And think about keeping your car key in a less obvious hiding spot," he advised as pulled open the door to climb inside his truck.

Greer's jaw dropped a little, which gave Mignon more chin to lick. She set the dog down and trotted after him, wrapping her fingers over the open window. "You're just going to leave now?"

His fingers closed over the key in the ignition, but didn't turn it. "What else do you figure I should do?"

Her lips parted slightly. "Can I pay you for the tow at least?"

He turned the key. "No need."

"Well, I should do something." She didn't step back from the truck, despite the engine leaping to life. "To thank you at least. Surely there's something I can do."

The "something" that leaped to mind wasn't exactly fit for sharing in polite company. Particularly with her elderly neighbor still watching them as though they were prime-time entertainment.

He said the next best option that came to mind. "Next time I need a lawyer, you can owe me one." He even managed a smile to go with the words.

Fortunately, it seemed like enough. She smiled back and patted the door once. "You'll never collect on that." Her voice was light.

"One thing I've learned in my life is to never say never." He looked away from her ringless ring finger. "Where'd that dog go?"

Greer looked around, giving him a close-up view of the tender skin on the back of her neck. She had a trio of tiny freckles just below the loose strands of hair. Like someone had dashed a few specks of cinnamon across a smooth layer of cream.

He focused on Mrs. Gunderson, who was skirting the back of his trailer, calling the dog's name. "Mignon, get out from under there, right now!"

Greer had joined in, crouching down to look under the vehicle.

He figured if he revved the engine, it might send the fat dog into cardiac arrest. He shut it off again and climbed out. "Where is he?"

"He's lying down right inside the back tire." Mrs. Gunderson looked like she was about to go down on her hands and knees. "Mignon, you naughty little thing. Come out here, right now. Oh, darn it, he seems to have found something he thinks is food."

"Why don't you get one of his usual treats?" Greer suggested.

"Good idea." Mrs. Gunderson set off across the street once more.

If he'd hoped that her departure would spur the dog to follow, he was wrong. He knelt on one knee to look under the trailer. "Come 'ere, pooch."

Mignon paid him no heed at all, except to move even farther beneath the trailer.

Greer crouched next to him. The bottom of her dress puddled around her. "He doesn't like strangers."

Ryder slid his hand out from beneath the soft, colorful fabric that covered it. "He wouldn't like getting flattened by my trailer, either."

"He'll come out for his treats," she assured him.

"Since he looks like he lives on treats, I hope so." It would take the better part of an hour to get home and he'd probably already used up Mrs. Pyle's allotment of patience. If the treat didn't work, he'd have to drag the little bugger out.

"She's actually gotten him to lose a couple pounds."

"He's still wider than he is tall. Reminds me of my aunt's dog, Brutus." He straightened and looked across the street, hoping to see Mrs. Gunderson heading back. Instead, she was just reaching the top of her porch stairs and he could feel the minutes ticking away.

Even though he didn't say anything, Greer could feel the impatience coming off Ryder in waves. She stood, hoping that Mrs. Gunderson moved with more speed than she usually did. It was obvious that he was anxious to be on his way. "Your aunt has an overweight poodle?"

He lifted his hat just long enough to shove his fingers through his thick brown hair. "Overweight pug." His blue gaze slid over her from beneath the hat brim as he pulled it low over his brow. "Adelaide spoils him rotten."

She couldn't help but smile. "A pug named Brutus?"

He shrugged. "She has a particular sense of irony."

"I love your aunt's name," she said. "Adelaide."

A dimple came and went in his lean cheek. "Coming from the woman who lives in that Victorian thing behind us, I'm not real surprised."

She leaned against the side rail of the trailer. "Does she live in New Mexico?" Greer and her sisters didn't know much about Ryder, but had learned that he'd lived in New Mexico before moving to Wyoming.

The brim of his hat dipped slightly. "She has a place near Taos."

"The only place I've ever been in New Mexico was the Albuquerque airport during a layover." She glanced toward her neighbor's house. The front door was still open, but there was no sign of Mrs. Gunderson yet. "Did you grow up there?"

The dimple came again, staying a little longer this time. "In the Albuquerque airport?"

"Ha ha."

His lips actually stretched into a smile. "Yeah. I spent most of my time in Taos."

So she now knew he had an aunt. But she still didn't know if he had parents. Siblings. Other ex-wives. Anybody else at all besides Layla. "What's it like there? It's pretty artsy, isn't it?"

"More so than Braden."

"Does your aunt get to visit you often?"

"She's never been here. She doesn't like to travel much anymore. If I want to see her, I have to go to her." He thumbed up the brim of his hat and squinted at the sky.

"You're anxious to go."

"Yup." He knelt down to look at the dog again. "My housekeeper's gonna be peeved." He gave a coaxing whistle. "Come 'ere, dog."

"Your housekeeper's Doreen Pyle?"

Still down on one knee, he looked up at Greer and something swooped inside her stomach. "Keeping close tabs on me?"

She ignored the strange sensation. "Braden is a small community. And I happen to know her grandson pretty well."

"Dating him, are you?"

She couldn't help the snort of laughter that escaped. "Since he's not legally an adult, hardly. Haven't even had a date in—" She broke off, appalled at herself, embarrassed by the speculative look he was giving her. She pointed, absurdly grateful for Mrs. Gunderson's timely reappearance on her front porch. Her neighbor was holding something in her hand, waving it in the air as she came down the steps. "There's the treat."

And sure enough, before his mistress had even gotten to the street, Mignon was scrabbling out from beneath the trailer, practically rolling over his feet as he bolted.

Ryder straightened and gave her that faint smile again. The one that barely curved his well-shaped lips, but still managed to reveal his dimple. "Never underestimate the power of a good treat."

Then he thumbed the brim of his hat in that way he had of doing. Sort of old-fashioned and, well, *rancherly*. He walked around his truck and climbed inside. A moment later, he'd started the engine and was driving away.

Mrs. Gunderson picked up Mignon, who was happily gnawing on his piece of doggy jerky, and stood next to Greer. "He's a good-looking one, isn't he?"

At least her elderly neighbor could explain away her breathlessness. She'd had to climb her porch stairs to retrieve the dog treats.

Greer, on the other hand, had no such excuse. "He's surprising, anyway." She gave Mignon's head a scratch. "I've got to go call my dad before he drives out to haul my car that no longer needs hauling."

Then she hurried inside, pretending not to hear Mrs. Gunderson's knowing chuckle.

CHAPTER THREE

"RYDER WILSON TOWED your truck?"

Greer tucked her office phone against her shoulder. "Hey, Maddie. Hold on." She didn't wait for her sister to reply, but clicked over to the other phone call while she scrolled through the emails on her computer. It was Monday morning. She wished she could say it was unusual coming in to find fifty emails all requiring immediate attention. The fact was, coming in to *only* fifty emails was a good start to a week.

"Mrs. Pyle, as I explained to your son last week, Judge Donnelly has refused another continuance in Anthony's case. He's already granted two, which is unusual. Your grandson's trial is going to be on Thursday and my associate Don Chatham will be handling it. He's our senior attorney, as you know, and handles most of the jury trials." After she had handled all the other steps, including negotiating plea deals. Which the prosecutor's office wasn't offering to Anthony this go-round.

Not surprising. It was an election year.

"I know Judge Donnelly." Doreen Pyle sounded tearful. "I can't be in court on Thursday. If I just went to him and asked—"

She shook her head, even though Doreen couldn't see. "I advise you not to speak directly to the judge, Mrs. Pyle."

"Then schedule a different date! You know how unreliable

my son is. Anthony needs his family there. If his father would have told me last week, I could have made arrangements. But I have to work!"

Doreen Pyle worked for Ryder Wilson.

Greer pressed her fingertips between her eyes to relieve the pain that had suddenly formed there and sighed. The only adult Anthony truly had in his corner was his grandmother. "I'll see what I can do, Mrs. Pyle. I'll call you later this afternoon. All right?"

"Thank you, Greer. Thank you so much."

She highly doubted that Mrs. Pyle would be thanking her later. "Don't get your hopes up too high," she warned before jabbing the blinking button on her phone to switch back to the other call.

"Sorry about that, Maddie." She sent off a two-line response to the email on her computer screen and started composing a new one to the prosecutor's office. She wouldn't present a motion to the court until the prosecutor agreed to another delay. "You all recovered from the baby shower?"

"The only thing that'll help me recover fully from anything these days will be going into labor. About Ryder—"

"Yes, he towed my truck." She switched the phone to her other shoulder and opened the desk drawer where she kept her active files. "I suppose Ali told you?" She'd caught their father before he'd made a needless trip out to Devil's Crossing but she hadn't told him the finer details of who'd taken care of the chore.

She pulled out the file she was seeking and flipped it open on her desk. Anthony Pyle. Seventeen. Charged with property destruction and defacement. It was his second charge and he was being tried in adult court. Anthony and his grandmother had good cause for worry since he was facing more than six months in jail if convicted.

Greer doubted that his father, Rocky, cared all that much about what happened. He provided for the basic needs of his son, but beyond that, the troubled boy was pretty much on his own. Rocky had told Greer outright that Anthony deserved what he got. Didn't matter to his father at all that the boy had consistently proclaimed his innocence. That the real culprit was his supposed friend—and the son of the man who owned the barn that had nearly burned down.

"Ali? No."

Greer held back a sigh. If Grant had told his wife that he'd seen Ryder with her, there was no way that Ali would have stayed quiet about it. And the fact that Grant hadn't told Ali just meant that he was still conflicted over everything that had happened with his sister.

"You know how news gets around," Maddie said.

In other words, Mrs. Gunderson had told someone she'd seen Ryder towing her car, and that someone had told someone, and so on and so forth.

Greer forestalled her sister's next question, knowing it was coming. "Ryder didn't have Layla with him."

"I heard. Did you know that his latest nanny quit on him?"

Greer's fingers paused on her computer keyboard. Doreen hadn't mentioned *that*. "That's the fourth one."

"Third," Maddie corrected. "Ray has been keeping track."

Greer spotted Keith Gowler in the hallway outside her office and waved to get his attention. He was one of the local private attorneys who took cases on behalf of the public defender's office because they were perpetually overworked and understaffed. "Is Ray concerned?"

"Not that he's said. We have no reason to think Layla's not being properly cared for."

"That's probably why Ryder was anxious to get moving the other evening, then. Doreen must have been watching Layla." And that was why she was upset about not being available for her grandson's trial.

"She's got a lot on her plate, too."

Greer glanced at Anthony's file. Despite the jurisdiction of the case, he was still a minor, which meant the case also involved Maddie's office. "Did you get notice of the trial date?"

"Thursday? Yes. I can't be there, though. Having another ultrasound at the hospital in Weaver and Linc will have kittens if I say I want to reschedule it."

"Everything okay?" she asked, alarm in her voice.

"Everything's fine, except I'm as big as a house and due in two weeks. And don't you start acting as bad as my husband. He's turned into a nervous Nellie these last few weeks. Driving me positively nuts."

"He's concerned. You're having your first baby."

"And I'm already thirty and yada yada. I know."

Keith stuck his head in her doorway. "Got the latest litter?"

She nodded at him and glanced at the round, schoolroom-style clock hanging above the door. It had a loud tick and tended to lose about five minutes every few days, but it had been a gift from one of her favorite law professors what felt like a hundred years ago. "Listen, Maddie, I've got a consult, so I need to go. But I want to know more about the ultrasound. We'll talk—"

"—later," her sister finished and hung up. At least Greer and Maddie were almost always on the same wavelength. It was too bad that Greer couldn't say the same about Ali.

She made a note on her calendar to call her. Maybe if Greer were the one to plan dinner next Monday, she'd get herself back in Ali's good graces. The three of them usually tried to get together for dinner on the first Monday of each month, but their schedules made it difficult. And when it came to canceling, Greer had been the worst offender. The fact that next Monday wasn't the first Monday of the month was immaterial. With Maddie ready to pop with the baby, this might be their only chance for a while.

Keith tossed himself down on the hard chair wedged into Greer's crowded office. "How many assignments this week?"

She closed Anthony's file and plucked a stack from the box on the floor behind her desk. "Too many. Take a look."

"I won't be able to take on as many as usual," he warned as he began flipping through the files. "Lydia and I have set the wedding date next month."

Even though she'd half expected the news, Greer was still surprised. It hadn't been that long since the lawyer was moping around from the supposedly broken heart Ali had caused him when they broke up, before she met Grant. Then he'd met Lydia when he'd taken on the defense case involving her son. "Congratulations. You're really doing it, huh?"

"I'd have married her six months ago, but she wanted to wait until Trevor's case was settled. Now it is and we can get on with our lives." He glanced up for a moment. "How's the Santiago case coming?"

"Pretrial motions after Labor Day. Michael has the investigator working overtime."

"I'll bet he does. Because your boss wants the case dismissed in the worst way."

"We'll see." Stormy Santiago would be the jewel in the prosecutor's reelection crown. She was beautiful. Manipulative. And charged with solicitation of murder. "Don's already prepping to go to trial on it."

"I'll bet he is. He gets her off and he'll be onto bigger pastures, whether he's best buddies with your boss or not. Mark my words."

Greer couldn't imagine Don wanting to leave their department, where he was a big fish in a small pond. "You think?"

Keith shrugged. He slid several folders from the stack toward her. "I can take these."

It was up to her to ensure the assignments were correctly recorded and submitted to the appropriate court clerk. Between municipal, circuit and district courts, it meant even more paperwork for her. "Great. See you in court."

Morning and afternoon sessions were held daily every Monday through Thursday, with Greer running between courtrooms as she handled arraignments and motions and pleadings and the myriad details involved when an individual was charged with a criminal offense. Occasionally, there was a reason for a Friday docket, which was a pain because they all had plenty of non-court details to take care of on Fridays. And increasingly on Saturdays and Sundays, too. Most of those days, Greer was meeting clients—quite often at the various municipal jails scattered around their region.

Such was the life of a public defender. Or in her case, the life of a public defender who got to do all the prep but rarely actually got to *defend*. It was up to Greer to prepare briefs, schedule conferences, take depositions and hunt down reluctant witnesses when she had to. She was the one who negotiated the plea deals that meant Don typically only had to show up in the office on Thursdays, when most of the trials were scheduled. She'd gotten a few bench trials, but thanks to Don and his buddy-buddy relationship with Michael Towers, their boss and the supervising attorney for the region, her experience in front of a jury was limited.

She also photocopied the case files and made the coffee.

But if Don were to ever leave…

She exhaled, pushing the unlikely possibility out of her mind, and sent off her message to the prosecutor. The rest of her email would have to wait. She shoved everything she would likely need into her bulging briefcase, grabbed the blazer that went with her skirt and hurried out of her office.

Michael was sitting behind his desk when she stuck her head in his office. "Any news yet on a new intern?" Their office hadn't had one for three months. Which was one of the reasons Greer had been on coffee and photocopy duty.

He shook his head, looking annoyed. Which for Michael was pretty much the status quo. "I have three other jurisdictions needing interns, too. When there's something you need to know, I'll tell you. Until then, do your job."

She managed not to bare her teeth at him and continued on her way. She didn't stop as she waved at Michael's wife,

Bernice, who'd been filling in for the secretary they couldn't afford to hire, even though she hopped up and scurried after her long enough to push a stack of pink message slips into the outer pocket of Greer's briefcase.

"Thanks, Bunny."

Greer left the civic plaza for the short walk to the courthouse. It was handy that the buildings were located within a few blocks of each other. It meant that she could leave her car in the capable hands of her dad for the day. Carter Templeton was retired with too much time on his hands and he'd offered to look at it. He might have spent most of his life in an office as an insurance broker, but there wasn't much that Carter couldn't fix when he wanted to. Which was a good thing for Greer, because she was presently pretty broke.

She was pretty broke almost all of the time.

It was something she'd expected when she'd taken the job with the public defender's office. And money had gotten even tighter when she'd thrown in with her two sisters to buy the fixer-upper Victorian—in which she was the only one still living. She couldn't very well start complaining about it now, though.

The irony was that both Maddie and Ali could now put whatever money they wanted into the house since they'd both married men who could afford to indulge their every little wish.

Now it was just Greer who was holding up the works.

She'd already remodeled her bedroom and bathroom when they'd first moved in. The rest of the house was in a terrible state of disrepair, though. But if she couldn't afford her fair third of the cost, then the work had to wait until she could.

She sidestepped a woman pushing a baby stroller on the sidewalk and jogged up the steps to the courthouse. There were thirty-two of them, in sets of eight. When she'd first started out, running up the steps had left her breathless. Six years later, she barely noticed them.

Inside, she joined the line at security and slid her bare arms into her navy blue blazer. Once through, she jogged up two more full flights of gleaming marble stairs to the third floor.

She slipped into Judge Waters's courtroom with two minutes to spare and was standing at the defendant's table with her files stacked in front of her before the judge entered, wearing his typically dour expression.

He looked over his half glasses. "Oh, goody." His voice was humorless as he took his seat behind the bench. "All of my favorite people are here. Actually on time for once." He poured himself a glass of water and shook out several antacid tablets from the economy-sized bottle sitting beside the water. "All right. As y'all ought to know by now, we'll break at noon and not a minute before. So don't bother asking. If you're not lucky enough to be out of the court's hair by noon, we'll resume at half past one and not one minute after."

He eyed the line of defendants waiting to be arraigned. They sat shoulder to shoulder, crammed into the hardwood bench adjacent to the defendant's table where Greer stood. After this group, there was another waiting, just as large.

Judge Waters shoved the tablets into his mouth. "Let's get started," he said around his crunching.

All in all, it was a pretty normal morning.

Normal ended at exactly twelve fifty-five.

She knew it, because the big clock on the corner of Braden Bank & Trust was right overhead when she spotted Ryder Wilson walking down the street.

He was carrying Layla.

Greer's heart nearly stopped beating. Heedless of traffic, she bolted across Main Street to intercept him.

A fine idea in theory. But she was wearing high heels and a narrow skirt, and had a ten-pound briefcase banging against her hip with every step she took. Speedy, she was not.

He'd reached the corner and would soon be out of sight.

She'd run track in high school, for God's sake.

She hopped around as she pulled off her pumps, and chased after him barefoot.

The cement was hot under her feet as she rounded the corner and spotted him pulling open the door to Braden Drugs halfway down the block.

"Ryder!"

He hesitated, glancing around over his shoulder, then let go of the door and waited for her.

"Hi!" She was more breathless from the sight of Layla than from the mad dash, and barely looked up at Ryder as she stopped. She knew her smile was too wide but couldn't do a thing about it as she leaned closer to Layla. "Hi, sweetheart. Look at you in your pretty pink sundress. You probably don't even remember me. But I sure remember you."

Layla waved the pink sippy cup by the handle she was clutching and showed off her pearly white teeth as she babbled nonsensically.

Everything inside Greer seized up. She wanted to take the baby in her arms so badly it hurt. She contented herself with stroking the tot's velvety cheek with her shaking fingertip. "I sure have missed you." The words came out sounding husky, and she cleared her throat before looking up at Ryder.

He was looking back at her warily, which she supposed she deserved, after chasing him down the way she had.

"What brings the two of you to town?"

He looked beyond her to the drugstore. "She's got some special vitamin stuff she's supposed to have. Aren't your feet burning?"

She looked down and felt the searing heat that was only slightly less intense than the heat that filled her cheeks. She quickly leaned over, putting her shoes back on. "Probably looks a little silly."

"Yep."

She huffed. "You didn't have to agree. Do you always say what you're thinking?"

"Not necessarily." His eyebrows quirked. It was her only hint that he was amused. "But I generally say what I mean."

Layla babbled and smacked the sippy cup against Greer's arm. "I think I recognize that cup," Greer said to her.

Layla jabbered back. Her bright green eyes latched onto Greer's.

She felt tears coming on. "I can't believe how much you've grown." The huskiness was back in her voice.

"You want to hold her?"

Now, given the opportunity, Greer was suddenly hesitant. "I don't know if she'll remember me. She might not—"

He dumped the baby in her arms.

Layla smiled brightly. She didn't care in the least that Greer's vision was blurred by tears as she looked down at her.

Greer wrapped her arms around the baby and cuddled her. "I thought she'd be heavier." She closed her eyes and rubbed her cheek against Layla's soft hair. "Nothing smells better," she murmured.

Ryder snorted slightly. "Sure, when she's not fillin' her diaper with something out of a horror flick."

Greer smiled. She caught Layla's fist and kissed it. "What's Daddy talking about, huh, baby? You're too perfect for anything like that."

"Excuse me."

They both looked over to see an elderly woman waiting to enter the door they were blocking.

"Sorry." Greer quickly moved out of the way while Ryder opened the door for her.

The woman beamed at him as she shuffled into the drugstore. "Thank you. It's so nice to see young families spend time together these days."

Greer bit the inside of her cheek, stifling the impulse to correct her. It was the same tactic she'd used many times in the courtroom.

Ryder let the door close after the woman. "Proof that appearances are deceiving."

Greer managed a smile. She was suddenly very aware of the time passing, but she didn't want to look at her watch or give up holding Layla a second sooner than she needed to. "What's special about the vitamins?"

He shrugged. "Something her pediatrician has her taking."

"Do you still take her to my uncle?" David Templeton's pediatrics practice in Braden was older than Greer. He'd been the first one to see Layla when Lincoln had discovered her left on the mansion's doorstep last December.

"You mean he hasn't told you?"

She gave him a look. "Wouldn't be very professional for him to talk about his patients to outsiders. And like it or not, that's what we are these days."

Ryder's lips formed a thin line.

Layla suddenly sighed deeply and plopped her head on Greer's shoulder.

Greer rubbed her back and kissed the top of her head. "I've heard about the nanny problems you've had."

"How?"

She stepped out of the way again when the shop door opened and a woman pushing two toddlers in a stroller came out. "Braden is a small town. Word gets around." She turned slightly so that Layla wasn't positioned directly in the sun. "Nannies don't hold to the same principles of confidentiality that a pediatrician's office does."

His lips twisted. "S'pose not." He reached for Layla, his hands brushing against Greer's bare arms as he lifted the tot away from her.

It was insane to feel suddenly shivery on what was such an infernally hot day.

She adjusted the wide bracelet-style watch on her wrist and wanted to curse. She was late getting back to the courthouse.

On foot from here, it would take at least twenty minutes. "I still feel I owe you a favor for helping me this weekend with my car."

"Was it the thermostat?"

"I don't know yet. My dad is looking at it. He's pretty good with cars. I told him what you thought, though." She shifted from one foot to the other and smoothed her hand down the front of her blouse, where it was tucked into the waist of her skirt. He'd taken a step toward the drugstore. "Maybe I could help you on the nanny front," she offered quickly.

"You?" He sounded incredulous. "Kind of a comedown in the world from lawyering to nannying, isn't it?"

"I don't mean *me* personally." She worked hard to keep from sounding as offended as she felt. She might not have a lot of experience with babies, but Layla wasn't just any baby, either. "I mean with advertising for a nanny. I'm on a lot of loops because of my work. I could post ads if you wanted."

His blue eyes gave away none of his thoughts. "I'll think about it."

She took that as a sign he was willing to negotiate. "I've got a lot of connections," she added. "I'd like to help."

Layla's head had found its way to his wide chest and she was contentedly gnawing the handle of her sippy cup.

"I suppose it wouldn't hurt," he said abruptly.

She'd fully expected him to say no. "Great! That's...that's really great." She cringed a little at her overenthusiasm, not to mention her lack of eloquence. She looked at her watch again and quickly leaned forward to kiss Layla's cheek. Then she started backing down the block. "I'll call you later to get the particulars. Pay range, hours, all that."

He resettled his black cowboy hat on his head, looking resigned. "Are you asking or telling?"

She knew her smile was once again too wide, but so what? She'd finally gotten to see Layla. And even if she earned Judge Waters's wrath for not making it back to court on time, she couldn't bring herself to care.

CHAPTER FOUR

RYDER SPOTTED THE little foreign job sitting in front of his house. It looked as out of place there as it had stalled on the side of the road out near Devil's Crossing.

The second thing he noticed was that Doreen Pyle's ancient pickup truck wasn't there.

When he'd set out that morning to get more hay cut, Mrs. Pyle had been sweeping up cereal after Layla overturned her favorite red bowl.

But now, Mrs. Pyle's truck was gone and the lady lawyer's was parked in its place.

It was too much to hope that she'd come all the way out here to tell him she'd found the perfect nanny candidate. She could've done that over the phone, the same way she'd gotten the particulars from him the other day.

He glanced at the cloudless sky. "What fresh new problem are you giving me now?"

As usual, he got no answer. The air remained hot and heavy, filled with the sound of buzzing insects.

He half expected to find Greer in the kitchen with Layla, but the room was empty when he went in.

He flipped on the faucet and sluiced cold water over his head.

Then he grabbed the dish towel hanging off the oven door to mop his face as he went in search of them.

There weren't a lot of rooms in the place, so it didn't take him long. He found both females in the living room, sprawled on his leather couch, sound asleep.

Layla wore a pink sleeveless T-shirt and diaper. She was lying on Greer's chest, who was similarly attired in a sleeveless pink shirt and denim cutoffs.

He looked away from her lightly tanned legs and quietly went up the iron-and-oak staircase. At the top, he crossed the catwalk that bisected the upper back half of the barn. All he had to do was look down and he could see his living area and who was occupying it.

Aside from the failed nannies and Mrs. Pyle, the last woman who'd spent any real time under his roof had been Daisy. When he thought about it, Mrs. Pyle had lasted longest.

He entered his bedroom. He'd put up sliding barn doors in the upper rooms after he'd taken custody of Layla. Before then, the only enclosed spaces had been the bathrooms. Two upstairs. One down.

He went into his bathroom now and flipped on the shower. Dust billowed from his clothes when he stepped out of them. He got into the shower before the water even had a chance to get warm.

He still had goose bumps when he stepped out a few minutes later, but at least he wasn't dripping sweat and covered in hay dust anymore.

He stepped over the dirty clothes, pulled on a pair of clean jeans and a white T-shirt from his drawer and went back downstairs.

They were still sleeping. He retrieved a bottle of cold water from the fridge in the kitchen, then wearily sat on the only piece of adult-sized furniture in the living room except for the couch. His aunt had designed the armless, triangular-backed chair during her furniture phase, and he had brought it with him along with the couch more for sentimental reasons than because it was comfortable.

He slouched down in the thing as much as he could and propped his bare feet on the arm of the couch by Greer's feet. Instead of opening the water bottle, he pressed it against his head and closed his eyes. Already the relief from the cold shower was waning and he caught himself having fond memories of the three feet of snow piled up against his house last March.

Not two minutes passed before Greer spoke, her voice barely above a whisper. "Do you think the heat's ever going to end?"

He didn't open his eyes. "I spent a summer near Phoenix once." Adelaide had been doing an exhibition there. "I was fifteen." He kept his voice low, too, because he knew what it was like when Layla didn't get in a decent nap. When he'd been rodeoing, he'd drawn broncs that'd been easier to handle. "It was like living inside a pizza oven."

"Descriptive. But you didn't answer my question."

He ignored that. "Where's Mrs. Pyle?"

"Still not answering my question. Obviously, Mrs. Pyle is at her grandson's trial."

He opened his eyes at that. The baby was still sleeping and Greer watched him over her head, eyes as dark and deep as the blackest night.

"What trial?"

"She didn't tell you?"

He spread his hands. "Obviously not."

"You do recall that Doreen Pyle *has* a grandson?"

He gave her a look.

"Anthony's seventeen. And he's being tried for burning down a barn."

Ryder swallowed an oath and pulled his feet off the couch. "She should have told me." He wasn't an ogre. "So why are *you* here?"

"Because I couldn't get the prosecution to agree to another continuance and Judge Donnelly has a stick up his—" Greer broke off with a grimace. "Anthony has a very competent trial lawyer representing him. Today, it's more important for him to have his grandmother there than me."

"Not because you wanted to spend time with Layla?"

"It's the one thing that made today tolerable. I've been working on Anthony's case since his prelim."

"Did he do it?"

"My client is innocent."

"Spoken like a defense lawyer."

"I am a defense lawyer. Just a poorly paid one, thanks to the great state of Wyoming."

"If he's your client, why is someone else handling the trial?"

Her lips twisted. "That, my friend, is the fifty-dollar question." She rolled carefully to one side so that she could deposit Layla on the couch cushion and then slid off the couch to sit on the floor.

It was almost as interesting as watching a circus contortionist.

Once she was on the floor with her back to the couch, she tugged her shirt down over her flat stomach where it had ridden up and blew out a breath. "This place of yours has a lot going for it, I'll grant you, but you need air-conditioning."

"I have a window rattler upstairs in my bedroom." He wondered why he didn't tell her there was another one in Layla's bedroom, too.

She slanted a look toward him from the corner of her eye. "Meaning?"

He smiled slightly. "Meaning I do have air-conditioning. Just not down here. I wish Mrs. Pyle would have told me."

"She must have her reasons. She's known since Monday."

He sat forward and offered her the unopened water bottle. "Why didn't you say something about the trial when you chased us down the street the other day?"

"Because it was Mrs. Pyle's business to tell you." Her fingers grazed his when she leaned over to take the water.

Adelaide had done her best to give him an appreciation of beauty and the visual arts. She'd always been asking him, *But what do you* see? and he never knew exactly what kind of answer she wanted. But he figured he must have learned something from her after all, given his appreciation of the way Greer tilted her head and tipped the bottle back, taking a prolonged drink. Her neck was long and lovely. Her profile pure. Watching her was almost enough to compensate for her and Mrs. Pyle's keeping him in the dark.

Greer handed him back the half-empty bottle.

Her lips were full and damp.

Even though he didn't need the trouble it would likely bring, he didn't look away from her when he took the bottle from her and finished it.

Her gaze flickered and she looked away as she pushed to her feet. She tugged at the hem of her T-shirt as she paced around the couch. "Did she give you any other reason to be quitting?"

"Maybe you should ask Mrs. Pyle."

She gave him a look and he relented, proving that he needed more willpower to resist the women in his life. "She tells me she's a housekeeper. Not a nanny."

"Because scrubbing floors is so much easier than heating a bottle?" Her voice rose a little and she pressed her lips together self-consciously.

"Layla doesn't use a bottle anymore. She only uses her cup. The pink cup. And if the pink cup isn't handy, she screams bloody murder until it is. Trust me, Counselor. Cleaning house is easier than childcare." He waved at Layla, who hadn't budged an inch from where she had rolled onto her side against the back couch cushion. She drooled all the time these days, and now was no exception. But the leather had survived him growing up, so he assumed it would survive a while longer.

"Did she say when she's leaving?"

"She gave me a week's notice."

"Even if we haven't found a nanny by then?" Greer propped her hands on her slender hips. "Did she say anything else?"

"Yeah. That I'd be better off finding a wife than a nanny."

Greer's eyebrows rose halfway up her forehead. Then she scrubbed her hands down her face. "I'm sorry."

"For what?"

She dropped her hands. "That she said something so...so insensitive!" She pressed her lips together again and watched Layla warily, as if expecting her to wake because her voice had risen once more.

"Insensitive how?"

A small line formed between her eyebrows. "Your wife passed away less than a year ago," she said huskily. "I'm sure remarrying is the furthest thing from your mind."

"It was until my housekeeper brought it up. But she had a valid point. Layla deserves a mother." At least he'd had Adelaide when his mother had died. He leaned back in the chair again and propped his feet once more on the couch arm. He linked his fingers across his stomach. "You never knew Daisy, did you?"

The line deepened slightly as she shook her head. "I never met her. But Grant has been talking more about Karen these days."

"The man actually talks?"

She gave him a look. "What she did has been hard on him, too. He was Karen's brother, but even then, the court wasn't ready or willing to hand over Layla to him."

He grunted. "She was never Karen to me. She was Daisy Miranda. That was the name she used when we met, the name she used when we got married and the name she used when she left me. She never said she had a brother at all. Either he didn't matter enough for her to mention, or I didn't matter enough. Considering the way things went down, I'll give you a guess which one I'm more inclined to believe."

Greer tucked her hair behind her ears. Her forehead had a

dewy sheen. "Regardless of her name, you loved her enough to marry her. You don't just get over that at the drop of a hat."

"You been married to someone who ran out on you? Ever gone through a bunch of tests just to make sure she didn't leave you with something catching to remember her by?"

"No, but—"

"Ever married at all?"

She needlessly retucked her hair. "No. But that doesn't mean I don't have feelings. That I have no appreciation for the pain involved when you lose someone. Hearts don't heal just because we decide they should."

He couldn't help the amusement that hit him.

And she saw it on his face. The line between her brows deepened even more. "What's so funny?"

He schooled his expression. "Nothing."

She let out a disgusted sound and his lips twitched again. Stopping the smile would've taken more willpower than he possessed.

She glared at him even harder and her eye got that little twitch she was prone to.

"Relax, Counselor. You don't have to worry that I'm withering away with grief or anything else because of my beloved wife. You do recall that *she* ran out on me, right?"

"And no matter what you say now, I'm sure that was very painful for you. But you know—" she waved her hands in invitation "—if you feel the need to pretend otherwise so as to maintain some false manly pride, be my guest."

He watched her for a moment. Then he pulled his feet off the couch again and sat forward. "Want a beer?"

She blinked. "What?"

He stood. Layla was still sound asleep. Snoring even, which meant that although he'd showered off the hay dust, she'd still probably gotten a whiff of it and her nose was getting congested. The pediatrician had warned him that Layla seemed to be developing some allergies. "A beer," he repeated, and headed into the kitchen, where he grabbed two cold bottles from the refrigerator.

Greer was standing in the same spot when he returned and handed her one. "It's five o'clock somewhere." He twisted off the cap and set it on the fireplace mantel.

Still looking suspicious, she slowly did the same.

He lightly tapped his bottle against hers and took a drink.

After some hesitation, she took a tiny sip.

"Let's go out back. It might be cooler."

She looked at Layla. "But—"

He scooped up the baby, who didn't even startle, and transferred her to the playpen. Then he picked up the baby monitor and turned it on, showing Greer the screen where the black-and-white image of his living space, including the playpen, was flickering to life. "Happy?"

Beer and monitor in hand, he headed out through the kitchen door, and Greer followed.

It wasn't any cooler outside. But at least there was a slight breeze and the gambrel roof provided shade from the sun. He gestured with his bottle to the picnic table and benches that he'd found stored in the root cellar when he'd bought the place.

"Wouldn't have expected something so fanciful from you," she said as she straddled one of the benches and set her bottle on the cheerfully painted table. "Flowers?"

He took the opposite bench. "Daisies." He set the baby monitor on the center of the weathered table and took a pull on the cold beer. "Twenty-five cents if you can guess who painted them."

"Ah." She nodded and fell silent.

He exhaled and turned so his back was against the table and he could stretch out his legs. The rolling hillside was his for almost as far as he could see. Beyond that was his by lease. His closest neighbor was ten miles away as the crow flew, and just to get to the highway meant driving down his seventeen-mile driveway, three miles of which were actually paved. Until he'd bought the place, he felt like he'd been looking for it his entire life.

But his housekeeper did have a point about his place being remote. "Mrs. Pyle's grandson going to get off?"

"It's a jury trial, so you never know until the verdict comes in. But I believe the facts are on Anthony's side."

"Doesn't it bug you not being there in court?"

"There are a lot of things about my job that bug me."

He took another drink and looked her way.

"Yes. It bugs me. But we've built a solid defense and Don Chatham—much as he annoys me personally—is a fine attorney. I can zealously represent my clients through the fairest plea negotiations to resolve their cases as well as anyone working in the PD's office. But when my client refuses to plea, or when they're truly better served going to trial?" She rolled the bottle between her fingertips. "Anthony *is* in good hands. Better than mine, when it comes down to it, since Don's experience before a jury exceeds mine by about a decade."

"When's the verdict likely to come in?"

"Before six tonight. The judge runs a tight ship and he likes to be home for dinner with his wife every night by seven. If the jury is still deliberating, he'll call a recess and resume tomorrow morning. But he'll be in a bad mood because he doesn't like working on Fridays any more than Don does. Did you move here because of Daisy?"

Her abrupt question was surprising. "No. We didn't meet until after that." He rolled his jaw around. "Not long after," he allowed.

"So why did you buy this place? Did you ranch in New Mexico?"

"I did a lot of ranch work. For other people. Along the way was some rodeoing. A few years in the service. Did you always want to be a lawyer?"

"What branch?"

"Army."

She smiled slightly. "My dad, too. Way before I was born, though." Her smile widened. "And I wanted to be a lawyer from the very first Perry Mason novel I read. My dad has a whole collection of them from when he was a kid and I started reading them one summer when I was grounded. I had romantic visions of defending the rights of the meek and the defenseless. And I also fancied following in Archer's path."

Ryder lifted his eyebrows.

"My older brother. Half brother, to be accurate. On my dad's side. I have a half sister on my mom's side who's also an attorney. But I didn't grow up with Rosalind the way I did with Archer. They're both in private practice."

"Classic yours, mine and ours situation?"

"Sort of. I have another half sister, too, who is a psychologist. Hayley lives in Weaver with her husband, Seth, and their baby. What about you?"

"No sisters. No brothers. Half or otherwise."

"But you have an aunt Adelaide with a pug named Brutus."

"Lawyers and their penchant for details."

"I'd be worried about my memory if I couldn't recall something you mentioned less than a week ago," she said drily. "What about your parents?"

"What about them?"

She waited a beat, and when he said nothing more, she took a sip of her beer. She squinted and her cheeks looked pinched. Her face was an open book, which for a lawyer was sort of a surprise. Maybe it was a good thing she didn't face juries very often. "Not your cup of tea?"

"It's fine."

He rolled his eyes and took the beer out of her hands. "I suppose you're a teetotaler."

"Not at all. I just... Well, wine is more my thing."

It was his turn to pull a face. "And not mine. Whiskey?"

"If the occasion calls for it."

"We've at least got that in common." He got up and she

looked alarmed. "Don't worry. I'm not bringing out a bottle of the good stuff. A cold beer at three on a hot afternoon is one thing. We'll save the whiskey for cold nights and staying warm. I'll get you a soda."

Greer chewed the inside of her cheek, watching Ryder head inside his house.

She thought she'd done pretty well not falling right off the couch when she'd wakened to find him sitting there. He'd obviously showered. His hair was dark and wet, slicked back from his chiseled features. His T-shirt was clinging to his broad shoulders. His feet sticking out from the bottom of his worn jeans had been bare.

And her mind had gone straight down the no-entry road paved with impossibility.

She hadn't expected to doze off along with Layla. But then again, she hadn't expected to be so pooped out after spending six hours taking care of the baby, either.

When she'd arrived out at the house, it had been early enough to relieve Doreen Pyle so she could get into town before court started. But Ryder hadn't been there, even though Greer had spent most of last night sleeplessly preparing herself for the encounter.

Doreen had told her that he'd headed out more than two hours earlier. "Haying," she'd said, as if that explained everything.

Foolishly, Greer had assumed that Doreen would have told her employer that Greer was pinch-hitting that day. And why.

She turned the baby monitor so she could see it better. Layla had turned around in a full circle inside the playpen, but still looked to be sleeping.

She reluctantly set the monitor on the table when Ryder returned. He set a bottle of cola in front of her. "Better?"

She rarely indulged, but it was still better than beer. And it was wonderfully cold. "Thank you."

His lips stretched into a brief smile. Then he sat down again, but this time he straddled his bench the same as her. "Why choose the public defender's office to zealously defend your clients?"

She'd been asked that question ever since she'd passed the bar. She'd always given the same answer. "Because I wanted to help people who really needed it." Her eyes strayed to the baby monitor. She couldn't help it. That grainy little image fascinated her.

"And do you?" His question dragged at her attention. "Help people who really need it?"

She twisted open the soda and took a long drink. The fact that she wasn't really sure what she was accomplishing anymore wasn't something she intended to share. "Everyone deserves a proper and fair defense," she finally said, which she believed right to her very core. "More than eighty percent of criminal defendants in this state end up in the public defender's office. I do my part as well as I can."

"Just not in front of a jury."

She realized she'd picked up the monitor again and made herself put it down. "Not generally. Although, honestly, I stay busier with my cases than Don does. We have a handful of trials a month. Unless it's something really big like the Santiago thing that's been on the news, Don spends most of his weekends fishing while I'm chasing around between courts and jails and—" She broke off. "I've never had a caseload that drops under one hundred clients at any given time."

The slashing dimple in his cheek appeared for a moment. "Do they all say they're innocent?"

She smiled wryly and let that one pass. "We cover a few counties here. But I know some offices with caseloads that are even heavier. We all make use of interns, but getting them can be sort of cutthroat." She shook her head. "The real problem is there's never enough money in the coffers to equip our office with everything and everyone we need."

"Now you sound like a politician."

On the monitor screen, Layla had turned around and was facing the other corner, her little rump up in the air. "Not in this lifetime," Greer responded. "Though I'd probably make more money if I were. Nobody I know has ever gotten rich working as a PD."

"Do you want to be rich?"

She laughed outright at that. "I'm more about being able to pay all the bills on time."

"What about that house of yours? That's gotta be a money pit."

"I'll take the fifth on that. I love my house. It has character."

"Like your car?"

She gave him her best stern look. The one she'd learned from her father. "Don't be dissing my car."

He lifted his hands in surrender.

"It *was* the thermostat, by the way. So thank you for that heads-up."

"Ever considered private practice?"

"Most lawyers do."

"Well, then? It's not like you don't have an in with people in the business."

"Much as I love Archer, I have no desire to actually *work* with him. Rosalind is with *her* father's practice down in Cheyenne and does mostly tax and corporate law. Bo-ho-ring. So—" She took another drink just so she wouldn't pick up the monitor again.

"So…?"

"Why are you so interested?"

"Shouldn't I know more about the woman who's been watching Layla behind my back?"

"For one day. Don't imply it's been a regular occurrence." She nudged the monitor with her fingertip. "We all fell in love with her, you know." She brushed her thumb across Layla's black-and-white image. "Right from the very beginning when Linc called in Maddie because he'd found a baby on his doorstep. The only identifying clue she had on her was the note Daisy left with her."

"'Jaxie, please take care of Layla for me,'" he recited evenly.

"Right. When Daisy cocktailed for Jax at his bar, she routinely called him that. That's the only reason we ever suspected she was Layla's mother in the first place."

Ryder's expression was inscrutable but she could easily imagine what his suspicions were. She'd had them herself. So had Linc. His brother, Jax, had been on one of his not-infrequent jaunts, which was why Linc hadn't immediately turned over the baby when he first discovered her. But whether or not Jax had been involved with Daisy in a more personal way, they'd nevertheless conclusively ruled him out as the baby's biological father last December.

She set the monitor down again. "By the time we knew about Daisy, though, Layla was already under the court's protection. The judge named Maddie as Layla's emergency foster parent while an investigation began." She was reiterating facts that he'd been told months ago.

"Your sister and Linc wanted to adopt her themselves. Before you ever even knew Daisy's brother existed."

She glanced at him. It wasn't a detail they'd shared when he took custody. "Who told you that?"

He swirled the liquid in his bottle and took a drink, making her wonder if he was stalling or if he was simply thirsty.

Then he turned the bottle upside down and poured out the remaining beer onto the grass beneath their feet. "Not cold enough," he said, and she thought he wasn't going to answer her at all.

But he surprised her.

He laid the empty bottle on its side on the table between them and slowly spun it. "As you've pointed out before, Counselor, word gets around in a small town." He stopped the bottle so it pointed her way. "Isn't it true?"

She was a lawyer. Not a liar. And what was the harm if he

knew the truth now? Maybe if he really understood, he wouldn't be so standoffish where her family and Layla was concerned. "They would have, but Maddie knew she and Linc would never get her. There were too many people in line ahead of them waiting to adopt a baby."

She clasped her hands on the table in front of her before she could pick up the monitor again. Her fascination with it was vaguely alarming. "The search for Daisy was leading nowhere and it was only a matter of time before Judge Stokes made a permanent ruling about placement. Not even the fact that Ali found Daisy's brother and discovered her real name was Karen Cooper changed that. We couldn't prove Layla was Karen's daughter and Grant's niece through his DNA because both he and Karen were adopted. Siblings by law, but not by genetics. Which meant that not even Grant could stop the legal forces at work. The one established fact the court recognized was that Layla had been abandoned and, as such, would benefit from placement in a suitable home through adoption. A family had even been selected." She sneaked a look at Ryder's face but his expression still told her nothing. She spread her fingers slightly, then pressed the tips of her thumbs together. "And then we discovered that your...that Karen had died in a car accident in Minnesota. Thanks to the photo that Grant and Ali found in her effects, we learned about you. Until then, we had no idea that Daisy Miranda or Karen Cooper had acquired a husband."

"The presumptive father, you mean."

She studied him. He'd had an opportunity to disprove it simply by requesting a paternity test.

But he hadn't.

Instead, he'd admitted—under oath—that he'd known about his absent wife's pregnancy. Combined with all their other information about Karen Cooper, it was enough for Judge Stokes to determine that Layla was legally Ryder's child. She'd been born during their marriage. No further questions asked. Certainly not about why Karen hadn't left their child with Ryder when she'd apparently decided parenthood wasn't for her.

The case may have been closed, but that didn't mean there weren't still questions.

"You didn't have to do it, you know," she said after a moment. "Claim Layla as your child. Not when we'd already failed so spectacularly to prove maternity." She didn't want to know if he'd lied under oath. It was hard enough suspecting that he had.

"It was the right thing to do."

"Even though *we* didn't know for certain that Daisy is... was Layla's mother." She could think of a dozen clients who wouldn't have done what he'd done. He'd told Ali when they'd first notified him that his wife hadn't been pregnant when she'd left him. Yet when he'd appeared before Judge Stokes, he'd attested that Daisy *had* notified him.

"How often do you run into someone named Layla?" He didn't wait for an answer as he spun the bottle again. "It was my mother's name. Daisy knew it. And I know Daisy liked it, because she told me once—in the beginning when I thought we actually had something—that if we ever had a baby girl, she wanted to name her Layla. Daisy *was* Layla's mother." He dropped his hand onto the bottle again, stopping its spinning once more. "It was the right thing to do," he repeated after a moment.

Greer's chest squeezed. He believed Daisy was Layla's real mother. But did he believe that Layla was his biological daughter?

She reached across the table and covered both his hand and the bottle with hers. "I'm sorry, Ryder. I really am." That he lost his wife. That he'd become a father in such an unconventional way. If she had questions, he surely had many more.

His jaw canted to one side. Then his blue eyes met hers and for some reason, an oil slick of panic formed inside her. She started to pull her hand back, but he turned his palm upward and caught hers.

"Sorry enough to marry me?"

CHAPTER FIVE

"MARRY YOU?"

Greer yanked on her hand and nearly fell off the bench when he let go of it. She caught herself, only to knock over the bottle of soda, which gushed out in a stream of bubbly foam, splashing over the front of her T-shirt and shorts. "Now look what you've done!"

It was obvious he was having a hard time not laughing. "Gonna sue me over it? You know, for a woman who looks like she can run the world, you're kind of a klutz. Did you really think I was serious?"

She plucked her wet shirt away from her belly. Now she wasn't just sweaty, she'd be sticky, too. And she'd never been klutzy. Until she was around him. "Of course not," she lied. "You're just full of funny things to say this after—" She broke off when he suddenly stood and went inside the house.

She muttered an oath after his departing backside and swiped her hand down her wet thighs.

He returned a moment later, holding a sleepy-looking Layla and a checkered dish towel that he tossed Greer's way. "She needs a fresh diaper."

"Am I supposed to take out an announcement in the newspaper?" She swiped the towel over her legs. She could feel the damn soda right through to the crotch of her cutoffs.

"You're pretty snarky when you're caught off guard, aren't you?" He went back inside.

Then she realized the baby monitor had gotten doused with soda, too. She snatched it off the table and started drying it with the towel.

The screen had gone black.

She carried it inside. Ryder was bending over Layla on the couch, changing the diaper. "Do you have any dried rice?" She didn't wait for an answer, but started opening cupboard doors. "Ali got her cell phone wet last year and kept it inside a container of rice for a day to dry. I had my doubts, but the thing worked afterward." Greer found plates. Drinking glasses. At least a dozen boxes of dry cereal. Only half of it was suitable for Layla, which gave her quite the insight into his preference for Froot Loops.

She moved on to the lower cabinets and drawers.

"No, I do not have rice."

He spoke from right behind her and she straightened like he'd poked her with an electric prod. "Oh." She slammed the drawer she'd just opened shut. "Well, then I don't know what you'll want to do about this." She set the monitor on the butcher-block counter. "More soda got on it than me."

He lifted an eyebrow as he settled Layla into the high chair and managed to fasten the little belt thing around her wriggling body. "You look pretty soaked."

It was all she could do not to pluck at the hem of her shorts. "Yeah, well, you shouldn't joke like that."

He slid the molded tray onto the high chair and grabbed one of the boxes of cereal. He dumped a healthy helping onto Layla's tray and she dived into it like she hadn't eaten in days.

There was no question that Layla liked her food. Greer had fed her both jars of the food that Doreen had left out, plus a cubed banana and a teething biscuit, right before her nap.

"Yeah, well, maybe I shouldn't be joking. Mrs. Pyle's the one who reminded me Layla'd be better off with a mama than a nanny. Not that I've had any luck keeping either one around," he added darkly.

She felt that slick panic again and opened her mouth to say something, but nothing came. Which was such an unfamiliar occurrence that she felt even more panicky. "You can't judge everyone based on Daisy and a flighty nanny," she finally managed to say.

"Three nannies," he reminded her. "Easier to discount one two-week wife than three nannies. Mrs. Pyle had a point."

She wasn't sure her eyebrows were ever going to come back down to their normal spot over her eyes. "On what planet?"

He slid a look her way. "I know I'm not Wyoming's biggest catch, but you really think I can't find a wife if I set my mind on it? At least this time, I'd be choosing with my head instead of my—"

"Heart?"

His lips twisted. "That wasn't exactly the body part I was thinking about."

She felt her cheeks heat, which was just ridiculous. It wasn't as though she was some innocent virgin. She was well versed in the facts of life, whether or not she'd acted on any of those facts lately.

"Anyway," he went on, "it wouldn't be a one-way deal." He'd pulled a covered bowl from the refrigerator and dumped the contents in a saucepan that he set over a flame on the stove. "I realize that she'd need to get something out of it, too. It'd be a business deal." He bent over, picking up the sippy cup that Layla had pitched to the floor. "Both parties benefit."

Greer nearly choked, looking away from the sight of his very, very fine jean-clad backside.

He set the cup back on the tray. "If you throw it, I'm going to take it away," he warned.

The baby laughed and swept her hands back and forth against the cereal, sending pieces shooting off the tray.

"Yeah, you laugh, you little terror," he muttered. "You know better." He went back to the stove to poke a fork at the concoction he was heating.

It all felt strangely surreal.

"I've always been better in business than relationships. So go with your strengths, right?" He glanced at her again.

"Marriage isn't a business deal."

He snorted. "Better a business deal than the real deal. As they say, Counselor, been there, done that. Not really a fan. You've been a lawyer for a while now. Haven't you seen the value of pragmatism over idealism?"

She wanted to deny it, but couldn't. "I don't think pragmatism is a basis for marriage, either."

"But it's a good basis for good business. At least that's been my experience. So—" he tested the temperature of the contents in his saucepan with his finger and pulled the pan off the flame "—like I said, Mrs. Pyle has a point. Two parents are supposed to be better than one. Didn't have two, myself, so I don't know about that. Maybe if I had—" He broke off, shaking his head and leaving Greer wondering.

He tipped the saucepan over a small bowl and grabbed a child-sized spoon from a drawer before flipping one of the table chairs around to face the high chair. "Every kid deserves a mother. Don't you agree?"

"Yes, but that doesn't mean I agree with this method of acquiring one!"

"People have been marrying for practical reasons a lot longer than they've been marrying for romantic ones. I could advertise for a wife just as easily as I can a nanny."

"You know what this sounds like to me? Like you've put all of five minutes of thought into it."

"And you'd be wrong. What happens to Layla if something happens to me?"

Her lips parted. "You... Well, Grant—"

"Daisy didn't dump Layla on Grant's doorstep. You think that was just an oversight? She didn't want him to have her!"

"You can't blame him for that! She didn't leave Layla with you, either!"

"Yeah, and that's something I get to live with. Daisy still named her after *my* mother. She was as unpredictable as the wind, but that means something to me."

She exhaled, feeling a pang inside. "Ryder. We'll find you a nanny. One who'll stay."

"If you were a kid, would you rather have a mom or a paid babysitter?" He didn't wait for her to answer. "Putting that aside for the moment, I'd rather have another plan in place for Layla if I get stomped out by a pissed-off bull one day."

"I've got to sit down." She grabbed one of the wood chairs from the table and sank down onto it. "I'm a lawyer. I appreciate your wisdom in planning for disasters, but I don't particularly want that vision in my head."

"You've heard worse in court, I'm sure."

She had, but that was different. "You can name anyone you want as a guardian for Layla if something were to happen to you. For heaven's sake, if you want to write up a will right now, I can help you. It doesn't mean you have to have a business-deal wife."

"Fine." He gestured with the spoon. "There's paper in that drawer. Get out a piece."

She slid open the drawer in question and pulled out the notepad and a short stub of a pencil. "You don't have to do it this very second."

"No time like the present." He scooped food into Layla's mouth.

"Maybe you should give it more thought," she suggested. "Deciding who would best—"

"I, Ryder Wilson, being of sound mind and body, yada yada. I assume you can fill in the blanks."

She exhaled noisily. "I'm not so sure about the soundness," she muttered. "But yes. So who do you want to name as guardian? Your aunt Adelaide?"

"She's already done her time raising me. You."

"Me, what?"

"You. Put your name down."

She dropped the pencil back into the drawer and shut it with a snap. "I don't find this funny."

"I don't find it funny, either, Counselor. There's no denying you've got a strong concern for Layla. But if your concern isn't that strong, no sweat." He scooped up another spoonful of the unidentifiable substance and evaded Layla's grasping hands to shovel it into her greedy mouth.

Something about his actions made Greer's insides feel wobbly. So she focused instead on the goopy little chunks on the spoon. "What *is* that?"

"Sweet potatoes, beets and ground chicken."

"Good grief."

"Don't knock it. I call it CPS."

"What?"

"Cow Pie Surprise."

She grimaced. "You just said it was chicken."

"It is. But doesn't matter what meat I add, it all looks the same. Like Cow Pie Surprise. But Layla loves it and she's sleeping better at night since I started spiking her food with meat." He gave Greer a sideways look. "You're not vegetarian or something, are you?"

She shook her head, keeping silent about her brief stint with the practice during her college years.

"Good." He focused back on Layla, slipping in a couple more bites before she managed to commandeer the spoon and whack it against the side of the tray. She chattered indecipherably, occasionally stopping long enough to focus on drumming her spoon or carefully choosing a round piece of cereal.

He tossed the bowl in the sink and wet a cloth to start wiping up the mess that was all over Layla's face and hands and hair and tray and clothes.

"Don't you have a bib?"

"Couple dozen of 'em. All came in the boxes of stuff your sister sent. Short-Stuff here doesn't like 'em." He freed the baby and set her down on the floor, and she immediately started crawling out of the room. "Decided a while ago that it wasn't worth the battle."

Having spent much of the day keeping up with Layla, Greer was less surprised by the rapid crawl than she was by Ryder's ease with Layla. She'd pictured him as struggling a bit more with the day-to-day needs of a baby.

"Do you have other children?"

His eyes narrowed and Greer knew she'd annoyed him. "D'you see any other kids here?"

She scooped up Layla before the baby could get too far. "Don't be so touchy." She much preferred taking the offensive tack to being on the defensive. "Nanny problems or not, you've obviously settled into the routine."

"Better than you expected."

"Not at all." *Liar, liar, pants on fire.*

"I've got roundup facing me whether this heat breaks soon or not, and it'll mean being gone a couple days. No matter what you think it looks like, I still need help. Nanny, wife or otherwise."

"And I'll remind you yet again that I have an entire family willing to help you out where Layla is concerned."

"Like Maddie? Your sister who is so pregnant she looks like she's about ready to explode?"

"How do you know what she looks like?"

"She was in Josephine's diner the other day."

"She didn't mention seeing you."

"She didn't."

He didn't elaborate, and Greer stomped on her impatience as though she were putting out a fire.

"I've already made some job postings for another nanny. It's only a matter of time before you find the right person. Here." She handed Layla to him. "I have briefs I need to prepare."

She'd even brought her case files with her, thinking she might have time to make some notes while Layla napped. But since Greer had napped right along with her, clearly *that* had been a silly notion. And even though she did have work to do, it was the sudden need to escape from Ryder that was driving her now.

"Briefs for a job that's not everything you'd hoped for."

"I didn't say that."

"You didn't have to." His gaze pinned hers and she felt uncomfortably like a witness about to perjure herself before the court.

She dragged her soda-moist shirt down around her soda-moist shorts. "I'll let you know when there are a few candidates—*nanny* candidates—for you to interview." She waved her hand carelessly. "But by all means, don't let that stop you from putting out word that you're wife-hunting if you're actually serious about that."

"Maybe I'll do that."

"If you do, I hope you'll look beyond the pool of cocktail waitresses at Magic Jax." The second she said it, she felt terrible. "I'm sorry. That was in poor taste."

"At least it was honest. You can let me know if you want to toss your name in the pool, after all."

She wasn't falling for that again. She snatched up her purse and her briefcase where she'd stashed them out of Layla's reach and hurried to the front door. "I'll be in touch about your will." She didn't wait for a response as she stepped outside and yanked the door closed.

She stood still for a moment and exhaled shakily. It was that time of day when the sun cast its rays beneath the covered front porch. It shone over her shoes. Her legs.

Marry Ryder.

She blinked several times, trying to ignore the words whispering through her mind.

Marry Ryder.

Try as she might, the thought would not be ignored.

"Get real," she whispered. He'd been no more serious about that than he had about naming her as Layla's guardian in his will. She stepped off the porch and strode decisively toward the car.

Marry.

Ryder.

Greer heard the front door open. "In the kitchen," she yelled, where she was putting the final touches on the tray of cold veggies and fruit. The heavens had finally smiled on her and her sisters' calendars, and Monday dinner was actually under way. She picked up the tray and carried it into the living room, where Maddie was struggling to lower herself onto the couch.

"Hold on. I'll help you." She set the tray on the coffee table, but Maddie waved her off.

"It's so hot," she grumbled, pushing her dark hair off her forehead.

"I've got lemonade or iced tea ready."

"Can you throw in some vodka?" Maddie made a face when Greer hesitated. "I'm joking." Even though she'd just sat, she pushed to her feet again and rubbed the small of her back. "Maybe."

The door opened and Ali blew in. "Have you heard Vivian's latest?"

Greer met Maddie's gaze before they both warily looked toward their sister. Where their paternal grandmother was concerned, anything was possible. Vivian Archer Templeton was nothing if not eccentric. And the fact that she was enormously wealthy thanks to Pennsylvania steel and several dead husbands meant she usually had no obstacles standing in the way of exercising those eccentricities.

"No," Maddie said cautiously. "What's she done now?"

"She went out on a *date* with Tom Hook!"

Greer stared. Tom Hook was an attorney. And a rancher. And a good twenty years younger than their eighty-ish grandmother. "Are you sure it was a date?"

Maddie let out a wry laugh. "Better a date than a marriage."

True enough. Their grandmother had already buried four husbands. "Vivian's always saying she has no interest in another husband because she's already had the love of her life in dear Arthur," Greer needlessly reminded them. He'd been the fourth of their grandmother's husbands. The only one who hadn't been rich. And Vivian made no secret of the fact that she would be happy to join him whenever the good Lord saw fit. After a life riddled with mistakes for which she'd been trying to make amends during the last few years, she maintained that Arthur was the one thing she ever did completely right.

"I'm guessing she's not looking for the love of her life," Ali said drily as she dropped her keys on the little table by the stairs. "Maybe she just wants some male companionship." She wiggled her eyebrows, looking devilish.

Greer made a face. "Don't be gross, baby sister."

Instead of getting Ali's goat, the reminder that she was the youngest of the triplets just made her laugh. "I'm a married woman now," she retorted, waggling her wedding rings. "Maybe I *like* thinking that I'll still be interested in that sort of thing when I'm Vivian's age."

"I'm even less eager to hear about your sex life than Vivian's."

Ali's eyes were merry. "Admit it, Greer. You're jealous. You need a date way worse than Vivian."

She rolled her eyes, ignoring the accusation that was too close to the truth. "So we can suspect why Vivian's dating Tom, but what's Tom up to?"

"Greer," Maddie chided. "Vivian's an intelligent, stylish woman."

"She's loaded," Ali said, ever blunt.

"Tom's not seeing her for her money," Maddie argued. "It

doesn't jibe with his personality at all. He's a good guy. Tell her I'm right, Greer."

"He's a good attorney," Greer allowed. "I always thought he had a lot of common sense. But to date Vivian? I don't know about that." She was as fond of their eccentric grandmother as her sisters were, but Tom and Vivian dating? "What if he's after her money?"

"You think if he were that she's too feeble to know?" Ali smiled wryly. "Fact is, *he's* the one we should probably be worried about. Vivian's pretty wily."

"It's just a date!" Maddie objected. "It's certainly not the craziest thing that's ever happened around here. And it doesn't have to mean marriage is afoot." She was still rubbing her back as she waddled into the kitchen. "Even for Vivian."

"Watch out for the two loose floorboards," Greer called out to her. What would her sisters say if she told them about Ryder's ridiculous wife idea? "I put a chair over them."

Maddie reappeared in the doorway. She was carrying a second tray and her cheek bulged out like a chipmunk's. "I wondered why it was sitting in the middle of the room," she said around her mouthful of food. She bent her knees enough so that she could slide the tray of cheese and crackers onto the coffee table without spilling the contents, then worked her way back down onto the couch. "When did we start having loose floorboards?"

"When did we not have them?" Ali responded. She sat down in the chair across from Maddie and pulled the trays closer, selecting a cluster of fat red grapes. "Are we having anything hot, or just cold stuff?"

"Just cold." Greer grabbed a fresh strawberry from the tray. "I have cold cuts and rolls, too, if you're interested."

"Much as I love sandwiches, it's too dang hot." Ali propped her sandaled feet on the edge of the couch. "Heard your esteemed colleague got Anthony Pyle off in court last week." She dangled her grapes in the air before plucking one from the stem.

"Must feel good to know your department has put another little punk back on the streets."

Greer's nerves tightened. Anthony's verdict hadn't come in until evening on the day that she'd babysat Layla. But instead of being in the courthouse as she should have been, she'd been pacing around her house trying to forget everything that Ryder had said. "It does feel good. Particularly since your department neglected to arrest the right person in the first place."

"Come on," Maddie said tiredly. "No arguments about work, okay?" She winced a little and rubbed her hand over her massive belly.

Greer peered at her. "When are you going to start your maternity leave from Family Services?"

"End of the week. I'm not due until next week, of course, but it's just starting to be too hard to get through—"

"—the doorways?"

Maddie elbowed Ali. "Ha ha. Soon enough you'll be in the same fix." She looked back at Greer. "The days," she finished. "Linc's been on my case to stop working for the past month, and my obstetrician for the past two weeks. Arguing with them both is too much work when—" She winced again and blew out a long breath.

"When you're this close to popping," Ali interjected. She closed her hand over Maddie's and squeezed. "You know you don't have to justify anything to us."

"Ali's right." Greer sat on the arm of the couch next to their pregnant sister. She rubbed Maddie's shoulder, left bare by the loose, sleeveless sundress she wore. "I'm just looking forward to meeting our new niece or nephew."

Maddie's lips stretched into a smile.

"Speaking of nieces and nephews..." Ali looked at Greer over Maddie's head. "Grant wants to know if there's anything we can do legally to ensure access to Layla. Are there visitation rights for uncles or something?"

Maddie made a sound. "Surely that's not necessary."

"It's been nearly six months," Ali said quietly. "Ryder hasn't made any attempts—"

"Has Grant?" Greer asked. She read the answer in Ali's expression. "Nothing will be accomplished if you and Grant take what Ryder will see as an adversarial angle."

Ali's chin came up. "And you know so much about Ryder's mind-set, do you?"

"I know that unless there's a custodial issue, a parent pretty much has the right to determine who has access to their own child!"

Ali looked annoyed.

"Remember that if it weren't for Ryder, Layla would have been adopted by now and off living in Florida where there would be *no* possibility at all for any of us to have some part in her life."

"That's right." Maddie was nodding. "Everyone just needs time. Things will work out for everyone. I know it will. We just have to have a little more patience. Meanwhile, I know there've been some problems with keeping a nanny, but Ray's last report to the court was positively glowing where Ryder's care of her is concerned."

"That's because Ryder *is* good with her. I've seen it for myself."

Both her sisters looked at her.

"I babysat for him last week. I filled in for Mrs. Pyle so she could be at court with her grandson."

Maddie's mouth formed an O. Ali looked annoyed.

"It was a last-minute decision," she added.

Ali held up her hand. "Thursday, Friday, Saturday." She ticked off on her fingers. "Sunday. Monday." She held up her hand. "Five days, Greer. It took you five days to tell us? What other secrets are you keeping?"

Greer pushed off the couch arm. "I'm not keeping secrets."

"What would you call it then?"

"Okay, fine." Ali had a point. "So I've... I've had a few encounters with Ryder lately."

Maddie's eyebrows rose. "A few?"

"How few?" Ali demanded. "And when?"

"Last week!" Greer hated feeling put on the hot seat, but knew she had only herself to blame for not telling them sooner. "I ran into him and Layla when I was on a break during court on Monday. It was just a coincidence." Though her chasing him right down the street hadn't been.

"So you think there's no reason to mention it?"

"No! I just—" She broke off. "I offered to help him find a nanny."

Maddie had closed her eyes and was breathing evenly. Ali, on the other hand, was watching Greer as though she'd committed a federal offense. "Why?"

"Because I wanted to help! You know that he was the one who got me to Maddie's shower."

"And why *did* he do that? He showed up just like that?" Ali snapped her fingers. "Out of the clear blue sky?"

"For God's sake, Ali. You're always suspicious. Yes, out of the clear blue sky! Maddie's been coaching us since you found Ryder not to push ourselves into his life until he gave some hint he'd welcome it. Well, he gave a hint! I didn't deliberately flag him down when I was stuck out by Devil's Crossing. But he helped and so I offered to help him in return. I'm not going to apologize for it. In fact, I would think you'd be glad for it!"

"Glad that you've been seeing my husband's *niece* without telling us a word about it? You *know* how important that is to Grant! Considering how estranged he'd been from Karen?"

Greer propped her fists on her hips. "I'm telling you now! Look, I know your husband is still dealing with his grief where his sister is concerned. But if he's been so concerned about Layla, why *hasn't he* gone banging on Ryder's door demanding to see her?" She waved at Maddie, who was looking pale. She'd always hated it when Greer and Ali went at it when they were kids, and things hadn't changed much since then. "Don't pretend that a man like your husband will follow *anyone's* advice if he doesn't agree with it! He blames Ryder and we all know it!"

"He *doesn't* blame Ryder! He blames himself!" Ali's raised voice echoed around the room. She was breathing hard. "And judging by Ryder's attitude these past months, he blames Grant, too."

The wind oozed out of Greer's sails. "Of course Grant's not responsible for what his sister did. Any more than Ryder is."

"I know that. And you know that. And my husband knows that, too. In here." Ali touched her forehead. "But in here," she said, tapping her chest, "it's still killing him."

Greer pushed aside the fruit and veggie tray and sat on the coffee table in front of her sisters. She grabbed Ali's hands and squeezed them. "It's not just hot monkey sex, right? The two of you are okay all the way around?"

Ali smiled slightly. She squeezed Greer's hands in return. "All the way around," she said huskily. "Grant is everything to me. I just want to be able to make this better for him."

"You will," Maddie murmured. "Just tell him about the baby."

"The baby," Greer echoed. "You think having another niece or nephew will make him less concerned with Layla?"

"Of course not," Maddie replied.

"She's talking about my baby."

Greer startled, looking at Ali. But Ali was looking at Maddie. "What I'd like to know is how *you* knew? I haven't told anyone yet that I'm pregnant!"

"I could just tell." Maddie blew out another audible breath as she scooted herself forward enough to push off the couch. "Now do me a favor, would you?" She pressed her hands against the small of her back and worked her way around the two of them. "Call *my* husband and tell him it's time."

Alarm slid through Greer's veins. "Time?"

"What d'you mean, *time*?" Ali looked even more alarmed.

"I mean baby time," Maddie exclaimed, thoroughly un-Maddie-like. "Now *move*!"

CHAPTER SIX

THE HANDS OF the clock on the hospital waiting room wall seemed like they had stopped moving.

No matter how urgently Maddie had entered the hospital six hours earlier, time seemed to be crawling now.

Greer's dad was pacing the perimeter of the room, his steps measured and deliberate. Her mom, Meredith, was curled up in one of the chairs, her long hair spread over her updrawn knees. Vivian was sitting next to her, dozing lightly over the *Chronicle of Philanthropy* magazine on her lap. Archer was on his way from Denver, where he'd been consulting on a case, and Hayley and Seth had left only an hour ago, because it was long past time to put baby Keely to bed. Then there were Ali and Grant. Greer's brother-in-law wore the broody sort of expression that never really left his darkly handsome face. But there was still tenderness in his face as he looked down at Ali's tousled head on his shoulder. She was asleep.

"How much longer d'you think it will take?" Carter finally stopped in front of Meredith.

"I left my crystal ball at home." She looked amused. "It's a baby. It'll take as long as it takes."

Her dad made a face. "What if something's gone wrong?"

Meredith smiled gently and took his hand. "Nothing's gone wrong," she assured him.

"You don't know that. Things go wrong all the time."

"Carter." She stood, wrapping her arms around his waist and looking up at him. "It was only a few months ago that Hayley had Keely. That all went perfectly. And things are going to go perfectly with Maddie, too."

He pressed his cheek to the top of her head.

Frankly, Greer sympathized more with her dad. Things did go wrong all the time. Her career proved that on a daily basis.

What's happens to Layla if something happens to me?

"I'm going down to the cafeteria," she said, pushing away the thought. "Get myself a coffee. Can I bring back anything?"

Grant raised his hand. "Coffee here. I'll go, though."

Greer waved away his offer. "And wake Sleeping Beauty?" In the commotion of getting everyone to the hospital, Greer couldn't help but wonder if Ali had told him yet that they were expecting. She suspected not.

"Your dad'll take some coffee, too, sweetheart."

"I don't suppose there's a chance for a cocktail here?" Vivian commented, opening her eyes.

Carter grimaced. He didn't have a lot of affection for his mother, but since she'd moved to Wyoming in hopes of making amends with him after years of estrangement, he'd at least gotten to the point where it wasn't always open warfare with her whenever they were in the same room. "It's a hospital, Mother, not a bar."

"You never did have a sense of humor." Vivian looked at Greer with a twinkle in her eye as she patted her handbag sitting on the chair beside her. "I have my own flask with me for emergencies just like this. Just enough to make a cup of the dreadful coffee they have here a little more palatable."

Greer smiled, though it was anyone's guess whether or not Vivian was being serious. Not that it mattered to her if her grandmother wanted to spike her coffee while they waited for the baby to arrive. As far as she was concerned, nearly anything that got them through was fine. "I'll be back in a few."

She left the waiting room and started toward the elevator, but then aimed for the stairs instead to prolong her journey. As she passed the window of the nursery, she slowed to look inside. A dozen transparent bassinets were lined up, four of them holding tiny occupants, wrapped so snugly in white blankets that they looked more like burritos than miniature human beings.

A blonde nurse wearing rubber-ducky-patterned scrubs walked into view and picked up one of the baby burritos, affording Greer a brief view of a scrunched-up red face and a shock of dark hair before the nurse carried the baby out of sight again.

Greer lifted her hand and lightly touched the glass pane with her fingertips as she lingered there.

When Daisy had left Layla on Linc's doorstep, they'd estimated she was about two or three months old.

Looking at the babies inside the nursery, Greer still found it unfathomable how Daisy could have done such a thing. If she had lived, if she'd been charged with child endangerment, if her case had managed to land on Greer's desk like so many others, would she have been able to do her client justice?

The blonde nurse returned to the area with the bassinets. She didn't even glance toward the window, which made Greer wonder if the view was one-way. She plucked another baby from its bassinet, but instead of carrying the infant out of sight, she sat down in one of the rocking chairs situated around the nursery and cradled the baby to her shoulder as she began rocking.

Greer finally turned away, but the hollowness that had opened inside her wouldn't go away.

It was still there when she went down the cement-walled staircase, footsteps echoing loudly on the metal stairs. At the bottom, she pushed through the door, and realized that the staircase hadn't let her out in the lobby like the elevator would have, but in the emergency room.

Since there had been plenty of times when she'd had to visit a new client in Weaver's ER, she knew most of the shortcuts. She headed past the empty waiting area and the registration desk, aiming for the hallway on the other side that would take her back into the main part of the hospital.

"Hey, Greer. Heard that Maddie came in earlier. How's she doing?" the nurse behind the desk asked.

Greer slowed. "Six hours and still at it." She smiled at Courtney Hyde, who'd been an ER nurse since well before Greer had learned that they were cousins a few years ago. "Thought you didn't work nights anymore?"

Courtney tucked her long gold hair behind her ear. "Don't usually. But we're shorthanded at the moment, so." She shrugged. "We're all doing our part." Then she smiled a little impishly. "And it gives Sadie an opportunity to have her daddy all to herself at bedtime. Yesterday when I got home, she'd convinced Mason to build her an 'ice palace'—" she air-quoted the term "—to sleep in, using every pillow and furniture cushion we have in the house. Sadie slept the divine sleep that only a three-year-old can sleep."

"And Mason?"

Courtney grinned. "My big tough husband had me schedule him for a massage just so he could work out the kinks from a night spent on the floor crammed inside an igloo of pillows."

Considering the fact that Mason Hyde was about six and a half feet tall, Greer could well believe it.

"I swear I'll never stop melting inside whenever I see the way he is with her, though," Courtney added, sighing a little. "Just wait. Someday you'll see what I mean."

Greer kept her smile in place, even though the image inside her head wasn't one of Mason Hyde and his little girl. It was of Ryder, scooping Cow Pie Surprise into Layla's greedy mouth.

"You going to be at the picnic?"

"Sorry?"

"Gloria and Squire are hosting a big ol' picnic next week out at the Double C. To celebrate Labor Day. Whole family will be there." Courtney's eyes twinkled. "That includes all of you Templetons now, too."

Greer chuckled wryly. "I kind of need to show my face at the county employee picnic that weekend. My boss's wife organizes it. Besides which, just because the Clay family lines have expanded our way doesn't necessarily mean we're welcome. If *my* grandmother finds out we're consorting with *your* grandfather, who knows how bad the fireworks will be."

"Old wounds," Courtney said dismissively. "Vivian might have shunned Squire's first wife sixty years ago, but she's apologized. It's high time he let it go. At least think about the picnic." She reached out an arm and picked up the phone when it started ringing. "Emergency," she answered. "Think about it," she mouthed silently to Greer.

Nodding, Greer left the other woman to her duties and continued on her way, only to stop short again when the double doors leading to the exam rooms swung open and Ryder appeared. He was holding Layla, wrapped in a blanket.

Alarm exploded inside her.

When he spotted her, his dark brows pulled together over his bloodshot blue eyes. He stopped several feet away. "What're you doing here?"

"What are *you* doing here?" Without thought, she closed the distance between them and put her hand on Layla's back through the blanket. The toddler's head was resting on his shoulder. Her eyes were closed, her cheeks flushed. "What's wrong?"

"Nothing."

The comment came from Caleb Buchanan, and Greer realized the pediatrician had followed Ryder through the double doors. "However, if she hasn't improved in the next twenty-four hours, give me or her regular pediatrician a call."

"Thanks." Ryder's jaw was dark with stubble and he looked like he hadn't slept in a couple days.

"And don't worry too much," Caleb added. "Kids run fevers.

As long as it doesn't get too high, her body's just doing what it's supposed to do."

When Ryder nodded, Caleb transferred his focus to Greer. "Heard Maddie was here. How's everyone doing?" Thanks to the prolificacy of Squire Clay's side of the family, Caleb was also a cousin. His pale blue scrubs did nothing to disguise his Superman-like physique. But Greer knew from experience that the doctor was singularly unconcerned with his looks.

"Fine. Anxious for the baby to get here. We've been waiting hours."

"Want me to check in on them?"

"That'd be great, if you've got the time. Everyone's up in the waiting room. I was just gonna grab some coffees from the cafeteria."

He smiled and patted her shoulder. "I'll see what I can find out." Then he retreated through the double doors.

Greer immediately focused on Ryder again. "How long has she been sick?"

"She didn't eat much of her dinner, but she seemed okay until she woke up crying a couple hours ago." He shifted the baby to his other shoulder. Layla didn't stir. "She threw up all over her crib, then threw up all over me and was hot as a pistol."

Greer couldn't help herself. She rubbed her hand soothingly over the thin blanket and the warm little body beneath. "Poor baby."

"Speaking of. Your sister's having hers?"

She nodded. "Whole family's been here at some point tonight."

"Hope everything goes okay." He took a step toward the sliding glass entrance doors.

"Ryder—"

He hesitated, waiting.

She wasn't sure why her mouth felt dry all of a sudden, but it did. "I... I haven't heard anything on the job postings yet. Have you?"

He shook his head. "Mrs. Pyle said she'd give me the rest of this week, after all." He shifted from one cowboy boot to the other. "Think she's feeling in a good mood after her grandson's acquittal last week."

"But not good enough to stay on indefinitely."

"She's a housekeeper. Not—"

"—a nanny," Greer finished along with him. "Well, I should get back up to the waiting room. They're probably wondering what's keeping me." She chewed the inside of her cheek. "I don't suppose you want to come..."

He was shaking his head even before her words trailed off. "Need to get her back in her own bed." He grimaced a little. "After I've gotten it all restored to rights, at least."

"Of course." She pushed her hands down into the back pockets of her lightweight cotton pants. It was silly of her to even have the notion. "Well." She edged toward the elevator. "Fingers crossed someone nibbles at one of the job posts."

The corner of his mouth lifted slightly and she felt certain he was thinking more about his wife idea than the nanny. "Yeah."

She took two more steps toward the elevator and jabbed her finger against the call button.

"Don't forget the cafeteria."

"What?" Her face warmed. "Oh. Right." The elevator doors slid open but she ignored them.

He smiled faintly. "G'night, Counselor."

She managed a faint smile, too, though it felt unsteady. "Good night, Ryder."

He carried Layla through the sliding door and disappeared into the darkness.

Greer swallowed and moistened her lips, then nearly jumped out of her skin when Courtney walked up and stopped next to her. She was carrying a stack of medical charts. "If I weren't already head over heels for my husband," she whispered conspiratorially, "I'd probably be sighing a little myself over that one."

"I'm not *sighing* over him."

Courtney grinned. "Sure you're not." With a quick wink, she backed her way through the double doors.

Left alone in the tiled room, Greer pressed her palms against her warm cheeks. She shook her head, trying to shake it off.

But it was no use.

And then her cell phone buzzed with a text from Ali. *Where are u?! Baby here!*

Forget the coffee.

She pushed the phone back into her pocket and darted for the elevator.

"If we're keeping you awake, Ms. Templeton, maybe you should consider another line of work."

Greer stared guiltily up at Judge Manetti as she tried to stop her yawn. It was a futile effort, though.

Just because she'd been at the hospital until three this morning celebrating the birth of her new nephew didn't mean she'd been allowed a respite from her duties at work.

"I'm sorry, Your Honor," she said once she could speak clearly. In the year since Steve Manetti had gone from being a fellow attorney to being a municipal court judge appointed by the mayor, she had almost gotten used to addressing him as such. But it had been hard, considering they'd been in elementary school together.

She glanced down at her copy of the day's docket before slipping the correct case file to the top of her pile. "My client, Mr. Jameson, wishes to enter a plea of not guilty."

Manetti looked resigned. "Of course he does." He looked over his steepled fingers at the skinny man standing hunched beside her. "Is that correct, Mr. Jameson?"

Johnny Jameson nodded jerkily. Every motion since he'd entered the courtroom betrayed the fact that he was high on something. Undoubtedly meth, which was what he was charged with possessing. Again. "Yessir."

Manetti looked at Greer, then down at his court calendar. "First available looks like the second Thursday of December."

She made a note. "Thank you, Your Honor."

Judge Manetti looked at the clock on the wall, then at the bailiff. "We'll break for lunch now."

"All rise," the bailiff intoned, and the small municipal courtroom filled with the rustling sounds of people standing. Manetti disappeared through his door and the courtroom started emptying.

Greer closed her case file and fixed her gaze on her client. "Johnny, the judge just gave you four months. I advise you to clean up your act before trial. Understand me?"

Johnny shrugged and twitched and avoided meeting her eyes. She shifted focus to Johnny's wife behind him. "Katie? Do you want another copy of the list of programs I gave you before?"

"No, ma'am." Katie Jameson was petite and polite and as clean as her husband was not. "Johnny's gonna be just fine by then. I promise you."

Greer dearly wished she could believe it. "All right, then." She pushed her files into her briefcase and shouldered the strap. "You know how to reach me if you need me. Mr. Chatham will be in touch with you to go through your testimony before December."

Johnny grunted a reply and shuffled his way out of the courtroom.

"You're a lot nicer than Mr. Chatham," Katie said, watching her husband go. "I wish you could handle Johnny's trial."

Greer smiled. "Don't worry. You and Johnny will be in good hands."

"Well, thank you for everything you've done so far."

It was a rare day when Greer received thanks for her service. More often than not, she busted her butt negotiating a deal for her client only to have him or her walk away without a single word of appreciation. She shook Katie's hand. "You're welcome,

Katie. Take care of yourself, okay? I meant it when I said you can call if you need me."

The young woman nodded, ducking her chin a little, then hurried after her husband.

Greer stifled another yawn as she walked out of the courtroom. She had two hours before her next appearance. If she'd had more than a few dollars left in her bank account after spending most of her paycheck on bills, she would have gone down to Josephine's for a sandwich. Instead, she walked back to her office, where she closed the door and kicked off her pumps. Then she sat down at her desk, and with a good old peanut-butter-and-jelly sandwich in one hand and a pencil in the other, she started in on the messages she hadn't been able to respond to before morning court.

She'd been at it for barely an hour when her office door opened and her boss tossed another stack of papers on her desk. "We're not getting an intern this round. There were only two available and the other offices needed them more." He pointed at the papers he'd left. "Plead all those out."

She swallowed the bite of sandwich that had momentarily stuck to the roof of her mouth and thumbed the latest pile. "What if they don't all want to plead?" She knew the futility of the question, but asked out of habit.

"Talk them into it," he said, and then left as unceremoniously as he'd entered. He always said that. Even though he knew some cases and some defendants never would plead.

Or should.

She glanced at the clock above the door. She started to lift her sandwich to her mouth, but her phone rang and she answered it. "Public defender's office."

There was a faint hesitation before a female spoke. "I'm calling about the job posting? The one for a nanny?"

Greer sat up straighter.

"This is the right number, isn't it?" The woman had a faint

accent that Greer couldn't place. "You said public defender's office?"

"Yes, yes, it's the right number." She set her sandwich down on the plastic wrap. "I'm Greer Templeton. I represent—" She cringed, realizing how that might sound. "I'm *assisting* a friend with his search for a nanny."

"He's not in trouble with the law?"

"No, not at all."

"That's a relief," the woman said with a little laugh. "The last thing I desire is another job that leaves me wanting. I prefer something that will be steady. And lasting. Your post said you're—he, your friend—is looking for a live-in? Is that written in stone?"

"It's probably negotiable. Why don't you give me your contact information and you can discuss it with him directly."

"Very good. My name is Eliane Dupre."

"Would you mind spelling—"

The caller laughed lightly. "Like Elaine but reverse the *i* and *a*. It's French."

Greer immediately imagined a beautiful, chic Parisian singing French lullabies to Layla while Ryder looked on. She cleared her throat, and her head of the image. "Is that where you're from? France?"

"Switzerland, actually. I moved to the States a few years ago with my husband. Alas, that didn't work out, but here I am. I'm a citizen," she said quickly, "in case that is a concern."

Her right to work should have been more of a concern to Greer, but her imagination was still going bananas. Swiss? Had Maria in *The Sound of Music* been Swiss? She sure got her man. No, that was Austria.

Still, the loving governess had captured the heart of the children and their father.

She shook her head at her own nonsense, making notes as Eliane provided her phone number and an address in Weaver in her musical, accented voice.

"You understand that the location where you'd be working is fairly remote?"

"Yes. Quite to my liking."

"How long have you lived in Weaver?"

"I've only been here a few weeks. I'm staying with an acquaintance while I look for employment. Shall I expect a call from your friend, then?"

There was no reason to hesitate, but Greer still felt like she had to push her way through the conversation. "Yes, I'll get your information to him as soon as I can."

"Thank you so much. Have a lovely day."

"You, too," Greer said faintly. But she said it to the dial tone, because Eliane had already ended the call.

She dropped the receiver back on the cradle and stared blindly at her notes. Then she snatched up the phone again and punched out Ryder's phone number.

Neither Mrs. Pyle, Ryder nor the machine picked up.

Was Layla still sick? Maybe Ryder had caught whatever bug she'd had. Or maybe her fever had gotten worse.

Greer rubbed at the pain between her eyebrows. "Stop imagining things," she muttered, "and be logical here."

She pulled up the information she had on record for Anthony Pyle. But when she called that number, there was no answer.

She hung up and looked at the time. She couldn't very well drive Eliane's information out to the Diamond-L and check on Ryder and Layla herself. Not when she was supposed to be back in court in less than an hour.

She looked at the docket she'd printed that morning. Hearing conferences and motions.

She reached for the phone again and dialed. This time, she received an answer. "Keith? It's Greer. Can you pinch-hit for me this afternoon? I know it's short notice, but I have a personal matter that's come up."

"Personal matter!" He sounded surprised. "You're joking, right?"

She made a face at the wall. "Does it sound like I'm joking?"

He chuckled. "I'm just yanking your chain. Nice to know that you're human like the rest of us. So, yeah. Sure. Just for today?"

"Just for today. I'll leave my files at the front desk with Bunny. Court's back in session at two."

"I'll be there," he promised. "Everything all right? I heard Maddie had the baby last night—"

"They're all fine," she assured him. It never failed to surprise her how quickly news spread in this town. "It's nothing to do with that. I really appreciate the favor. I'll owe you one."

"And I plan on collecting," he said with a laugh before hanging up.

Now that she'd made the decision, she tossed the rest of her sandwich in the trash. The bread was already getting stale, anyway. She bundled up everything that Keith might need for the afternoon and left it with Bunny Towers. Then she went back to retrieve her shoes and purse and left the office.

Not even Michael noticed, which had her wondering why she'd never tried taking off an afternoon before. No matter what she did, her boss seemed to remain unimpressed.

It took nearly an hour to get to Ryder's place. There were no vehicles parked on the gravel outside the house. Even though she'd seen it more than once now, the sight of the converted barn was still arresting. The only barn conversions she'd ever seen before were in magazines and on home decorating shows.

No doubt, Eliane-of-the-beautiful-accent would only add another layer of interest to the surroundings.

"Get your brain out of high school," she muttered, and snatched up her purse before marching to the front door. There was no answer when she knocked, but the door was unlocked when she tried it. She cautiously pushed it open. "Hello? Mrs. Pyle?" She stepped inside. "Ryder?"

The last time she'd been there, the house had been as tidy as a pin.

Now it looked like a tornado had hit.

Layla's toys were everywhere. Laundry was piled on the armless chair, overflowing onto the floor. The couch was nearly hidden beneath a plastic bin that she felt certain contained the baby gear that Maddie and Linc had given Ryder when they'd turned Layla over to him.

She dropped her purse on top of it and walked into the kitchen. Cereal crunched under her shoes. The sink was filled halfway to the top with dirty dishes.

She crunched her way to the back door and looked out at the picnic table with its painted daisies. It hadn't even been a week since she'd been there, but the grass was already overgrown.

Weren't Swiss people notoriously tidy? Maybe Eliane would take one look and run for the hills.

The thought should have been worrying.

The fact that it was not was an entirely different cause for concern.

She left the door open slightly to allow for some fresh air—hot as it was—and went upstairs.

Layla's nursery was empty. The mattress had been stripped of bedding. It was probably sitting in the pile of laundry downstairs.

The air was stuffy here, too. One window held a boxy air conditioner. It wasn't running, and Greer left it off. She went to the second window and opened it; the hot breeze fluttered at the simple white curtains.

She left Layla's room, intending to go back downstairs, but she hesitated, looking down the hall toward the other open door. She could see the foot of a bed where a navy blue quilt was piled half on and half off the mattress. A pair of cowboy boots were lying haphazardly on the wood floor.

Unquestionably, the room was Ryder's.

When she'd babysat Layla, the sliding door to the room had been closed.

She knew the house was empty.

Still, Greer's heart beat a little faster as she stepped closer to the room. She peered around the edge of the doorway. The dresser was wide, with six drawers. One framed picture sat on top, but otherwise it was bare.

His bed was big with an iron-railed headboard. Three white pillows were bunched messily at the head of the mattress. Instead of a nightstand next to the bed, there was a saddletree complete with a fancy-looking tooled leather saddle. An industrial sort of lamp was attached directly to the wall. There was an enormous unadorned window next to the bed, and before she knew it, she'd walked across the room to look out.

Directly below was the picnic table.

She wondered how often he looked out and thought about his late wife.

She wondered if he'd look out and still think about her when he had a delectable Swiss confection under his roof tending to his child.

Disgusted with herself, she turned away from the window. She bent down slightly to look at the framed photograph on his dresser. It was an old-fashioned black-and-white wedding photo. Maybe his parents? Or the aunt named Adelaide? Then she heard a faint sound and her nervousness ratcheted up.

She darted out of the bedroom and was heading to the staircase when Ryder—looking entirely incongruous in cowboy hat and boots with a pink-patterned baby carrier strapped across his chest—appeared.

Even before he saw her, his eyes were narrowed. "What're you doing here?"

CHAPTER SEVEN

WHAT'RE YOU DOING HERE?

Ryder's question seemed to echo around her.

He looked hot and sweaty, as did Layla in the carrier, and Greer's mouth went dry.

Not only from nearly being caught out snooping in his bedroom, but from the strange swooping feeling in her stomach caused by the sight of him.

"Greer?"

She felt like her brains were scrambled and gestured vaguely toward Layla's bedroom. "I was...ah—"

"Never mind." In a move that she knew from personal experience was more difficult than he made it look, he unfastened Layla from the carrier and handed her to Greer. "Take her for a few minutes while I clean up."

Layla's green eyes were bright and merry as she looked at Greer. She was wearing a yellow T-shirt that felt damp and a pair of yellow shorts with a ruffle across her butt. Her reddish-blond curls were spiked with perspiration. "Is she still running a fever?"

"Nah. Even on a cold day the carrier gets hot." He pulled off his hat as he brushed past Greer, smelling like sunshine and fresh hay. He continued along the hallway, pulling off not only the carrier, but his T-shirt, as well. "She popped out two more teeth this morning, though. I don't care what that doc said last night about teething not causing a fever. Soon as those teeth showed up, she was right as rain, just like my aunt Adelaide predicted." He stepped inside his bedroom and looked at Greer. "Be down in a few." Then he pulled on the rustic metal handle and slid the door closed.

She closed her eyes. But the image of his bare chest remained. Heaven help her.

She opened them again to find Layla smiling brightly at her, displaying the new additions to her bottom row of teeth. She jabbered and patted Greer's face.

Greer caught the baby's hand and kissed it. "Hello to you, too, sweetheart."

She heard a couple thuds from behind Ryder's bedroom door. It was much too easy imagining him sitting on the foot of that messy, wide bed, pulling off his boots and tossing them aside.

After the boots would come the jeans—

"Let's go downstairs," she whispered quickly to Layla, who laughed as if Greer had said something wonderfully funny.

"At least *you* think it's funny." Greer hurried to the staircase. "You have a lot in common with your aunt Ali, that's for sure."

Once downstairs, she settled Layla into her high chair. It was much cleaner than the kitchen counters were, so she had to give Ryder points for that.

She opened the back door wider so there was more air flowing, then found a clean cloth in a drawer. She wet it down with cool water and worked it over Layla's face and head. Layla took it as a game, of course, and slyly evaded most of Greer's swipes before gaining control of the cloth, which she proceeded to shove into her mouth.

Chewing on a wet washcloth wasn't the worst thing Greer could think of, so she let the baby have it and turned her attention to the dishes in the sink. They weren't quite as dirty as she'd first thought. At least they'd been rinsed.

Loading the dishwasher didn't take much time. She found the soap and started it. But the sound of the dishwasher wasn't enough to block the sound of water running overhead, and Greer's imagination ran amok again.

To combat it, she found another cloth and furiously began wiping down the counters. When she was done with that, she found the broom and swept up the scattered cereal crumbs. And when she was done with *that*, she grabbed an armful of clothes from the pile on the chair and blindly shoved it into the washing machine located in a sunny room right off the kitchen.

The cheeriness of the room was almost enough to make up for the laundry drudgery, and she wondered if he'd made it that way for Daisy.

With the washing machine now running, too, she went back into the kitchen, lifted Layla out of the high chair and took her outside.

"You like this soft grass as much as I do?" Greer unfastened the narrow straps around her ankles and kicked off her high-heeled shoes, curling her toes in the tall grass. She bent over Layla, holding her hands as the baby pushed up and down on her bent knees, chortling.

"Wait until next year. You're going to be running all over the grass on your own." They slowly aimed toward the picnic table. But they made it only partway before Layla plopped down on her diaper-padded, ruffle-covered butt. She grabbed at the grass undulating around her and yanked, then looked surprised when the soft blades tore free.

Greer tugged her skirt above her knees so she could sit in the grass with her. She mimicked Layla's grass grab and then held open her hands so the pieces of green blew away on the breeze.

Layla opened her palms and her grass blew away, too. Instead of laughing, though, her brows pulled together and her face scrunched.

Greer laughed. "Silly girl." She tore off another handful of grass and let it go again. "See it blow away?" She leaned over and nuzzled her nose against Layla's palms. "Smells so good." Then she rubbed her nose against Layla's and plucked a single blade of grass and tickled her cheek with the end of it. "Smells kind of like your daddy, doesn't it?"

"Mama mamamama!" Layla laughed and grabbed the grass, but missed and rolled onto her side. She immediately popped up and crawled over to Greer, clambering onto her lap.

Knowing Layla hadn't really said *mama* didn't stop Greer's heart from lurching. She wrapped her arm around Layla's warm body and kissed the top of her head.

Then they both yanked hunks of grass free and tossed them into the air.

He had a perfect view of them from his bedroom window.

Ryder dragged the towel over his head and down his chest. The water in the shower hadn't been much above tepid to begin with, but it had turned altogether cold after only a few minutes.

Probably a good thing.

Below, Layla had crawled onto Greer's lap. As he watched, Greer rolled onto her back, heedless of her silk blouse and her hair that today had been pulled back into a smooth knot behind her head. She pushed Layla up into the air above her, and even through his closed window, he could hear her peals of laughter.

He'd been cursing Mrs. Pyle's absence after she'd promised him another week of work. With no alternative, it had meant hauling a baby around with him on a tractor for half the day. Which meant he still wasn't finished haying. He was falling behind on everything.

But right now, looking down at Greer and the baby, he almost didn't care.

Almost.

As if she sensed him watching, Greer suddenly looked up at his window. It was too far for him to see her exact expression, but he had no trouble imagining her dark brown eyes.

They were mesmerizing, those eyes of hers. They kept entering his thoughts at all hours of the day.

And the night.

The air-conditioner kicked on, blowing cold air over him and drowning out the sound of Layla's high-pitched squeals.

He took a step back and blew out a long breath, not even aware that he'd been holding it.

"You're losing it, man," he muttered to himself, roughly dragging the towel over his head once more before tossing it aside. It knocked over his grandparents' picture and he automatically set it to rights while he pulled out the last clean shirt he possessed, plus a pair of jeans that weren't so clean. He quickly got dressed and went downstairs.

As soon as he walked through the kitchen, he understood why his shower water had been cold. Both the washing machine and the dishwasher were going.

It wasn't Mrs. Pyle's doing, that was for certain.

The mug tree sitting on one corner of the butcher-block island had three clean mugs still hanging from the metal branches. He took two, filled them with water and pushed open the wooden screen door.

When it slammed shut behind him, Greer froze and looked his way. Her face was as flushed as Layla's and dark strands of hair had worked loose to cling to her neck.

The ivory blouse she wore had come partially free from the waist of her light gray skirt. As if she were following the progression of his gaze, she suddenly pushed the hem of her skirt down her thighs and swept her legs to one side as she set Layla down on the grass. "It's still crazy hot," she commented, not exactly looking his way. "What happened to Mrs. Pyle?"

"Her grandson." He was as barefoot as the two females, and the earth beneath his feet felt cooler than anything else as he walked toward them. It was no wonder Greer had chosen to sit in the grass rather than at the picnic table. He extended one of the mugs to her. "It's just water."

She smiled a little as she took it from him. "Thank you." Before she could get the cup to her mouth, though, Layla launched herself at it, and Greer wasn't quite quick enough to avoid her. Half the water sloshed out of the cup and onto her blouse, rendering several inches of silky fabric nearly transparent.

Ryder was polite enough not to comment, but too male to look away. He could see the scrolling lacework of blue thread beneath the wet patch and had no trouble at all imagining the soft flesh beneath that.

Greer plucked at the fabric, though as far as he could tell, she only succeeded in pulling the rest of the blouse loose from the skirt. She took a sip of what was left of the water, then held it to Layla's mouth. "What's going on with Anthony? He was just acquitted last week."

"And he turned around and got picked up on drunk driving last night."

She jerked, giving him a sharp look that was echoed somewhat by the sharp look that Layla gave *her*. "What? Where? I haven't heard about it."

"I don't know where." He sat on the grass, leaning his back against the picnic table. "I just know she dropped everything and immediately took off to rescue him." Mrs. Pyle had given him the courtesy of a rushed phone call, but that was it.

Greer frowned, then focused once more on Layla, who'd started fussing for the mug of water. "I'm sorry, sweetheart. It's empty now. See?" She turned the mug upside down and glanced back at Ryder. "You make that sound like a bad thing."

"I don't have a lot of sympathy for people who drink and drive."

"Because of what happened to Layla's mother."

"Because of what happened to my mother." The second the words were out, he regretted them. "Here." He leaned forward and poured half his water into her mug, then sat back again. "You obviously didn't come out here because Mrs. Pyle asked you to sub for her." He repeated what he'd asked when he walked into his house and found her there. "So what *are* you doing here?"

"Someone called me about the nanny position."

"You must be pretty excited about the prospect to drive out here to tell me. I do have a phone, you know."

"Which nobody answered when I called. And then after last night... Layla's fever and all." She lifted one shoulder, watching Layla, who'd lost interest in the mug and had started crawling toward the far side of the picnic table. "I was concerned. So I drove out."

"And found the place looking like a bomb had hit."

"You want me to say it wasn't that bad?"

"I have a feeling you're not much for lies, even the polite ones."

She got on her hands and knees and crawled after Layla. "I did watch her for the better part of a day," she reminded him. "I can appreciate that she's kind of a force of nature." She looked over her shoulder at him for a moment. "Toss in last night's trip to the hospital, and a messy house doesn't seem so strange."

The afternoon was admittedly hot. But that wasn't the cause for the furnace suddenly cranking up inside him. He looked away from the shapely butt closely outlined by pale gray fabric. "What did she sound like?"

"Who? Oh, right." Greer pushed herself up to sit on the bench. "Her name's Eliane. Eliane Dupre."

"French."

She gave him a surprised look.

"I knew an Eliane once."

Surprise slid into something else. Something on the verge of pinched and suspicious. "Oh?"

"She was a model for Adelaide during her nudes phase."

"Excuse me?"

"My aunt's an artist." And Eliane had been an incredible tutor for a horny seventeen-year-old. He didn't share that part, though, much as he was coming to enjoy the game of keeping the lady lawyer a little off-balance. It was his one way of feeling like things were sort of even between them. "What else did you learn besides her name?"

Greer was still giving him a measuring look.

Or maybe she was just trying to keep her eye from twitching.

"She's currently staying in Weaver. She did ask if the live-in part was negotiable. So when you talk with her, be prepared."

"What else?"

"She's from Switzerland. Divorced, it sounds like. And looking for a steady job. I have her phone number in my purse."

He pushed to his feet. "Let's do it, then."

Greer's expression didn't change as she lifted Layla and stood. But he still had the sense that he'd surprised her. And not necessarily in a good way.

They went inside and she handed him a slip of paper from her purse. Then she carried Layla back outside.

To give him privacy? Or because she wasn't interested in the conversation in the first place?

Even wondering was stupid. Pointless.

Maybe he needed more sleep.

He snatched the phone off the hook and looked at the paper.

Greer's handwriting was slightly slanted and neat. *Spare*, as Adelaide would say. There were no curlicues. No extra tails or circles. While he dialed the number, his mind's eye imagined her hand quickly recording the information on the paper.

Daisy's handwriting had been all over the place. All loopy letters and heart-dotted *i*'s.

He pushed away the thought. He definitely needed more sleep.

The phone rang four times before it went to voice mail. He wasn't sure if he was disappointed or not. He left his name and number and hung up, then went back outside. It was hotter outside than in, but at least the air was moving.

This time Greer was sitting at the table bouncing Layla on her lap.

"No answer. I left a message."

"I'm sure she'll call you back. She sounded pretty interested to me."

The wet patch on her blouse had dried. No more intriguing glimpses of white lace with blue threads. But there was a smudge of green on her thigh. "You have grass stains."

Her eyebrows rose, then she quickly looked down at herself. She swiped her hand at the mark. "Dry cleaners will get it out. Hopefully." Her shoulders rose and fell as she took a deep breath. "I should be going."

"Back to the office, I suppose."

She glanced at the narrow watch on her wrist. "Court should be finished for the day, but yes, I probably should go back. Start reviewing everything for tomorrow's docket."

"Probably." He waited a beat, but she didn't move an inch. "Or—"

Her gaze slid toward him.

"Or I could pull out a couple steaks." He jerked his thumb toward the covered grill. "Throw 'em on the grill after I give Short-Stuff a badly needed bath."

Greer's lips parted slightly. The top one was a little fuller than the bottom, he realized.

"Or you could give her a bath," he said casually. "If you wanted."

Her lips twitched. "I do like steak. Medium rare."

"I wouldn't do well-done even if you asked."

She ran her fingers over Layla's curls. "You feed her *after* her bath?"

"Counselor, sometimes I'm feeding her ten times a day. I learned real quick there's no point in sweating about the order of things when it comes to her."

"My mother would love you," she murmured. She stood with Layla. "And I'm clearly not above a bribe, whether there's dinner payment or not." She marched past him into the house.

He scrubbed his hand down his face and followed her inside. She was fastening Layla into the high chair.

"Have any of your cow pie stuff?"

"Not today." He took the last banana from the holder and started peeling it. "Personally, I hate bananas, but she loves 'em." He tossed the browning peel in the trash, then cut the fruit into small chunks and dropped them into a shallow plastic bowl that he set in front of Layla.

She was already starting to look heavy-lidded, but she dived into the bowl with both hands. "Greedy girl." He plucked a mushy piece of banana from her cheek and fed it to her.

Greer was watching him when he turned away. "What?"

She just shook her head slightly and cleared her throat. "What else besides overripe banana? Does she still have a bottle?"

"Formula, but she wants it in her cup." He looked in the sink. "I loaded everything in the dishwasher."

He pulled it open and steam spewed out. He plucked out the cup and lid, then closed the door and started it up again. He rinsed both pieces under cold water, then filled it with premixed formula. "There's a container in the fridge with some cooked vegetables. She didn't eat 'em last night."

Greer went to the refrigerator and opened it.

He glanced over. "Top shelf. Red lid."

She pulled out the glass container and peeled off the lid. "Yum. Carrots and peas."

"Don't knock it." He gave Layla her sippy cup, then took the container from Greer, dumped the vegetables in a pan and set it on the stove.

"Wouldn't the microwave be faster?"

"Yep." He made a face as he lit the flame under the pan. "Adelaide'll lecture me for a week about the dangers."

"There are dangers?"

"Probably not as many as my aunt can name." He jabbed a spoon at the vegetables. "It's one of those lose-the-battle-win-the-war things, I think."

"You're in a war with the microwave?"

He chuckled. "More like a war with my aunt over the microwave. You might say she's a little—" He broke off when the phone rang. "Eccentric," he finished. "Watch these, would you?"

"An eccentric aunt who paints nudes and names her dog Brutus. She sounds like quite a woman. You mention her a lot." Greer's fingers brushed his as she took over the spoon. "Afraid I'm not much of a cook."

"She photographs nudes," he corrected. "Among other things. And I'm afraid I'm not much of a cook, either. But I like to eat, so—" He picked up the ringing phone. "Diamond-L."

"Is this Mr. Wilson?" The voice was female. Accented. "I'm Eliane Dupre."

"Eliane," he repeated, watching Greer turn toward the stove so that her slender back was to him.

Her shoulders were noticeably tight beneath the thin, silky blouse.

Interesting.

The conversation was brief.

Greer's back was still to him when he hung up. She was stirring the vegetables so diligently, he figured they'd end up mushier than the banana. He moved next to her and turned off the heat beneath the pan.

"I'm meeting her tomorrow over lunch at Josephine's," he said.

She gave him an overbright smile. "Great." She brushed her hands down the sides of her skirt. "You know, I just remembered I *do* have to go back to the office before tomorrow morning. So I'm going to have to pass on the bribery, after all." As she spoke, she was backing out of the kitchen, stopping only long enough to lean over and kiss Layla's head as she passed.

"You sure?" He tested the vegetables. Definitely mushy. But at least not too hot. He dumped some into Layla's now-empty banana bowl.

Greer's head bobbed. "I'm sure. Let me know how it, uh, how

it goes tomorrow." She grabbed her purse that was sitting on the couch and clutched it to her waist with both hands.

"Will do."

"Great." Her head bobbed a few more times. "Well, good... good luck." She quickly turned on her bare feet and hurried to the front door.

"By the way, what did she have?"

She'd made it to the vestibule and she gave him a startled look. "Excuse me?"

"Your sister."

She looked even more deer-in-the-headlights. "Maddie! She had a boy. Seven pounds, thirteen ounces. Twenty-one inches long. They named him Liam Gustav after Linc's grandfather. Mommy and son are doing well." She smiled quickly and yanked open the front door. "Daddy is, reportedly, a basket case." She lifted her hand in a quick wave and darted out the door, closing it behind her.

He waited.

But she didn't come back.

Even though her feet were bare, since her high-heeled pumps were still out back, lying in the grass.

He looked at Layla.

She was plucking a pea out of the carrots with one hand and clutching her pink cup with the other.

"Interesting, indeed," he told her.

She smacked her cup against the high chair tray and gave him a beatific smile. "Bye bye bye bye!"

"You got that right, Short-Stuff. She sure did go bye-bye." He chucked her lightly under the chin. "But I'm betting she'll be back."

CHAPTER EIGHT

"WHAT THE HELL did you do to your feet?"

Greer looked up to see Ali standing in the doorway to her office and yanked her feet down from where they were propped on the corner of her desk. "Nothing." She tugged her black skirt down around her knees.

"You have bandage strips all over the soles of your feet."

"I know you're in uniform, but you can stop the interrogation. Bandage strips aren't a criminal offense." Greer slid her feet into the shoes under her desk. She was still embarrassed over the way she'd raced out of Ryder's place the evening before. She didn't particularly want to explain why to her sister. "What brings you to the dark side?"

"Glad you're finally ready to admit the truth about your work." Ali grinned and threw herself down on the chair inside the doorway. She leaned back and propped her heavy department-issue boots on the corner of the desk.

"Hey!" Greer shoved at them. "Just because I did, doesn't mean you can. Have a little respect, please."

"For the dark side? Never." She put her feet on the floor, still smiling.

"You're in an awfully good mood," Greer complained. "If

you've come to brag about the latest night or morning or afternoon of hot sex you've had with your new husband, spare me."

Ali looked at her fingernails. "Well, it is pretty brag-worthy," she drawled.

"Save me."

"You don't need saving. You need sexing."

"Ali, for God's sake."

Her sister laughed silently. "Your chain is so easy to yank these days."

"And if you weren't pregnant, I'd yank yours but good. Speaking of." She pinned her sister with her fiercest lawyer look. "Have you told Grant?"

"Yes."

"And?"

"Between looking like he wanted to pass out and suddenly treating me like I'm made of Dresden Porcelain, I think he's pretty much okay with it." Her expression sobered. "He still needs to create some kind of relationship with Layla, though. He's not going to let it go, Greer. He can't."

"Nor should he even think he has to." She dropped her head onto her hands, pressing her fingertips into her scalp. She exhaled and lifted her head. "Ryder's coming along, Ali." She hoped. "Is that what you came here to find out?"

"Actually, I came here to invite you to lunch. Josephine's. On me."

"Oh, that's right. You're not living only on a public servant's salary anymore. You have a bestselling thriller writer as a husband now."

"Poke as much as you want. Do you care for a free lunch or don't you?"

"I do." She glanced at her watch. "It'll have to be quick, though. I have less than an hour before I need to be over at the courthouse."

"Yeah, yeah." Ali pushed to her feet. "I know the drill. Josephine's pretty much makes a living off the police department and the courthouse. It's always quick." She waited while Greer collected her purse and they left her office. "Seriously." Ali gave her a sidelong look. "What is going on with your feet? You're limping. You didn't actually fall through one of the floorboards in the kitchen, did you?"

"Of course not. I just, uh, just broke a glass."

Ali pushed through the entrance door first. "You never could lie for squat." She stopped short. "Hello, Mr. Towers. Out enjoying the weather?" She smiled the same sweet smile she'd used all her life when she didn't particularly like someone. "I've heard you like things hot."

Michael looked right through Ali to focus on Greer. "I learned that you didn't take the plea on Dilley."

"The client refused."

Her boss looked particularly annoyed. "I told you to plead them all."

"I cannot force a client to accept a deal! Particularly one that isn't even a good deal. Come on, Michael. We're better than that, aren't we?"

His jaw flexed. His gaze slid to Ali, then back to Greer. "We'll talk about it later," he said brusquely and pushed past them, going inside.

"How do you stand working for him?" Her sister made no effort to lower her voice.

Greer closed her hand around Ali's arm, squeezing as she pulled her farther away from the office. "Michael has a lot on his plate."

"Yeah, Stormy Santiago, from what I hear."

"It's a big case."

"Considering he's sleeping with her, yeah."

Greer dropped her hand from her sister's arm. "What?"

Ali gave her an incredulous look. "Don't tell me you haven't heard the rumors."

"Michael Towers is not sleeping with Stormy Santiago," Greer said under her breath. "He could get disbarred!"

"And maybe he should." Ali's voice was flat. Disregarding the fact that she was jaywalking, Ali set off across the street, leaving Greer to catch up.

"He's also happily married," Greer said when they reached the sidewalk on the other side.

Ali just shook her head. "And I thought Maddie was the naive one. Maybe you're just so busy with your clients that you can't notice what's going on right in your own office." She pulled open the door to Josephine's and gestured. "Age before beauty, dear sister."

Greer went inside, only to stop short at the sight of Ryder sitting in a booth across from a very attractive blonde.

Ali practically bumped into her. But she couldn't fail to notice, either. "*Who* is that?"

"Eliane Dupre," she said in a low voice, steering her sister toward an empty booth on the opposite side of the nearly full restaurant.

"And who is Eliane Dupre?" Ali asked with an exaggerated accent once they were seated. She looked over her shoulder in Ryder's direction.

Maybe the next Mrs. Ryder Wilson.

Greer kept the thought to herself. "Don't stare. They might notice you."

Ali looked back at her and spread her hands. "So?"

"Eliane is interested in the nanny position. She responded to one of the notices I placed for Ryder."

"Ah."

"Mrs. Pyle must be back. Otherwise he'd have Layla with him."

"Too bad. *I* would've loved a chance to see her."

Greer snatched one of the laminated menus out from where they were tucked against the sugar shaker and the bottles of ketchup and hot sauce. It didn't matter that she knew the contents by heart. She still made a point of reading it. Or pretending to read it.

"How's that new baby doing?" Josephine herself said, stopping at the table and without asking, setting glasses of water in front of them before flipping over both of their mugs to slosh steaming coffee into them.

"Liam's perfect," Ali said. Her gaze slid over Greer. "Went over to see them at the hospital yesterday evening. Maddie's supposed to be released today sometime."

"Give her and Linc my best when you see them. You two know what you'd like today?"

"French dip," Ali said immediately. It was pretty much what she always ordered.

"Chef's salad." It was pretty much what Greer always ordered, too. She slid the menu back where it belonged.

"Coming up." Josephine headed back toward the kitchen.

"I suppose that was a dig about me not going to the hospital last night."

"It wasn't a dig. More like a...curiosity. I was there for a few hours. Mom and Dad came by. Vivian. Squire and Gloria Clay. Fortunately, Vivian had already left before they got there. We all sort of just assumed you'd show up after court was through for the day."

Greer grimaced. "I wasn't in court yesterday afternoon. Keith Gowler stepped in for me. Did I tell you that he and Lydia Oakes are getting married?"

Ali wasn't sidetracked. "You took off work? That's the second time this month. You never do that."

"Well, I did. I'll go see Maddie and the baby tonight when they're home." From across the busy diner, she heard a laugh and looked over toward Ryder's booth. His back was to her. But that only meant she had a perfect view of the fair Eliane.

Despite Greer's ripe imagination where the nanny applicant had been concerned, she'd nevertheless pictured someone older. Someone old enough to have left her own country for another. Someone old enough to have a failed marriage under her belt.

But Eliane—with her long, shiny, corn silk–colored hair and perfectly proportioned features—looked no older than Greer.

Younger, even.

"Because of Ryder?"

She belatedly tuned back into Ali. "What?"

Ali turned sideways in the booth. A move clearly designed so that she could look at the man in question without craning her head around.

Greer's lagging brain caught up. "I took off work because of *Layla*," she corrected.

Ali unrolled her knife and fork from the paper napkin. "Sure you did."

"Ali—" She broke off when another musical laugh filtered through the general noisiness of the diner. She exhaled and rubbed her fingertips against her scalp again.

"Having headaches a lot these days?"

"No," she lied.

Ali just watched her.

Greer dropped her hands. The sight of Ryder's booth in her peripheral vision was maddening. "Change seats with me."

Ali's brows disappeared beneath her bangs. But she slid out of the booth and they traded places. Greer pushed Ali's coffee mug over to her and wrapped her fingers around her own. She swallowed. "What if I told you I might have the solution to all of our problems where Layla is concerned?"

Ali mirrored her position: arms resting on the Formica tabletop, hands cupped around her mug. Her voice was just as low as Greer's. "The only problem we have with Layla is Ryder refusing all the offers of help he's gotten from us these past months. The fact that he's still keeping us all at a distance."

"Particularly your husband."

"He *is* her uncle. So what's the solution? Did you find some legal loophole?"

"It's something legal," Greer allowed. "But not a loophole." And she was insane to even be mentioning it to Ali. Much less to think that somewhere along the line, she'd even been giving it the slightest consideration.

"Just cut the mystery, Greer. What?"

Greer exhaled. "Ryder mentioned finding a wife instead of a nanny. You know. For Layla's sake." She took a quick, nervous sip of coffee.

Ali immediately looked toward his booth. "Are you kid—" She broke off when Josephine appeared, carrying their lunch plates.

She started to set down the meals, but stopped. "You switched places. I remember when you used to do that when you were girls, trying to pass for one another."

Ali flicked her streaky hair. "Don't think we'd have much luck on that anymore," she said lightly. "Don't s'pose you have any of that chocolate cream pie left, do you? I thought I'd take a slice home to Grant."

"I'll package one up for you," Josephine promised, and headed off.

"He's buried himself in a new manuscript he started," Ali confided.

"I thought he never intended to write another T. C. Grant book."

"I don't know if it will be another CCT Rules military thriller or not." Ali picked up half of her sandwich. "For all I know, it might be a children's book. I'm just thrilled that he's feeling an urge to write again. As for Ryder—" She broke off, glancing around and lowering her voice. "You think he's going to marry the nanny?"

Greer pressed the tip of her tongue against the back of her teeth for a moment. "Or...someone else," she said huskily. "Me, for instance."

The sandwich dropped right out of Ali's hand, landing on the little cup of au jus and sending it splashing across the table toward Greer.

Greer barely noticed until Ali slapped a napkin over the spill before it dripped onto Greer's lap.

Then her sister sat back on her side of the booth and stared at her with wide eyes. "How long have you two been..." She trailed off and waved her hand.

"We haven't been." Greer mimicked the wave. She didn't mention the fact that she'd thought about it often enough.

Ali leaned closer. "Yet he *proposed* to you."

"N-not really." He'd been joking. Hadn't he? "But the subject has come up. It would just be a business arrangement," she clarified. "Not a romantic one."

Ali sat back again. She picked up a french fry and pointed it at Greer. "Are you crazy?" She shoved the fry in her mouth.

"Nobody thought the idea was more insane than me." Greer forced herself to pick up her fork and at least look like she was eating. "At first."

"When did all this come up?" Ali waved another fry.

"Last week."

Ali suddenly dropped her french fry and assumed an overly casual smile.

And the back of Greer's neck prickled.

A second later, Ryder was passing their table. He was following Eliane, his hand lightly touching her arm as they progressed through the busy diner. They made a striking couple. Both tall. Both perfect specimens of their gender.

His blue eyes moved over Greer's face and he gave a faint nod.

Heaven help me.

Then he was reaching around Eliane to open the door for her, and they were gone.

Greer's breath leaked out of her. She actually felt shaky.

"Here." Ali pushed a water glass into Greer's hand. "Drink. You look like you're going to pass out."

"I've never passed out and I'm not going to start now." Still, she sucked down half the contents. Then she picked up her fork and jabbed it into her salad, even though the thought of food was vaguely nauseating.

She was well aware of Ali's concern, which was the only reason she was able to swallow the chunk of ham and lettuce. But as soon as had, she set her fork down again. "Layla deserves a mother," she said huskily.

Ali's eyes immediately glistened. "You can't marry someone just because you love a little girl," she said softly.

"Want to bet?" Greer cleared her throat, but it still felt tight. "I also love my sisters. And if I did this, Layla *would* be part of our family. For real. For good. You know I would be able to make certain of it."

"And you? What about you?"

"What about me? I'd be getting the best part of the deal. Layla."

"You know that's not what I mean."

Greer swallowed. "You know I've never thought about the whole marriage thing. My career's been everything."

"Are you sure this isn't *about* your career?" Ali pushed aside her plate of food and leaned her arms on the table again. "Six months ago you told me you were thinking about quitting. Remember that?"

"Trust you to throw a moment of weakness in my face."

But Ali didn't bite. She just sat there, watching Greer, eyes more knowing than Greer wanted them to be.

"It's not about my career," she finally said. "At least I don't think it is. Entirely, anyway."

"Gotta say, Greer. I'm feeling a little freaked out at this indecisive version of you."

"Yeah, well, I'm a little freaked out by the settled-and-married-gonna-have-a-baby version of you. Maddie was one thing. She's had *mama* written all over her since she was playing with dolls. You used to cut off the heads of your dolls and shoot them out of your slingshot."

Ali snorted softly. "I did not."

"Just about. You were both the ultimate tomboy and the ultimate flirt. Everything you want to try your hand at, you succeed at. I'm sure you'll be the same way with motherhood."

"So says Madame Lawyer," Ali said drily. "Maybe I had to try so hard because you've always been the brilliant one. Well. Until now." She spread her palms. "You cannot marry a man you don't love, Greer. Not even for Layla."

"Even if it means solving this problem between Grant and Ryder? I'm at a crossroads here. All I have to do is turn the right way! Maddie's a mom. You're going to be a mom. Well, maybe I want to be one, too!" So what if he'd been joking? He'd been serious enough about the will. She could do a business deal just as well as *Eliane*.

"What happens if you meet someone you really *do* love?"

"I'm thirty years old. It hasn't happened yet."

"You're already talking yourself into it. I can tell."

Maybe she was.

"If you do this, what're you going to tell Mom and Dad? The truth? Or are you going to try making up some story about a sudden romance between the two of you? Because we all know what a rotten liar you are. They'll see right through it. And Mom'll be brokenhearted at the thought of you locked in a loveless marriage."

Greer exhaled. "It wouldn't be like her history with Rosalind's dad."

"She stayed married to Martin Pastore for years because of Rosalind. How's it different?"

"Well, for one thing, Ryder isn't like Martin!" Her encounters with their mother's first husband were mercifully few and far between. "He's not cold and controlling."

"Could've fooled me by the way he's acted for the last six months."

"You don't know him. He's…warm and…and loyal."

"Sounds like a lapdog."

Greer glared.

"Oh, come on. You left yourself wide open for that one."

"You're impossible."

"Admittedly, he's an awful good-looking lapdog. We've grown up around guys in boots and cowboy hats. He does the whole rancher look better than most."

"He does the entire *male* look better than most." She dropped her head into her hands again and massaged her temples. Then she raised her head again and looked at her watch. "I have to get to court."

"You didn't eat anything."

"Trust me. Judge Waters isn't going to care about that." She slid out of the booth. "I appreciate the thought, though." She headed for the door.

Ali followed her, calling out to Josephine that she'd be right back. Then she pursued Greer right out onto the sidewalk. "Promise me you'll think about this a little longer."

A gust of hot wind buffeted the striped awning over the door and she glanced up, absently noticing the clouds gathering overhead. Maybe the weatherman was finally going to get a prediction right.

"All I've been doing is thinking. Maybe it's time I stopped and just—" She broke off. Shook her head.

"Tossed a coin?"

She managed a faint smile. "Maybe."

Ali grabbed her hands and squeezed them. "Greer, I know what marriage is really supposed to be. I want that for you."

Her throat tightened. "Baby sister, I'll never forgive you if you make me cry now."

Ali made a face.

Greer kissed her cheek and pulled away, checked the street for traffic, and started across.

Ali's voice followed her. "What *did* you do to your feet?"

Greer waved her arm without answering and quickened her pace, trying harder to ignore the tiny cuts she'd gotten from the gravel outside Ryder's house.

She was breathless when she rushed past Bunny Towers sitting at the reception desk and headed straight for her office.

"Oh, Greer. You have some—"

Greer nearly skidded to a halt at the sight of Ryder leaning against her desk. His arms were crossed over his wide chest. He'd set his cowboy hat on the desk beside him.

She swiped her palms down the sides of her black skirt and briskly entered her office, moving around to the opposite side of her desk. "I have to be in court in a few minutes." She started shoving files into her briefcase, heedless of whether or not they were the right ones. "The interview with Eliane went well?"

"She's ready to start tomorrow if I say the word. Didn't even ask about the live-in part. She also agreed to sign an agreement that she'd stay at least six months."

Greer felt a pang in her chest. Who was it that said timing was everything? "I see. Did you tell her about your other idea?"

His eyes narrowed slightly. "You haven't tossed your name in the pool. Does it matter to you?"

She pulled out the will she'd drafted for him and handed it to him. "Not as long as you sign that." Not as long as he didn't decide the lovely Eliane would make a lovely mama and there was no need to plan for disasters.

He tossed the document down onto her desk. "No. I didn't tell her. Yet."

She shoved in a few more files, then hefted the strap over her shoulder. "A live-in nanny's a lot easier to manage than a wife." She edged out from behind her desk again and scooted past him to the door. "I'll cancel the job postings when I finish with court today. Thanks for coming by to tell me."

"I came to bring those, too." He nodded toward the chair sitting inside her doorway and she felt her cheeks turn hot.

Her high-heeled shoes were sitting there.

The same pale gray high-heeled shoes that she'd left in the grass at his place the night before when she'd run out on him like the devil was at her heels.

"Right," she said in a clipped tone. "Thank you. I'm sorry if that took you out of your way."

"Not out of my way. I was in town, anyway."

The clock on the wall above her head seemed to be ticking more loudly than usual. "Did Eliane, uh, remind you of your aunt's model?"

His lips twitched slightly and she wished the floor would open up and swallow her.

"Hey. Didn't expect to catch you."

She whirled to see Ali striding up the hall carrying two plastic bags containing takeout.

"Figured you might as well have your uneaten lunch for—" Ali obviously noticed Ryder then. "Dinner, instead," she finished more slowly. "I'll just stash it in the break room fridge for you. Leave you two to...talk...or whatever."

"No need." Ryder straightened away from the desk and slid his hat in place with a smooth motion. "I was just dropping off those." He pointed at the shoes. "Your sister left 'em behind last night."

Greer cringed even as she saw her sister's gaze drop to the chair.

Ryder's chin dipped a fraction as he thumbed the brim of his hat and turned sideways to go past Greer through the doorway. His arm still managed to brush against hers and she felt hotter inside than ever.

Tick.

Tick.

The clock above Greer sounded louder and louder as Ali slowly looked from the shoes back to Greer.

Her mouth felt dry, which was ridiculous. Ali was her sister. Together with Maddie, they were triplets, for God's sake. "It's not what you're thinking."

Tick.

"Sure," Ali finally said. "Circumstantial evidence, right?"

"Exactly!"

"I think I'm worrying about the wrong thing."

"You don't have to worry about anything, period."

Ali pointed. "You can tell yourself this is about Layla. And you can tell yourself this is about your job. About being at a crossroads. And I get that it's all true. But if you think you're considering marrying Ryder only because of all that, you're dreaming, big sister. So what happens if you end up actually going through with this, only to realize you're not on the business track at all, but *he* is?"

"That's not going to happen," Greer said flatly. "And it's all semantics, anyway. He's set to offer the job to Eliane."

"The job of wife?"

"Nanny!"

"Are you sure about that?"

Tick.

CHAPTER NINE

"TEMPLETON! GET YOUR rear end in here."

Greer's shoulders slumped at the command.

She dumped her overstuffed briefcase on her desk and backtracked to Michael Towers's office. *You bellowed?* "Yes?"

"Shut the door."

After her encounters with Ryder and Ali, she'd had a crappy afternoon in court. She'd been late getting to two different arraignments. One of her clients already facing a misdemeanor drug charge got popped with a second offense, meaning she'd lost all the ground she'd made on negotiating a fair plea deal. And she'd gotten into an entirely uncharacteristic argument with Steve Manetti about Anthony Pyle's DUI charge, nearly earning herself a contempt charge.

She closed the door uneasily.

"Sit."

Michael's office was twice the size of hers. Which still meant that there was only room for two chairs. She nudged the one on the right slightly and sat. "If this is about Manetti, I can expl—"

"I warned you to plead out Dilley."

Her lips parted. She swallowed what she'd been going to say about Judge Manetti.

"I tried," she said. "Mr. Dilley refused. He's insistent on having his day in court."

"You have more clients going to trial than any other attorney in my jurisdictions." He was drumming the end of his pencil against his ink blotter. "I think you'd be more effective in Hale's office."

"Hale!" She popped to her feet and the chair wobbled behind her. "He's eighty-five miles away!"

"He's getting ready to retire. You'd be the senior attorney on staff. You could take as many cases as you want to trial."

"Sure. In municipal court." It was the only one located in Lillyette, Wyoming. "Which is in session maybe three times a week. On a busy week. You're punishing me for something. What?"

"I'm not punishing you. I'm trying to promote you."

"By sending me to Lillyette." Braden was a booming metropolis in comparison to the tiny town. "What if I turn down this...kind...promotion?"

Michael stared back at her, unmoving.

Her jaw was so tight it ached. "I see." She aligned the chair neatly where it belonged. She felt blindsided. She'd never lost a job in her life. But she knew that if she didn't accept the reassignment, that was what would happen. "When do you need my decision?"

"End of the week."

She supposed it was better than at the end of this little tête-à-tête. Unable to get out a polite response, she nodded and left his office.

She returned to her own. It was a closet of a space. But whether she'd been feeling frustrated there or not, it had been hers.

Her eyes suddenly burned. Blinking hard, she emptied her briefcase of files and loaded it up for the following day. She scrolled through her email and sent a few brief replies.

Then she shut down the computer, shouldered her briefcase

once more and looked up at the clock above the door. As usual, it was a few minutes behind.

She set down her briefcase and moved the chair so she could stand on it to reach the clock. She pulled it off the wall and adjusted the time.

She started to hang it back in place but hesitated. It would just continue to tick along, losing time along the way.

She inhaled deeply and held the clock against her chest as she exhaled.

Tick. Tick.

She climbed off the chair. Moved it back against the wall.

Then she tucked the clock inside her briefcase and left.

Ryder barely heard the knock on his front door above the sound of thunder. The clouds had been building all afternoon. But it hadn't helped with the heat. And aside from the noise, there hadn't been any rain.

The knock sounded again. He closed the logbook he kept on his livestock and went to the door.

Greer stood on his front step.

Her windblown hair gleamed in the porch light. She was still wearing the closely fitted white blouse and black skirt from this afternoon. But she'd unbuttoned a couple of the buttons and rolled up the sleeves. She had bright orange flip-flops on her feet.

And a bottle of whiskey in her hand.

She held it up for his inspection. He looked from the familiar label to her face. It wasn't the finest whiskey on the planet. But in his experience, it did the job pretty well. "Does the occasion call for it?"

"You tell me. I think I quit my job today."

Without asking, she stepped inside, brushing past him.

Another low rumble of thunder rolled through the night. Greer's car, parked on the gravel, was little more than a shadow.

Layla had been asleep for the last few hours. Hopefully she

would sleep all the way through to morning, though with the thunder he wasn't going to hold his breath.

He closed the door.

Greer had sat down on one side of his leather couch and propped her feet on the coffee table. The fluorescent orange flip-flops looked more like they belonged on a teenager. But the slender ankles and long calves belonged to a grown woman.

He sat down on the other side of the couch—one full cushion between them—and took the bottle from her. He, too, propped a bare foot on the coffee table. He peeled off the seal on the bottle and pulled out the cork. "Ladies first."

Her dark eyes slid over him as she took the bottle. She lifted it to her lips and took a sip.

He expected a cough. A sputter. Something.

She merely squinted a little, obviously savoring the taste as she swallowed.

When he'd ridden rodeo, the girls had tended toward beer. Daisy had liked a strawberry daiquiri, sweet as hell and topped with hefty swirls of whipped cream. Eliane—the model, not the nanny—had given him his first taste of red wine before Adelaide caught them. Instead of firing Eliane, his aunt had sat down and poured herself a glass, too. Then made him finish the bottle.

To this day, he couldn't drink wine without thinking about that.

It occurred to him now that there was something a little dangerous about being turned on by the way Greer drank a shot of whiskey straight from the bottle.

She handed it to him.

Their fingers brushed. Him, taking. Her, not yet releasing.

"When Daisy first left, I spent a fair amount of time in Jax's company."

Her fingers slid away from his. Away from the bottle. "You must have loved her very much."

"I thought I did. Enough to give her a wedding ring." Just

not *the* ring. His grandmother's ring. The one his aunt had kept in safekeeping for him since he'd been a kid. Since she'd taken him in when there was no one else to do so.

He took a drink, squinting a little at the familiar burn and savoring the warmth as it slid down his throat. "Adelaide says I've got a hero complex. That marrying Daisy was more about trying to save her than loving her."

"What do you think?"

He thought about his mother, who'd been just as troubled as his erstwhile bride. He took another drink and handed Greer the bottle.

She cradled it, running her thumb slowly over the black label. Her nails were short. Neat. No-nonsense. "I've never loved anyone like that," she murmured. "I think it might not be in my makeup."

"Just don't tell me you're a virgin," he muttered.

If he'd thought he would set her off guard, he was mistaken. She made a dismissive sound. "Sex and love don't have to be the same thing."

"Adelaide would agree."

"I think I'd like your aunt. You talk about her, but you don't talk about anyone else in your family."

"There wasn't anyone else."

Greer studied him for a moment, then looked away. She took another sip. A longer one this time. She tilted her head back a little and her eyelids drifted closed.

He got up and opened the kitchen door. The breeze was finally cooler. He stood in the doorway for a long minute and felt the base of his spine prickle when she came up to stand beside him in her silly orange flip-flops.

"D'you think it'll actually rain?" Her voice was little more than a whisper.

"Finished haying this morning. It can rain for a week straight, as far as I'm concerned."

She pressed her fingertips against the wooden frame of the simple screen door. "Layla?"

"Asleep."

She pushed open the screen door and went outside, taking the whiskey bottle with her. Ryder hadn't turned on the back porch light. Her blouse showed white in the light coming from the kitchen, but the rest of her melted into the darkness.

He caught the door before it could snap shut and followed her out, holding the screen until it sighed silently closed.

He sat on the end of the picnic table, watching the gleam of her blouse moving around as she swished her feet through the grass. Her restlessness was as palpable as the weight of thunder overhead.

"How old are you, Ryder?" Her voice sounded farther away than she appeared.

"Thirty-four." He cupped his hands around the edge of the table. The wood felt rough. It would be full of splinters if he didn't sand it down sometime soon. While he was at it, he could slop a coat of barn-red paint over the whole thing. Cover up all the flowery stuff.

"I'm thirty."

"Are we trading statistics? Want to know my boot size?" He listened to the grass swishing and wasn't sure if it was from her feet or from the breeze. But the gleam of her blouse was getting closer and then she stopped a few feet away from him. "Thirteen."

"Did you give Eliane the word?"

"No."

She took another sip from the bottle, then stepped close enough to set it next to his hip. "Why?"

He moved it down to the bench seat. "Why do you think you quit your job today?"

She started to move again, but he reached out and caught her hands and she went still. Her palms were small. Her long fingers curled down over his. He could see the faint sheen of moisture on her lips.

"Because I don't want to drive eighty-five miles to work every day. Or move eighty-five miles away from my home. Because." She took a step closer. She exhaled a shaky-sounding sigh. "Because."

He let go of her hands and slid his palm behind her neck. Her skin was warm. Silkier even than his imagination had promised. But that was as far as he went. He didn't pull her forward. Didn't make another single move.

It was one of the hardest attempts at self-control he'd ever made.

"Were you really joking the other day?"

He didn't have to ask what she meant. He didn't have to think about the answer. "No. Are you tossing your name in the pool?"

After a moment she took another step forward and stopped against the edge of the table, between his thighs. When she drew breath, he could feel the press of her breasts against his chest.

"If we do this—" his voice felt like it was coming from somewhere way down inside "—I know what I get out of it. What do you get out of it?"

"Are we talking about marriage?" Her fingertips drifted over his knees, slowly grazing their way higher up his thighs, leaving heat in their wake even through his denim jeans. "Or this?"

He pressed his hands over hers, flattening them. Stilling their progress. "Counselor, I know what you'll get out of *this*."

She leaned closer, bringing with her the seductive scents of warmth and whiskey and woman. The breeze blew over them, and her hair danced against his neck. Her lips brushed against his jaw, slid delicately across his chin. Then she found his mouth for a moment that was strangely endless but much too brief. Her fingers pressed into his thighs. "I get the assurance that Layla will be part of our lives. Permanently. If you want to marry to give her a mother, then I want to *be* her mother. Legally."

He caught her behind the neck again, pulling back so he

could see her face. But it was too dark. The sky too black with clouds. Her cheekbones were a faint highlight. Her lips a dark invitation. And her thickly lashed, deep brown eyes...they were the most mysterious abyss of all. "You want to adopt Layla."

"Is that so strange?"

He wasn't sure what it was, except that it made something inside his chest feel strange. "I'll consider it. What else?"

"Our wills. Anything happens to us both, then Layla goes to Grant and Ali. Those are my terms."

"What about starting your own legal firm?"

"Maybe someday when I've won the lottery and can afford it, I'll have one."

He moved his hand along her neck and over her shoulder. The gleam of white fabric looked crisp but did a poor job of hiding the heat radiating from her. "I could stake you."

"It's not just money. An office. Equipment. All that sort of thing. It's time. Time I won't have much of, if I'm out here taking care of Layla."

"You're a lawyer. Your greatest equipment is your brain. And you can turn that fancy-ass Victorian house you're supposedly renovating into an office."

Her hands slid out from beneath his as she stepped back from him. Cool air seemed to flow between them. "You're full of ideas all of a sudden."

"I've given it a thought or two."

"Why does it matter to you? I've already said that Layla is what's important."

"Because I'm never going to be the cause of a woman giving up her dream." He reached for the bottle of whiskey and cradled it in his hand.

She was silent for a moment while the thunder rumbled. "Is this about Daisy?"

"The only dream that Daisy claimed to have was being married to me." He scratched at the edge of the bottle label with his fingernail. "Whatever her real dreams were, she obviously never shared them with me." He figured it was progress that he could make the observation without feeling much of anything.

"What's your dream?"

He spread his arms. "This place."

"The Diamond-L."

"Named for my mother. The original Layla. You want me to talk about her?" He felt the label tear. "She was born here. In Wyoming."

He felt her surprise.

"Her dad—my grandfather—was a minister. Moving his family from one small town to another every few years. They died before I was born. But my mom dreamed of adventure. Of seeing more of the world than a string of tiny towns needing a preacher. Finding the end of the rainbow. And she gave it all up because she got pregnant with a baby she wasn't at all equipped to handle." He took a last burning sip of whiskey before tossing the bottle away into the dark, even though it meant a waste of perfectly good liquor. "She was an alcoholic. One night, she got behind the wheel of a car, drunk, and killed herself as well as two other people."

"Oh, Ryder." Greer's sigh was louder than her words. "How old were you?"

"Eight."

"Your father?"

"She never said who he was."

"And your aunt?"

"Adelaide didn't know who he was, either. She was the only one left to take me in. She's not my real aunt. She was my grandmother's best friend. She was there when my mother lost her mother. And she was there when I lost mine. Adelaide gave me a home." He felt a raindrop on his hand. "I asked her why once. She said it was the right thing to do."

Greer stepped close again and slid her arms around his shoulders. "The Victorian would make a good office," she whispered.

"I'll consider it. Put your arms around me."

He didn't need to be told, though it was a novel enough occurrence that it appealed to him. Her waist was so slender, his fingers could span it. But as he slowly ran his hands down over the flare of her hips, he discarded the notion that he'd ever considered her too skinny for his tastes.

"If we do this, it doesn't change anything." She arched slightly when his hands drifted down over her rear. "Layla will have two parents. We'll raise her together. But the deal between us stays—"

"—business." He'd discovered the zipper on the back of her skirt and slowly drew it down. The skirt came loose and slid down her thighs. All she wore beneath was a scrap of lace.

"That's right." She angled her head and brushed her lips against his ear. "Business," she breathed.

He slid his fingers along her slender neck. Felt the pulse throbbing at the base. The way she swallowed when his fingers curled beneath her chin. He nudged at it slightly, lifting it. "You saying this is a one-and-done, Counselor?"

"I'm saying let's not call this marriage something it's not. It'll be a marriage of convenience. Pure and simple."

He lowered his head and slowly rubbed his lips across hers. Felt the softening. The parting. The invitation.

He lifted his head again. Eased his fingers behind the nape of her neck once more. "I'm not thinking too many pure thoughts at the moment."

Her breasts rose and fell, pressing against him. Retreating. "Neither am I. As long as we don't confuse this with something it's not, I don't see the problem. Just because marrying would be convenient doesn't mean it has to be sterile. It'd be a different matter if we weren't attracted to each other. But we are." Her lips were close to his, her whisper soft yet clear. "So we might as well be realistic from the start."

"Realistic. Works for me."

She took a deep breath again. Her breasts pressed against his chest and stayed there. "And…and if…*when* it stops working, when Layla's older, we'll end the deal. No fuss. No muss." She waited a beat. "As long as I'm just as much her legal parent as you. My family—*all* of my family—becomes her family. That means Grant, too."

He felt another plop of warm rain. This time on his arm. "If I agree to you adopting her, you have to agree about your own practice."

"Negotiation?"

"You told me you were good at it."

"Okay. Agreed."

The second she said the words, he closed his hands around her hips again, pulling her in tighter. She was warm. Soft. "It's going to rain."

"As far as I'm concerned, it can rain for a week." He felt her words against his lips.

He smiled slightly and pushed her away. Only a few inches. "Take off your shirt, Counselor."

She made a soft sound. He sensed more than saw her dark eyes on him. "I'd rather you take it off me."

There were invitations to ignore.

There were ones he couldn't.

His fingers brushed against her skin as he found the tiny buttons on her shirt. Impatience raged inside him, but he took his time. One button. Two. All the way down, until it took only a nudge of his fingers and the shirt fell away, too. The bra and panties she wore were as white as the shirt had been. But lacy. Stretchy. No protection at all when he tugged them off.

And then she took a full step backward, giving him enough room to push off the table and pull his shirt over his head. He unfastened his belt and jeans and shoved them down his legs.

Then she crowded close again, slipping her hand under his boxer briefs. She inhaled audibly when she closed her fingers around him. "Perfect," she breathed.

He looked up at the sky, dragging in an audible breath of his own. Another raindrop hit him square on the face. His shoulder. His back. "I should take you inside."

"I'm not sugar." She dragged his briefs down, bending her knees, going down with them, setting them aside when he stepped out of them. But she didn't stand back up. "I'm not the Wicked Witch. I won't melt from some water." Her hair brushed his knee. His thigh. And her lips...

"Maybe not," he said. Her mouth closed over him and he exhaled roughly. He slid his fingers through her hair. He couldn't help himself. She had a lot of hair. The strands were silky. Slippery. He wanted to wrap his fingers in it and hold her. His hands were actually shaking from resisting the urge. "But what you're doing feels damn—" another oath slid through his teeth "—wicked."

The air suddenly felt electric and thunder cracked. She made a sound. Sexy. Greedy. And took him even deeper.

He let her go. Let her do as she pleased. And oh, how it pleased. For as long as he could hold out. Then a flash of soft light flickered in the distance, giving shape to the canopy of clouds. Giving shape to the woman kneeling before him.

"Enough." It was a rough order. A rough plea. He pulled away. Pulled her up. Maybe it wasn't going to be one-and-done. Maybe they'd manage a year. Two. Before convenience didn't matter to her so much and she'd want more out of life than a business deal of a marriage.

But he wanted more this time—this first time—than just *this*.

Another fat raindrop splashed on his shoulder as he drew her up to him and found her mouth with his. Found her breasts with his hands. And she was right there with him. Pressing herself against him, her nipples tight points against his palms. Her tongue mingling with his, her hands dragging up and down his spine before closing over his head.

He could feel her heart pounding as hard as his own as he lifted her against him. Her legs slid along his thighs and wrapped around his hips. And then she cried out when he slid inside her, and he froze. Because she was so tight. So small in comparison to him, and he was suddenly afraid of hurting her.

Thunder cracked overhead and the clouds finally opened up, drenching them in seconds.

Holding her ought to have been impossible. Water rained down on them, making her flesh slick. But she simply twined herself around him, holding him tightly gloved within. "Don't stop now." She sounded exultant as she dragged his mouth back to hers.

And then everything that was perfect overrode his fear.

Wet inside.

Wet outside.

And she wanted him as much as he wanted her. He backed up until he felt the table. There'd be time for bed later. Time for every other thing he could possibly imagine. He ignored the rough, splintering wood as he leaned against it and took her slight weight in his hands and thrust.

"Yes." She arched in perfect counterpoint.

Again. And again. And again. He wanted to go on and on and on, but he knew he wouldn't last. Not with the way he could feel her quickening. Tightening. Shuddering.

Lightning flashed.

Her head dropped back but she clung to him. "Yes!"

The rain fell and the world shrank down to this one woman in his arms.

And he let himself go.

"Yessssss."

CHAPTER TEN

"YES. I DO."

Judge Stokes smiled at Ryder and turned to Greer to repeat the vow. "And will you, Greer Templeton, take this man, Ryder Wilson, to be your lawfully wedded husband? To have and to hold, in sickness and in health, for richer or for poorer? Forsaking all others and keeping only to him?"

It was vaguely surreal, standing there in Judge Stokes's chambers.

But there was nothing surreal about Greer's answer. Since she'd made the decision to marry Ryder, she hadn't suffered any second thoughts. "Yes," she said just as clearly as he had. "I do."

The judge smiled benevolently at them. With his white hair and beard, and his tendency toward wearing red shirts, he looked a bit like Santa Claus. Even though it was only the end of August. "Then—" he closed his small black book "—by the authority vested in me by the State of Wyoming, and with a great deal of personal delight I might add, I declare you to be husband and wife." He spread his hands. "Congratulations. You may kiss your bride."

Ryder, looking uncommonly urbane in a dark gray suit with

a lighter gray striped tie knotted around his neck, turned to her. He took her hands and his thumb brushed over the narrow platinum band he'd given her. His thick hair was brushed back from his face. There was no hatband mark in evidence. His jaw was clean-shaven and his blue eyes were brilliant. When he leaned down, instead of his usual scent of hay or grass or fresh open air, he smelled faintly woodsy. Exotic.

He was entirely *un*-rancherly.

And for the first time in thirty-six hours—since the night she'd gone to his house and she'd thrown herself, mind and body, into his marriage plan—she felt a wrinkle of unease.

How well did she really know this man to whom she'd just promised herself? This rancher who had a beautiful gray suit that looked as if it had been custom tailored just sitting around in his closet?

Was it a leftover from his Vegas wedding to Daisy?

It was just a suit, she reminded herself. She'd pulled her dress from her closet, too.

Then his eyes met hers, and it felt as though he knew exactly how she was feeling.

"We can do this," he murmured. Low. For her ears only.

She gave a tiny nod.

The faint lines beside his eyes crinkled slightly and his dimple appeared. Then his lips brushed slowly, lightly across hers.

It was barely a kiss. Yet it was still enough to make her feel warm way down inside.

But there was no time to dwell on it, because the judge's wife and his usual clerk, Sue, who were acting as their witnesses, had started clapping. Layla, dressed in a ruffled yellow jumper, jabbered and clapped her hands, too. Sue had insisted on holding her during the ceremony.

"Just lovely," Mrs. Stokes said. "So romantic."

Greer bit back a spurt of amusement that she knew Ryder felt, as well, and relaxed even more.

They were of one mind when it came to that particular element of marriage. They could rock each other's socks off in the bedroom while Layla slept. Or on a picnic table in the rain. Or in his shower that ought to have been too cramped, but wasn't. All of which they'd done in the span of a mere day.

But this legal union of theirs wasn't about romance. It was because of Layla, and for no other reason.

"If I could get your signatures here?" Sue pointed to the marriage license they'd obtained just that morning from the county clerk's office. She evaded Layla's grab for the pen and handed it to Ryder.

He signed the document and handed the pen to Greer before lifting Layla out of Sue's arms. "Thanks."

"My pleasure. It's just so exciting to see a happy ending for all of you."

Greer finished signing her name next to Ryder's and she capped the pen before handing it back. "Thanks, Sue."

"I still can't believe you did this without your family, though. They're going to be so surprised."

"We didn't want anything or anyone—not even family—delaying it," Greer explained smoothly.

"That's how it is, isn't it?" Sue's eyes sparkled. "When you know you absolutely can't spend one more minute without committing to the person you love?"

"It was like that for us, wasn't it, Horvald?" Mrs. Stokes commented as she signed the witness line.

It was easier to let them think that than to tell them the truth. That Greer hadn't wanted to give her family a chance to talk her out of it. Which they would surely have done, no matter how much they, too, loved Layla.

Ryder had disagreed with her. Said they should wait, at least long enough to tell her family. It wasn't about seeking approval or blessings. It was about respecting them enough to give them the truth.

Greer had prevailed, though. They'd made the decision. If

they'd waited, they'd have had to wait through Labor Day holiday weekend to be married. Meaning she'd also have to wait four more days to file the petition to adopt Layla.

Sue took up the pen and signed after Mrs. Stokes. Then the court clerk set the document on the judge's desk. "Congratulations again." Sue linked her arm through Mrs. Stokes's and the two of them left the judge's chambers.

"All right." The judge signed the license with a flourish after they'd gone. "I guess I can trust you to turn that in to the recorder's office." He slid the paperwork into its envelope and handed it to Greer. "And now for your next item of business."

He moved another document to the center of his desk. "I've reviewed your petition for Layla's adoption and everything is in order." As he spoke, he signed his name and then he flipped open an enormous date book in which, Greer knew, he kept all of his case schedules. It didn't matter that Sue managed his official calendar by more efficient—namely computerized—methods. Horvald Stokes still liked his old-fashioned calendar. And it was legend how he'd never once made a scheduling mistake.

He flipped through it, studying and muttering to himself under his breath. Then he went back a few pages. Then forward again. And finally he stopped. "Hearing will be November 19." He made the notation in his book and then on the petition. "That's before Thanksgiving."

For the first time that day, Greer's smile felt shaky. Becoming Layla's mother was the crux of the matter, the reason they were there at all. When they were done, Layla would have a father and a mother. The hearing in November would be little more than a formality before Judge Stokes could sign the final decree. "Sounds perfect to me, Your Honor."

"It really is my genuine pleasure." He stood and pulled one of the black robes off the coat stand behind his desk and slipped his arms into the voluminous sleeves. "Layla had a rocky start through no fault of her own. I'm more than pleased that things have resolved themselves in this manner."

A manner that Greer never would have imagined six months ago.

Her throat felt tight. "Thank you again for fitting us into your schedule today."

He winked. "Fifteen minutes for a good cause."

Sue returned then and gathered up both the thick, stapled document that he'd signed and his oversize date book. "Both parties for your next case are present, Judge Stokes, whenever you're ready."

He nodded and she went through the doorway that Greer knew led directly from his chambers into his courtroom. The fact that he zipped up his robe before he headed toward the door meant he was prepared to get straight to business. "Will we be seeing you at the county picnic this weekend?"

Greer moistened her lips and adjusted the band of black velvet fabric around her waist. By itself, her knee-length ivory cotton sundress had seemed a little too casual to wear to her own wedding. Marriage of convenience or not. After seeing Ryder's suit, she was glad she'd made her outfit a bit more formal by adding the wide black belt. The black touches were repeated in the jet clip she'd pinned into her chignon and her black suede pumps.

"I'm afraid not. I've left the public defender's office." She'd turned in her notice to Michael the day before. He'd been livid and told her she needn't serve out the two weeks. Considering the choice he'd given her, she felt like she was the one who had a right to be livid. "I'm cleaning out my desk when we're finished here, actually."

The judge was clearly surprised. "You're not leaving the practice of law, I hope. You're an incredibly valuable part of the legal community, Greer."

The praise was as unexpected as it was touching and she didn't know quite what to say.

"She's opening her own firm," Ryder said.

Greer understood why it was so important to Ryder, even though, in her own mind, it was a much hazier proposition.

The judge's expression cleared. "Good for you! I look forward to you really spreading your wings." His smile broadened. "And one day, Mrs. Wilson," he said, winking, "I'll expect to see you on the bench." He pulled open the door and went into his courtroom.

Which left Greer alone with Ryder.

Her husband.

They'd married so quickly she hadn't even thought whether she was going to take his name. Mrs. Wilson...

Layla was yanking on his tie, jabbering away in her sweet little-girl babble, and Greer pushed away the thought.

"That went smoothly," she said. "Don't you think?"

"It was smooth enough." He tugged at his tie, but Layla looked ready to do battle over it. "I should have said before— you look real pretty."

She dashed her hand quickly down the skirt of her dress, suddenly feeling self-conscious. "I guess the dress did the job. It's ancient. Back from law school days. You...you look very nice, too." She snatched up the small black clutch she'd brought with her, along with the entirely unexpected nosegay of fresh lavender stalks wrapped in gray ribbon that he'd given her. "I guess you must subscribe to the theory that every man should have a decent suit in his closet."

His dimple appeared. "I was afraid it would be a little tight. Last time I put it on was at least five years ago." He looked at Layla, chuckling. "Gonna need a new tie now, though."

So. *Not* the suit from his Vegas wedding.

She lifted the bouquet and inhaled the soothing fragrance. "Looks like it fits you just fine," she managed, and led the way out of the judge's office.

As she clutched the lavender, she noticed how foreign the shining ring felt on her wedding finger. It was a little too loose.

She honestly wasn't sure what had surprised her more.

The flowers or the ring.

He'd chosen both. She couldn't imagine when he'd had the time.

She reminded herself that the ring would simply take some getting used to. As would chasing after Layla instead of chasing clients right here among these courtrooms every day.

Simple enough.

They'd reached the wide central staircase. Her high heels clicked on the marble as she started down. It was only ten in the morning. But it was a Friday, which meant that most of the courtrooms weren't in use and the building was pretty empty.

The recorder's office on the first floor was open every weekday, though, and they stopped there to turn in their signed wedding license.

"Don't forget this." The girl working behind the counter was new. She didn't know Greer. She was holding out the certificate portion of the wedding license. Though it was nothing more than a souvenir, the reality suddenly sank in.

Greer's head swam. She took the certificate, feeling embarrassed by the way her fingers visibly trembled. "Thank you." She went to tuck the folded paper in her clutch, but the thick parchment slid out of her grasp. She knelt down to grab it.

When she rose, she swayed.

Ryder's hand closed over her elbow, steadying her. "When's the last time you ate?"

"Yesterday evening." She'd spent the night before at home, wrapping up the details of her resignation. Contacting her former clients and letting them know that she wasn't abandoning them, even though it felt like it. That someone else from her office would be taking good care of them.

She'd fallen asleep in the middle of making case file notes for the attorney who would come after her.

When she'd woken up, she had a crease in her cheek from

the folders and a stiff neck from sleeping with her head on her desk. She still felt a little stiff now.

"Let's get you fed, then," he said, caressing her neck, his fingertips somehow magically discerning the tight spots.

"After I clean out my office."

His hand closed around her shoulders. "Your office can wait." Holding her in one arm and Layla in the other, he headed toward the courthouse exit.

"But—"

He didn't slow his long, measured strides. "What's left that matters, Greer? You told me about the clock."

"I don't know," she admitted. "I have stuff there still."

"Paper clips?" They'd reached the courthouse doors and he let go of her to hold one open. "Face it, Counselor. If anything else had truly mattered, you'd have taken it the same time you took the clock."

She hated to admit he was right. "I need to at least drop off the box of files I still have."

"Fine." When they stepped outside, they were greeted by clear blue skies. The heat had broken a little. "*After* you've eaten."

"Is this what being married to you is going to be like? You telling me what's what?" She stopped on the courthouse steps, tucking her clutch beneath her arm and pointing her lavender bouquet at him. Layla was playing with his ear and yanking on his tie as though it was a rein.

"It is when I know I'm right." He tried to smooth his tie; the attempt seemed futile. He took Greer's hand in his and they began to descend the courthouse steps.

That's when she saw them.

Her parents. Vivian. Her brother and sisters. Their husbands. All of them were there. Even Rosalind, who hadn't visited Braden in years.

Greer yanked her hand from Ryder's. "What did you do?"

"You want Layla to be part of your family. So." He took her

hand again, firmly, and nodded toward the not-so-small crowd assembled at the bottom of the stairs. "I called them. Last time I got married it was supposedly for the right reasons. We eloped. Never told a soul until after the fact. And you know how that turned out. So I'm doing things differently this time. I'm not going to pretend we're living in a vacuum. We can't shut out the people who care about us the most." He looked into her eyes, his expression intense. "They're gonna say we didn't marry for the right reasons but I don't care. Our reasons are our own. As long as you and I are on the same page, we're good." He squeezed her hand. "We are good," he repeated. "*Showing* them is the only way they'll get on board."

She moistened her lips. "I'm not so sure I like it when you're right."

He smiled faintly. "You'll get used to it in time."

A fine idea in theory. So why did it make her feel increasingly disconcerted?

Adjustments, Greer.

She tugged his tie away from Layla and smoothed it down the front of his hard chest. Her fingers wanted to linger. Her common sense insisted otherwise. "I guess now I don't have to keep running scenarios in my mind about how to tell my parents."

His dimple appeared. "There you go."

"Have you told Adelaide?"

He smiled slightly. "Who do you think reminded me that a bride should have flowers on her wedding day?"

And just like that, her chest felt tight all over again. "You called my family, but will she come, too?"

He shook his head. "She doesn't travel anymore, remember?"

"Has she met Layla?"

"I had sort of figured I'd visit for Christmas. A few days. Can't spare a lot of time away from the ranch." He was silent for a moment. "We could go. You know. As a family."

"That sounds nice." She lifted her small bouquet and inhaled the lovely, calming scent, though it wasn't quite enough to soothe away the disconcerting butterflies flitting around inside her. "Did she tell you to choose fresh lavender, too?"

"Didn't need to. They were the only flowers that seemed fitting for a woman who lives in a house like yours."

"Lived," she corrected, and looked down at her family. "Well. We can't stand here forever, I suppose. At least they're smiling."

"Yep." He muttered an oath when Layla yanked his tie again. "You're gonna strangle me with it, aren't you, Short-Stuff?"

"I'll take her." Greer handed him her clutch and bouquet, lifted Layla out of his arms and propped her on her hip. Then she took back her bouquet.

He gave her clutch a wry look, then slid it into his pocket. "Ready?"

She nodded.

And they continued down the stairs.

They'd barely made it to the bottom before a collective command came for them to stop where they were. Out came a half dozen cell phones to take their pictures. But then, clearly too excited to wait a second longer, Meredith darted up to greet them, throwing her arms around Greer and Layla, engulfing them in her familiar, uniquely Meredith fragrance.

"Oh, my darlings," she cried, and somehow Greer managed to lose Layla to Meredith in the embrace. But then her mom always had been sly that way. She kissed the baby's face. "You've grown so much! And you!" Meredith dragged Ryder's head down and gave him a smacking kiss on the cheek before he had a hope in heaven of avoiding it. He gave Greer a vaguely startled look. "I knew you were a special man," Meredith was saying, "and when you called us last night, I—"

"Last night!" Greer gave him a look.

"You were home doing your thing. I was doing mine."

Meredith laced her free arm through Ryder's and pulled him the rest of the way down the steps. Since his hand was locked onto Greer's, that meant she went, too, and they didn't stop until they came up against her father's stalwart body. Carter's service in the military might have ended decades earlier, before Greer, Ali and Maddie were even an idea, but he still carried himself as though he wore a uniform and a chest full of medals.

He and Ryder were about the same height. But Ryder's brawny build, hidden so spectacularly beneath his tailored suit, made him seem even larger than her dad.

The men were eyeing each other. Taking measure.

Predictably, her dad went on the offensive. "Guess you didn't figure you needed to call and get permission to marry my daughter before you just did it."

"Dad! I don't need—" Greer broke off when he lifted his hand. She looked to her mother. "Mom."

Meredith just gave her an amused look. She was as unconventional as her husband was conventional, and yet together, they were the perfect couple.

"If I'd done that, and Greer had found out, I'm pretty sure she wouldn't be standing here this morning with my ring on her finger," Ryder replied easily.

"Darn right," Greer started, only to break off again when her dad gave her the same silencing look he'd given all of them growing up.

"The fact that you didn't call for permission makes me feel you know my girl pretty well. The fact that you let us know so we could be here this morning makes me think you've got a few good brain cells."

"Dad!"

"But the fact that my girl chose you, well, that says a lot, too." He looked over at Greer's sisters. "I didn't raise any of my daughters to choose badly. So." He stuck out his hand. "Welcome to the family, son."

It was ridiculous, but Greer's eyes stung a little as her father shook Ryder's hand.

After that, it was pretty much a free-for-all. She wasn't sure if they would have made it from the courthouse steps to Josephine's diner if Ryder hadn't taken charge and made it happen.

There was a general jostling for seats and the usual chaos of menus and ordering for such a large party, but the diner was half-empty and nobody else there seemed to mind.

Greer now had stiff competition for Layla's attention. Between Ali and Maddie and her mother fawning, Layla was wholly and delightedly occupied. Linc, with tiny Liam sleeping against his shoulder, was holding his own in a debate about politics with Vivian and Hayley's husband, Seth, who had tiny Keely sleeping against his shoulder. Hayley was trying in vain to change the subject before Carter blew a gasket and jumped into the lively exchange. At the other end of the tables, Rosalind and Archer were giving each other the same fulminating glares they'd always exchanged growing up. Which left Grant. Sitting on the other side of Ryder.

Greer considered offering to switch seats with Ryder, but decided not to. Instead, she just stood up from her own chair and crouched a little, wedging herself in the narrow space between them. A human buffer between her new husband and his former brother-in-law.

The looks she earned from both of them were nearly identical.

She wanted to point that out but knew better. Among her relatives, there was already the likely explosion over politics before too long. She didn't want to chance adding more combustible material because of Ryder's and Grant's mutual grudges.

The fact that Grant had accompanied Ali was promising as far as Greer was concerned, and she gave him a bright smile. "Ali tells me you're working on something new. I think that's great. How's it coming?"

"Fair."

She looked from him to Ryder. Grant's hair was blacker than Ryder's, his blue eyes lighter. Grant had a swimmer's build. Ryder, a linebacker's. Grant was an author who'd already made a fortune several times over with his military thrillers. Ryder was a rancher, whose resources were considerably more modest. They couldn't be more different.

Their only common ground was Layla and the mother who'd abandoned her.

"Ryder was in the army," she said brightly. She rested her hand on his shoulder. "How long were you in?"

He knew what she was trying to do. She could tell. "Four years. Right outta high school."

"And you, Grant?" She glanced at Ryder again. "He served in the air force. That's how he started writing the CCT Rules series. From his experiences there." She looked from Ryder's face to Grant's. "You put in a fair amount of time, didn't—"

"Yoohoo!" The loud greeting came from across the diner and Greer automatically glanced over. Ryder, on the other hand, shoved back his seat with an exclamation and strode toward the tall, gangly woman who'd entered the restaurant.

She had hair dyed black, and turquoise dripping from her ears and her neck and surrounding nearly every finger. A designer dog carrier hung from one skinny shoulder and Greer could hear the yapping of a dog.

There was no question in Greer's mind who the woman was when Ryder swung her right off her feet in a boisterous hug.

No matter what he'd said, Adelaide had still come.

Across the table, Vivian suddenly stood. She was staring at the woman, too. "Oh, my word! That's Adelaide Arians."

"Who the hell's Adelaide Arians?" Grant asked.

"She raised Ryder." Greer had to push the words through the ache in her throat. Across the restaurant, Ryder had set Adelaide back on her feet and she'd handed him something. As Greer watched, he shook his head as if refusing, but then he looked her way and seemed to still.

"She's only considered one of the seminal artists of our age," Vivian was saying as if it were a fact any person should know. "Her work hangs in the Museum of Modern Art! Wyoming and *culture* are simply two different universes," she huffed.

"Sometimes I wonder why I bothered coming here." She tugged at the sleeves of her Chanel suit, and the diamonds on her fingers winked.

"Spoken like the snob you are," Carter observed acidly.

"Dad," Hayley started to caution. She was always trying to be the peacemaker between their father and his mother.

"The apple doesn't fall far from the tree, son." Vivian spoke right over her. "You just save your judgment for *me*."

"You are *impossible*!" At the other end of the table, Rosalind had risen from her seat and was glaring at Archer. In turn, he wore the goading expression he always had around her. "Just crawl back under your rock!" Rosalind was practically shrieking.

Liam and Keely were no longer sleeping like little angels against their daddies' shoulders. They both were crying. Which had their mamas jostling to get out of their chairs to resolve the situation.

Layla was banging her sippy cup against the table and joyfully knocking down the towers of plastic creamer containers that Meredith built for her.

And there was Ryder, drawing his aunt up to their table, which had suddenly lost its collective mind. Whatever his aunt had given him was no longer in evidence.

"And this must be her." Adelaide had an unexpectedly booming voice that carried over the bedlam. She gave Greer an appraising look, but there was a glint of humor in her heavily made-up eyes and a smile on her deeply red lips that helped calm the sudden butterflies inside Greer's stomach. "I've got to say, Ryder my boy, your taste has sure improved since that last one."

Grant shoved his chair back and stood. He tossed down his napkin and walked out of the restaurant.

"Oh, dear." Adelaide's voice could have filled an auditorium without need for a microphone. She set the dog carrier on the chair he'd abandoned. "Did I say something wrong?"

Ryder looked at Greer.

She exhaled. "So. Not everything can go as smoothly as it did with the judge."

He frowned. But the lines beside his eyes crinkled slightly and his dimple came out of hiding.

Greer held out her hand toward his aunt. "I'm very pleased to meet you, Ms. Arians. I'm Greer."

"Call me Adelaide," she boomed, and jerked Greer into a nearly bone-crushing hug. "Oh, yes, indeed, the next few months are going to be *great fun!*"

She let go of Greer so suddenly, she had to catch her balance. "You're going to stay for a while, then?"

"Right through Christmas, sugar pie." Adelaide adjusted the eye-popping tie-dyed scarf she wore around her wrinkled neck. "Now where's the little peanut at the center of all these goings-on? Oh, there you are." She strode around the table. "Cute little thing!"

Layla's eyes went round as saucers as she stared warily up at the tall, loud Adelaide. She banged her cup a few times, but without her usual emphatic enthusiasm. Then she opened her mouth and wailed.

Adelaide whipped one of her chunky rings off a finger and waved it in front of Layla. The distraction worked enough to have Layla grabbing the bauble, but not enough to silence her plaintive howling. Adelaide laughed delightedly. "Little thing already knows what she likes and doesn't like!"

"She's gonna put that ring in her mouth," Ryder warned.

"And why not? You used to do that when you were a little mite, too. Stone's the size of a golf ball. She's not gonna choke on it!" She stood there, hands on her skinny hips, and grinned down at Layla.

Greer's arm brushed Ryder's. She was curious about what Adelaide had given him, but figured if he wanted to mention it, he would. Meanwhile, the cacophony around them was only increasing, made worse by the dog's shrill yipping from inside the carrier. She had to raise her voice. "Still think the one-big-family thing is going to be all it's cracked up to be?"

He dropped his arm around her shoulder. "Time'll tell, Counselor. Time'll tell."

CHAPTER ELEVEN

"...Happy birthday, dear Layla, happy birthday to you!"

While their party guests finished singing, Greer set the cake she'd gotten from Tabby Clay in front of Layla. It was shaped like an enormous white cupcake with huge swirls of pink frosting on top, and had a single oversize white candle.

"No, no, no," Layla chanted as she looked at the confection facing her. It had become her favorite word of late. Along with "Dadda" and "bye-bye" and "sus-suh," which Greer had figured out was her version of "Short-Stuff." She even had a name for Brutus and Adelaide.

But there had been no more instances of "mama," inadvertent or otherwise.

"Yes, yes, yes," Greer told her, and shooed Brutus away so she could scoot Layla's chair with its booster seat closer to the table. "It's the prettiest cake for the prettiest girl."

"You guys need to sit next to her," Maddie ordered, gesturing at Ryder. "I want a picture of the three of you together." She had Liam strapped to her chest in a fabric carrier and a camera in her hand.

It was October 27.

And though they'd planned to have Layla's first birthday party outdoors, an early snow had put paid to the notion. Which was why the family was instead crowding around the dinner table inside.

"So we don't really know for sure this is her birthday?" Even after two months with them, Adelaide's voice could still reach the back row of an auditorium.

Greer, sitting down on one side of Layla, looked over at Ryder, who'd pulled out the chair on the other side.

He returned her wry look. "No, we don't know for sure," he told his aunt, not for the first time, "but since we could never find out exactly where or when she was born, it's as close as we can determine. So this is what we've chosen."

"You know it was your grandmother's birthday, too!" Adelaide now had her camera out. But since she was just as likely to take a photo of a dust mote that caught her interest as she was to capture Layla's expression when she smashed her hands into the cake, Greer was glad Maddie was there with the fancy digital camera that Linc had gotten after Liam's birth.

Ryder caught Greer's eye above Layla and winked. He hadn't shaved in the last few days, and Greer hadn't quite decided whether she liked the stubbled look or not. "I know it was, Adelaide," he said patiently.

"Don't you think it'll be confusing if you ever find out where and when she really *was* born?"

"It won't really matter," Meredith answered before they could. She slipped closer to the table, snapping off pictures with her cell phone while skillfully managing not to trip over Brutus. "Layla's going to have a brand-new birth certificate once the adoption's final."

Ryder's hand went to the back of Layla's chair, and his fingers came close to touching Greer's.

But didn't.

"You going to let my niece demolish that cake, or what?" That came from Grant, who was leaning against the couch with Ali beside him.

It might have been two months since he'd walked out on

Greer and Ryder's wedding breakfast, but there had been little sign of softening between Ryder and him. The two men were grudgingly polite whenever there was a family event, like today, but that was as far as it went.

Frankly, it made Greer want to smack their two stubborn heads together. But generally, she didn't have time to worry about it too much. Not with taking care of Layla, who was walking now and getting into everything. It was almost impossible to take the toddler with her to the Victorian, where she was trying to supervise the work of the two-man crew Ryder had found. Luckily, Meredith had come to the rescue. She never missed an opportunity to babysit. She'd started on the day of the wedding, insisting that Ryder and Greer should have a proper wedding night.

What Ryder and Greer had had was an awkward wedding night spent sleeping on opposite sides of his wide bed. As if their marathon of lovemaking the night of the rainstorm had never occurred.

She'd never believed that night would be a one-and-done, as he put it. Yet it basically was. Sure, they'd indulged themselves several times that night. So was it a one-and-done or three-and-done? What was the difference?

There had been no repeat performance.

"Of course she's going to demolish her cake," she assured Grant, blocking the memories as she drew it a little closer to Layla. "This is all yours, sweetie." She pulled one of Layla's fingers through the icing and caught it in her mouth, sucking it off noisily. It was more whipped cream than frosting. "Yum yum."

"Num!" Layla lovingly patted Greer's face. Her green eyes were full of devotion. "Nummy."

Feeling like her heart would burst, Greer pressed a kiss to their toddler's palm. She couldn't keep herself from looking up at Ryder.

He was grinning; he looked dark and piratical with his short, stubbly beard. "Nummy, indeed."

She tried to ignore the heat shimmering through her, but it was futile.

Instead, she turned her focus back to Layla. Camera shutters clicked all around them as she suddenly launched herself toward her cake, squealing with pure, excited delight, sending Brutus into a frenzy of yipping.

It was, Greer decided, a very perfect first birthday for their little girl.

Eventually, though, it was time to clean up the mess.

Not surprisingly, at that exact moment, everyone conveniently found something else to do.

Vivian and Meredith took off in Vivian's ostentatious Rolls-Royce; heaven only knew where or for what purpose. Her grandmother was a terrible driver, but as long as Vivian didn't run her car over something or someone, Greer wasn't going to worry about it. Maddie and Ali were upstairs, giving Layla and Liam a bath. And all of the men, along with Adelaide and the dog, were out checking the cows Ryder had gathered in the big pasture over the last few weeks.

With the dishwasher already full, Greer set herself to the enormous stack of dishes still waiting on the counter and in the sink. She moved them aside, fit the stopper in the drain, squirted dish soap under the running water and got to work.

Overhead, she could hear laughter from the bath and she smiled to herself.

It hadn't been a bad two months since she and Ryder signed their name on that marriage certificate. Moments like this—even elbow-deep in dish water and dirty dishes—were pretty sweet. Ryder had been able to catch up on his nonstop chores and Greer hadn't even missed the PD's office too badly. Particularly once the scandal broke that Michael Towers really was sleeping with their most notorious client, Stormy Santiago. From what Greer had been hearing, nobody from the office was escaping entirely unscathed. There were rumors that a new supervising attorney was going to be brought in from Cheyenne.

Most important of all, though, Layla was thriving.

Greer let out a long breath and turned on the tap to rinse the stockpot she'd just washed.

"That's a big sigh."

She startled, looking over to see Grant closing the kitchen door. "Decide one cow looks pretty much like the next?" she asked.

A smile touched his aquamarine-colored eyes. "Something like that."

She hesitated, wanting to say something, but not knowing what. Instead, she turned back to the stockpot and tipped it upside down on the towel she'd spread on the counter for the clean dishes. "Ali's upstairs. I'm sure Layla and Liam have both had plenty of time in the tub by now."

He didn't head upstairs to retrieve his wife, though. He stopped next to Greer, picked up one of the towels from the pile she'd pulled from the drawer and lifted the stockpot.

"Thanks."

"That was good chili you made. Reminded me of my mom's cooking."

She shoved her hands back into the water. The suds were all but gone. "Thank Adelaide. She supervised. On top of all the other stuff she's done, she wrote a cookbook more than twenty years ago. There are a few used copies still out there. Selling for a ridiculous amount of money online."

"She's something, that aunt of his." He didn't look at her as he ran the towel over the pot. "Whatever comes into her head seems to go right out her mouth."

"At broadcast decibels," Greer added wryly. "I thought at first that maybe she was hard of hearing, but she's not. I think she could hear a pin drop from a mile away. It's just her way."

"Ali says you must be pretty cozy here, all three of you. There are only two bedrooms?"

"Yeah." She rinsed the last pot and handed it to him, then let out the water so she could start with fresh. She had all of the glassware yet to wash. "We've got Layla's crib in with us." More often than not, the toddler ended up in bed with them, usually sprawled sideways and somehow taking up the lion's share of the mattress. Fortunately, Ryder had drawn the line at Brutus coming into the room. Adelaide's rotund pug seemed to think he owned the place now and he'd have been up with them for sure.

"I'm surprised Adelaide didn't take up Vivian's offer to stay with her in Weaver. She's got a lot more space."

"Ryder would sleep on the floor before he'd let Adelaide stay somewhere else. I know she's a bit of a character, but she means a great deal to him. Her coming here at all is major. She doesn't travel." She chanced a quick glance at Grant's profile as she stoppered the sink again and waited for it to fill once more. She knew he'd had a troubled early childhood until he'd been adopted as an adolescent by the same family who'd adopted his sister. "He lost his mother when he was young, too."

"Ali told me."

She turned off the faucet and set a few glasses in the water. "Oh, stuff it," she said under her breath, and angled sideways to look straight at him. "He blames himself, too, Grant. For what happened. Daisy, Karen, whatever name she went by, she was his *wife*. She didn't turn to him any more than she turned to you when she chose to leave her baby with someone else."

He cleared his throat. His jaw looked tight. "I was her big brother a lot longer than she was his wife," he said in a low voice.

"So that means his self-blame is misdemeanor level but yours is felony grade?" She shook her head. "It doesn't work that way, Grant. You must know that. Time is not the measure. You've been married less than a year to my sister. If—God forbid—something happened to her, would your loss be less devastating than mine or Maddie's? We shared our mother's womb."

Heedless of the water still on her hands, she closed her fingers over his arm. "You and Ryder knew your sister in different ways. She didn't tell you everything. She certainly didn't tell him everything. She married him entirely under false pretenses. Whatever your childhoods were like, as an adult, Daisy did some things that were terribly wrong. I get that she was troubled. I do. But she abandoned her child when she had other options she could have taken! Maybe she regretted it but didn't know how to make it right before it was too late. I know that's what Ali says you believe. And maybe she didn't regret what she'd done at all. Regardless, what she did was what *she* did. What she did not do, *she* did not do. Neither you nor Ryder was her keeper. And you're both losing out, because out of all the people Layla has in her life, the two of you were the ones closest to her real mother!"

Greer's eyes were suddenly burning. "I'm adopting your niece. I don't see how I can possibly love her more than I already do. We can give her an official birthday and a new birth certificate. But one day Layla is going to want to know about her biological mother. Who else is going to be able to give her the answers she needs besides you and Ryder? Seems to me that would be a lot easier if the two of you would stop acting like adversaries and start acting like what you are! Two men who cared deeply for the same woman who deeply hurt you both!"

She huffed out a breath and turned to plunge her hands back in the suds. "I'm sorry." The glasses clinked as she grabbed one and started scrubbing it with her dishrag. "I'm sure Ali won't appreciate me sticking my nose into your business."

"As you've just eloquently put it, Karen wasn't only my business." He gently pulled the glass away from her furious scrubbing. "That's quite a closing argument you give." His hand lingered on the glistening glass after he'd rinsed it and turned it upside down onto the cloth. "I just wish things had been different," he said after a moment.

"I'm sure you do." Her eyes were still burning. She couldn't bring herself to say that she wished things had been different, too.

Because if they were different, she believed Ryder would still be with Daisy. Because that was the kind of man he was.

The kind of man who did what was right.

Her stomach suddenly churning, she pulled her hands from the water and hastily dried them. "I'm just going to run up and see what's going on with bath time. The babies must be prunes by now." She hurried out of the kitchen, but instead of heading up the stairs, she bolted for the bathroom behind them and slammed the door shut. She barely made it to the commode in time to lose all of the dinner she'd eaten.

Afterward, feeling breathless and weak, she just sat there on the wood-tiled floor, her head resting against the wall.

It had been two months since she and Ryder had stood in front of Judge Stokes and repeated those simple vows.

It had also been two months since she'd had a period. And this was the fourth time in as many days that she'd lost her cookies after supper.

That little implant in her arm had proven itself to truly be pointless.

She hadn't taken a test. But she knew the truth, anyway.

She was pregnant.

The house had been quiet for hours since the party when Ryder quietly stepped into the dark bedroom and slid the heavy door shut.

He didn't need a light to see. The moonlight shining through the windows gave him plenty.

He expected to see Layla's crib empty. But there was a bump in one corner: her diapered fanny sticking up in the air.

There was also a bump visible on the far edge of the bed. The sheet and blanket were pulled up high, only leaving visible Greer's gleaming brown hair spread out against the stark white pillow.

He turned away from the sight and exchanged his flannel

shirt and jeans for the ragged sweatpants that he'd taken to wearing to bed ever since he'd gotten himself a wife.

The irony wasn't lost on him.

He could say he'd gotten into the habit because his aunt was right there under their roof, snoring away in the second bedroom. He could say it was because they had a toddler in the room.

He could say it.

Couldn't make himself believe it.

He went into the bathroom and quietly closed the door before turning on the light. He brushed his teeth and when he was finished, rubbed his hand down his unshaven jaw. The beard was part laziness, part convenience. It helped keep his face warmer when he was out on horseback gathering cows and the wind was cold and whipping over him.

Mostly, though, it was just his way of being able to face himself in the mirror every morning.

He tossed the soft, plush hand towel over the hook next to the sink. Somewhere along the way since he'd married Greer, things like threadbare towels and wrinkled bedding had been replaced by thick terry cloth and smooth, crisp sheets. There were clean clothes in his drawers and sprigs of fresh flowers stuck inside glass jars on the dinner table. And though Greer claimed not to be much of a cook, Layla had learned there were good things to eat besides Cow Pie Surprise. Greer hadn't just kept to the inside of the house, either. The picnic table he'd intended to sand and repaint had gotten sanded, all right. Just not by him. And the daisies he'd thought to cover with red paint, she'd sealed with shellac instead.

Greer's mark was everywhere. Even when it meant preserving something he hadn't really cared to preserve.

He went back into the bedroom and lowered himself to his edge of the bed.

It had been two months of nights lying on his side, one pillow jammed under his neck. Watching her in the moonlight as she slept on the other edge.

As always, she wore striped pajamas. The kind with the buttoned top and the pull-on pants. She had them in yellow. And blue. And red and purple and pink.

The few months that Daisy had been there, she'd worn slippery satiny lace things or nothing at all. The bed he'd had then had been smaller. There hadn't been so much space between them.

He'd gotten rid of the bed.

Gotten rid of the slippery satiny lace things, along with every other item she'd left behind, except the picnic table. And he'd only kept that because it was practical.

He'd never figured striped two-piece pajamas were a particularly sexy thing to wear to bed.

Until he'd spent two months of nights thinking about reaching across the great divide to unbutton that buttoned top. To slide those pull-on pants off.

Thoughts like that tended to make a long night even longer. So he'd started earlier in the morning with chores. Gone later at night before finishing.

Every square foot of his ranch was benefiting from the extra hours of attention.

Except for the 150 square feet right here in his own bedroom.

He could have made things easier on himself. Could have refrained from insisting Adelaide stay with them even though she'd clearly been interested in taking Vivian up on her offer to stay at her place. The two women couldn't be more different; the one thing they had in common was that they both were uniquely eccentric. Yet they'd hit it off. Ryder knew that big house Vivian had built on the edge of Weaver had more than enough space for a half dozen Adelaides and their pain-in-the-butt pugs.

Yeah, Ryder could have let Adelaide accept Vivian's invitation. If he had, Layla's crib wouldn't be blocking half his dresser drawers. He wouldn't be waking up six nights out of seven to her toddler feet kicking him as she rolled around in her sleep, unfettered in the space between Ryder's edge of the bed and Greer's because she wasn't even sleeping in her crib.

It was his own fault.

The night of their courtroom wedding, he should have pulled Greer across the mattress. Should have met her halfway.

He should have started as he meant to continue. Should have given her his grandmother's wedding ring that Adelaide had produced when she'd shown up so unexpectedly on their wedding day. Should have made love with her on their wedding night.

But he hadn't. And he was damned if he knew why.

The ring was sitting in its box inside the dresser half-blocked by Layla's crib.

And here they were.

As far apart as humanly possible on a king-size bed.

He lifted his head, rebunched the pillow and turned to face the saddle propped on the saddletree. If he moved the damn thing to the tack room where it belonged, there'd be room for the crib there instead.

But he was proud of that saddle. He'd won it at the National Finals the last year he'd competed. The same year he'd won the money that he'd kept so carefully in savings because ranching was never a sure thing and he'd wanted to be certain he had enough to carry him when times were lean.

The money that he was dipping into now just to make sure his wife from the other edge of the bed had a place to hang her legal shingle that didn't have rotting floorboards and dicey electrical wiring.

Two minutes later, cursing inside his head, he turned over again to stare at his sleeping wife's back.

Only she'd turned, too.

And she wasn't asleep.

And so there they lay. Facing each other across the great divide. Her eyes were dark pools of mystery.

Finally, she whispered, "What are you thinking?"

He cast around for something to say. "It was a nice party."

"Mm." She shifted a little. "Even after Brutus jumped on the counter to eat the leftover cake." She tucked her hands beneath her cheek in the same manner as Adelaide's angels from her ceramic phase. "Can I ask you a question?"

She was still whispering. Probably didn't need to. At least not for Layla's sake. Lately, the baby had been able to sleep through anything. Not even Adelaide's booming voice disturbed her anymore.

"What?"

"Why didn't you want to do the paternity test?"

Of all the things she might have asked, that was the last thing he expected.

She shifted again, and for half a moment, he thought maybe she was shifting closer. An inch. Even two.

But no. Nearly an entire mattress still lay between them.

"What purpose would it have served? Soon as I learned her name, I knew I was going to take her."

"But don't you want to *know*?"

"Have it confirmed that on top of everything, she cheated on me?"

"It might confirm that she didn't."

"And which is worse?"

Greer didn't respond to that. She turned her head slightly and he knew she was looking toward the crib. At Layla inside it. "Are you afraid it will change how you feel about her?"

"No."

"Are you lying?"

He thought about not answering. But there was enough distance between them just from the gulf of mattress. "Maybe." He wasn't proud of it. "She's mine. *Ours*," he corrected before she could. The adoption wasn't yet final, but it might as well have been. "I don't want what the DNA test says to matter, and that is more about Layla's mother than it is about Layla."

Greer was silent for so long, he thought maybe she was simply going to turn over once more. Turn her back to him. But she didn't. "Do you still love her?" she finally asked in her hushed voice.

"No. And you don't have to ask if I'm lying. The answer's no." On that his head was clear. He wished it were as clear when it came to the woman lying across from him.

"There might come a day when Layla wants to know."

He knew she meant about the DNA. "That's another matter." He'd given it some thought. "I already have a DNA profile. If it ever comes time to use it, it'll be waiting."

She pushed up onto her elbow, obviously surprised. Her hair had grown since they'd said "I do." It curled around her shoulders now. Softer. Lusher. It was almost as unfamiliar as his beard. "You do?"

"That last year I was bronc bustin'." He pushed up onto his elbow, too, and nodded his head toward the saddle behind him. "When I won that. I was served with a paternity suit. The girl was looking for a piece of my winnings. She thought I'd just let her take it. But I knew it was bull. I'd slept with her, but that baby wasn't mine. Test proved it."

"But Layla's different?"

"Layla had no one else. She was my wife's child."

She lowered herself back down off her elbow with her hands tucked beneath her chin. "So it was the right thing to do," she whispered.

He lay back down, too. Bunched the pillow beneath his neck. There was no need to answer, but he did. "Yes."

She exhaled softly. Leaving him wondering what she was thinking.

All he had to do was ask.

All he had to do was stretch his arm toward her. Offer his hand.

It wasn't too late to break the habit of two months of long nights. The great divide could be breached. Could be destroyed.

All it would take was a step.

He shifted and in the moonlight he could see the way she tensed.

He lifted his head, rebunched his pillow and closed his eyes.

CHAPTER TWELVE

"Happy Thanksgiving!"

Greer smiled at her mom as she walked into the house where she'd grown up. Layla was walking at her side. Her steps were the sweet, plopping sort of steps that all toddlers took at first. She had one hand clasped in Greer's, the other in Ryder's.

"Happy Thanksgiving. Smells great in here."

Despite the bare, frozen ground outside, the house was warm. Greer noticed Meredith's feet were typically bare as she hurried out of the kitchen and across the foyer to give them a hug. The tiny bells around her ankle jingled and Layla immediately crouched down, trying to catch them. "Bell," she said clearly.

"That's right, darling. Grandma's bells." Meredith scooped up the baby and nuzzled her nose. Layla's rosy-gold hair would probably never be as thick as Greer's mom's, but it might turn out to be just as curly. "Did you get it?"

Greer held up the envelope she was carrying. "It's official. I picked up our copy of the final adoption decree yesterday just before the recorder's office closed for the holiday." She pulled out the document and handed to her mother.

"Well." Meredith was teary as she paged through it before setting it on the entryway table. Her gaze shifted from Ryder to Greer. "Congratulations, Mommy."

If they only knew.

Greer blinked back the moisture in her own eyes. She glanced at Ryder and quickly looked away. She still hadn't told him that she was pregnant. She hadn't told anyone, except her doctor.

"It's a fabulous day," Adelaide practically shouted in greeting, coming inside behind them. She was carrying Brutus inside his expensive leather transport. "Meredith, I've decided I need to photograph you."

Her mom's eyebrows flew up. "Whatever for, Adelaide?"

"Just be glad she's out of her nude phase," Ryder commented drily.

He was still wearing the closely cut beard he'd started before Layla's birthday. Now the stubble was full-on beard. Still short. Still groomed. But his dimple was hidden.

"She'd still be a fine-looking nude," Carter said as he walked past. He was carrying two bottles of beer and handed one to Ryder.

"Dad!"

Meredith was smiling, though, and the look that passed between her parents was almost too intimate to bear.

"Pardon me while I go throw up," she muttered for effect as she walked around them and headed into the kitchen. Her mother's laughter followed her.

Fortunately, Greer's after-dinner morning sickness had faded. Unfortunately, she knew she was going to have to fess up sooner rather than later to everyone—her husband most particularly. So far, she hadn't even let her belt out a notch; her stomach was as flat as ever. The obstetrician she'd sneaked over to Weaver to see had needlessly reminded her it wasn't going to be long, though. When Maddie was carrying Liam, she'd been visibly pregnant at four months. Same with Ali, who was now six months along.

Greer could either admit the truth in the next few weeks, or she'd be showing it, if her sisters were anything to go by.

But that didn't mean she was going to worry about the fallout today.

Not when it was Thanksgiving. Not when she felt positively ravenous and there was a veritable feast for the taking.

Every inch of kitchen counter was covered with trays of food. She grazed along, plucking olives and candied pecans with equal enthusiasm. Within minutes, she could hear more people arriving. More family members. More friends. Even Vivian, despite the ongoing animosity between her and Greer's dad and uncle. And soon the house was bulging at the seams.

There was laughter and squabbling and it was all dear and familiar. And despite the secret she harbored, Greer felt herself relax. Even when she and Ryder were sitting so close to each other at the crowded table that the length of his strong thigh burned against hers, and they couldn't lift their forks without brushing against each other.

After the glorious feast, it was football. The options were to watch it on television or play it on the winter-dead front yard, where Archer was warming up, tossing the football around with their cousins and their brothers-in-law.

Ali intercepted the ball and looked toward her sisters and their cousins. "Guys against the girls? Cousins against cousins? What'd we do last year?"

"Cousins," Maddie reminded her with a laugh. "And it was a slaughter."

"Only because Seth turned out to be a ringer." Quinn was the eldest of their cousins and, like Archer, had only sisters. "I say Templetons against the spouses!"

His wife, Penny, rubbed her hands together and laughed. "I'm game for that. Means I've got nearly all the guys on my side!"

Ali looked toward Greer where she stood on the sidelines.

"Count me out," Greer said hastily. She had her hands tucked into her armpits and was stomping her feet to keep them warm. The snow in October had been a onetime occurrence and melted away, but the temperatures had hovered around freezing ever since. "It's too cold!"

"What a wuss you've become," Ali chided with a laugh. "Go

find Maddie, then. And Ryder. It's his first Thanksgiving game, same as Grant and Linc." Her smile was devilish. "Gotta initiate these men of ours into the family just right." She tossed the ball from one bare hand to her other. "Rules are same as always. No tackle. Just touch."

"Think you've been touched enough," Archer called to her. "Don't know what's bigger, that football or your belly."

Ali preened, tucking the ball under her arm as she framed her bulging bump against the Green Bay sweatshirt she wore in honor of their father's favorite team.

Then Grant, the guy responsible for her baby bump, came up behind her, poked the ball free, and the game was on in earnest even though the teams weren't entirely present and accounted for.

But that was always how it went.

The most basic rule of Templeton Family Football was for everyone to have fun. The second basic rule was for everyone to stay out of the hospital.

Greer was smiling as she went back inside. She found Maddie in the study, nursing Liam while she ate another piece of pumpkin pie with her fingers. Greer let her be and went to find Ryder. He wasn't in the family room, where her dad and uncle were sprawled out in front of the large-screen television. Nor in the kitchen, where her mom and aunt were still cleaning up the dishes.

"Have you seen Ryder?"

Meredith pointed toward the screened sunporch off the kitchen. Beyond that, Greer could see him and Adelaide sitting outside on the park-style bench in the middle of the flower garden. Right now, the only flowers in view were the brightly painted metal ones that were planted in the ground on long metal spikes. Layla was chasing after Brutus as he ran around the yard sniffing every blade of dead grass.

Greer smiled at the picture they all made and opened the kitchen door, going out to the sunporch. She peeled back a corner of the thick clear plastic that her dad hung up in the screened openings so that Meredith could enjoy the space whether it was cold or not. "Ry—"

"Why haven't you?" From all the way across the yard, Adelaide's voice wasn't quite megaphone-ish, but it was still audible.

Something about the tone made Greer swallow the rest of her husband's name.

"It's my decision, Adelaide." Ryder's voice was much quieter. Underlaid with steel.

Disquiet slithered down her spine. One part of her urged retreat. The other part refused. Morbid curiosity kept her pinned to the spot, prepared to witness disaster.

"If I wanted to give her the ring, I would have."

"It's a mistake, Ryder."

Oblivious to their audience, Ryder shoved off the filigreed bench. "Consider it one more mistake I've made when it comes to marriage." He whistled sharply. "Brutus. No." The dog had started digging near the base of a tree. His words had no effect on the little dog. "Adelaide—"

"Brutus, come." At least the pug sometimes listened to his mistress. The dog retreated and hopped up onto Adelaide's lap.

Ryder swung Layla up high and she laughed merrily, sinking her hands into his hair when he put her on his shoulders as he headed in Greer's direction.

Closer. Closer.

She exhaled, finally managing to drag her mired feet free as she hurried back into the house before he could see her.

She caught the glance her mother gave her as she scurried through the kitchen. "Cold out there," she said a little too loudly.

"Your dad's got a fire going—"

Greer waved her hand in acknowledgment as she fairly skidded around the corner and escaped into the hallway by the front door.

She sucked in a breath, pressing her palm against her belly, knowing she had to keep it together even though inside she felt like she was unraveling.

Ryder never said what he didn't mean.

No matter what he'd said the day they got married, he obviously considered the business of *their* marriage as one more mistake.

"There you are." The man in her thoughts rounded the corner of the hallway and she froze. Layla was no longer on his shoulders. "Adelaide's getting pretty tired. I thought I'd run her back to the ranch."

"I can do it," she heard herself offer. "Layla's going to need her bath and bed soon, anyway. Your...your presence is wanted on the football field."

Even as she said the words, the front door flew open and Grant rushed in. His hair was windblown, his cheeks ruddy. "Tell me you played football."

Ryder's eyes narrowed slightly. "Running back, but not since high school. Helluva while ago."

Grant beckoned. "Better'n nothing." He looked at Greer. "I'm pretty sure we've been sandbagged. Archer—"

Any other day, Greer would have enjoyed the moment. "All-state quarterback."

"And my wife? What was she? All-state sneak?"

"Track. All three of us." She spread her hands, managing a smile even though it felt as brittle as her insides. "We grew up on football. Dad didn't care whether we were girls and more interested in horses and ballet or not."

"Should've known." Grant turned to Ryder. "We spouses lose this game and you know it's gonna follow us the rest of our married lives." He clapped his hand over Ryder's shoulder. "It's a matter of pride."

Ryder looked her way.

"It's a matter of pride," she parroted. "Vivian'll give you a ride home. I'm sure she'd be happy to detour to the ranch on her way back to Weaver."

"She'd be happy, but I've seen her drive." Still, he was smiling a little as he went out the door with Grant.

As if all was right.

As if it mattered to him that losing this first game might seal his fate for all their Thanksgiving football games to come.

She looked out at the two of them jogging out to join the scrimmage. She called after them. "Just remember, no tackling!" If her voice sounded thick, it didn't matter.

She was the only one who noticed.

She closed the door.

The adoption decree was sitting on the table against the opposite wall. She picked it up and slid it carefully back into its envelope.

Then she went to retrieve her daughter and Adelaide and her yapping dog, and they went home.

She was glad that all of her passengers fell asleep on the way.

It meant that they never saw the tears sliding silently down her cheeks.

"Here." Ali handed Greer a hanger. "Try that one."

Greer slid the red tunic off the hanger and pulled it over her head. It hung past her hips over her long black palazzo pants She turned sideways to view herself in the full-length mirror.

The small bulge of her abdomen was disguised among the ridges of the cable knit.

She exhaled. "Okay. This one'll work." She dashed her fingers through her hair. She hadn't had it cut in months. Not since she'd left the PD's office. With the help of her prenatal vitamins, it was growing even faster than usual. It was already down to her shoulder blades.

Unfortunately, her good hair days weren't making up for all that was wrong.

Ali just shook her head, looking decidedly Buddha-like as she sat cross-legged on the counter in Greer's bathroom at the Victorian. "You should've told him by now, Greer."

"I will." She lifted her chin as she peered into the mirror and applied some blush so that her face wouldn't look quite so washed out against the brilliant vermilion tunic. "Adelaide is leaving the day after Christmas. I'll tell him about the baby after she's gone. That's only four days from now."

Ali folded her hands atop her round belly. While Greer was hiding the changes in her body, her sister was delighting in showing off hers. At that moment, she wore a clingy white sweater and burgundy leggings that outlined every lush curve she'd developed.

And why not?

Ali and Grant were besotted with each other. She had no reason whatsoever to want to hide what that love had produced.

It was Greer's bad luck that she'd somehow fallen in love with her own husband. She knew when he learned about the baby, she wouldn't be just another mark in his column of marital mistakes. She—and their baby—would become his next "right thing to do."

And it was almost more than she could bear.

She didn't want to be his responsibility. And she didn't want to be his business partner in this sterile marriage.

"I still can't believe Ryder hasn't noticed," Ali was saying. "Maybe you can hide that bump under thick sweaters and shapeless pajamas, but your boobs are another story. Is the guy blind?"

Greer tossed the blush in the vanity drawer and pulled out the mascara. They'd met at the Victorian—which was still undergoing renovations—to finish wrapping the Christmas gifts they'd been stashing away there, before heading over to Maddie and Linc's place. They were hosting a party for his employees at Swift Oil.

Grant was waiting downstairs in what was originally the living room, but was now a framework for a reception area and two offices.

Ryder hadn't come at all. He'd been moving the bulls to

their new pasture that day and the task was taking longer than he'd planned.

Greer suspected he was just as relieved as she was that he had a valid reason to miss the party.

"He doesn't have to be blind when he doesn't look to begin with." Her voice was flat.

"I don't know." Her sister was unconvinced. "You guys still share a bed."

Greer cursed softly when she smudged her mascara. "A bed where he stays on his side and I stay on mine. And never the twain shall meet."

"Seems to me you could twain your way over to him if you wanted to. You did it before. That's how you got yourself in the family way."

Greer ignored that as she snatched a tissue from the box next to Ali's knee and dabbed away the mess she'd made.

It was too bad she couldn't dab away the mess of her marriage with a simple swipe.

"I should have never confided in you in the first place," she told her. Not about the rainstorm. Definitely not about the great divide that existed between her side of the bed and his.

"I think you needed to tell somebody," Ali said quietly. Her eyes were sympathetic. Ali was always easier to take when she was full of sass and vinegar than when she wasn't.

Greer cleared her throat as she balled up the tissue and tossed it in the trash. "You just happened to catch me in a bad moment."

"Sure. Sitting on the side of the road near Devil's Crossing bawling your eyes out. A little more than a bad moment in my view, but if that's what you want to call it."

She'd been on her way back from an appointment with her obstetrician in Weaver. She'd started blubbering near the spot where Ryder had rescued her that day in August, which now felt so long ago. She had pulled off the road before she ran off it. Ali, in her patrol car, had spotted her. And the entire story had come pouring out of Greer, along with her hiccupping sobs.

"Hormones." Finished with the mascara, Greer capped the tube and tossed it next to the blush, then shut the drawer with a slap. "I'm ready." She tugged her pants hem from beneath her high heel where it had caught.

"More like a broken heart," her sister was muttering under her breath as she unfolded her legs and slid off the counter. "I warned you that something like this would happen." She followed Greer through the bedroom and downstairs.

While Greer didn't appreciate the "I told you so," she did appreciate Ali's return to form.

"Finally," Grant said when he spotted them. "Sooner we get to this deal, sooner we can leave. We're already going to be late."

"Party animal," Ali joked. She lifted her hair when he helped her on with her coat.

Grant's smile was slanted. "I'll party your socks off when we get home."

"Well, now, that *is* a good reason to get moving along."

Greer grabbed her coat and headed out the door. She didn't begrudge her sister's happiness. Truly, she didn't. But her hormones were at work again, and she really didn't want to have to go back upstairs and redo her mascara again.

She paused on the front porch as she pulled on her coat. Every house down the hill from the Victorian was outlined in bright Christmas lights. There still hadn't been any snow since October, but it was pretty all the same.

At the ranch, Ryder had put up the Christmas tree he'd cut down himself. He'd left the decorating of it to Greer and Adelaide, though. The results had been interesting, to say the least. Adelaide's unusual eye might be highly regarded at MoMA, but Greer was probably a little too traditional to fully appreciate the strange paper clip–shaped objects juxtaposed with the popcorn garland she was used to.

She stifled a sigh, climbed behind the wheel of her car and pulled away from the curb. Ali and Grant were in their SUV behind her. She'd become accustomed to using Ryder's truck, because Layla's car seat fit so much better into it. But Layla was back at the ranch with Adelaide. Ryder's aunt had declined the invitation, saying that two parties within just a few days of each other were more than she was used to. And Vivian's annual fete was the night after next on Christmas Eve.

Greer wondered if Ryder would find an excuse to miss that party, too. If he did, it was going to be a little harder for her to explain away his absence. Her brother-in-law's company party was one thing. Vivian's, quite another.

As Grant had predicted, the party was in full swing when they arrived at the Swift mansion.

Greer left her coat in the foyer with the teenager who'd been hired to handle them and aimed straight for the bar. She longed for a cocktail, but made do with cranberry juice and lime. Then she filled a small plate with brownies that she knew Maddie had made from scratch and a half dozen other little morsels.

If anyone did notice her bump, they'd just figure it was from gorging herself.

Christmas music was playing in the background, loud enough to cover awkward silences as employees settled in but not so loud that it was annoying. If Vivian held true to form for *her* party, she'd have a live quartet. When it came to her grandmother, expense was no object. She imported the musicians from wherever she needed to.

Greer wandered through the house, smiling and greeting those she knew as if she wouldn't want to be anywhere else. There wasn't a corner or a banister that hadn't been decked with garland and holly, and the tree that stood in the curve of the staircase was covered in pretty red-and-gold ornaments. She stood admiring it, sipping her juice.

"Looks a little more like a normal tree than ours."

Greer jerked, splashing cranberry juice against her sweater. She blotted the spot with her cocktail napkin and stared at Ryder. "I thought you weren't coming." He was wearing an off-white henley with his jeans, and it just wasn't fair that he should look so good when she felt so bad.

"I thought I wasn't." He shrugged. "But I got the bulls settled finally and decided to come." His blue eyes roved over her face, but they didn't give a clue to what he was thinking. They might be married, but she felt like she knew him no better than she had when they'd first met.

He took the napkin from her, folded it over and pressed it against her sweater. "Would you have preferred I hadn't?"

Her heart felt like it was beating unevenly and she hoped he couldn't feel it, too. "Of course not," she managed smoothly. "You just surprised me, that's all." She tugged the napkin away from him and crumpled it. "There's a bar and an entire spread." She gestured with the hand holding her plate of food. "You should go help yourself. Maddie's brownies will go fast."

His gaze seemed to rest on her face again for a moment too long before he headed off.

She blamed the impression on her guilty conscience.

No matter how strained things were between them, she knew she needed to tell him about the baby.

This time, there'd be no room for him to doubt the paternity. It was the only positive note that she could think of in what felt like an intolerable situation.

"That you, Greer?"

She looked away from watching Ryder to see a familiar face. "Judge Manetti!"

He smiled. "It used to be Steve, remember? We're not in my courtroom now." He leaned over and kissed her cheek. "When I saw you at first, I thought you were Maddie." He waved his fingers. "The hair's longer. You're looking good. Heard you got married. It must suit you."

She kept her smile in place. It took an effort, but she'd had a lot of practice. "I didn't know you were part of Swift Oil."

"My wife started there a few months ago." He looked around

the room. "Always wondered what it was like inside this old mansion. Pretty impressive."

It was a little easier to smile at that. "I think so, too. How're things over at civic plaza?"

"Crazy. You know about—" He broke off and nodded. "Of course you know about it. Heard they've got a short list for the top spot in your old office."

From the corner of her eye, she saw Ryder returning. "Oh? Someone from Cheyenne, I suppose."

He shook his head. "You really don't know?"

"I really don't—ah. Keith Gowler? He's got the trial experience. I think he's pretty happy being in private practice, though. Means he can take cases for PD when he chooses."

"Not Keith. You."

She blinked, then shook her head. "No. Not possible. There're too many other attorneys in line ahead of me. And I quit, remember?"

Ryder stopped next to her and set his hand against the small of her back. She nearly spilled her drink again. "Friend of yours?"

She turned and set the cranberry juice on the edge of a stair tread at the level of her head, along with her still-full plate. "This is Judge Steve Manetti," she introduced. "Steve, my...my—"

"Ryder Wilson." He stuck out his hand. In comparison to Steve's, his was large. Square. A working man's hand.

She moistened her lips, reminding herself to keep a friendly smile in place. "Steve and I have known each other since elementary school."

"I was just telling your wife that she's on the short list for replacing Towers."

Ryder's brow furrowed. "She's opening her own practice."

"No kidding!" Steve gave her a surprised look. "I hadn't heard that. Not that you wouldn't be great at it, but I always thought you had the public defender's office running in your veins."

"Guess not," Ryder answered before she could. His fingers curled against her spine. "If you'll excuse us, there's someone we need to see."

The judge smiled as Ryder ushered her away, but Greer recognized the speculation in his gaze. As soon as they were out of earshot, though, she jerked away from Ryder. "I didn't know caveman was your style. What was that all about?"

"You're not going to work for the PD office again."

She felt her eyebrows shoot up her forehead. "First of all, I haven't heard this short-list rumor. And second of all, even if I had, I would think that's my decision, wouldn't you?"

"Working in that office ran you ragged. And that's when you were an expendable peon."

She stiffened. "Good to know you had such respect for the work I did there!"

His lips tightened. "That's not what I meant and you know it."

She propped her hands on her hips and angled her head, looking up at him. "No, I don't know it. Why don't you explain it to me?"

"You really want to run that place? What about Layla? Months ago, you told me she was what was important and I believed you. Who's going to take care of *our daughter* when you're spending eighty hours a week defending drunk drivers and shoplifters?"

She gaped. "If that's the way you feel, why on earth did you ever insist on my opening my own practice? And don't go on about it being my *dream*! You think I'd be able to grow a practice from scratch with Layla on my hip 24/7?"

"You'd be calling your own shots," he said through his teeth. "Controlling your own schedule. You'd still have time to be a mother. Or now that you've finally got that right legally, has it lost the luster? You want to dump her off on someone else while you go off to do your own thing?"

She could barely form words for the fury building in her. She was literally seeing red. "You can regret marrying me."

Her fingers curled into fists as she pushed past him. "But don't you *ever* compare me to Daisy."

He caught her arm. "Where are you going?"

She yanked free. "Away from you."

The foyer had become a traffic jam of people arriving at the party. Greer veered away and started up the staircase instead.

"Dammit, Greer." He was on her heel. As unconcerned as she was that they'd begun drawing attention. He closed his hand over her shoulder and she lost it.

Quite. Simply. Lost it.

She whirled on him. *"Don't touch me!"*

He swore and started to reach for her again.

That he kept doing so now infuriated her, when he hadn't reached for her at all in the way that mattered most ever since they'd been married. She swatted his hands away, taking another step. But her heel caught again in the long hem of her pants and she stumbled. She steadied herself, though, grabbing the banister, and blindly took another step.

Right into the plate that she'd set on one of the treads. Her shoe slid through brownies and ranch dressing and she felt herself falling backward, arms flailing. Some part of her mind heard someone gasp. Another part saw Ryder's blue eyes as he tried to catch her.

And then she landed on her back and bounced against the banister so hard the Christmas tree next to the staircase rocked.

And then she saw no more.

CHAPTER THIRTEEN

"How is she?"

From the hard plastic chair he'd been camped in, Ryder lifted his head and looked from Meredith and Carter to Greer. She was lying asleep in the hospital bed. The white bandage on her forehead was partially hidden by her hair. The rest of the damage from her fall was harder to see. Harder to predict.

Which was why she was still lying in the hospital bed at all thirty-six hours later.

His jaw ached. "She hasn't lost the baby." *Yet.* He didn't say that part. But it felt like the word echoed around the small curtained-off area all the same.

He still was trying to resolve the fact that he'd learned she was carrying his child at the same time he'd learned she was very much in danger of losing it.

Now his wife was being carefully sedated while they waited.

Meredith's hand shook as she pressed it to her mouth.

"She's going to be all right," Carter told her, kissing her forehead. His arm was around her shoulder. "Nothing is going to happen to our girl on Christmas Eve."

Ryder wished he were so convinced.

Meredith finally lowered her hand. "Where's Layla?"

"Ali picked her up this morning." Much as he loved Adelaide, she wasn't up to the task of keeping up with an active one-year-old for more than a few hours at a time.

"That's good." Meredith nodded. She scooted past Ryder's legs until she reached the head of the bed, and then dropped a tender kiss on her daughter's forehead.

Ryder looked away, pinching the bridge of his nose.

"Have you gotten any sleep?" That was from Carter.

He shook his head. How could he sleep? Every time he closed his eyes, he saw Greer tumbling backward down those stairs.

"Maybe you should."

He shook his head.

"At least take a break."

He shook his head.

Carter stopped making suggestions. He sighed and squeezed Ryder's shoulder. "She's going to be all right, son. If the baby—" He broke off and cleared his throat. "I know you don't want to hear it. But there can be other babies."

But Ryder knew otherwise. This baby was their only chance. Greer was never going to forgive him no matter what happened. He was never going to forgive himself.

He propped his elbows on his knees again and stared at the floor.

Eventually, Meredith and Carter left with promises to return later. They'd bring him something to eat. They'd bring him something to drink.

It didn't really matter to him.

The only thing that did was lying in a hospital bed.

Inevitably, more family members visited. Hayley. Archer. Cousins he knew. Cousins he didn't.

Nobody stayed long. There wasn't space for more than the one chair Ryder was occupying. And he was too selfish to give up his spot by Greer's bed, even to all the other people who loved her, too. Finally, he must have dozed off. But he jerked awake when he heard a baby cry.

But when he opened his eyes, there was no baby. Only his wife. Eyes still closed. Breath so faint that he had to stare hard at the pale blue–dotted gown covering her chest to be certain that it was moving.

"How is she?"

How many times had he heard the question? A dozen? Two? He focused on the petite woman standing inside the curtain. "Vivian? What're you doing here?"

"Checking on my granddaughter, of course." She slipped past him to peer closely at Greer. "You're a Templeton," she told her. "We're many things, but we're not weak." She kissed Greer's forehead, much like Meredith had, and straightened.

Her face seemed more lined. Wearier. He offered her the chair.

She took it and held her pocketbook on her lap with both hands. "I've spent so many days in my life at a hospital." She shook her head slightly and reached out to squeeze his hand. "It's Christmas Eve. Nothing's going to happen to our girl on Christmas Eve."

"That's what Carter said."

Her lips curved in a smile. Bittersweet. "He's like his father," she murmured.

Then it occurred to him. "Your party is tonight."

"It's on hold."

"Greer said you invited a hundred people."

She waved her fingers dismissively. "And they'll likely come when I reschedule. When you and Greer can both be there."

"I don't know if that's gonna happen," he admitted in a low voice.

She smiled gently. "I do." Then she pushed to her feet. "I've picked up Adelaide. She wanted me to see Greer first, but she's in the waiting room."

"That was nice of you, Vivian. Thank you."

"Don't get too sentimental on me. I have a selfish motivation, as well. She and Brutus will be coming home to stay with me. I convinced her to stay awhile." She reached up and patted his cheek. "And that's final, dear boy." Then she tugged on the hem of her nubby-looking pink suit and left.

Ryder moved back next to the bed. Greer's hand was cool when he picked it up. He pressed it to his mouth, warming it. He was still like that when he heard the curtain swish again.

Adelaide stood there.

He exhaled and lowered Greer's hand to the bed. Then he stood and let his aunt wrap her skinny, surprisingly strong arms around him. "You love her," she said in a whisper. He hadn't ever heard her speak so softly. "You need to tell her."

"How do you know I haven't?"

She pulled back and gave him a look out of those crazy made-up eyes of hers. "I've been living in the same house as the two of you for four months. How do you think I know?" Then she set a familiar-looking ring box in his hand.

He slid his jaw to one side. Then the other. "How'd you find it?"

Now she just looked droll. "You've always hidden your treasures in your sock drawer. Not very imaginative if I must say, and it was quite the nuisance getting past Layla's crib to get the drawer all the way open."

There was nothing to be amused about. Yet he still felt a faint smile lift his lips. Then he looked back at his wife. Lying in that bed.

And he closed his eyes.

"Ryder," Adelaide whispered. "Have faith."

"Faith hasn't gotten me very far before, Adelaide. You know that."

"You just weren't looking." She gestured toward the bed with her turquoise-laden hand. "What do you see when you look at her?"

My life.

"Tell her you love her. Give her your granny's ring. I know you said before that you were afraid to. Afraid she wouldn't want it. Wouldn't understand the treasure you were trying to give. This last thing that remains from your family." She squeezed his hand around the ring box. "And I'm telling you that she will." She went from squeezing his fingers to squeezing his jaw. "What do you *see* when you look at her, Ryder?"

His eyes burned. "My life."

She gave a great sigh and smiled. She pulled on his jaw until he lowered his head and she kissed his forehead, like she'd done about a million times before.

Then she, too, went back outside the curtain.

Ryder pushed open the ring box. The box alone was ancient. The filigreed diamond ring inside was from the 1920s. He slid it free from the fading blue velvet. It was so small it didn't fit over the tip of his finger.

He sat down beside the bed again. Slowly picked up Greer's hand. It was still cool. Too cool.

When they'd brought her to the hospital, they'd taken her jewelry. Her wedding band. Her earrings. Placed them in a plastic bag that they'd given to him. He wasn't sure where he'd even put it.

He slowly slid his grandmother's ring over Greer's wedding finger. He didn't expect it to fit. But it did. "With this ring," he whispered huskily.

"I thee wed." Her words were faint, her touch lighter than a whisper as she curled her fingers down over his.

His heart charged into his throat and he looked up at her face. Her eyes were barely open but a tear slid from the corner of her eye. "The baby..." Her lashes closed.

He leaned close and smoothed away that tear. "The baby's okay." His voice was rough. "You're okay. All you have to do is rest."

Her lashes lifted again. A little more this time. Her hand slowly rose. The back of her knuckles grazed his cheek. "You're crying. Just tell me the truth. The baby—"

"Is going to be okay."

Her eyes drifted closed again. "I should've told you." Another tear slid from her eye. "I'm so sorry I didn't tell you the truth."

"I should've seen." He cupped her head in his hand. "I should have seen all along. And you are the truth." He pressed his mouth against hers. "You're my truth. I just didn't let myself see it. You're my wife, Greer. For all the right reasons, you're my wife." He pulled in a shaky breath. "So just get better and come home with me and Layla. You can work any damn job you want. Just…don't give up on me. Don't give up on our family."

Her eyes opened again and she stared up at him. "I thought you gave up on me," she whispered.

"Not in this lifetime," he promised thickly. He pressed another shaking kiss to her lips, and her hand lifted, closing around his neck.

"Don't leave me."

He shook his head, but her eyes had closed again. He lowered the rail on the side of the bed. Carefully, gingerly, with the same caution he'd felt when he'd first taken Layla all those months ago, he moved her an inch. Two. Just enough that he could slide onto the edge of the hospital bed with her. It was crowded. He had to curl one arm awkwardly above her just to be sure that he wouldn't jostle her. Jostle their baby. But he managed.

"I love you, Greer."

She exhaled. Turned her head toward him. "Love…you…" Her fingers brushed his cheek. "No more great…divide."

A soft sound escaped him. "No more great divide," he promised. "Never again."

And then he closed his eyes, cradling his life against him.

And they both slept.

EPILOGUE

"Welcome home, Mrs. Wilson."

Greer smiled up at Ryder as he carried her across the threshold of their house. It was an interesting experience. He carried her. She carried Layla. "We could've walked, you know. The doctors said the baby was okay. So long as I don't try running a marathon, we're all good."

"I know." He shouldered the door closed behind him. "But then I wouldn't have this opportunity to impress my ladies with my manliness as we made the trek through the deep, freezing snow."

Greer pressed her cheek against his chest and looked at their daughter. "Daddy's very silly today. Two snowflakes. That's what we trekked through."

Layla's green eyes were bright. "Dadda!"

Ryder's dimple appeared. "Daddy's very happy today," he corrected. He carried the two of them right through the house and deposited them carefully on the couch. He peeled off his coat and pitched it aside, then sat down beside them, his fingers twining through Greer's. "It's Christmas Day and I've got the very best presents. Because Mommy's home."

"Mama!"

Greer went still. "Did she just—"

"She did. Who's Mama, Short-Stuff?"

"Mama." Layla patted Greer's cheek and pressed a wet kiss on it. Then she patted Ryder's face, kissing his clean-shaven jaw. "Dadda."

She clambered off Greer's lap and ran over to the oddly decorated Christmas tree. She started tearing into the wrapped presents beneath it. "Sus-suhs," she chanted.

"She's gonna demolish them all," Ryder commented.

"Probably." Greer slid her fingers through his and pulled his hand over the baby nestled inside her. "I wouldn't be too concerned. Most of them are hers, anyway. Between you and me and Adelaide, we might have gone a little overboard with the gifts."

"It's our first Christmas together. Overboard is expected."

"Now you sound like Vivian."

He grinned. "She rescheduled that party of hers for tomorrow night, you know. Just like that." He snapped his fingers.

"The advantages of outrageous wealth."

"Mama." Layla toddled back to the couch, her fists filled with the shreds of Christmas wrapping paper. She dropped it on Greer's lap.

"For me?"

Bright-eyed, Layla returned to the tree and started back in on the presents.

"We could go over to your parents', you know. Everyone's there. Hoping to see you."

She shook her head and wrapped her arms around his neck. "Maybe later. Right now…right now, everything I never even knew I wanted is right here."

His eyes smiled into hers. "Merry Christmas, Layla's mommy."

She smiled back. He thought he'd gotten the best gift. But

she knew better. They'd all gotten the best gift. And she was going to treasure it for now and for always.

"Merry Christmas, Layla's daddy."

* * * * *

Keep reading for an excerpt of
Snowbound Reunion In Japan
by Nina Milne.
Find it in the
Christmas Together...Forever anthology,
out now!

PROLOGUE

THEA GLANCED AT her watch and quickened her footsteps; she didn't want to be late, especially as her family would ask why, and Thea really didn't want to tell them she'd been in the office. On a Sunday morning. Again.

She knew her mum, her dad and both her sisters, older sister Sienna and younger sister Eliza, all worried about how hard Thea worked.

She sighed. She wished they would get it—she *wanted* to work, *needed* to work, because the prospect of partnership was so tantalisingly close. Her jaw clenched in determination; she would achieve her ambition, and once she'd attained partnership she'd be off on to the next rung, climbing higher and higher. And if she smashed through a few glass ceilings on the way all the better.

She approached the Chiswick pub overlooking the Thames where they were meeting for Sunday lunch, a traditional venue for family get-togethers, usually for some occasion, a birthday or a celebration. But today her mum had called and suggested an impromptu meal.

Thea felt a welcome sense of familiarity as she entered the pub, with its polished wooden tables, the staff carrying loaded plates, the tantalising smell of food and its view of the river with boats moored by the side.

Tradition was important to the Kendalls. It bonded them together. Thea wondered if it was too early to bring up the subject of Christmas. Not that any planning was necessary; Christmas was the most cherished Kendall tradition of all.

She spotted her family and waved, heading over with a broad smile.

'Good day at the office?' Eliza greeted her with a cheeky grin.

'No comment,' Thea quipped back, as she blew everyone a kiss and sat down.

'Excellent. Now you're here, let's order,' her mum said, and Thea glanced at her in surprise.

Lila Kendall was usually happy to have a catch-up and linger over her food and drink choices. Even at a Sunday lunch there would normally be some discussion over which roast to go for, whether to try the vegetarian option, whether to have a glass of wine or a soft drink.

But clearly not today.

In record time the family were sitting with their plates in front of them and Thea was sure her mum was avoiding everyone's eye, her gaze fixed on her food or occasionally flickering to her unusually quiet father.

Thea helped herself to extra gravy and decided to offer a cheerful conversational topic. 'This is lovely. It's making me think about Christmas dinner, even if it's only October.'

She gave a small happy sigh as she pictured the turkey with all the trimmings, the crackers, the massive box of chocolates Sienna always brought, and the amicable bickering over the last favourite, sitting in their Christmas pyjamas watching Christmas movies on the massive overstuffed sofa in her parents' living room.

'Actually…' her mum said.

The word fell heavy as a stone and Thea felt a sudden sense of foreboding.

Lila trailed off and looked at her husband, then resumed again.

'There's something we want to tell you.'

The sense of foreboding deepened.

'We want to do something different this Christmas.'

There was a beat of confused silence before Eliza summed up what they were all thinking as she stuttered, 'Wh...what?'

'Like your mum said,' her dad started, 'we've decided to do something different for Christmas. We've booked a month-long cruise!'

The words came out in a rush and he looked at his wife. They exchanged a quick smile that spoke of relief that they'd got the words out, imparted their news.

The statement seemed to reverberate around the table as Thea struggled to actually absorb its meaning, aware of a childish urge to cover her ears. Now silence stretched, and she was aware of how they must look, a frozen tableau of shock, with her sisters clearly as stunned as she was as they stared at their parents.

Until finally Sienna pushed her chair backwards, almost as if she were going to leave, flee the scene. 'I should have known there was an ulterior motive for this spontaneous lunch,' she muttered.

But Thea couldn't see how anyone could have predicted this.

Her mum took a deep breath. 'It's our fortieth wedding anniversary this year. We wanted to do something just for ourselves.' Her voice held a near plea. 'You have your own lives, your own circles of friends. I thought you might appreciate the chance to do something different.'

Thea had absolutely no idea why her mum would think anything of the sort. This was *Christmas*. She could see a similar sense of disbelief and bewilderment on her siblings' faces, knew that for all three of them Christmas was all about coming home, being together. It offered comfort and certainty and happiness. Her parents must know that.

'Next you're going to tell us you've sold the family house,' she said. She knew she sounded sulky but she couldn't help it. It might be ridiculous, but she felt betrayed and bereft. She loved their traditional Kendall Christmas and she'd thought her parents did too.

Her dad sighed, exchanged a glance with his wife. 'Why would we do that?'

Sienna leant forward. 'Well, why would you do *this*?'

It was a question that held all the outrage that Thea felt too, and yet it was a good question—one that stopped Thea in her tracks.

Why *would* her parents do this? Her parents were the most amazing people Thea knew, especially her mother. All evidence showed that her mum put her family first, she always had, and Thea felt a familiar sense of admiration when she recalled exactly how true that was.

When Eliza had been diagnosed with acute myeloid leukaemia aged six it had, of course, impacted on all of them. Thea could still feel the fear, the terror, that had gripped her eleven-year-old self. But it had been their mum who had completely changed her life from thereon in, had given up her career plans and ambitions and centred her life around her youngest daughter.

Because although Eliza had gone into remission, the illness had returned when she was a teenager and there had been other illnesses in between. And always, always, the overhanging shadow of worry.

Yet thanks to her parents the Kendalls had always been a happy family—a family who pulled together, a family who loved spending time together, especially at Christmas. And so much of that was down to her mum. Again, Thea felt admiration, but as always it was tinged with a sense of her own inadequacy.

Because she knew she could never be like her mum, could never sacrifice so much and never show even a smidgeon of resentment. Still be calm and loving and the rock they all depended on, despite her whole life being upended by Eliza's illness. Thea knew she could never be that selfless, could never risk not being a good enough parent.

For a second sadness touched her, even though she knew her decision to be the right one—she *knew* it wasn't possible to have it all. So motherhood was not for her. Her career was too important and she'd invested too much in it.

But her mother wasn't like Thea, and she would know how important Christmas was to her daughters. So what was going on?

Thea blinked, realising she'd been so caught up in her thoughts she'd missed the ensuing conversation.

She caught the tail end of her mother's words to Eliza. 'It's like a ton weight from all of our shoulders.'

She knew her mother was reminding them of their massive relief that Eliza had had the all-clear, had been given her final discharge from the hospital.

Thea saw emotion skitter across Eliza's face and then, 'It sounds wonderful,' Eliza said.

'Really?' their mum asked.

Thea could hear the mixture of disbelief and hope in her voice and the penny dropped. Her parents were free—free from anxiety and worry—and they wanted to celebrate forty years of marriage alone.

She nodded, and knew her sisters had got it too as Sienna chipped in, 'Of course I understand.'

Eliza launched into all the reasons why of course their parents must go. Then they turned to looked at Thea, and gamely she did her bit, because her parents deserved this.

'Absolutely you must go,' she said firmly, as Eliza rose to her feet and went to hug her parents before turning to her sisters.

'Sienna, Thea, come and help me get another round of drinks.'

Thea glanced at her little sister, heard the underlying quaver in her voice and got to her feet, waiting as Sienna followed suit and headed after Eliza. Then she flashed her best, most reassuring smile at her parents. 'Truly,' she said. 'We all get it. I think the cruise is a wonderful idea too.'

Once the sisters were out of their parents' sight, Eliza pulled them down onto some chairs at another table, Sienna on one side of her, Thea the other. Thea felt a rush of love for her little sister, and could only imagine how she must be feeling.

'You OK?' she asked her.

In an almost synchronised movement she and Sienna both reached out to cover their sister's hand, and Thea knew Sienna felt the same protective urge she did. She suspected it would take more than an all-clear to remove that instinct. But right now they were all in the same boat, adrift on an unfamiliar sea where Christmas was no longer a given.

'I can't believe this,' she said.

'We have to let them go,' Eliza said, her voice full of determination.

Sienna sighed. 'I just don't understand... This seems to have come out of nowhere.'

And in that instant Thea knew that this was even worse for Sienna than it was for her—Sienna was coming to terms with so much this year, and needed the security blanket of a traditional Christmas.

Eliza removed her hands in a gentle movement. 'It's time. They've spent years worrying about me. You all have. They deserve this break, a chance to concentrate on themselves again.'

Thea knew Eliza was completely right.

Sienna nodded. 'Agreed. But is it wrong that I'm an adult but still love going to our parents' house for Christmas to spend time with my family?'

'Me too,' said Thea.

'We all do,' said Eliza. 'But this year it has to be different.'

Thea gave a small groan as different scenarios chased through her mind. Should the three of them still get together in the Kendall family home? Or go and have a meal in a restaurant? Perhaps they could book a hotel somewhere? Every idea felt wrong.

'What will we do instead?'

She saw Eliza's eyes light up. 'We should do something different too,' she said. 'Let's make a pact.'

Sienna's brow furrowed. 'A pact? We haven't done that since we were teenagers.'

Thea laughed, relieved to have a memory to look back on. 'And that leave-the-windows-open pact so that we could sneak in and out didn't exactly work.' She pushed up the sleeve of her jumper and looked ruefully at the small scar on her elbow. 'I have the scar to prove it.'

Eliza grinned, but wasn't to be distracted. 'This will be our Christmas pact. To have a Christmas adventure of our own. I think we should all step outside our comfort zones and each go away for Christmas.'

'By ourselves?' Sienna choked out. 'Even you?'

'Yes, even you, Eliza?' Thea asked, and then wished the words back as she saw the stubborn tilt to Eliza's chin.

Sympathy touched her. How must it feel to always be cosseted and protected? At Eliza's age Thea had already finished uni and had been on the first rung of her career ladder. She had been on her way to success and her first promotion, a big step on her way to the partnership that she craved...that she was now so close to. If she stayed focused, with her eye on the prize, as she knew so well how to do, she knew it was within reach.

'Especially me,' Eliza said. 'Our Christmas pact will be that we each go away for two weeks—one before and one during Christmas. We will choose for each other, and do it in secret. Each destination will be a complete surprise. We'll pack each other's cases, and only find out our destination when we arrive at the airport.'

Eliza sounded very sure of her plan, although Thea was pretty sure it could only just have occurred to her.

'She's lost it,' said Thea, shaking her head and smiling at Sienna, sure that her sister would agree it was a terrible idea. Christmas alone? Plus, it was completely impractical—no way could Thea take a two-week holiday from work. The idea was preposterous.

'She has,' agreed Sienna. 'But it's not the worst idea I've heard.'

'Huh?' Thea gazed open-mouthed at her older sister.

'I like the idea that we will challenge ourselves,' Sienna said.

'It could be brilliant,' Eliza said.

And, seeing how vital, how excited Eliza looked, Thea swallowed her protests. She understood that her baby sister wanted to stretch her fledgling wings.

Then, her sister's face fell. 'Oh, but how will I pay?'

Thea glanced at Sienna. That was an easy fix—both of them earned more than enough to cover this idea, however harebrained it was.

'We can cover it,' she said.

'But that's not fair.'

Thea could see the frustration on Eliza's face.

'It's just how it is. No argument. This is a brilliant idea and it's happening.'

Eliza hesitated, and then gave a massive smile and a small nod that conveyed more than words could.

'I like it that we get to pick for each other,' said Thea.

At least she could find something positive to say. Because she and Sienna could make sure that their sister went somewhere safe. In fact, Thea already had an idea. And she and Eliza could pick somewhere amazing for Sienna to go, somewhere her sister could truly relax and escape from the year she'd had.

'So we're really going to do this?' asked Eliza.

Sienna nodded. 'We're doing it,' she said confidently. 'Right, Thea?'

Thea nodded too, and laughed, hoping it didn't sound too fake. 'What have I just let myself in for?' she asked.

She hoped she sounded light-hearted even as she wondered exactly that. But surely there would be loopholes. At least the pact didn't mean she had to promise not to work at all. Maybe her sisters would pick somewhere in Europe, somewhere from where she could pop across to London in an emergency, or for a sneaky meeting.

Sienna held out one fist, her knuckles facing her sisters. 'To the Christmas pact.'

'To the Christmas pact!' Thea and Eliza replied, bumping their fists against Sienna's.

MILLS & BOON

Want to know more about your favourite series or discover a new one?

Experience the variety of romance that Mills & Boon has to offer at our website:

millsandboon.com.au

Shop all of our categories and discover the one that's right for you.

MODERN

DESIRE

MEDICAL

INTRIGUE

ROMANTIC SUSPENSE

WESTERN

HISTORICAL

FOREVER
EBOOK ONLY

HEART
EBOOK ONLY

f @millsandboonaustralia 🐦 📷 @millsandboonaus

Subscribe and fall in love with a Mills & Boon series today!

You'll be among the first to read stories delivered to your door monthly and enjoy great savings.

MILLS & BOON SUBSCRIPTIONS

HOW TO JOIN

1

Visit our website
millsandboon.com.au/pages/print-subscriptions

2

Select your favourite series
Choose how many books. We offer monthly as well as pre-paid payment options.

3

Sit back and relax
Your books will be delivered directly to your door.